A LOVE FORBIDDEN

Robbed of marriage to the man she loved, Leah Bryce rears his daughter Miriam as her own. But her bitterness leads her to treat the girl cruelly, and when Miriam falls pregnant, Leah refuses to let her marry. Leah's own son Ralph has always loved the girl he believes to be his sister, and when he discovers Miriam's seducer has no intention of standing by her, he takes a terrible revenge: Saul Marsh will leave no other woman pregnant. Even on her deathbed Leah seeks to ruin the girl's happiness. Only when Leah's malign influence is finally removed can Miriam find joy at last.

A LOVE FORBIDDEN

A LOVE FORBIDDEN

by

Meg Hutchinson

Magna Large Print Books
Long Preston, North Yorkshire,
BD23 4ND, England.

British Library Cataloguing in Publication Data.

Hutchinson, Meg
    A love forbidden.

    A catalogue record of this book is
    available from the British Library

    ISBN   0-7505-1701-8

First published in Great Britain in 1999 by Hodder & Stoughton
A division of Hodder Headline PLC

Copyright © 1999 Meg Hutchinson

Cover illustration © Len Thurston by arrangement with
Hodder & Stoughton Ltd.

Published in Large Print 2001 by arrangement with
Hodder & Stoughton Ltd.

Magna Large Print is an imprint of Library Magna Books Ltd.

Printed and bound in Great Britain by
T.J. (International) Ltd., Cornwall, PL28 8RW

For all my colleagues at Lyng Junior and Infant School with whom I shared so many happy years, and especially for Graham. We shared the same sense of humour.

Chapter One

'You be nothing but a trollop – a dirty, stinking, bloody little trollop!'

Leah Bryce's already narrow face seemed to become even narrower, her sharp features more drawn, her usually colourless eyes blazing with old hatred and new spite.

'Who have you been with? Lying out on the heath with some man, giving yourself like a whore! Or be it more than one? Be it that you have lain with so many you don't know who has left you with his bastard?'

'Mother, please, it wasn't like that...'

Leah's hand lashed out, catching her daughter's face, hurling her sideways against the dresser, sending plates toppling from the shelves. 'Wasn't like that?' she spat, thin lips drawn back in a snarl. 'Wasn't like that! Then what *was* it like?' Grabbing the girl's shoulders, she hauled her upright. 'Don't be telling me I'm wrong, that you don't have a child inside you. There were no cloths from you last month and none the month before that. No show of blood for almost a three-month and you regular as night following day since you were ten year old. Ain't nothing but a man causes that to stop, so don't be telling me you don't be carrying!'

Her shoulders slumping, the girl pressed her hands to her face, sobs shaking her thin frame.

9

'I knew I was right!' The vindictive gleam in her eyes changing to one of triumph, Leah drew a paper from her pocket, slamming it on to the table that half filled the kitchen.

'I guessed what this was the minute I found it. I knew then that what I suspected was true. Well?' Leah's open palm came hard down again on the table. 'Look at it. Look at the marks you yourself have made on it, then tell me those marks don't number the days since last you had a flow of blood! Look at it!' The last was screamed as she grabbed a handful of the girl's hair, savagely twisting it about a closed hand, yanking her head back on her neck and forcing her to look up.

The pencil marks blurred into one long continuous line, the tears in Miriam Bryce's eyes seeming to make it move and slide across the paper like a thick black worm. The paper had been hidden beneath the flock mattress of her bed, but not well enough from the prying eyes and poking fingers of her mother.

'Yes, they mark the days sure enough.' Leah pushed with the hand that was folded in the girl's hair, throwing her once more violently against the heavy oak dresser. 'But they don't mark *all* the days of your sins, I'll be bound! It's my guess you've been at your dirty little games much longer than is written there.'

'No!' Eyes green as newly sprouted grass sparkling under dew, Miriam looked through her tears at the woman who not once in her memory had ever given her a loving word. Who since the earliest time she could remember had shown her

10

only harshness – a harshness that since she had grown into a beauty had turned to spite. 'I am not what you accuse me of being. I am not a whore.'

'Then what would you call yourself?' Both hands coming palm down on the table, Leah leaned forward, glaring at the girl who cowered on its other side. 'You ain't what I accuse you of, so what are you? Any woman who lies with all for the asking be a whore in my book, and in that of any other decent body.'

'I do not lie with any man for the asking.' Miriam's head came up, sun slanting in at the room's one window, sprinkling the rich russet of her hair with threads of gold. 'There has been only one.'

Slowly drawing herself upright, Leah Bryce's mouth curved into a cold, loveless smile. 'So, there has been only one, and that makes you less than a whore! Go ask the priest at St Matthew's if lying with just one man outside the marriage bed makes you less than a whore. Ask him if a seventeen-year-old girl with a bastard in her belly be any better than a trollop.'

'Yes, I am pregnant,' Miriam said with quiet dignity. 'And I do not defend what we have done. We both know it to be wrong, but the child I carry will not be born a bastard. We are going to be married just as soon as the banns can be called.'

'We?' Leah's thin lips tightened. 'You say *we*. Just who is the man can't wait for his pleasure but takes it afore placing a ring upon your finger?'

11

'You know him well enough, we have loved each other since being children. We always intended to marry. His name is Saul Marsh.'

Across the table Leah Bryce's eyes glittered above that cold smile, giving her narrow face the look of a fox with a fresh kill. Marsh! His mother was a widow the same as herself and she too had only the money her son earned to keep her from the workhouse. Now he was about to bring home a wife and soon a child. Two more mouths to feed and probably one more each year. Inside Leah the smile widened. Perhaps the workhouse would soon be called upon to take in more than one old woman!

'Then Marsh knows about his love child, you have told him?' She caught the look behind her daughter's eyes, one that told her all she wanted to know. He had not yet heard of the child.

'I ... I shall tell him this evening, when his shift at the mine is finished.'

'Then tell him this an' all,' snapped Leah. 'You have four years before you be of the age to marry without my given word.'

Miriam's eyes widened and her words tumbled out in a rush. 'You ... you would not deny us?'

Leah sank to the floor, gathering the pieces of broken china slowly into her apron. Behind the shelter of the table she heard the girl's sharp intake of breath, and the smile that rose to her own lips was warm with the pleasure of spite. She wanted nothing more than to have the child she loathed taken from beneath her roof, nothing more except the satisfaction of seeing her suffer. The girl could marry, but only after her father's dues had been paid.

The pieces collected, Leah rose to her feet, malice burnishing her dull brown eyes to the colour of beaten copper. 'You will not have the condoning of what you have done from me,' she said evenly, eyes fixed on the girl's stricken face. 'That which is in your belly will come out a bastard and that it will remain, till you be twenty-one. By that time Marsh may have another wench in the family way, one who can marry afore you.'

Her lovely face crumpling, Miriam stared at her mother. 'Why?' she asked, tears coursing down her cheeks. 'Why do you treat me the way you do? What have I ever done to make you hate me so much?'

Holding the apron bunched about the broken china, Leah's fingers tightened and her eyes flashed venom.

'You lived,' she said quietly. 'You *lived.*'

Ralph Bryce placed the last of the numbered tokens on the tub he had filled with newly hewn coal then called for the donkey boy to push it along the rails to the shaft bottom. Using the strip of cloth wound about his neck to wipe the sweat from his eyes, he squatted on his haunches, leaning his bare back against the coal seam glittering like black diamonds in the gleam from his Davy lamp. It was well named 'the deep seam'. Thirty feet thick and running for miles beneath the ground, it had yielded a rich harvest for the coal masters, and today he felt as though he personally had dug every ounce.

'Another shift finished, Ralph lad.'

'Arrh,' he agreed wearily.

'Then let's be getting up above. We be spending that much time down here my old woman be getting to think I've got meself a fresh 'un!'

'Now what could you be doing with another woman?' Hands hanging tiredly over his knees, Ralph smiled, his teeth gleaming white in the pool of light cast by the lamp.

'Not a lot, Ralph lad, not a lot for sure. It be all I can manage to keep my Sarah happy. Once a week it has to be, but I tells her that more than that sends you blind!'

Chuckling low in his throat, the other man gathered up the pick he had laid aside on the ground and, bent almost double against the tunnel that was less than half his height, began to shuffle his way back towards the shaft.

Pushing himself up from his haunches, the shovel with which he had loaded coal into the tub grasped firmly by its wooden haft, Ralph followed, his head almost on his chest to avoid striking the jagged outcrops of coal jutting from the roof only inches above it.

'Will you be laying the dust along of Banjo's?' his workmate asked.

'Not this shift,' Ralph answered, spitting out the coal dust raised by the other man's feet. Since the wage paid by the owner of the Grace Mary mine had been reduced by six shillings a tub, a tankard of ale at the beer house was one of the things he must do without. Keeping the house and feeding three mouths left little over to pay for ale. Saturday evening was the one time he made

14

an exception, and then two tankards was all he allowed himself.

Reaching the end of the tunnel that the two of them had burrowed through the massive vein of coal over the months, they stepped into the iron cage, Ralph tugging the rope that rang the bell in the winding house.

Rising slowly through darkness so deep their lamps were helpless against it, both men held their silence, each feeling relief seep through him at the end of a fifteen-hour day.

'You'll be needing no bath tonight,' the man winding the cage remarked as it reached the surface. 'It be raining heavens hard.'

'In that case, I reckon I'll take the time to drink a second tankard at Banjo's.' Ralph's shift mate grinned, blinking against the purple evening that both men found brilliant after the stygian blackness of the mine. 'It'll mean less time spent listening to my Sarah chuntering.'

'That wife of your'n might do her share of grumbling, but you would come off badly without her!' the winder called as they trudged across the yard towards the checking shed, hurriedly slipping on shirt and coat that had been removed at the coal face, their hob-nailed clogs squelching in the slimy clay of wet coal dust.

Removing the brass disc hung about his neck, Ralph handed it to another man who barely glanced at it before draping it over one of a line of nails driven into the brick wall and equally sullenly took the lamp, placing it on a long wooden bench that ran beneath.

Calling a goodnight that received no answer, they stepped from the shed, turning up their collars against the rain before setting off on the mile-long walk across the empty heath, following the track that would lead them safely past mines whose disused shafts lay open, ready to claim any who did not have the sixth sense born into miners.

Snap tins wedged under their arm, bottles that had held their drink of cold tea shoved into a coat pocket, the two bent their heads to the driving rain and trudged in silence, steps quickening as they reached the surer ground of Gypsy Lane. Passing the boiler-making works that loomed black and huge out of the night, they crossed Fishers Bridge spanning the canal.

Coming to the tramway that skirted the village, Ralph took his leave, turning in the direction of a house that stood some distance away across the heath while his workmate went eagerly in the direction of the beer house.

Glad to be alone, Ralph slowed his steps, lifting his face to the rain, wanting it to wash away the misery lodged like a stone in the pit of his stomach. He should be used to the pain of it by now, it had been with him for years, growing as he watched her grow. But the sting of it cut deeper with each new day that dawned; days that brought the fear of losing her to another man, the agony of thinking of her in someone else's arms, in someone else's bed. It was a fear and an agony that was ripping the heart from him, that made his life a living torment, yet it was a torment he could not end for what could come of the love that filled him, that kept sleep from him night after night, the deep needful love of a man for a woman? The love that no man should have for his sister.

Across the darkness of the heath the yellow glow of oil lamps spilled from the window of the cottage that had once stood surrounded by fields of crops and animals. But the dairy cow had long since gone, the plough horse been sold and the corn and wheat fields reclaimed by gorse and broom. Only the chickens kept by his mother remained of the life that used to be.

Would it have been more pleasant? he wondered as he walked on. Working by the light of day, seeing her go about her chores, watching her lithe young body as she brought his midday meal to the fields, sun glinting on her russet-coloured hair, seeing her lift her lovely face to smile into his eyes? Feeling the pain surge afresh in his chest, Ralph knew that way of life could only have worsened the hurt inside him. Far better for him to be shut away in the dark bowels of the mine; shut away with his shameful secret.

'You be fair soaked.' Leah turned from emptying a kettle full of boiling water into the tin bath set before the fire. 'Let me take that coat from you.' Placing the huge smoke-blackened kettle on the hob of the shiny blackleaded grate, she eased the wet coat from Ralph's shoulders spreading it across the back of a chair drawn over to where the fire's heat would reach it. She had seen many such nights as this and was well prepared. A bath to wash the dirt away and put warmth into her

17

son's bones, and lamb broth with suet dumplings to satisfy his hunger.

Taking the striped twill shirt as he pulled it off, she felt a surge almost of pride sweep through her. Her son was a fine figure of a man. There were those in Brades Village would be proud to have him as a husband. But he had shown no interest in any girl. She crumpled the shirt in her arms. None except...

'There be cold water in the pail.' She indicated a bucket stood in the hearth. The same cold fear gnawed in her stomach, one she had felt for the last ten years. 'Give a shout when you be finished, and I'll bring you in a clean shirt.'

'Where's Miriam?'

Leah's heart sank. If she told him the girl had not been home all evening then Ralph would insist on going out to find her, out into the rain and cold again, and all for a dirty little slut.

'We were out of flour and I need it for to-morrow's baking.' The lie came easily from a tongue long practised in the art and no blush stained her cheeks.

'You sent her for flour ... in weather like this!' Ralph hesitated, one boot half unlaced.

'It were not raining when her went.'

He lifted his eyes to his mother, experiencing the same rush of suspicion he always did when Miriam's whereabouts were in question. Too many occasions in childhood on which he'd found his sister with weals red on her arms, or marked across her face, had taken the trust from him and even now they were both older it had not returned. There was something about his

18

mother, something that caused her to hate her own daughter; he had seen it often in her face, heard it in the way she spoke to the girl. It was unnatural, and more than that it was dangerous. One day that hatred would become too strong, one day it would threaten all their lives.

'What time was that?' he asked, lowering his foot to the floor.

'Not much after three.'

Ralph glanced at the enamelled tin clock on the mantelshelf 'That's nigh on five hours ago. She should have been back long since.'

Leah saw the quick leap of concern darken his eyes and the coldness of her own fear mounted. They were both worried over Miriam but not for the same reason.

'I asked her to look in on Martha Lloyd.' She hitched the shirt in her arms before letting them come to rest under her flat breasts. 'Her Isaac has not been at all well since Advent. The cold and damp plague his bones. It be likely they be pressing her to wait of their lad coming in from the pit so he can fetch her home.'

'Happen you're right.' Ralph lifted his foot again, fingers busy with the leather bootlace.

'Of course I be right. Give the lad time to wash the coal dust from his body and take a bite to eat and he'll bring her.' Turning towards the door that gave on to the stairs, Leah felt hope quicken within her, easing some of the cold fear in her stomach. The girl had been gone long enough for her tears to give way to hunger and cold, to have begun the return home, to cross the heath in the dark... With luck she was already lying at

19

the bottom of some pit shaft!

He would come. Miriam drew her shawl closer about her shoulders, shivering in the damp night air. Saul would know where to find her. They often came to this hollow they had found at the foot of the straggling limestone hill, its entrance hidden by clumps of gorse. Here they could be together, and for a short precious time she was free from her brother's watchful, suspicious gaze, and the acid tongue of her mother. Why was it that Leah hated her so? It had been that way ever since Miriam could remember. Many times after her father's death she had cried herself to sleep, her back stinging from the bite of the belt he'd never used on her but which her mother had kept especially to beat her with. Often her mouth had bled from the sharp slaps her mother would give without the need for reason; blows she still inflicted whenever Ralph was not home.

Feeling the blood pound in her veins Miriam pressed deeper into the hollow, knowing the tremor was not solely due to the cold. Ralph had always defended her, protected her from their mother's cruelty whenever he could, yet there was something in him that frightened her, something she did not understand but saw in his face each time he looked at her; a sadness that haunted the depths of his eyes. Yet when she smiled at him he turned from her as though she had struck him.

But would he defend her now, seeing the sin she had committed, or would his anger blaze forth as their mother's had done? Would he too turn from her? But even should he not, he could only shield her from Leah's vindictive spite when he was at home, and that was for just a few hours in the evening.

In the distance a vixen screamed, the sound ringing over the silent heath, and Miriam pressed a hand to her mouth to hold in a frightened cry. The folk in the village said the screams and calls heard on the heath at night were the spirits of men lost in the mines, trying to find their way home.

They were old wives' tales, Ralph had said when he had heard her sobbing in the night. Told to frighten wayward children. There was no truth in what they said, there were no such things as ghosts and spirits. Nevertheless Miriam had stayed a long time awake, needing the re-assurance of his arms holding her fast. But that had been long ago in childhood. Her hand closed over her mouth, her eyes wide with fear she pressed backward until her spine came flat against the rock, her stare fixed on the entrance to her hiding place, blood curdling in her veins as the fox screamed again.

What if Saul did not come? Sobs she could not hold back escaped through her fingers, echoing from the rock face, their sound joining together like the voices of some unseen choir, blending and rising, the noise filling her with terror, tracing her spine with icy fingers.

What if he did not truly love her after all, if he had merely used her and now wanted no more to do with her? Thoughts tumbled through her mind, adding fresh fuel to the fear that riddled

21

her. Maybe he would refuse to accept that the child she carried was his. He too might think, as her mother did, that she had lain with others beside him. But she had not. Dear God, he must believe she had not!

But if he did turn his back, refuse to marry her? The thought refused to be banished. What would she do? Would her mother allow her to stay at home? And if she did, would the child be subject to the same cruel treatment that had been meted out to Miriam?

'No!' she cried aloud. 'Don't let that happen to our child. Please, Saul ... don't let that happen.'

Drawing up her legs to her chest, arms folded about them, she let her head sink down until it rested on her knees.

'Please,' she sobbed quietly. 'Please send him to me.'

Chapter Two

Ralph Bryce glanced at the tin clock on the shelf above the fireplace. It wanted ten minutes to nine o'clock. Nine o'clock and she still wasn't home! Martha Lloyd's son had had time enough to wash and eat half an hour gone. What in the world was keeping them?

'There be a fresh roly-poly with jam from the summer strawberries.' Leah rose from the table, glancing at the half-eaten bowl of broth Ralph had pushed away. He had not taken near as much as a man working the pit needed.

Ralph shook his head. 'I want nothing more.'

'But you've eaten next to nothing, you need...'

'I said, I want nothing more!' he interrupted, both fists hitting the table, setting the spoons rattling against the dishes.

'Roly-poly be your favourite pudding, that be why Miriam made it special this morning. Her feelings will be hurt if you leaves it untouched.'

It sounded casual enough but Leah knew what she was about. Chance was he would eat what Miriam had cooked. He ate less and less, each mealtime hardly worth the bother, and she knew why; she had trodden that same path many years since. She had known the yearning, the burning in the night, the long hours of the day when every glimpse of the loved one was a torment you longed for and a torture that clawed out your heart when that sight was denied.

'I'll cut you a piece, it be all ready.'

'Leave the pudding, Mother!' Ralph caught her wrist as Leah began to collect the used soup bowls.

Looking into her son's eyes, she felt a tremor of fear touch her spine. Fear, anguish and misery swirled together in their dark depths, but more terrifying still was their utter desolation. A desolation that seemed to say he was a lost man already, one who need pay no heed to his actions.

'But Miriam...'

'Yes, Miriam.' His fingers tightening, Ralph stared into his mother's face, fighting the suspicion mounting in his mind. 'Where is she, Mother? Did you really send her to buy flour and pay a call on the Lloyds, or is she out on the heath somewhere, nursing yet another of your hidings?'

'I told you...' Leah tried to break free but he pulled at her arm, dragging her halfway across the table, tipping over cups and milk jug put out ready for later.

'I know what you told me...'

His voice was quiet, its very calmness bringing a fresh jolt to Leah's nerves. He was her son, but he was a man grown, a man who flamed with desire for a woman in the knowledge he could never have her. It was enough to drive him to recklessness.

'...and I know it be a lie. Tell me where she be.' The hand that held Leah's crushed it tight and his eyes became pits of fire. 'Tell me true, Mother, or I swear before the Lord God Himself, I will do to you what you have done to her many a time. Have you raised your hand to her?'

'Yes, I raised my hand to her!' Rage and hatred burst out in a violent explosion, the strength of it dragging Leah free from Ralph's grip. 'The dirty, no-good little trollop! I raised my hand to her and will do the same and more the minute she shows herself in this house again.'

Slowly Ralph straightened, nursing calmness like a weapon in his hand. 'Why do you call her a trollop?'

Why!' Leah laughed derisively, the sound harsh in the quiet room. 'What else would you call a wench with a babby on the way and no marriage lines in her hand?'

A child! Ralph felt the blood drain from his

heart. Miriam with child? It was a lie ... another of the lies dreamed up by his mother to cover her treatment of the girl. Yet the thought did nothing to still the drumbeats of dread hammering in his brain.

'There – there be the evidence of her whoring.' Drawing the slip of paper from the pocket of her skirt, Leah threw it across the table. 'It were in her room, beneath the mattress of her bed. She thought it would be safe there, that her filthy goings on would not be found out. But it was. Look at it!' Reaching across the table, she smoothed the paper then stood back, face triumphant. 'Look at it. Each mark be a day of waiting – waiting for that which tells a woman there be no child in her womb. Count them,' she crowed, 'count them for yourself. There be more than makes up one month or two; near enough three. She be nigh on three months gone. Now what do you think to your precious Miriam?'

Ralph stared at the paper, seeing the pencil marks show black in the glow of the lamp, and felt each one strike him like an arrow to the heart.

'Did she say these ... these marks stood for days of waiting?' He forced out the words which threatened to choke him. 'Or is that the meaning *YOU* have put upon them?'

He had always taken the girl's word over hers. Leah tasted satisfaction sweet on her tongue. But this time he would be forced to believe, and with that belief accept that the wish of his heart had been granted to another.

'There were no need for my putting a meaning

on them, that were already clear to see.'

'But did *she* say what they stood for?' His stomach tightening, Ralph looked at the smile curving his mother's thin mouth, and in that instant hated her.

'What else could her say?' The smile widened, the faded eyes glittered. Cold and colourless as glass. 'When faced with that paper, the truth had to be told, and that being a child be well on the way.'

'Whose? Whose is it?'

It was a cry of torment as Ralph seemed to crumple, his shoulders sagging, his face turned away. A cry that should have wrung any mother's heart, should have elicited only pity. But there was no room for pity in Leah Bryce's heart, and there would be no mercy. There had been none for her, no mercy when her heart was breaking, and she would give none.

'There could well be doubt about that.' She watched the hand he lifted to the mantelshelf whiten at the knuckles as he gripped it. 'The time her's been at the game, who knows how many men have lain with her? There might be many along of Brades Village could lay claim, but many will keep a still tongue.'

'You would be wise to keep your own still on that score.' Ralph gazed into the heart of the fire that burned no brighter than his own bitterness.

'Oh, arrh, keep quiet about that! Make no mention of the number of men having taken Miriam's services. Well, that you might hush up but the result won't be so easily set aside. In another month or so the signs will be there for all to read. For all to know her be no more than a dirty little trollop.'

'Did she name the man?'

Leah read the emotions pent up in him, the despair and grief that in a moment could change to anger. Yet even knowing this could not curb the spite frothing inside her.

'Her put no name to any of them,' she lied.

A heavy silence settled over the room, seeming to swallow the very air. From her place beside the table, Leah watched her son's other hand slowly rise to the shelf, ornamented with a crocheted runner and plaster figures won at the yearly Wakes; watched him lean heavily against it, eyes fixed on the fire.

'There could be no more than one.' The words came after long seconds, but he did not turn nor did he lift his eyes from the fire.

'No?' Leah laughed again, with a repellent mixture of bitterness and satisfaction. 'But then, you would tell yourself that, wouldn't you? You won't believe the truth when it hits you like a ton of bricks. Her could never do wrong in your eyes. Well, you be going to have to face up to it now for it will soon be obvious not only to your eyes but to all in Brades Village. Your sister, the girl you have doted on nearly the whole of your life, your innocent little Miriam ... where be her innocence now?'

'She did not go to the village, did she?' Ralph held on to the shelf, feeling that if he let go he would not have the strength to stand. 'Tell me true, Mother. For if I find you lie, I'll not be responsible for my actions.'

'How am I to tell where her went?' Leah answered, the threat of his words lost in the pleasure that suffused her, the satisfaction of seeing her own years of heartbreak brought to a fitting culmination. The man could not be made to suffer but his daughter could, and if her son suffered in the paying, then so be it. 'I faced her with the paper lying on that table, faced her with the fact that near three month had gone by and there had been no discharge of blood. We won't hide behind the niceties Ralph, you be old enough and wise enough to understand the meaning of my words. I asked if there were reason other than her carrying of a child and she admitted there were none, that she was near enough three month pregnant. When I asked who it were by...'

'Careful, Mother!' Dropping his arm, Ralph turned to her, his face a mask of pain. 'Let your words be none but true, let them be hers and hers alone.'

It had taken long years for her revenge to reach its gathering, but now it had begun, she could await its harvest. Eyes on his, voice empty of all but a quiet vehemence, Leah answered him. 'Her told me straight out and with no trace of remorse, no inkling of shame, that her were with child. When I said the baby would be born a bastard her denied it, saying a marriage had been planned.'

'A marriage!' Ralph breathed. 'Then she does know the man?'

'Her named one.' Leah could not resist the barb. 'One likely to accept the blame more

28

readily than the rest, I shouldn't wonder, though he be a fool if he does...'

'His name!' Ralph's cry bounced off the whitewashed walls, setting the crystal pendants that hung from Leah's prized lamp ringing with the reverberation.

'Saul Marsh.' Leah reached once more for the bowls in which she had served their broth. 'Her said it were Saul Marsh.'

After carrying the bowls into the scullery, she returned for the kettle she had refilled and set it on the bracket swung over the fire. Her son disappeared for a moment then came downstairs, the blanket from his bed draped over one arm.

'Where be you going with that?'

'To find her.' Dropping the blanket on to the table, he reached for his jacket, shoving his arms into the still-damp sleeves.

'You'll not find her at the Marsh house. Amy Marsh ain't one to take kindly to her son's fornication. Your sister will find no welcome there.'

'I won't find her at the Lloyds either, will I, Mother? Because you didn't send her there. You didn't send her anywhere, and nor did you try to stop her leaving. You drove her out with your slaps and your vicious tongue, out on to the heath whose shafts be ready to trap anyone without their wits about them, much less a girl blind with her own tears!'

'No, I *didn't* try to stop her!' Banging the kettle on to the hob, Leah felt the hatred flow again, felt the wretchedness and misery of years rise in an unquenchable stream, let it pour from her as she

29

turned to face him. 'And I won't try to find her and neither should you. The wench is a trollop, a dirty whore. There be no place for her here, I'll take no bastard under my roof.'

'There will be no bastard.' Ralph tucked muffler ends under his armpits before buttoning the jacket. 'They will be married as Miriam said.'

'So, you think it's to be done her way? Once again it be what her wants and no mind to me!' Leah's mouth thinned, drawing her face to a foxlike pointedness. 'Well, you take heed of me, Ralph Bryce, for I be going to tell you what I told her. There be four years to go afore her can wed without my consent. That child in her belly will be born a bastard whether the man that put it there be willing or no, and it will remain that way for I will not give that word and you can't!'

Ralph stared at the woman standing opposite him, one who had had the rearing of him, one with whom he had lived every day of his twenty-three years, yet only at this moment did he feel he really knew her. 'You would let a child be born a bastard? Let it grow with that stigma hanging over its head?'

'Her should have thought of that afore her opened her legs!' spat Leah. 'They both should, instead of giving way to their animal lust.'

Picking up the blanket, he turned towards the door.

'You may find her,' Leah shouted as his hand lifted the latch, 'but you'll not bring her here. This be my house and it won't see the rearing of a bastard. Marsh had the pleasure but it would be we had the paying of it, we the feeding and the clothing.'

'And the love, Mother.' Ralph's hand rested on the latch. 'You say nothing of love.'

'I can feel no love for a bastard!'

'As you have never felt any for its mother.' He turned his head, eyes sweeping her face. 'Why is that, I wonder? What turned you so sour you can't stand the sight of your own child? What is it fills your soul so there is no room left for love?'

'You love enough for two!' Cold eyes glittering, Leah spoke with a viper's tongue. 'You have done all your life. Don't think I don't know. That I haven't known these ten years. Yours don't be the love of a brother for his sister, it be the love of a man for a woman. Yours be the feelings that should only be those of a husband. But that you can never be, for the woman you lust after be your own close kin. You be in love with your own sister!'

Head lowered against the stinging rain, Ralph walked on across the heath, trusting his long acquaintance with it to guide his feet to solid ground. The land all around Brades Village was riddled with mine shafts sunk by long-gone colliers who had left behind unhealed scars on the earth, black water-filled holes that could swallow a man without trace. Had one already taken Miriam? The thought stopped the heart in his body. He almost cried out. She could not be dead ... she *must* not be dead. He would find her; he *had* to find her or stop living himself.

One hand holding the lapels of his jacket closed

31

beneath his throat, the other supporting the blanket he had stowed beneath it to keep dry, he paused, eyes screwed up against the rain, trying to penetrate the shadows. But the cloud-bound sky held the secrets of the heath, allowing only Derby's Hill to show itself, black and menacing against the moonless sky.

Would she have come this way? He had no way of knowing. Would she have gone to the Marsh house? Had she been there already and found the kind of welcome his mother had spoken of?

Looking behind him, his glance cut through the rain towards Brades Village and as he stared the steel foundries that formed its bones opened their furnaces, throwing the light of their fiery heart into a wide arc overhead. Crimson and scarlet it leaped into the sky, piercing the sable depths, lighting the ground about him with a luminescent blush.

Was she somewhere in that village, somewhere with Saul Marsh? His own thoughts a whip that cut deep into his flesh, the rain drove into his mouth as he moaned softly, 'Why, Lord ... why was this pain given to me?'

Like laughter from hell, the bark of a dog fox came clear and sharp from the shadowy hills and Ralph knew there would be no other answer to his question.

Scanning the heath beneath the fading glow from the sky, he searched for any glimpse of a figure moving among the gorse, but as the darkness closed in on him, he saw nothing.

'Miriam!' He hurled the cry into the night then stood still a moment, listening for an answer.

When none came he moved on, steps turned away from the village and Brades Farm. Without Miriam he would not return again to that house. There could be no life for him there, no life for him anywhere if she were not part of it.

Carefully, each step not knowing what lay beneath, he walked on, every few minutes pausing to call her name; but each time the echo spent itself searching for an answer that did not come.

Reluctant to cease its assault the rain eased only slowly, resisting the efforts of a light breeze to sweep it away, grudgingly conceding only as the grey veil of dawn swept the horizon. Cold eating into him, Ralph sank on to an outcrop of limestone washed white by the downpour. It was useless to call any more, she would not hear; she would never hear anything again. The sister he loved was gone.

The *sister* he loved! Slumping forward, he rested his arms on his knees. '*Yours don't be the love of a brother for his sister...*' the words his mother had taunted him with rang in his head, words he had not denied '*...it be the love of a man for a woman. Yours be the feelings that should only be those of a husband ... you be in love with your own sister.*'

No, he had not denied those words. How could he? They were true and he was trapped by a love he could never fulfil, a love the world condemned. A deep, heart-rending love for a girl, but that girl his own sister.

A few yards from his feet, flushed from the cover of bracken and grass, a partridge burst

33

upward in flight, the beat of its wings and the startled 'chirrick' of its call shattering the silence.

Catching the flash of an orange throat, its feathers the colour of rust in the pale dawn, he watched the bird rise effortlessly into the sky, easily escaping the threat it sensed upon the ground. It was an example he should have followed long ago; he should have left Brades Farm and the threat it held for him. Even now it was not too late. Ralph laughed softly to himself. That was the biggest lie of all. It had been too late for the past ten years. It would always be too late.

His glance leaving the bird, he turned again to the clump of bracken that had sheltered it. What had caused it to break cover? A stoat, maybe, or a weasel. His eyes followed the line of rock to where it curved away into a natural half circle, then to the gorse growing thickly at its base. Derby's Hill, part of the Ragley Hills which were filled with caves and hollows. Perhaps there was one there behind that screen of gorse? The lair of wild things ... or perhaps the hiding place of a girl?

Leah Bryce glanced at the clock on the mantelshelf It had been nine hours since Ralph had left the house, hours in which she had waited and prayed that the girl might be dead. If Miriam had never been born, none of this would have happened. Ralph would likely be married by this time, wed to some wench from the village. But had there never been a Miriam, would that have healed the wound in her own soul? Rising from

34

the chair she had drawn to the side of the fire, Leah pressed her hands to her back, feeling the pull of aching muscles.

Had Ralph gone straight to the mine without coming home? His shift began at four which was three hours gone. Reaching for the poker, she raked the fire lying low behind the bars, drawing the blanket of ash into the steel pan set beneath the basket. Should she take a meal out to the Grace Mary? Fetching the bucket of coals kept beside the scullery door, she tipped it on to the fire then emptied the ash pan into it, sweeping the hearth with a small brass-handled brush. Unless she took food to the pit Ralph would go without eating for near enough twenty-four hours – too long for any man, much less one hacking away at a coal face.

Taking the bucket across the yard, she tipped the ash on to the heap, blowing down her nose at the film of dust lifted on the breeze. He must have gone on to the mine. Ralph was not one to miss his shift, he knew how much they depended on his work. As he knew there was always another ready to step into his shoes, ready to snatch the living from him.

One hand brushing away a loose strand of sandy hair that blew across her eyes, Leah stared at the tall foundry stacks, their thick black smoke curling into the rain-washed sky. There was precious little for any man in Brades Village. Here almost every life was sacrificed to coal or steel, every penny hard wrung from the owners. But one man had broken free, one man had gone, leaving behind a young woman who'd

35

vowed revenge. Turning towards the scullery, Leah breathed a name, one that stung like bitter aloes on her tongue.

Once more in the house, she turned out the lamp she had kept burning all night. She would wash her face and tidy her hair then see to Ralph's snap tin and filling a bottle with tea.

Her toilet finished, she bent to a chest set below the window of her bedroom, slowly pulling open a drawer. Tracing her fingers over heavily frilled white cotton pillow cases, she felt the old bitterness fill her. These had been part of her bottom drawer, the linen she had collected against her marriage. They had held her dreams, heard her whispered longings. Then *she* had come to Brades Village, a girl with eyes the colour of spring grass and curls shining like polished mahogany, and Leah's dreams had died. It had wanted one week to her marriage day when they had left, and her dreams had been buried in this drawer. In their place had been born a desire stronger than love, a desire for revenge.

Glance lifting to the window, Leah caught her breath. There ... coming from the direction of Derby's Hill... Rubbing a hand over the glass pane, wiping away the mist of her breath, she looked at it more intently. A man and a woman. It *was* him. It was Ralph, and the woman with him... There could be no mistake. No other woman in Brades Village had hair the colour of dark fire. He had found her. Leah pushed the drawer savagely back into place. He had found Miriam ... but she was still his sister.

Chapter Three

'I told you not to bring her back here!' Leah stood in the doorway, her scrawny body quivering with a rage that gave life to her faded eyes.

'Get out of the way, Mother.' Ralph felt his sister slump against his side. He had found her in the gorse-screened hollow, huddled against the rock, limbs stiff from cold. He had wrapped her in the blanket then held her until it was light. She had cried herself to sleep in his arms and his own tears had fallen silently with hers, bringing no comfort. Today Miriam would have her love, but for Ralph Bryce today and every day after it would be empty.

'I said, there be no place here for bastards!' Leah's thin mouth clamped as she lifted one arm to the door jamb, barring their entry.

'Then there be no place for me either.' Meeting his mother's furious gaze, Ralph spoke calmly, his anger of the night before no longer evident. 'You turn Miriam away and you turn me away. What is it to be?'

There was no question that he meant what he said. Leah dropped her arm, stepping aside for him to enter, then watched as he carried the blanket-wrapped figure upstairs.

'She'll need a hot drink and something to eat.' Returning two minutes later, Ralph walked to the fireplace, holding out his hands to the heat.

'It won't be from my getting!' Leah slammed the door that still stood open to the sharp morning air.

'Then it will have to be from mine.' Lifting the gently bubbling kettle from the bracket, he poured water into the teapot ready on the hob.

'How could you bring her back to this house? How can you run about nursing her after what her's done?'

Fetching milk from the cool jar in the scullery, Ralph poured a little into a cup before answering. 'She needs help, Mother.'

'Help!' Leah's hands curled into tight balls. 'Her needed none to get herself in trouble.'

Ralph glanced up from his task. What Miriam had done was a shameful thing, it would cause hurt to any mother, but what he saw in Leah was more than shame, more than anger. It was satisfaction.

'Miriam is very young.'

'Oh, arrh, and that be an excuse, be it?'

'No, not an excuse.'

'Then what? Her be seventeen nigh on, and that be old enough for any wench to know right from wrong.'

His fingers clenched about the spoon, Ralph drew a long breath before placing it on the cracked dish kept for the purpose. 'Age is no barrier against mistakes,' he said, carrying the cup towards the stairs. 'We all make them, and nature itself is no exception. Only for those mistakes there is no cure, eh, Mother?'

No cure for the mistakes nature makes? Leah

listened to the heavy tread of his clogs on the bare wooden stairs. But it was no mistake of nature caused Ralph's pain...

'She's asleep.' Bringing the tea down with him, he set the cup on the table, lowering himself into the chair in which his mother had spent the night. 'But she needs to be got out of her clothes, they're still damp from the rain.'

'Her can lie in them as they be!' Leah said stubbornly. 'And when her wakes, her will go from this house.'

'If you don't take the clothes from her, I will. The choice is yours.'

'You be no better than the slut you carried home! We all makes mistakes, you said so yourself. But thinking that to strip her body of its clothes will strip your loins of the fire that burns them will be your mistake. It will only cause it to burn brighter, turning your days to misery and your nights to living torment.'

'They're that already.' Ralph stared into the glowing coals. 'They're that already.'

Leah looked at the sleeping girl she had dressed in a calico night gown; at skin so creamy soft it was like the statue of the Virgin in St Matthew's. Alabaster, folk said it was, Leah didn't know, but its beauty was not lost on her and nor was the beauty of the girl in the bed. But this girl was no virgin.

Taking up the bundle of damp clothing, she returned to the kitchen.

'There be broth in the pot,' she said, placing the clothes on the rack strung over the fireplace. 'I'll warm you up a bowl afore you go to the pit.'

'I'll not be going to the pit.'

'Not going?' Leah paused, the ladle in her hand. 'But you can't go missing a whole day's work.'

'My place will have been taken on the shift.'

'Arrh, that will, but there'll be other tunnels you can work. They won't turn you away. The gaffer there knows you be a good worker. He'll let you go down, you'll see. You'll be all right.'

'And what of Miriam?' Ralph looked up from the chair. 'How all right will she be once I am down the mine?'

Placing the small pot over the fire Leah remained still. 'I told you, there'll be no staying here for her. When her wakes, her leaves this house for good.'

When he replied, Ralph's voice held a softness that presaged a storm. 'No, Mother, Miriam will not leave this house. Not until the day of her marriage.'

'This be *my* house!' Leah exclaimed. 'Mine! And I be the one to say who will live in it.'

'Yes, it is your house,' Ralph agreed, his quiet tone edged like fine steel. 'But it is *my* money that keeps it. *My* back that is bent fifteen hours a day – kneeling in sludge, breathing in the black dust of coal to earn it. And without it where will you be, Mother? How will you keep your house without a wage coming in? There's no place for women in the coal mines any more, and there's none in the steel or iron foundries.'

Throwing the ladle aside, Leah rounded on him, her thin lips turned inward. 'Then p'raps I'll do the same as your sister has been doing – I'll go whoring for my keep!'

Catching the cold eyes Ralph held them, his own mouth a straight line. 'If that is your choice, Mother. But you'll have to give your customers more pleasure than ever you gave my father or your living will be a poor one.'

'The sort of pleasure *her* gave Saul Marsh? The pleasure her will go on giving him? The pleasure you can't ever know – least not with her. Yet her be the one you want. That's so, isn't it ... you want your own sister!'

Yes, she was the one he wanted. Ralph felt his heart shrivel within him. The one woman in the world he wanted, the one he would die for, but she was the only one denied him.

'I told you last night to think carefully.' He pushed himself up from his chair. 'Miriam stays here until her wedding and I'll stay for life. But send her away and I go too, and when that happens you'll never see me again. Oh, I know that in itself will cause no heartbreak. You have had little more love for me than for your daughter. But it could well cause the loss of this house.'

Her son's leaving would be hard but it would not cause Leah heartbreak. That prerogative was not his; her heart had been broken long ago, and like a soap bubble could only be broken once.

'The day of her wedding could be a long time coming.' Leah swung the soup pot away from the fire. 'Do you think Saul Marsh will want her once he knows what her carries in her belly? Do you think any man will? No one wants another man's leavings.'

41

'Saul Marsh will take her,' Ralph answered grimly. 'He will take her or take his last breath.'

'I have done wrong, I know, and I'm sorry.' Miriam gazed up at her brother, her eyes moist and green as dew on grass. 'I never meant for it to happen. I never meant to hurt Mother or you.'

'You have given me no hurt,' Ralph lied.

'But I have shamed you both. The village will be full of gossip once it becomes known.'

'They will talk but not for long. You're not the first girl to try the bed before buying it.'

'Oh, Ralph!' Her long lashes dropped, shielding her eyes from his. 'I feel so ashamed. If only I could undo what I have done.'

'You speak as though the blame is all yours, but it isn't. The man should have had more control. He's not a lad, too naive to know the consequences of what he's doing.'

'So should I.' Her lashes lifting, she looked up at him again. 'But sometimes love is too strong, and we are in love, Ralph. Very much in love.'

Love is sometimes too strong. Turning away from her bedside, he walked over to the window, knowing that to look at her another moment, her face wet with tears, would be to lose control of himself.

Behind him Miriam sobbed. 'Don't hate me, Ralph, please don't hate me!'

The longing of years overcame him then, like a tidal wave washing away his strength of will. Turning back to the bed, he sat beside her holding her close, his mouth against her hair. 'I don't hate you,' he murmured. 'I could never hate you. You are my sister, the one I love more than anything on earth.'

His sister! Pressing his face to her hair, Ralph felt the warm tears slide down his cheeks.

'Have you told him?' Her sobs dying down, he eased her back on to the pillows, moving quickly away so she would not see the marks of his own tears.

'I intended to last night. I thought he would come to the hollow, to our special place, but he did not. I waited so long, but Saul did not come. It must have been because of the rain.' Her voice rose defensively. 'He would not expect me to go there in such a downpour.'

Wouldn't he? The thought jarred in Ralph's mind. Had Saul not gone to the hollow because of the rain or was it the thought of what he might have to face there that had kept him away? *Do you really think Saul Marsh will want her once he knows what she carries in her belly?* His mother's words rang in his head. Should that prove the case, should Saul Marsh turn his back on Miriam, he wouldn't live another day!

'But I shall tell him tonight. He will come tonight. But ... but that will do no good...' Miriam's eyes widened as memory brought fresh despair. '...Mother said she will not give her consent, she will not permit me to marry. Our child will be born a bastard!'

'You will not go to the heath tonight or any other night.' Ralph swung round to face her but remained at the window. 'Marsh will come here to this house, as he should have done from the start. Your marriage will be arranged and you

43

need have no fear of Mother. She will place no obstacle in your path.'

'But if I do not go to the hollow, Saul will think I no longer wish to see him. How can he think otherwise without word from me?'

Ralph looked into eyes bright with the beginnings of fever. 'Write him a note telling him to come here. I'll take it to the place where you meet. He'll find it there.'

He had placed the paper in the hollow. Rolled tightly and wedged in the neck of a bottle, he'd stood it in the centre of the clearing. That had been just before sunset. Now, as the last mauve streaks melted into grey, he watched the figure of a man stride across the heath, his sure tread that of one familiar with his surroundings. Hidden behind the rock, Ralph watched Saul Marsh enter the hollow, caught the flare of a match, flickering through from the mouth where he had pushed aside the growth, then watched as he quickly emerged, carefully replacing the short stubby branches of the bushes, masking any sign of entry. Then, after glancing about him, he walked away.

'*Do you think Saul Marsh will want her...?*' Sitting in the lee of the rock, watching the man's figure merge into the shadows, Ralph felt coldness grip him. Saul Marsh would not want the responsibility of a child, nor would he want Miriam.

'How be that sister of yours?' Ralph's workmate asked as they followed the ritual of handing in

44

their number discs and lamps. 'My Sarah feared it might be the pneumonia.'

'We were worried for a while.' Ralph drew on his shirt then slipped the length of rag from about his neck, replacing it with a muffler, tucking the ends under his arms as he pulled on his jacket.

'Could have been a nasty business.' The older man followed Ralph's lead, buttoning his own jacket across his chest. 'Getting catched crossing the heath in pouring rain, that be no joke. Reckon her be lucky to come off light as her has.'

If a month hovering on the brink of death could be called coming off light then, yes, Miriam had been fortunate, Ralph thought as they walked. But it had been a month where every moment had been torment for him. He had come to the mine every day, for once in his life blessing the hours spent in darkness where none could see the fear in his face, fear that she might die; only the thought that he must live long enough to avenge her keeping him sane. Then walking home, worry over his mother's state of mind dogging every step. He had warned her what would happen should she not take care of Miriam and so far his words had carried weight. But for how much longer?

'You tell your mother I be asking after the little wench, and tell her me and my Sarah will be happy to call once her be completely well.'

Ralph nodded, murmuring his thanks, but inside knew there would be no calls made on Leah Bryce. She had never been over friendly with the village folk nor encouraged them to call at Brades Farm. 'I keep myself to myself and my business my own,' she had told Ralph once when he had asked why it was they never joined the May Day celebrations, and why as children he and Miriam had not been allowed to go on church picnics.

'Will you be calling in to Banjo's this evening?'

The question took him by surprise. Ralph had not realised they had crossed Fishers Bridge and now stood beside the tramway that followed Freeth Street.

'I have to see how Mother is. It takes it out of her, running up and down stairs all day, then having to be up in the night too.' It was just an excuse, though. Ralph guessed his mother did little running up and down to his sister, and it was he himself who sat up all night.

'Arrh, I understand, lad.' The older man smiled sympathetically. 'Ain't no easy job looking after the sick, what with everything else her be called on to do. Makes a difference when there be none other to help. It be a pity there were no more children born to her.'

A pity! Ralph stifled the cynical laughter in his throat. Leah's having no other children was a blessing on the unborn. His mother had no real love for the two she had. Why suppose a third would have fared better?

Turning towards the house set apart from the village, he felt the familiar dread in his bones, a feeling that had been with him since Miriam's birth; a fear that some day he would find her gone. It had been bad enough when as a lad he had raced home from school, then from thirteen years old back from the mine, all from a fear of her somehow being taken away. In the month since learning of her love for Saul Marsh the dread had become worse, a thing that gnawed at him every hour of the day and long into the night. Marsh had not come for her yet, and though deep in his soul Ralph knew he would never come, still the fear haunted him.

Entering the house through the scullery, he removed his clogs, setting them on a sheet of newspaper kept for the purpose beside the door.

'You be home then?' Leah came to stand in the small passageway that linked scullery and living room.

'Has Marsh called?'

Her mouth twisting, she took the jacket Ralph slid from his shoulders. 'You asks the same thing every time you come in, and today the answer be no different. I've seen neither hide nor hair of the man, nor do I expect to.'

It was like having a sentence of death lifted. Ralph felt the hot joy of reprieve flood through his veins, but it was only momentary. Tonight Marsh might well come to the house, come to claim Miriam. And if he did? Pulling the shirt over his head, he remembered what his mother had said on the night she told him of Miriam's disgrace at Marsh's hands. '...*I will not give that word and you can't!*' Would she still refuse to let her daughter wed ... allow an innocent child to be born a bastard? Either way there could be only sadness for Ralph.

'The bath be ready afore the fire.' Leah took his shirt. She would collect his trousers when he

47

called to say it was fitting, then carry them out into the yard to beat some of the coal dust from them.

She had seen the relief in his eyes when he heard Marsh had not come to the house. But it would avail him nothing. Leah threw coat and trousers across the rope strung from the brew-house wall to a stake driven into the ground at the bottom of the yard. Ralph and Miriam Bryce were brother and sister, and however strongly he felt for her, he would break no law of man or church.

Dressed in the fresh clothes she had left airing above the fire, Ralph brought out the tin bath, emptying the blackfilmed water into the channel that spanned the yard. Gathering his work clothes as he hung the bath on its nail on the brew-house wall, she followed him into the house.

'How has she been today?'

Lifting a cloth-wrapped basin from a pot set on the hob, his mother carried it to the table, flicking her fingers as the heat scared them. Gingerly pulling free the knots in the scalding cloth, she took her time answering.

'Your sister has been well enough,' she said as the cloth came away and she turned over the basin to reveal a steaming steak and kidney pudding.

'Has she eaten?'

Slicing into the pudding, Leah slid a large portion on to a plate, spooning extra meat and rich gravy beside it. She knew what it was he really wanted to say, the same as she had known

48

these last four weeks. The question forever on his tongue which he lacked the will to ask.

'I took her in breakfast and a meal at midday.' Leah turned back to the fireplace, bringing a bowl of boiled potatoes to the table. She could have told him that both were left untouched when she'd carried the dishes back into the scullery, but she kept her own counsel.

'I'll take her up a tray and make up the fire in her room.'

'There be no need.' Leah sat herself down at the table. 'You can take your own meal in peace, I've seen to her supper and the fire. Set yourself down and eat.'

They ate in silence, Leah not missing his glances first towards the clock then the window. Was he still expecting Saul Marsh to turn up here? He'd far better expect the Second Coming, it would happen quicker.

The meal over, she cleared the table before brewing a pot of tea.

'I reckon Miriam would enjoy a cup.'

'Arrh, I reckon that an' all. Mebbe you'd take some up to her while I see to washing them crocks.'

Ralph's smile was brief but genuine, pleased his mother had given him the excuse he felt necessary for him to enter his sister's room. 'You just leave the dishes, Mother. I'll wash them later.'

Waiting until he left the room, Leah gathered the tea cups. There would be no dishes left for a man's washing in her house. And nor would a bastard be reared beneath its roof.

Chapter Four

'Has Saul been?' Miriam looked anxiously at her brother, standing at the foot of her bed. 'I ask Mother every day and she always says he hasn't called, but he must have. Why does she say otherwise? Why lie to me?'

Ralph did not have to look at her to know her pain, it rang in her voice. He had hoped not to be asked that question, not to have to inflict further pain upon her. But she had asked and now he must answer.

'Mother isn't lying to you.' He said it gently but the cry from the bed made it sound as though he had struck her.

'But it's been almost a month!' She stared at him through a mist of tears. 'He wouldn't stay away on purpose. Saul wouldn't turn his back on me. He loves me as I love him.'

As she loved him! Ralph found he could not breathe, a lump in his throat cutting off the air from his lungs. Dear God, why did those words hurt him so?

'He does not know,' Miriam cried, her own pain blinding her to her brother's. 'Saul cannot know what has happened or he would come. Ralph...' She looked up, tears turning her eyes to green crystal. 'You ... you did take my letter, didn't you?'

He knew there was no accusation in her words,

no real doubt that he had done as she had asked; they were rather a subconscious realisation of the truth, a truth she was trying desperately to stave off. She did not voice the question she really wanted to ask.

'I took your letter,' he said, turning towards the window so she would not see the heartache in his eyes. 'I put it where you asked, in the hollow where I found you.'

'Then some animal has carried it away. That must be the reason Saul has not come.'

There was desperation in her voice, a clutching at any straw of hope.

'I will go to the hollow and check tonight. But most likely the reason he has not visited is because you have been so ill. Pneumonia is a dangerous sickness, you could so easily have died. Likely Saul has been advised to stay away until he is sent for.'

'How would he know I was ill if he has not called at the house? Mother has not been down to the village.'

It was a shrewd question. Obviously she had thought long and hard, searching for answers yet not finding any.

'Likely 'cos of me.' Ralph stared from the window deep into the shadows gathering about the heath. Purple and grey they mingled together, cloaking the hollow that lay against Derby's Hill, keeping the secret it held. 'I talked of your illness to the men at the mine and they'll have talked of it in their homes. It would not be long before the whole of Brades Village had heard.'

51

'And if the note is gone?'

His eyes still on the shadows forming and reforming, deepening to black, Ralph answered quietly, 'If it is gone then I will bring him to you.'

'Ralph!' she called anxiously as he reached the door. 'Mother said she would not give her consent for us to marry.'

His fingers closed about the door handle. 'You will have a wedding,' he muttered. Then, under his breath, 'Even if I have to fight for it.'

There were no paths leading across this part of the heath. The coal and the limestone had been worked out long ago and the scrub and gorse returned to cover the wounds if not to heal them. But Ralph had walked this ground since childhood and now he moved quickly and confidently, hampered only by the spells of darkness when the moon was banked by cloud.

Instinct told him what he would find in that hollow. He had seen Saul Marsh enter and leave swiftly and with that had come the certain knowledge that he had no intention of calling to see the girl he had seduced, and certainly none of marrying her. But that would be knocked out of him. Miriam would be left with no man's bastard.

Reaching the place, Ralph shoved aside the screen of gorse, bending almost double to squeeze through the narrow entrance. Once inside he took a box of matches from his pocket and struck one, peering through its short-lived brilliance. It was still there, as he had known it would be. Letting the spent match fall to the floor, he struck another, seeing in its light the bottle standing on a flat piece of stone, the rolled paper wedged in its throat. Had Marsh read it? Had he even bothered to look at it, or had he guessed what it held and turned tail without lifting the paper from the bottle?

Flame touching his fingertips, Ralph dropped the match, a curse escaping his lips. But it was not solely the match he cursed. He damned himself too for what he was about to do. Yet do it he must. He must know whether Marsh had left a reply to Miriam's note, or left her nothing at all.

The position of the bottle imprinted on his brain, he reached through the darkness, fingers closing about the paper. Unrolling it, he struck another match, holding its flame to shed light on the pencilled lines.

Marsh knew. Ralph held the burning match to a corner of the paper. She had written it there for him to see, told him of the coming child, but he had made no move to see her, no attempt to claim the child as his own.

But claim it he would, and tonight! The paper turning black and crisp, Ralph watched the last vestige swallowed by the flames then left the cave.

Her son had gone from the house, gone without speaking. But it had needed no words to tell her where he was gone, or which man he would be seeking. Leah sat beside the fire, a half-finished rag rug draped across her lap. She had seen it in his face as he had grabbed at his jacket, seen the mask of bitterness and rage. Taking a narrow strip of cloth from a heap on the table she drew it through the hole she'd pegged into the rough hessian. The rage he could burn out, but the fires of hell would not burn away his bitterness. Only she could quench that, and though purgatory opened at her feet she never would. She stared into the fire. The peg idle in her hand, she watched the flame spurt blue-tipped crimson darts that danced as her jealousy had danced, glowed as the pain in her heart had glowed.

She had come to Brades Village, the daughter of a carpenter brought to work at the Hall. She had come with her soft smile, her pretty curls that gleamed like burnished mahogany, and a face so beautiful it captivated every man. But the one she had chosen, the one she had taken, had been already betrothed, promised to marry Leah Thompson. But that promise had come to mean nothing for when the carpenter and his daughter moved on, Leah's husband-to-be went with them.

And she had been left to face the stares and the gossip of the village, the object of their snide remarks. And when she had become the bride of William Bryce, still they had pointed the finger, murmured she had taken him as second best.

They had moved then, taken the house at Brades Farm, putting a distance between them and the village. But the gossip had never really died; it remained in the whispers that followed her whenever she had gone to the shops, quiet half-spoken innuendos that had cut into her until finally she had gone there only when lack of provisions forced her to do so. Leah had severed friendships, keeping strictly to herself But that had proved no salve to the infection that ate at her core; provided no cure for what smarted like an ulcer in her heart. That had stayed with her, not even the birth of her son easing it.

Then had come the birth of Miriam. Leah stabbed the peg into the hessian. Ralph had been not quite six years old. From the cradle they had been close, a feeling that the passage of years had only intensified until it was stronger in Ralph than the usual affection of brother for sister. Leah pulled another strip of cloth through the hessian. He had watched over Miriam from the beginning, guarding her, defending her, fighting with any who dared speak a sharp word to her; until now those feelings had become a bond, a cord that tied his heart, the lynch-pin that held his soul; a love as strong as the one his mother had felt all those years ago, and like hers a love that would have no answer.

She had kept a good home for the man she had married, seen to his needs, but he had soon come to realise theirs could be no marriage of love, and when he turned away from her she had felt no sense of loss, no deprivation, it had merely given her the freedom to dream of the revenge she knew would one day be hers; and now that revenge was drawing close. The sins of the fathers... Leah laughed softly as she drew another clipping of rag through the hessian. They would certainly be visited upon *these* children, the daughter and the son.

He had not found Marsh. Ralph walked on,

hands in his pockets, Sunday boots crushing the long grass of Derby's Hill. He had searched the village last night, called at the beer house, but there had been no sign. At last he had returned home to his mother's caustic remarks.

'So he's done a moonlight flit...'

Sinking to the ground, he plucked a stalk of grass, twisting it between his fingers as the words spoken the night before returned to mind.

'I said you would find no sign of him. He don't intend to tie himself to wife and child. He took his pleasure and now he be gone – leaving us to pay for it!'

'You won't have to pay!' he had answered, frustration and anger sharp within him. 'I will find the money it takes to keep the child.'

'And that will be the all of it, will it? Money will take care of everything. And what of a name? Can you give it that? Can you wed its mother and take away the shame of what's been done? Oh, that's what you'd like to do, but you can't. You can't give her child your name, it will be born a bastard ... and a bastard it will be all its life!'

'We can move away ... right away where we are not known.'

Leah had taken the poker, raking ash from the fire as she laughed. 'Move away? Go some place where you can pretend the child be yours, pretend its mother be your wife? That be nearer the truth. Find a place where you can live out your ungodly dreams, where you can...'

She had got no further. Ralph had spun her around, wrenching the poker from her hand and raising it above her head, every fibre in him

56

wanting to smash it down into her face. But even as the rage scared him he knew it was not his mother's spite he wanted to stop; that harming her would not bring respite from his hurt. He had released her then, thrown down the poker to clatter against the fireplace. The noise had brought Miriam from her bed.

Breath harsh in his throat, he dropped his head into his hands as the image of her flooded into his mind. She had looked so pale, but in a strange way that only added to her beauty. Her long hair, for once unbraided, fell in a red-brown cloud about her shoulders. Her grass-green eyes were lit with anxiety, lips parted from the effort of breathing. He had felt a rush of feeling that left him light-headed.

'Saul?' The word had trembled on her tongue. 'Have you seen Saul?'

It should have been no surprise to him yet it hit him like a douche of cold water, leaving him numb.

'No, he hasn't seen Marsh.' It was Leah who answered, mouth tight as she looked at her daughter. 'Nor will you. He be gone from Brades Village. You'll be having no marriage to Saul Marsh. He's turned his back on you and what you carry inside you. But I'll not have the shame of it here under my roof. I provide lodging for no bastard and its mother!'

'Is it true, Ralph?' Miriam had asked softly, fearing his answer. 'Has Saul left?'

'I could not find him.' It had to be said. Cruel as it was, it would be more cruel to lie.

And the note? This time it was her eyes alone

57

that spoke. She saw the reply he could not hide and with a sob crumpled to the floor.

He had lifted her in his arms, feeling how frail her body was beneath the thick cotton night gown. Carrying her upstairs, he placed her back in bed, covering her with the patterned quilt as Leah followed him into the room.

'Don't mention Miriam leaving this house again,' he had said as they both stood looking down at the still figure, her long lashes dark smudges on her pale cheeks. 'I won't have her made any more afraid than she is now. She has enough to worry over.'

'Aarh, that her has. But there be more coming yet. Once that babby be here and no father to keep it, that'll be when her real worries start.'

'I will keep it.' He had stared down at his sister's pale face. 'The child will want for nothing.'

'Except a name!' Leah had turned away then, going to the door that gave on to the tiny landing. 'The money you earn may feed it and clothe it and no doubt provide it with a home, but it will not protect it from wagging tongues and pointing fingers. What will you tell it?' She turned briefly to look at him then, her faded eyes filled with a bitter light. 'What do you tell a bastard when it asks who its father is?'

Ralph had made no answer for he had none to make. The village talking of the child's parentage was one thing, but when the child itself should ask... In that at least there could be no arguing with his mother, for what would they reply?

Now, lifting his face to a sky stippled with the

pearl and gold of a June evening, he closed his eyes. 'I will take care of it,' he murmured softly into the vastness. 'I will take care of both of them, they will always be safe with me. Only take this love away – let me feel for Miriam as a man ought for a sister. Lift this burden from my shoulders for I don't know how much longer I can bear it.'

Venting a long sigh which seemed to hold within it the tears of a lifetime he sat there for several minutes, the last warmth of the sun bathing his face. At last, reluctant to face the world again, he slowly opened his eyes.

Light was gradually giving way to shadows that sought the hollows between rocks, painted the outline of the gorse bushes over the tussocky grass. In an hour or so it would be dark. But it was not fear of night which forced him to move so much as fear of his mother's baleful influence at home.

Why, in God's name, why did she have a hatred for Miriam? It wasn't natural. But then, was her taunting of him natural? Any other mother would try to help, or at least talk to her son of the hurt she knew to be slowly destroying him. But not her, not his mother. She seemed rather to revel in it. And now he had given her his ultimatum – that Miriam should stay at home for as long as need be or he would leave with her and Leah could fend for herself – now there was no telling to what lengths she would go; as signs of the child grew more evident in Miriam, so would the anger in their mother. An anger that would no longer be satisfied by giving her daughter a beating.

Half rising from the ground, Ralph sank down quickly again, catching sight of two people coming towards him across the open heath. A man and his girl out for their Sunday stroll. He would stay put until they'd passed. Screwing up his eyes against the glancing sun, he watched them come, feeling a growing sense of unease.

The man was tall and lean, his movements easy as he bent over the girl, laughing down at her. But it was his hair that drew Ralph's attention. Catching the rays of the sun, it gleamed like newly made butterscotch. Saul Marsh had hair that colour!

His gaze keener, he watched them take a few more steps. Then, pulling the girl by the hand, the man half turned to catch her in his arms – and as he did so the breath stopped in Ralph's throat. He had not been mistaken. This was Saul Marsh.

He heard the girl's excited giggles carry across the heath, saw Marsh close his mouth on hers as he lowered her to the ground. Ralph felt contempt strong and sour within him. This girl was not even to be afforded the shelter of a cave.

They had not seen him. Sitting where he was, he must be hidden from view. He could wait, go to Brades Village later tonight and take Marsh then. To take him now would only be to embarrass the girl. Though she might well come to know a deeper shame, as Miriam had done.

Below him he heard the squeals the girl gave as her skirts were pushed up, easily muffled as Marsh shifted above her.

Was that how it had been with Miriam? Had

her cries been so easily overcome? Contempt melting before the white heat of fury, Ralph rose to his feet. Had Marsh taken Miriam knowing she was to be just one more pawn in his filthy game, knowing he had no intention of making her his wife?

His steps muffled by the coarse grass, he strode downhill to where they lay, the girl's eyes closed, her legs spread wide. Lifting one foot, Ralph shoved it hard against the other man's thigh.

One glance from the startled girl, her breasts exposed by her unbuttoned blouse, legs pale and bare from hip to white knee-stocking topping black Sunday boots, had her wriggling from beneath her lover, snatching at her blouse as she scrambled to her feet.

'What the bloody hell...!' Pushing himself to his feet, Saul Marsh glared at the intruder then stepped back as recognition came.

'*That's* what the bloody hell!' Ralph's fist smashed into the other man's mouth, sending him crashing to the ground. Standing over him, Ralph glared down at the bleeding face, seething with rage. 'You've played the same game with my sister, the game you were at just now. You read the note she sent for you...'

'What note?' Saul played for time. Ralph Bryce was no weakling and the temper he was in was dangerous.

'It's no use pretending you didn't read it.' Ralph's voice was icy calm, thinly covering the fires that burned beneath the surface. He glanced to the figure of the girl, now running away across the heath. 'She escaped lightly, but you will not.'

He returned his gaze to the man lying before him, fingers closing the buttons of his trousers.

'Read what?' Saul eased himself back along the ground. 'I don't know what you're talking about.'

Disgust adding to his rage, Ralph stepped forward, closing the distance Marsh had gained. 'I saw you. I watched you go into that hollow beneath the hill. I saw the light of the match you struck, the same as I saw you come out and brush back the gorse so it would seem no one had been there. You know my sister is pregnant and you know who the father is! You are going to marry her, Marsh, and you are going to tell her so right now.'

'Like bloody hell I am!' Drawing up one knee, Saul kicked out, landing his foot in the base of Ralph's stomach, jumping to his feet as Ralph reeled backward. 'I'm not ready for marrying yet!' he panted. 'And when I am it won't be to a village nobody with less than twopence to her name. A bloody little trull only too happy to oblige!'

Fighting the pain lancing through his stomach, Ralph looked at the man facing him: his legs apart and bent at the knee, body half crouched, both arms lifted in the stance of a bare knuckle fighter. Except that one hand held a knife.

'Your sister were willing enough.' His mouth widening in a sneer, Saul shifted his weight from one foot to the other. 'I got plenty from her, and it were not complaint. She knew what she was about.'

'She's little more than a child!' Anger tightening his throat, Ralph lunged forward, gasping as the blade sliced across his hand.

'She was old enough!' Saul shouted back. 'Old enough to know one and one can come out three.'

The scornful words and the contempt in his face fed the rage in Ralph, fanning the flames higher. 'You were the one should have known – known I would not let you shirk your responsibility.'

'And what do you reckon to do?' Marsh taunted him, balancing the knife in his hand. 'Drag me to the altar?'

'If I have to.' From the corner of his eye Ralph saw the glint of sunlight on steel.

'Some hope you have of that,' Saul laughed. 'I'm a long way off marrying, and when I do your sister will not be first choice.'

Quick as lightning Ralph kicked out at the hand holding the knife, following it up with a swift punch to the groin. A second one to the jaw lifted the other man clean off his feet, sending him spinning round to fall face down.

'My sister will not be your first choice?' Ralph breathed as he straddled the fallen man, one hand holding a fistful of shining hair, pulling his head back painfully.

'She ... she wouldn't even be the last!' croaked the other man defiantly. 'I want a woman with money, not a twopenny whore!'

Reaching out for the knife, Ralph felt a strange calmness descend on him. Still holding the handful of hair, he rolled Marsh on to his back, looking down into that sneering face. 'If my sister cannot be the first,' he whispered, lifting the knife high, 'then let her be the last.' Bringing the blade down, he slashed away a line of trouser buttons and ripped away the torn cloth with the other hand.

With a screech of sudden fear, Marsh clawed at the face above him but Ralph was too deeply buried in a terrible calm to hear the pain of it. Raising the knife again, he looked into eyes no longer sneering but darting in a terrified dance as he fastened a hand about Marsh's naked genitals.

'Let her be the last,' he whispered again, the icy calmness of his voice lending it added terror. 'You will leave no other woman with child!'

Chapter Five

Ethan Rawley touched a heel to the flank of the silver-grey stallion. His father had not wanted him to take the horse; it was unpredictable, he said. But Ethan had taken it regardless of its flighty reputation. He was tired of being so carefully watched over. His father meant well, meant him the best; he had proved that again and again with all the doctors he had engaged, and Ethan appreciated it, but at the end of the day it had become wearisome.

Only he himself could do anything about it, the last doctor, more truthful than the rest, had told them. He it was had locked away his tongue and he alone had the key to release it.

Almost at the foot of Derby's Hill, Ethan

looked out across the stretch of heathland dotted with clumps of rock amid the green of gorse and broom, and the brown shades of bracken. He had been fourteen years old... They had come riding here on the hill, his mother on a bay mare and he on a black gelding. Laughing, she had challenged him to a race home, spurring her mare as she spoke. Ethan's hand closed convulsively on the reins as the memory, never far away, rushed in on him. He had called 'Cheat!' as he too spurred his horse, sending it flying after the mare. What happened then had become his own private nightmare, one that revisited him almost nightly. Ten years ago it had threatened his sanity. Now he could control the emotions it still aroused but even the man he had become could not prevent the tears that followed it.

He had drawn level with her, riding side by side. She had laughed across at him, eyes sparkling, cheeks pink from the rush of air, then she had raised her short riding whip.

Closing his eyes. Ethan tried to clear his mind, dreading the rest, but when he opened them the images remained.

His mother had raised her whip, bringing it sharp down on her mare's flank, then... As though in slow motion the pictures passed before his inner eyes. The bay mare seemed to buck, then her forelegs folded and her quarters rose, and his mother's arms seemed to reach out towards him as she was thrown from the side saddle; he had seen terror replace joy at the last as her mouth opened to scream his name.

It had taken less than a moment, but in that

moment they had both known. She was dead before he reached her. He had held her in his arms, her head lolling sideways on a broken neck, lovely eyes closed forever. From that moment on Ethan had not spoken a single word.

It had not been his fault, his father had assured him. No one could have known the mare would catch her foot in a pot-hole. But to a young lad who felt responsible for his mother's safety, the words were as chaff in the wind. Since that day Ethan had remained in his own silent world, allowing no one in to comfort him.

Somewhere across the heath a bird trilled the song that heralded the time to roost, the sound intruding on his memories, pushing them aside. Glancing at a sky rosy with the hues of dusk, he touched his heel again to the stallion's flank, then the crop to its shoulder as it refused to move. Twice more he tried. When the animal persisted in its refusal, he climbed from the saddle. It probably sensed a rabbit or some other beast caught in a trap; he knew men from the villages set them here.

Careful of where he placed his feet, he searched the immediate vicinity, finding nothing. His father had said the horse was unpredictable! Halfway back into the saddle, he heard a faint moan. This was no animal. Someone was lying out here in pain.

Throwing the reins over a tall bush, he followed the sound, coming to a hollow between two jagged outcrops of rock. At the bottom, lying face down, was the figure of a man.

Slithering on the shale-covered ground, Ethan

reached the figure then retched as he gently turned it over. The hands clutched to the groin were covered in blood. The man had been castrated!

Ralph had been so good to her. Ever since childhood he had cared for her, protecting her, shielding her against their mother's spite, just as he had yesterday.

Miriam sat on the edge of her narrow iron-framed bed. Asking herself why her mother detested her would bring no answer. It had always been that way and probably always would be. But Ralph ... she could not expect him to spend the rest of his life standing between her and their mother. He was a man full-grown. Even if there were no girl in his life now, the time must come when there was. He would want a wife, a family of his own to love and care for, and that was only right. She must make way for them; leave this house and give her brother a chance to live his own life.

Going to the chest, which apart from the bed and a small cane-seated chair was the only piece of furniture in the room, she took a petticoat from a drawer and laid it on the bed. She would not be able to carry much with her. Not that she had a lot to take, her mother had never seen the need to buy her many clothes. Fripperies, she'd called them, begrudging Miriam much more than a Sunday dress. And underwear? One to wash and one to wear was deemed sufficient.

Laying spare bodice and bloomers with the petticoat, Miriam took her one and only dress

67

from the chest. It had been bought two Christmases ago and then only after pressure from Ralph. Miriam held the dress against her, the soft claret wool warm against her breasts. Her mother had protested strongly against the buying of it. Too expensive, she'd said. Who in their right mind would pay three pounds two and six for a frock? It was money wasted! But Ralph had paid it. Miriam herself had not wanted him to, for she knew it must be every penny he had ever managed to save, but he had smiled and said it would only be wasted if the dress went to anyone but her. *'It was made for you, Miriam,'* he had said, smile deepening. *'No one else should have it.'*

She had felt so wonderful that Christmas morning, going to church in her new dress, her hair caught up in pink ribbons that had been another gift from Ralph. But her happiness had been short-lived. The moment they were home her mother had ordered her to change into her everyday skirt and blouse and the dress had been put away. Easter and Christmas, that was the only time she was allowed to wear it. She would have worn it again this year for she had not grown much, but now...

Placing the dress back in the chest, she stared at the deep rich colour, then slowly closed the drawer.

Wrapping her few clothes in her petticoat, she reached for her shawl draped over the back of the chair. Her mother would be downstairs! Miriam's hand tightened on the shawl. Would Leah try to prevent her from leaving? But then, why should she? Why hold on to something she hated? Surely this was her golden opportunity to be rid of the daughter she did not love.

What would she tell Ralph when he returned? That she thought Miriam asleep in her bed? That she had not seen her leave? Doubtless Mother would have a ready answer.

Passing the shawl about her shoulders, Miriam tied the corners together beneath her breasts. If only she could have seen Ralph before she left, to tell him no girl could have a more kind and thoughtful brother or one who was loved more by his sister. But she could not. To stay until he came would mean more argument between him and their mother. Better she should go now.

Taking up the bundle of clothes, she walked quickly from the room.

'Where do you think you be going?' Leah looked up sharply as her daughter came down the stairs.

'I don't know, Mother,' she answered quietly. 'I only know it will be better for all of us if I leave.'

'And how will you keep yourself?'

'I'll find work.'

'Oh, so you'll find work?' Leah was scathing. 'And who do you think will take you on? Or if they do, how long will they keep you once they see what's in your belly? That won't stay hid for long! And then what?'

Miriam felt a fresh chill run down her spine. She had not really given any thought to the long-term consequences of leaving this house, only of escaping her mother's vicious tongue. What would she do if she could not find employment and a place to live ... go to the workhouse?

The very thought made her tremble, but a life in that place could be no worse than the one she led here ... except here she had Ralph. But she could not hold on to her brother forever. He too had a life to make.

'You have no need to worry, Mother.' She hitched the small bundle in her arms. 'Whatever happens to me, I shall not return here. You will have what you have always wanted ... me gone from your life.'

'If you be thinking to go to Saul Marsh, then save yourself the trouble. It be plain he don't want you or he would have been here long afore.'

It was meant to hurt and it did. Miriam had thought long and hard, still trying to find excuses for his not coming, and though she now realised the truth, the pain of hearing it was no less sharp.

'I shall not go to Saul.' Crossing the kitchen, she halted with her hand on the door latch. 'Tell Ralph I love him,' she said softly. 'I love him very much.'

She loved him very much. But not as much as he loved her. Leah took the poker in her hand, stabbing it into the bed of the fire. She had thought to prevent a marriage and that way extract the payment due to her, a payment the girl's suffering would make. But maybe this way would be better. She would not see it but she could picture it. Placing the poker back in the hearth, Leah stared into the glowing coals. Pregnant and alone, without a penny to bless herself with ... yes, the dues of her father would be paid.

The bundle of clothes weighed almost nothing yet, her arms aching from holding it, Miriam stopped to rest. Lowering her burden to the ground, she stretched her back. She had not thought to tire so soon. Was it the carrying of the child or her recent illness that made her feel so weak? Lowering herself to the ground, she gazed back the way she had come. She had not gone past Derby's Hill, would never go that way again. That was part of the past, part of an unhappiness she would never truly put behind her. But it was over. From now on she must look to the future, one that would include her child.

In the distance Brades Village huddled beneath a darkening sky. She had thought Saul loved her. Believed him when he'd said she was the centre of his life, that he wanted to marry her. But they had been words of deception, lies to seduce her. He wanted only that one particular pleasure a woman can give to a man, but she had found it out too late. Now she was to pay the piper alone.

Miriam took up her bundle. She must find somewhere to spend the night. But the heath was no place to wander in the dark, it would be more prudent to follow the road.

How far she walked she could not say, knowing only the heaviness of each step, a heaviness that was echoed in her heart. Would Ralph go on searching for Saul Marsh? Her brother was never anything but gentle with her but she had seen his temper flare whenever he thought her insulted or threatened; many a boy had gone home from school with a black eye after a tussle with him in

71

the school yard and more than one man had nursed a bloody mouth after a comment Ralph found displeasing. But that too was over, in the past.

Tears blinding her eyes, she stumbled and the bundle fell from her arms. That was the only part of leaving Brades Village that caused her any real pain: the fact that she would not see her brother again. It was an underhand way of doing things. Miriam passed a hand across her face, wiping away the tears. But how could she have done otherwise? How could she have waited for Ralph to come home? He would not have allowed her to leave, or not without leaving with her. And what good would that have done? It would only have meant two of them without shelter and no place in which to seek it.

But what of his anger when he did return to the house to find her gone? Would he accept it ... or would he set out in search of her?

She thought she knew the answer to that and summoned the strength to continue, deaf to a jangling noise on the road behind her. She had to go on, get as far away from the village as she could.

Dark skirts and shawl blending with the dusk, she bent to retrieve her bundle. She was straightening up as the cart passed, the edge of one wheel striking her back.

'You be all right, miss, but you have to lie still. The doctor says there be no bones broke but you need to lie still.'

The voice was gentle. Why was it so gentle?

Miriam's brow furrowed as she struggled with the problem. It should not be so soft, the words spoken with concern; that was not the way a woman usually spoke to her.

'It's all right, miss,' the too-gentle voice came again. 'You had a nasty bump but you need have no worries, you will be well looked after here.'

Her eyelids lifting, Miriam stared at the face hovering above her: a plump round smiling face topped by a white cap set on grey hair plaited around the ears. 'What...?' She tried to push herself up but the sharp pain lancing through her back had her gasping.

'Now you just settle yourself.' A smile spreading itself over the plump face, Miriam was pressed gently back on the pillows. 'There be time for asking questions later. Right now you are going to drink this soup and then you are going to sleep. No! There will be no arguments from you, miss. You be going to do as you are told, at least till the doctor gives you leave to get up. Now drink your soup like a good girl, and tomorrow we'll see about fetching your folks.'

Drinking the soup, Miriam watched the woman add a few coals to the fire burning in a small prettily patterned iron grate. Why did everything feel so strange ... and apart from the feeling of strangeness, why was her mind so empty?

'That's a good girl!' The woman bustled back to the bed, taking the empty soup cup from Miriam. 'Now, a good night's sleep and you'll feel a whole lot better come morning.'

Miriam opened her mouth. There was something she should ask. But what was it? The pain

73

in her head chased away the questions she ought to be asking. She *had* to remember, she *had* to ask... But as sleep overwhelmed her only emptiness remained.

'Is it all right to come in, Mrs Baxter?'

'Yes, Mr Ethan.' Tray in hand, the woman turned towards the man standing at the doorway of the bedroom. 'She be just about asleep though, I reckon.'

'But is she all right?'

'You heard for yourself what the doctor said. No bones broken.'

'Yes, I heard, but it was what I did not hear that has me worried.' He came to stand beside the bed, the movements of his tall body fluid and easy. 'Broken bones can be mended, but a bump to the head ... she didn't seem to know where she was or where she was going.'

'Neither would you after being knocked unconscious by a wagon,' Sally Baxter replied with deliberate tartness. With two injured people in the house she did not want another giving way to guilt, especially when it was no fault of his. 'It be my guess the girl was only half conscious when you talked to her. Small wonder she couldn't place her whereabouts.'

'She looks so pale, so thin.'

Using the tray, she edged him from the room. The girl was thin enough now, but given what was inside her that would not last long. But Ethan must not learn of the child the stranger was carrying, he felt beholden enough already. Should he discover what the doctor had told Sally, he was like to let her stay. An offer the girl

74

would not refuse. Balancing the tray in one hand, Sally closed the bedroom door. Judging by the look of her she had never had a decent meal in her life, and the bruises on her body did not speak of a loving home.

'Best leave her to sleep,' Sally urged. 'She'll likely enough answer all your questions in the morning.'

'I hope you are right, Mrs Baxter,' he answered though his glance returned to the closed door.

''Course I be right ... don't I always tell you true?'

Ethan Crawley's handsome face creased into a smile. 'You always told me what I wanted to hear, even though *I* never told you what it was. Isn't that what they call feminine intuition?'

'I don't know what other folk call it.' Sally ushered him before her down the back stairs. 'But I calls it common sense. A woman gets to know the mind of a lad she has charge of most of the time. It gets so she knows what's forming in his mind afore he be fully aware of it himself.'

Reaching the corridor that led to the kitchen, he stopped. 'Mind reading!' he laughed. 'I always had a feeling you could read my mind. I can see now I'm going to have to exercise caution in your presence from now on.'

'Never mind caution,' Sally Baxter chided him. 'You just carry on exercising that tongue of yours ... oh, Lord, Mr Ethan, it be so good to hear you talk! I hadn't never thought to hear it again. But like my mother always said, God is good. He don't never send adversity without providing a blessing somewhere along with it, and this be the

75

greatest blessing He could give both you and your father.'

Ethan smiled again, touching a finger to the tear spilling from the woman's eye. She had always been so kind, treating him more like a son than the child of her employer, especially after... 'Thank you, Mrs Baxter,' he said, refusing to succumb to the memories struggling for possession. 'But sometimes I wonder!'

By the light of the gas lamps set at intervals along the corridor, her round face shone with curiosity. 'Wonder what, Mr Ethan?'

Walking in the direction of the hall, putting a safe distance between himself and the house-keeper, Ethan laughed over his shoulder. 'I wonder how long it will be before you tell me to hold my tongue!'

Her own silent laughter jiggling her several chins, Sally Baxter made for the kitchen, carrying the tray into the scullery. It had been a long time, but now, thanks be to God, the unhappiness was over.

'Be the girl all right?' her husband asked as she returned from the scullery and set about stowing the bowl and tray in their respective places.

'Her body be all of one piece. 'Cept it ain't.'

'There you go again, Sally Baxter!' He shook his grey head, amusement flickering in his eyes. 'I don't believe you'll ever be able to say a thing without denying it at the same time. How can a body be all of one piece and at the same time not?'

'Well, that's the way her be.' Going to the fire-place, Sally swung the kettle over the coals on its bracket. 'That wench's body don't exactly be one on its own – there be another inside it.'

Tying a dark blue apron about his middle, Ezra Baxter bent to the task of cleaning boots. 'The young wench be expecting? Did the doctor say so?'

'No,' Sally answered. 'But I don't need no doctor to tell me her be carrying!'

'She be lucky not to have lost it then, being struck by a wagon.' Ezra smeared polish over leather.

Spooning tea into a blue and white patterned teapot, Sally pulled a wry face. 'If you ask me, that be the worst of the luck that one has had tonight.'

Experience telling Ezra his wife would continue to answer questions, whether asked or not, he silently carried on polishing.

'It be plain as a pikestaff.' After scalding the tea in the pot, Sally bustled about the large kitchen fetching cups to the table. 'That wench has been shown the door. Whether it be by her own folk or not, she's been thrown out. I bet you a pound to a penny she got herself in trouble and the man has refused to marry her.'

'You can't know that.' Ezra breathed on the toe cap of the boot stretched over one hand then rubbed it briskly with a cloth.

Lifting the bead-edged cover from a jug that matched the teapot, Sally poured milk liberally into the cups. 'Maybe I don't have it written in black and white, but then I don't need no affidavit. That girl is wearing no wedding ring!'

'That doesn't mean she's not married.' Ezra

placed the boots aside.

'And it don't mean she is!' Sally returned tritely. 'You mark my words, Ezra Baxter, that girl be no man's wife!'

After returning polish and brushes to a small room adjoining the scullery, he accepted the tea his wife offered, taking it to a chair set against the highly polished cast-iron range. 'Well, married or not it makes no difference. The girl will be sent on her way as soon as she's recovered.'

'I wouldn't be too sure of that!' Sally sipped her tea thoughtfully. 'I wouldn't be sure at all.'

'I took the stallion out to Derby's Hill, I often ride there.' Ethan Rawley eased his long legs out in front of him, head resting against the wing armchair. 'When he refused to budge, I thought he was just living up to his reputation of being damned awkward. But after I got down to investigate, I saw that chap lying in a hollow. I went down to him, not knowing what to expect, and it was beyond any imagining.'

'A nasty business.' Clayton Rawley shook his head slowly. 'The man is lucky to be alive.'

'I think whoever did that intended him to stay alive, otherwise a knife in the heart would have done a much better job. But why was he not killed, Father ... why would someone injure him so badly yet not kill him?'

Father! Clayton Rawley's heart glowed at the sound of that word. Ten years his son had remained silent, never speaking, whatever the circumstance. But now his tongue was freed, the bonds that had held him were broken; and much as he pitied the man lying upstairs, Clayton could not help but feel a greater gratitude. This was the way of Providence, he told himself. The man would have suffered those injuries anyway; he could have lain out there on the heath undiscovered for days, probably died. As it was he would live, though what kind of life? Providence may have fashioned the way but it had extracted a high price. One man's suffering for another's healing.

'Who can tell why he was not killed?' Clayton answered his son. 'I can only say that the man ... or woman ... who did him such an injury was either truly evil or so full of rage as to have given way under its influence. The doctor is convinced that had you not found him he would not have been alive come morning. Was he able to speak? Did he tell you what had occurred?'

'No.' Ethan sipped the brandy his father had pressed into his hand. 'He was pretty far gone, almost unconscious. I could tell from the state of his clothes that he must have lost a great deal of blood. To drag him up that slope and get him on to a horse would likely have exacerbated the bleeding, but I doubt I could have managed to lift him by myself. The nearest help was Portway Farm. You probably know it, Father? It lies at the foot of the hill over from Brades Village.'

Clayton nodded but made no answer, the thrill of hearing his son speak making more impression on him than the words.

'I rode there for a wagon and someone to help me lift the injured man into it. The farmer had a wagon and horse, but when I said to send a rider here to the Hall he told me that one horse was all he had. So we sent his son here on my horse with instructions to have things ready.'

Sipping his own brandy, Clayton relived his moment of terror at seeing the stallion with another rider on its back; felt again the horror of anticipating news of an accident. Then his disbelief on hearing the rider say, 'Mr Ethan told me to tell you...'

'I was unsure at first,' Ethan was saying. 'That stallion isn't exactly easy to handle. But when he let the lad fondle his muzzle, I guessed it would be all right.' He shrugged. 'I had very little choice. If I had not stayed with the wagon they could have spent a day looking for the man. One part of the heath looks very like another.'

'And the girl?'

'God knows, Father!' The tension that had held him since his discovery this afternoon showing in his face, Ethan rose to his feet, brandy glass gripped between his fingers. 'One moment the road was empty. The next...' He turned to the fireplace and stared into the fire.

'You were not to know she was there,' Clayton said gently. 'It will do no good to blame yourself.'

'I should have been driving the wagon! The farmer could just as easily have ridden in the back with the injured man.'

Placing his glass on the small sofa table at his side, Clayton kept his voice deliberately matter of fact. To blame himself for the girl's accident might put Ethan back where he was a few hours ago – in a world his father could not enter. 'What you say is true, but it makes very little sense. The farmer could have ridden in the back of the wagon and left you to drive a horse that was unfamiliar with your voice or your hand on the reins – and that over territory you know yourself to be dangerous. I think, of the two of you, he showed the more common sense.'

'Of course you are right, Father ... it's just that I feel so responsible.'

Clayton smiled, pride obvious in the light that shone in his eyes. It was good that his son felt responsibility towards others. One day there would be many men working for him and he would hold a measure of responsibility for each of them. He had made a good start.

'Responsibility and blame are not necessarily bed fellows, Ethan. I want you to feel the first but take care where you attach the second. Bent close to the ground, as the farmer says she was, dressed in dark clothing, she was all but invisible. And, fortunately, she seems to have come to little real harm.'

Ethan turned to face his father, tension still clearly marked between his brows. 'Can we count her not being able to recall who she is, or where she was going, as fortunate?'

'But do we know that was a result of the accident on the road?' Clayton met his son's glance. 'Do we know she had those memories before that wagon hit her? Can we be positive she was perfectly lucid before sustaining that bump to her head? Be sensible, Ethan. You did what any responsible person would have done. You had her put in the wagon and brought here to be cared for. And she will be, for as long as it takes. Only do not hang blame like a millstone about your neck. The doctor told us it is probably no more than a mild concussion that will pass within a few days.'

'And if it does not?'

'Then we can only see that she is looked after,' Clayton replied, seeing his frown deepen. 'She will have a home here, and judging by what I saw when she was carried in, it will be a better one than she has had for some long time.'

A home, yes. Ethan turned away again, his eyes on the dancing flames. But what was a new home worth if your world had suddenly been snatched away?

Chapter Six

Miriam lay still. Behind her eyes a dull ache throbbed. She had wakened with the dawn but when she tried to rise from the bed a pain shot through her back. But this was wrong. She should not lie abed, her...

She probed the darkness that was her mind. Her what? What or who caused her to feel that lying in bed was wrong? But the answer remained concealed, as though by a thick curtain. Opening her eyes, she glanced about the room, a vague feeling that all was not as it should be the only light in the darkness that filled her.

A narrow pencil line of light where the curtains met in the middle was just enough to reveal the outlines of the furniture and this too added to her alarm, the feeling that something was wrong. She had to get up before ... but the rest of it slipped away. Catching her breath with the pain of it, she threw off the covers, forcing herself to stand.

Moving slowly, each step an effort, she reached the window, wincing as she reached up to draw back the curtains.

Behind Miriam the bedroom door creaked a little on its hinge. Somewhere in the empty darkness of her mind the sound found an echo and the cry broke instinctively from her lips. 'I am up ... I am up!'

Sally Baxter caught the fear behind the words and saw it in the eyes that met hers. Her suppositions of the night before were confirmed. This wench had been hard dealt with!

'I see you are, but you shouldn't be. You should lie still until the doctor says you be fit to move.' Sally took a couple of steps forward then stopped as the girl drew back, fear bright as fever in her wide eyes. She was no more than a child ... a slip of a girl. A rush of warmth and pity swept through Sally. From what she could guess there might have been wrongdoing on her part, but the dread on the girl's face was living proof there had been a whole lot more on someone else's.

'C'mon now, me wench. There be nothing to be afraid of.' Sally reached out one hand then let it fall as the girl whimpered. 'You had a bit of a tumble last night. It be better you rest in bed for a day or two.'

'No ... it is wrong ... I should not lie in bed, I...'

83

Puzzlement mixing with fright, Miriam glanced behind Sally to the door, her expression saying she expected someone else to come in.

'You be bound to be feeling a mite mixed up,' Sally returned with calm practicality. 'That's not to be wondered at after a bump on the head. You get yourself back in that bed and I'll send you up a cup of tea and a bite of breakfast, that will bring the colour back to your cheeks.' But memories? She closed the door behind her. What would bring those back?

Miriam stood, her eyes on the closed door, sounds and blurred pictures confused in her mind. She had heard a shout, then felt a blow to her back. Then a man bending over her, his face anxious. Another, deeper voice, had followed, and then the sensation of being lifted ... a wagon. She had been put into a wagon. Then a woman's voice and hands more gentle than... She shivered as another memory began to rise, but it fell back into the depths before she could recognise it. Those hands had taken her clothes, bathed her face and body before putting her into this. Miriam looked down at the oversized calico night gown. And all the time that voice had talked, softly, soothingly, not like...

'Eh, miss, you'll take a chill standing there in the cold.'

A girl no older than herself, dressed in grey apron over a brown dress, a cap covering every vestige of her hair, tapped on the door before carrying a bucket of coals into the room. Kneeling before the fireplace, she began to clear the grate of dead cinders before laying sticks

84

criss-cross over a layer of tightly crumpled newspaper. Taking a match box from her pocket, she struck one, holding it to the papers until they flamed.

Miriam felt the emptiness inside her ebb and flow as she watched the girl place first egg-sized pieces of coal over the sticks, then several larger lumps over them. Thoughts, intangible as mist, drifted hazily in her mind. Who was the woman who had dressed her in this night gown? Who was this girl? Should she know them?

Scooping ash into the bucket, the girl swept the hearth before rising to her feet. 'There you go.' She fanned a breath along the small mantelpiece. 'Ain't no dust, but it be as well to make sure. Mrs Baxter will run a finger across this shelf sure as my name be Ginny Jinks.'

'Mrs Baxter?'

Bucket in hand, the girl looked at Miriam, a tiny frown puckering what little brow showed beneath the cap. 'Arrh, Mrs Baxter. She was up here a minute or two ago, and if she said you was to get into bed then I would do it if I were you. Don't take kindly to having her orders flounced, don't Sally Baxter.'

'My clothes?' Miriam plucked at the rough cotton gown.

'Oh, they be ready for you when the doctor says you be fit to go on your way.'

Go on her way? Miriam watched the door close a second time. To where? Wisps of something elusive and fragile drifted into her mind then were gone, disappearing like spindrift on the wind, leaving her with the same frightening

85

emptiness. A heaviness pulling at her limbs, she sagged on to the bed.

Why were those women strangers to her? Why did this room feel so wrong? And, worst of all, why could she not remember what had happened before that blow to her back?

How could Miriam have left the house without their mother seeing? Wiping the sweat from his eyes with the cloth tied about his neck, Ralph squatted on his haunches as the donkey boy loaded lumps of coal into the bogey. Leah had been down the yard using the privy, or so she said, but in his bones Ralph knew his mother lied. It would be nearer the truth to say she had watched the girl go; probably helped her through the door with a blow to the face or a boot to her rear. His hand tightened on the handle of his pick. God, if he found that were so...

'You can put your marker on now, Mr Bryce.' The whites of his eyes all that showed in the blackness of the mine, the lad still spoke respectfully.

Laying aside the pick and taking a metal disc from his pocket, Ralph hung it on the side of the wooden truck filled to capacity with coal, then set his shoulder against it, using his weight to set it in motion on the steel lines set into the floor of the narrow tunnel.

'Thanks, Mr Bryce.' A flash of teeth joined the white circles, the light of Ralph's lamp reflecting the only patches of the lad's skin that were not thickly coated with black dust, hardened to a coat by sweat. 'Do this tub be the last for today?'

Ralph nodded, the light from his lamp dancing a weird measure over the shiny coal walls of the tunnel.

'Can I go up top with this then?'

'Reckon so, lad.' Sweat trickling into his eyes, Ralph wiped the cloth once more over his face.

The white teeth flashed again and the lad bent to push the bogey back along the tunnel towards the shaft. 'I'll tell the winding shed you be coming up.'

Sinking down, Ralph rested his back against a coal wall glistening with moisture. He had searched for his sister. Every moment free from the mine he had searched, looking for her in every place he guessed she might be, and in some his heart told him she would not. But all the hours spent walking, all the questions asked had brought no reward. For all anyone seemed to know, Miriam had vanished from the face of the earth.

And every time he returned to the house Leah had been waiting, coldness in the set of her mouth, animosity touching her eyes. If only he knew why, knew what had happened in mother's life, then he might understand. But she had never told him of any cause, any reason that could give rise to this loathing of Miriam.

Around him water dripped steadily on to the ground, like the ticking of a hundred clocks, each sound a measure of his life. Ralph lifted the ends of his neck cloth, pressing it hard against his eyes. If only his life could stop, if never again he had to face the pain of living! But things could not be ordered that way. He had to go on despite everything, go on until he found her. And then? Bent almost double in the low-ceilinged tunnel he had been set to work alone, he followed the steel bogey lines. It would be no different. His life would go on, just as long as Miriam needed it to.

'She has been with us two weeks now.' Clayton Rawley looked at the plump woman standing before his desk in the booklined study. 'What is your opinion, Mrs Baxter?'

'Well, sir, the doctor says she be well enough.'

Folding his hands and resting them on the well-polished mahogany, he spoke again. 'I have the doctor's opinion, Mrs Baxter. Now I am asking for yours.'

Sally Baxter eased her weight from one foot to the other. 'It be like the doctor says. The girl be near enough healed in her body.'

'But?' Clayton asked the question quietly but there was no mistaking the firmness behind it.

'It be her mind, Mr Rawley, sir.' Sally fidgeted with a corner of her snow white apron. 'Or rather, I should say her memory. There be nothing amiss with her mind, that girl be as sound in that as you or me, it be her memory as is lacking. Seems she has no recollection of anything before Mr Ethan brought her to the Hall.'

'I had assumed as much. Tell me, Mrs Baxter, have you any suspicion she may be concealing something from us?'

The girl had never mentioned her condition, it was true. Sally thought quickly. She was almost sure the doctor had somehow not included it when discussing her with Clayton Rawley. It was strange, for would he not have detected the pregnancy? But then again, he had examined only the girl's back, and it was only gut feeling had revealed the truth to Sally Baxter rather than the size of the girl's belly. Being called out from a good night's supper and a better night's drinking had possibly diminished the doctor's attentiveness, and he had seen the patient only once more and that to determine her recovery from concussion. No, by some quirk of fate, her employer had no idea the girl he'd taken into his house was with child.

'I think she's telling us all she knows,' Sally answered, not sure why she deliberately withheld what she herself suspected. 'As for what she can't recall...'

'And what do you think that is?'

Sally's fingers played with the corner of her apron. 'Not good, sir. The girl's body were fair covered with bruises. She's been knocked about, and by my reckoning, more than once. Whether it be by her family or otherwise, I have no way of knowing. She has told me no more than she has told you. But whoever it were had no love for the girl.'

'Do you think maybe she was running away?'

'There be no way of telling.' Sally shook her head slightly. 'If she was then I would have thought her to be carrying at least a change of clothing with her.'

'But there was nothing.'

'She had only the clothes she stood up in.'

'Stood is hardly the right word!' He brought his

hands down in one sharp movement, letting them lie still as he muttered, 'Why in heaven's name did she have to be on the road at that time of night?'

Sally made no answer. What her employer really meant was, why did it have to be his son who had run the girl down?

'She had no personal possessions, anything that will help identify her?'

'No, sir. Nor have I heard of a girl gone missing from the village. Seems like she don't be from these parts.'

'Then what brought her here?' He glanced up as he spoke. 'Was she visiting? Relatives or friends maybe? We must make enquiries, there has to be an explanation.'

'For what, Father?'

Clayton Rawley smiled as his son entered the study. Tall and lithe as whipcord, riding habit accentuating rather than disguising his wide shoulders, Ethan made an imposing figure. And a handsome one too, Clayton noted proudly, with his mother's midnight blue eyes and sculpted features.

'Mrs Baxter and I were just speaking of the girl you picked up on the road.'

Knocked down would have been a fairer description, Ethan thought, but, sparing his father's feelings, made no comment.

'She is no worse?'

'No different from when you spoke to her yesterday,' the housekeeper reassured him quickly.

'But no better? There has been no return of

memory?' As Sally shook her head, he glanced again at his father. 'Should we not get a second opinion, bring someone from London to take a look at her?'

Reluctant to deny his son anything, Clayton nodded. 'If that is what you wish, Ethan, then of course we will ask a specialist to examine the girl, but I think perhaps it may be a little early for that. She has had quite a shock and the effects of that can take some time to wear off. Two weeks is really very little. Give the girl a while longer and if she still cannot remember, then we will take further advice. How do you feel about that?'

'Of course, Father. Two weeks is a little too soon for worry.'

Clayton Rawley's gut tightened with suspicion. 'Worry' his son had said. Did he feel more than responsible for that girl? Was there something between them? Had he been visiting her when he went riding that afternoon?

His face betraying none of the sudden turmoil inside him, Clayton unfolded his hands, laying them palm down as he looked again at his house-keeper. 'Now, Mrs Baxter, you say this girl is well? Does that mean she is fit enough to...'

'We can't send her away, Father!'

Clayton's gut tightened again. That interruption had been a little too vehement.

'Allow me to finish, Ethan, please.'

'My apologies, Father.' He lowered himself into another of the leather armchairs but his whole body was visibly tense. What exactly did his father have in mind? Having her placed in an institution ... was that what he planned? Yet only

91

a moment since he had spoken of having her examined by a specialist, but he had not specified where such an examination would take place; it could just as easily be done in the workhouse as here. Resentment building hotly inside him, Ethan watched his father covertly. They had never before had a disagreement. In fact, for the last ten years, his own muteness had precluded any proper conversation. He hoped it would not lead to dissension between them, but he could not stand quietly by and see that girl put back on the road when she had no idea who she was or where she belonged.

'Is she fit enough to work?' Clayton went on quietly.

Sally had dropped the corner of her apron when her employer's tone sharpened towards his son. Now she folded her hands across her stomach. 'I reckon she is, sir, depending on the nature of the work she be asked to do.'

Smiling, Clayton shook his head. 'You are as suspicious of me as my son, Mrs Baxter. I assure you both, I have no intention of putting her out on the road nor do I intend setting her to making chain in some back-street workshop. I had rather thought of some post here at Brade Hall. That is, if you are willing to have the supervision of another maid?'

'I am, sir.' Sally beamed. He had no need to ask, she would do as she was ordered, same as any other body in his pay, but he had always treated her with politeness and respect and in return she would turn the earth over in the heavens for him and his son.

'Then if the girl agrees, the matter is settled. Let Baxter know she will be paid the same wage as others her age, supposing he can guess what that may be.'

'We will manage, sir.' Bobbing a curtsey, Sally left the study, asking herself on the way to the kitchen what would happen when the girl's pregnancy began to show.

'I'm sorry I jumped the gun, Father.' The tension that had held him loosened and Ethan relaxed. 'I should have known you would not put the girl out.'

Pushing himself to his feet, Clayton went to stand against the fireplace. Beautifully patterned tiles set inside an ornate wooden surround picked out the colours of the heavy chenille drapes hanging from the high, faintly Gothic-styled windows; the gleam of the heavy brass fender and firedogs echoed the gold-tooled bindings of the books.

'You seem more than anxious about the girl.' He stared into the fire's heart. 'You would tell me, Ethan, if there was anything between you and her? If ... if perhaps she was not a stranger you found wandering on the road?'

'But of course I would,' laughed Ethan. 'We've never had secrets, Father, and I am not about to have any now. I never saw that girl before the evening I brought her here. If I sound anxious for her welfare it is because I feel responsible for what happened. Oh, I know ... I know!' He raised his hands in a defensive gesture as his father turned to face him. 'It was not my fault. But knowing that does not make it any easier.

Coincidence or not, Father, I can't help but feel as I do. Thank you for giving her work here.'

'She will be useful about the place, I have no doubt.' Clayton answered, his earlier suspicions evaporating. 'Besides which, the girl has a pretty face which will make a pleasant change. Though don't go telling Mrs Baxter what I said.'

'That is one secret we will both keep.' Ethan stood up and would have left but his father spoke again.

'Talking of secrets, the fellow you found on Derby's Hill? He has said nothing of his attacker. Do you think he is deliberately hiding something?'

Ethan laughed again, the sound deep and musical in his throat. 'You know, Father, you sound rather like Doctor Watson in those dreadful Sherlock Holmes stories. He was always suspicious of everyone then ended up getting it wrong.'

'Dreadful stories or not, you appear to have read them.'

'They *are* entertaining, Father ... if a little old-fashioned.'

'Like a certain parent you know?'

'Something like him.' Ethan joined his smile to that of his father. 'But, seriously, the fellow is possibly withholding something, unless of course he was attacked from behind. That way he would not have seen who it was.'

Taking a cigar from a humidor on his desk, Clayton lit it with a spill held to the fire. After drawing deeply for several moments he exhaled, sending a filmy cloud of smoke towards the

ceiling. 'There does not seem to be any indication of an attack from the rear. There's no
injury to his head, no marks on his back that
would point to his being struck from behind.'

'A bit of a puzzle, eh?'

'Mmm.' Blowing out another stream of smoke,
Clayton held the cigar between his fingers,
studying its glowing tip. 'As you say, puzzling.
But what I find even more puzzling is the reason
this...'

'Saul Marsh.'

'Ah, yes, Saul Marsh! I find the reason he gives
for being attacked rather less than plausible.
Robbery? Well, yes, probably there was someone
with even less than he had, but from the look of
him and what was left of his clothing, I'd say that
he had precious little in his pockets.' The cigar
held between first and second finger, Clayton
tapped it with the third, sending a shower of
downy ash floating into the hearth. 'Supposing I
am correct in that surmise, what other cause
would there be for his being attacked?'

'A dispute over an inheritance? Which son has
the family farm and which the pig?'

Clayton smiled at the picture the words
conjured up in his mind but he could see the
logic of them. Family feuds were not the sole
province of the rich. A man might as easily fight
over a pig as a palace. Tempers could run high
and blood hot in matters such as inheritance, and
men stoop to many acts to achieve what they saw
as their due; but to wreak such a terrible
vengeance, to deprive a man of all that made him
a man... Yes, claim to inheritance could be the

force that drove a man to do that to another ... or claim to a woman!

'But you do not think that was the cause?' Ethan had watched his father's thoughts chase across his face.

'What do I not think the cause?'

'Why, fighting for the pig, Watson. Fighting for the pig!'

'No, I do not.' Smoke narrowing his eyes, Clayton watched his son's tall figure move towards the door. Love was the strongest of all emotions, the most potent force of body or mind, and it was the closest kin to hatred. Love could cherish or it could kill.

Pig or palace? Clayton drew on the cigar, his son's laughter drifting back to him from the hall. He was willing to wager the man lying upstairs had neither ... but a girl?

'Elementary!' He smiled. His son was not the only reader of the famous Conan Doyle.

Chapter Seven

Miriam looked at the bundle of clothes the woman had placed on the bed. Dark skirt topped with neatly folded blouse and underwear, the shabbiness of which even careful laundering could not disguise.

'There be no more call for you to stay cooped up in this room.' Sally Baxter watched the young girl's face. This was the first time she had seen her own clothes since that accident; it could be they would bring some response, some spark of memory.

Miriam stretched out a hand, touching the plain cotton petticoat, the rough serge skirt.

'They be your clothes,' Sally said. 'Your own and nobody else's.'

Her clothes! Miriam stared at the anonymous bundle. How could they be hers? She did not recognise them, they held no meaning for her.

'I reckon they be your everyday things.' Sally's eyes remained fixed on her pale features, watching for the faintest flicker, the slightest change. There had been none so far, not the least sign since the girl had been brought here; but she must be sure this loss of memory was not some fabrication. That it was not a story cunningly concocted to get the girl a place to live.

'But your Sunday dress will be prettier. What colour is it?'

It was a subtle question, designed to take the girl off guard, but as she lifted her head her eyes were empty.

Inside Sally felt a mixture of emotions: gladness the girl was not deceiving her, and sadness that she was lost in a world that held nothing. No mother, no love, only a dark relentless void.

'Well, no matter.' She forced cheerfulness into her voice. 'No doubt we can find you a Sunday frock from somewhere, but right now you get yourself into them. I'll send Ginny up in a couple of ticks to bring you downstairs.'

The door closing behind the plump figure, Miriam picked up the petticoat, pressing it to her

97

face. Why had she been on the road at night? Where had she been going to ... or coming from? If only she could remember! A sob worked its way to her lips but was forced back by the cloth held tight against her mouth. The people of this house had been kind to her, caring for her as...

As whom? Miriam's breath stuck in her throat as a door creaked open in her mind, then her shoulders sagged as it shut tight. Had someone cared for her? Had she been loved by a father or a mother? Her eyelids pressed down painfully as she tried to prise open that mental door, tried to reach whatever lay behind it. But it would not budge.

Defeated, she climbed from the bed, pulling the calico night gown off over her head, catching sight of fading bruises on her arms and above her breasts. Were *they* signs of love, evidence of a caring family? Recovering her memory might bring more than answers, it might bring misery. Reaching for the underwear, Miriam began to dress.

'Ah, you be dressed already.' Ginny breezed into the bedroom before the sound of her tap on the door had died away. 'Mrs Baxter thought you could maybe do with some help, you not having been out of bed for some time.'

Not having been out of bed? Miriam thought of the long hours, of the nights she had paced this room trying to remember, always trying to remember: watching the arrival of each grey dawn, another day that brought no offering to fill the vacuum of her memory. But she kept the thoughts to herself as she fastened the tiny cloth-covered buttons of her blouse.

'I can manage, thank you.' Crossing to a table that held mirror, brush and comb, she tried to smile at the young girl watching her. 'Ginny ... I want to say thank you to you for helping to take care of me. I ... I shall miss you.'

'Miss me! How come? I ain't going anywhere.'

But *she* was. Miriam pulled the brush through her hair. But where? Where was she going?

'It's time for me to leave.' Coiling her long hair about her fingers, Miriam lifted it on to the back of her head, securing it with some of the pins lying in a glass bowl.

Ginny had already set about remaking the bed, her quick hands smoothing the twill sheets and plumping the flock filled pillows. 'Who said?' she puffed, as she threw the quilt over the bed. 'Who said for you to leave?'

Her hair fastened, Miriam joined in tidying the bed then picked up the night gown from where she had dropped it on to a chair. 'Where do I put this?'

A frown puckering her plain face, Ginny paused from her last-minute check of the smooth sheets. 'Put it? That be your night gown. You'll be sleeping in that again tonight, we don't get a fresh one every night, we don't be one of the nobs.'

Miriam glanced at the gown now folded in her hands. 'I'm sorry, I seem to have misled you. I wasn't expecting a fresh night gown, I was wanting to put this with the laundry before I leave.'

'There you go again!' Ginny gave the bed a

final pat. 'Going on about leaving. Do you mean you haven't been looked after proper?'

'Oh, no, it's not that!' Miriam felt a tide of colour sweep her cheeks.

'Then what is it? Anyone would think your bottom be on fire, you be so anxious to go!'

'Mrs Baxter brought me my clothes.'

'And you thought they were your marching orders? It ain't so, it ain't so at all. You ain't going to be told to leave, you're going to be asked to stay.'

Miriam's hands tightened on the folded night gown. 'Stay!'

'Yes.' The frown disappeared from the other girl's brow, chased by a smile that lent her plain face a temporary prettiness. 'Mrs Baxter said the master told her to offer you a place here at the Hall. So you see, you'll be wanting that night gown again tonight ... that is, supposing you choose to stay?'

What other choice had she? The colour ebbing from her cheeks, Miriam clutched the night gown, lips compressed against the tears that rose to her throat. These people had been so very kind to her, caring for her the same way...

Again that closed door opened the tiniest fraction, allowing an elusive, tantalising gleam to flicker in the shadows, a half-formed something that reached for her mind and then was drawn back, locked away once more in impenetrable darkness.

'It ain't a bad house to be in.' Ginny prised the gown from Miriam's fingers, misreading the sudden pallor of her cheeks. 'I tell you, I'd rather be at Brade Hall than sweating away making nails like a good many women down there in the village. That sort of work kills horses! Was that what you was doing for your living?'

Had she made nails? Miriam probed the shadows. Had that been her work? Was it her employment that had been responsible for the bruises that adorned her arms and body?

Placing the night gown on the bed, Ginny turned towards the door. 'Well, whether you stay or not, I have to be getting back to the kitchen or Mrs Baxter will have my guts for garters!'

Saul Marsh eased himself higher in the bed. The sting at the base of his stomach was markedly less but he was in no hurry for that to be known. He was comfortable here in this house, every comfort given, every need satisfied. Yes, he was very comfortable and that was how he meant to keep it, just so long as he could. His mother would have asked around for him, but she wouldn't in a hundred years expect to find him tucked up at Brade Hall, and he had no intention of enlightening her.

He had not quite finished with the village, not yet. There was still the matter of Ralph Bryce to deal with, and he *would* be dealt with. But not by the law. That way too much would be brought to light, such as the reason for Bryce's attacking him and in particular the circumstances of it.

Relaxing against the pillow, Saul smiled thinly. She had been so easy. Not willing, not easy in that way. But it had been no real contest just the same. She had fallen for his patter hook, line and sinker, believed every single word. Believed he was in love with her. The malicious smile playing about his mouth, he stared up at the ceiling. She was pretty enough, and her body slim and satisfying, but Miriam Bryce was not for him, and nor was any other Brades Village girl. When he took a wife it would be one could bring him more than a comely body. She must bring money, enough to ensure her husband never spent another day below ground digging in the bowels of the earth for nothing but a few coppers. In fact, she would have to bring enough money to ensure he never had to do another day's work so long as he lived.

He had come to see the other side of the coin since being brought to this house. Saul glanced about the room. Blue velvet, thicker than the quilt on his mother's bed, fell in graceful folds from high windows. Set below them a writing bureau complemented matching bedside tables, and at the fireside a comfortable brocade-covered chair echoed the deep blue of the carpet. There were no pegged rugs here, no living room doubling as kitchen, and no curtains that boasted as many holes as a colander.

Yes, this and no less than this was what he wanted from life, and what he had every intention life should bring him.

But he must be careful. At the first opportunity he must silence Ralph Bryce, could take no chance of his speaking out. Once he was dealt with there would be no danger from the girl. She would make no claim, not without her brother to back her, and neither would the mother. What proof would they have? A girl who was willing to give herself to one man may just as eagerly give herself to others. Would Leah Bryce risk that sort of gossip? No, she would not! That woman wrapped privacy about herself like a shawl. And the child the girl carried? What of it? No, there was no proof.

The smile on his mouth widening, Saul settled back against the downy soft pillows, luxuriating in the feel of them against his shoulders, revelling in a comfort he had never known in his life, but which from now on he meant to enjoy; all he had to do was tread softly. He was handsome enough and possessed an attraction for women, the girls of Brades Village had more than confirmed that; he had taken his pick of them. And women were women whatever walk of life they came from.

Pretty Edwina would prove no real challenge. She was already a daily visitor here and it was Saul Marsh she sat and chatted to.

Edwina Sadler, only daughter of Obadiah Sadler of Sadler's Brick and Tile and owner of Hange collieries. Yes, the wealthy Edwina would do very nicely.

And if she wanted children? So what! The little rich girl had to find out sooner or later that she could not necessarily have everything she wanted; and by the time she did it would be too late!

'Can you stand to have visitors, old man?'

Wiping the smile from his mouth, Saul turned his head to the door, blinking as though waking suddenly from sleep.

'Oh, Saul! I am so sorry. We've woken you and

it's all my fault. I asked Ethan to bring me up to see you.'

'Don't apologise for saving my life, Miss Sadler.' Saul gave the wry smile he had practised so often. 'I wasn't sleeping, I was dying ... of boredom! So, you see, you came just in time.'

'How sweet, to pretend to be pleased to see us.' Edwina Sadler's ready smile was clear to see as she came closer to the bed.

His glance taking in the deep pink costume frogged with burgundy, matching hat set at an angle over sherry-coloured hair, wide dark eyes smiling down at him, Saul nodded inwardly. Edwina Sadler *would* do. At least until he felt ready for a change!

'I am not pretending, Miss Sadler. Boredom was sitting very heavily upon me, but your companion has threatened to sit there even more heavily should I attempt to leave this bed.'

'And I mean it!' Drawing an armchair to the bedside, Ethan Rawley settled the young woman into it before seating himself on the end of the bed. 'You are going to stay put for as long as it takes, so stop bleating.'

'Bleating?' Eyes darkly appealing as liquid chocolate held Saul's. 'Does he really bleat, Ethan?'

Ethan hoisted one leg, folding it on the bed as he answered. 'Like a ewe that's lost its lamb. Goes on about being a nuisance to us and a hindrance to the staff. But I tell him he is no nuisance to Father or myself. And as for the staff, they positively fawn on him, especially Ginny. Mrs Baxter tells me she will not let the new girl get a look in so far as bringing the handsome Saul his meals.'

His own glance dropping to Edwina's breasts as she questioned Ethan, Saul felt again that inward satisfaction. She could provide him with a pleasant life in more ways than one.

'New girl?'

Ethan's own smile suddenly widened. 'Yes, you remember. I told you about her ... the girl we found on the road?'

'Ah, the mysterious beauty!' Edwina returned her attention to Saul. 'The girl without a yesterday.'

'She sounds intriguing. Beautiful *and* mysterious. That could prove a heady combination.'

Edwina's laugh rang out. 'I think it has done already. Ethan is quite taken with her.'

Pushing himself up, Saul took care to show just the right amount of pain in his face, to allow a carefully pitched groan to escape his lips and the wry smile not quite to reach his eyes as Edwina reached a sympathetic hand towards him. So Ethan had a fancy for another girl? That was all to the good, an obstacle removed from his own path. He had wondered about the state of things between these two. Now it seemed he need wonder no more.

'Don't be ridiculous, Edwina.' Ethan laughed but tell-tale colour touched his cheeks.

'Why do you call her the girl without a yesterday?'

'Because that's what she is. Hasn't Ethan told you about her?'

Saul shook his head slowly. 'No. He's not told

me about any girl.'

'That proves it then.' Edwina laughed again, but this time the sound was short and high-pitched. 'He's keeping her a secret, keeping her to himself.'

'Edwina, I wish you wouldn't talk such nonsense!' Ethan protested. 'I am not keeping the girl a secret. I have not mentioned her to Saul for the simple reason that I could not imagine his being at all interested.'

Leaning close to him, her perfume delicate in his nostrils, Edwina whispered loudly, 'Do you believe him, Saul? Does he really suppose you are not at all interested, or is it that he wants no rival for the auburn-haired beauty?'

Jumping up from his seat on the bed, Ethan walked around to the other side. Placing both hands on Edwina's shoulders, he pretended to shake her. 'Now look here, Miss Sadler, either you behave or you go home right now.'

Raising a hand to the one that rested on her shoulder, Edwina tapped it playfully but her dark eyes held a warmth born of something other than mirth as she retorted, 'You are a bully, Ethan Rawley, and you always were.'

'What do you say, Saul?' Ethan lifted his glance but his hands stayed where they were. 'Do you think I am a bully?'

'I would never dream of contradicting a lady.' Saul's smile was designed to charm birds from the sky. 'Especially one so beautiful as Miss Sadler.'

'That is below the belt.' Ethan swung away, chuckling deep in his throat. 'You two are ganging up on me. What is a chap to do?'

'You could always tell Saul about...'

'I know, I know. The girl with no yesterday.' Falling silent, his face serious, Ethan stood at the bottom of the bed, fingers on the mahogany foot board.

'It was the same evening we brought you down from Derby's Hill. We were on the road that leads on to Tividale. It was almost dark and the driver of the cart we were in did not see the girl. Her dark clothing was lost among the shadows and as we passed the wheel of the cart struck her. She was unconscious when we picked her up. The blow to her back bowled her forward and she struck her head. We brought her here and had her looked at by the same doctor as we called to you. He said there may be some slight concussion, but apart from that the accident had caused no serious harm. And that is the way it has proved. Except that she appears to have no memory of her life before the mishap.'

'You mean, the accident caused her to lose it?'

'It may be, Saul, but we cannot be sure. It could be her memory was already lost before she was knocked down by us. Perhaps it had already happened.'

'Maybe that was why she was running away?'

Ethan turned his head sharply. 'We cannot be sure of that either, Edwina! What is to say she was running away, where is the evidence? She had no bag with her, no belongings.'

'Did you check, Ethan?' Edwina's expression too had relinquished its smile, matching that of the man for seriousness. 'Did you search the road, or the verge of the heath? Did you think to look for anything the girl may have been carrying?'

'No.' His gaze fell away. 'No, we didn't search.'

Gentle and quiet but still firm, she asked, 'Then how can you be sure the girl had nothing with her?'

'It was several days before we searched.' Ethan's lips were tight. 'Only when we were afraid her memory might be some time returning did we try to find out if she had been carrying a bag, or something that might point to her identity. I rode over every inch of the spot where it happened, as well as the heath. Had she had a bag or anything of the sort I thought I might find it, or at least what the foxes had left of it. But there was nothing.'

'What about the farmer, the one whose cart you used?'

Pushing himself away from the bed, Ethan crossed to the window, one hand holding the blue velvet drape. 'Mrs Baxter had the same notion. She thought maybe on the homeward journey he'd come across something. But when I rode over to see him, he said he had seen nothing. What could he or his lad be expected to see in the dark?'

Edwina pursed her lips, her eyes thoughtful, but made no answer.

Saul watched the figure at the window. They had become friends. He had every reason to think that friendship may extend to the offer of a home here once he was well. Ethan's father had said he was pleased Saul and his son got on so well together, that he was welcome to stay as long as he wished. Yet this talk of a girl wandering the road, with no sign of who she might be, somehow unnerved him. Seemed to cast a shadow over his own hopes. Running the tip of his tongue over lips gone suddenly dry, he asked, 'You think the girl was on her way to Tividale?'

Turning so his back was to the window, his hair burnished to bronze by the late-June sun, Ethan shook his head. 'That is all I can guess. Less than half a mile further on the road branches to lead to the Hall, and the girl certainly did not live here. She must have been coming from Brades Village; she may have been visiting there and returning home.'

Or maybe she lived in Brades Village or the edge of it! The sickness increasing in his stomach, Saul's fingers tightened on the sheets. He needed to think, go over every eventuality. Bringing a trace of pain to his mouth, he closed his eyes, sinking back against the pillows.

'There now.' Catching the look she was meant to, Edwina rose from the chair. 'We have tired Saul with our talk, we must go and leave him to rest.' Bending over him, she touched a hand lightly to his. 'May I come again soon, Saul?'

Making no answer, he smiled weakly. She would come, and keep on coming, and nothing and no one would stop her.

After waiting for the door to close, he opened his eyes, questions whirling madly around his brain. Could the girl they spoke of be Miriam Bryce? It was not impossible. Leah would not have taken kindly to the news that her daughter

109

was pregnant, nor to hearing her son say the father had refused to accept the child as his. Scandal, and of such a sort, was a thing the oh-so-private Leah Bryce would not face up to willingly. Showing her daughter the door would be much more typical of the woman's character. But was the girl Miriam? Unresolved, the question hammered away at him. Edwina had said she was a beauty. Miriam Bryce was beautiful, but so were other women. Ethan had said no belongings had been found, but did every girl carry her personal belongings each time she left the house? She was alone on the road ... why should she not be? She had been coming from the direction of Brades Village ... so what? There were many people in the village had visits from relatives.

One by one his brain laughed away questions and suppositions, but there was one last question it could not laugh away. If the girl Ethan Rawley had knocked down was Miriam Bryce, why had he made no reference to her pregnancy? Saul's mind told him the logical answer was that the girl was not carrying a child and therefore was not Miriam Bryce.

His mind told him! Saul stared at the closed door. So why the churning in his stomach? Why did he suddenly feel so threatened?

Chapter Eight

Miriam tied the white apron about her waist, smoothing its folds over her stomach. She could not remember her name or what her life had been like before coming to this house but she had not forgotten the ways of a woman's body. There had been no monthly flow of blood from her, and though there was as yet not so much thickening of her waist and stomach that could not be disguised by her skirt, there was that regular morning nausea that had her retching in the privy.

Her eyes straying about the new room she had been given since becoming a paid servant, she caught sight of her reflection in the small oval mirror set above the wash-stand. A face pale almost as the apron she smoothed, seemed too small to hold those wide eyes, their green depths wreathed in unspoken sadness.

She was with child! Lifting her left hand, she stared at the slim fingers each devoid of a ring. She was to have a child, but whose? Had the life she could not remember held a husband ... or had she been a...

No! She closed her eyes, refusing to acknowledge the rest of the thought. Surely she would have remembered that? But she remembered nothing. Where, when or by whom she had conceived were concealed in the mists of memory, hidden from her conscious mind by a dark cloud, a nebulous shroud that moved and parted, showing small inroads that beckoned, then rolled together shutting off the way when she tried to follow them.

How many months was she gone? Opening her eyes, she stared again at her waxen face. How long before everyone would be able to see her condition? She would not be able to stay here after that. The master would not welcome a servant who was pregnant without a husband.

Then where would she go, and how would she manage? Miriam shivered from cold fear of the ordeal that faced her. There was no place for such as her. No place but the workhouse!

'A cup of tea, Emma?' Mrs Baxter used the name they had given her. 'A loan,' she had said, smiling, 'Just till you get your own back.'

'No, thank you, Mrs Baxter,' Miriam refused politely, wanting only to spend her precious free time in the garden.

'Well, sit yourself down anyway, girl. There are things I must say and now is as good a time as any.'

Miriam's heart skipped a beat. Was she to be dismissed? Sitting at the table she waited, watching the housekeeper pour tea from a heavy china pot.

'I don't know whether you be aware of it or not...'

Miriam watched as two spoons of sugar were dropped into the cup, her heart dropping with them.

'...could be as that concussion as might have took your memory has also took away your recollection of the condition you be in. The fact is, I believe as how you could be expecting.'

Sally Baxter lifted the cup to her lips, studying the girl over its rim. She had a natural politeness about her, a way of answering that, while not servile, was respectful. She would have made a much better upstairs maid than Ginny, but given the way things were that had been ruled out from the beginning. It had been many years since a pregnant woman had walked the rooms of Brade Hall but Clayton Rawley was not blind nor was he a fool. This girl's condition would not escape him for very long.

'You know what that means?'

A touch of pink staining the ivory of her cheeks, Miriam met the older woman's eyes with honesty in her own. 'Yes,' she answered softly. 'I am to have a child.'

'How far on are you?'

'I don't know.'

'But you were carrying when Mr Ethan brought you here. Is that why you were on the road, had you been turned out?'

'I cannot be absolutely sure, yet I feel I must have been.' Miriam drew a long breath but the look in her eyes did not waver and her voice when she spoke was firm. 'Mrs Baxter, I think I cannot have been married, that the child I carry has no father, or at least not one who lays claim to it. Whoever my parents are, I feel that this was unacceptable to them and I was made to leave, but I do not think I was a whore.'

113

There was no anger in the statement, no accusation and no self-recrimination. The honesty in the girl's eyes shone forth like a beacon.

'No, Emma, I don't think you were,' Sally Baxter replied with the same honesty. There was something about this young woman that poured scorn on the very idea.

'I did not realise the ... the way I was, not when I first arrived. Believe me, Mrs Baxter, I did not feel sure until...' Miriam broke off. She may not have been sure in the beginning, but after the attacks of nausea she should have spoken out. Hiding it was a form of lying, and painful as lies were to tell, they were more painful still when they were found out.

'Until you were sick each morning in the privy!' The housekeeper smiled briefly. 'There don't be much goes on in Brade Hall that I don't know about.'

Miriam's glance flickered to the door of the kitchen.

'Don't be worryin' over the others.' Sally's own glance stayed on her frightened face. 'Nobody else knows and I don't be going to tell them.'

Standing up, Miriam began to untie her apron. She could leave that here in the kitchen. The rest of the things she had on were her own, so Ginny had told her, and there was nothing else of hers in the bedroom, nothing to collect.

Placing her cup in its saucer, Sally watched the apron being lifted over the girl's head. 'What do you be doing?'

Folding it neatly, Miriam placed it on the

corner of the pine dresser that took up the whole of one wall. 'I will leave now. Please be kind enough to thank Mr Rawley for his goodness in having me in his home. And thank you too, you have been more than kind.'

'So you be going to leave?' Sally glared at the face that had appeared at the scullery door, sending Ginny scuttling back whence she came. 'To go where?'

'There's only one place.'

'That being the poor house?' Sally's mouth tightened. 'What sort of prospect be that for a child?'

Miriam's mouth trembled. 'The only sort I can give it. But after the birth, when I have my strength back, then I will find work...'

'You'll not get your strength back in that place,' Sally snorted. 'I ain't never yet knowed of a body coming out of there with any strength. As for you – look at yourself! You don't be any thicker through than a kipper between the eyes! How long do you think you'd last in such a place?'

'The child would last,' Miriam answered. 'That is the only thing that matters. It did not ask to be conceived, that was my doing.'

'Not all of it. Half at least be down to some man! Though how can he be called a man when you be left to pay the piper for the tune he danced to?'

A tune they had both danced to. Miriam felt the touch of shame. A cold frightening touch. She had done wrong, no lack of memory could disguise that. Now she must pay, but not the child. No harm must come to it. The workhouse might prove a poor home but it was one she had to give.

There were ways... Sally Baxter poured a second cup of tea, adding milk, slowly stirring in sugar. Old Harriet Coates along of Rounds Green was said to know how to get rid of children from the womb. But this girl ... she would have no dealings with Harriet, that much showed in her face.

'So you intends to go through with it?' she asked over the rim of the cup.

'If you mean, do I intend to have the child, yes, I mean to go through with it,' Miriam answered as the other woman knew she would. 'I can at least give it the love it deserves.'

'Arrh, you can do that. Supposing you ain't worked to death afore it sees its first birthday.'

'Maybe it will not be so awful as we think.'

'You think what you will, wench, but you ain't lived as long as I have. I tell you, I've seen whole families go on the road sooner than set foot in that place.'

'I do not have any option. Save risk the child being born under a hedge.'

Sally set down her cup. She had thought long and hard on this, talked it over with Baxter, gone over all the pros and cons, listened to reasons why she should not become involved with the girl Ethan Rawley had found wandering the road, a girl who was likely no better than she should be. But through all the discussions, all the argument, one thing had remained clear in her mind. She liked the girl she had named Emma, liked and trusted her, with a trust that went deep. This girl was no common prostitute. The child she carried had been got from love. The real pity was that the love seemed to have been on her side only. Looking the girl square in the face, she said, 'It don't have to be born under a hedge, and it don't have to be born in the workhouse neither.'

'Then where?' It was almost a cry. 'It cannot be here. I will not take further advantage of Mr Rawley.'

'He don't have to be taken advantage of,' Sally went on calmly. 'You will continue to do the work you are set – pregnancy be no disability, though I've known it to be treated as such. And I still have a couple of skirts and blouses I've long grown too fat to wear. They will cover you well enough for the time you have left.'

'I do not want to deceive the Rawleys.'

'And I ain't asking you to. I just say there be no need to say anything for a three-month or more. By that time we can have things the child will need, woollies and the like.'

'But where...'

'You leave that to Sally Baxter.' She smiled. 'Trust me, child, you won't give birth under no hedge.'

Standing naked before the long, walnut-cased cheval mirror of the dressing room that adjoined his bedroom, Saul Marsh stared at the jagged scar that ran across his inner thigh and down into his crotch.

Ralph Bryce had done this to him. Had slashed his manhood then left him to bleed to death there on the heath. Only he had not died!

Tracing the tip of one finger along the pearl-coloured flesh of the newly healed scar, he remembered again the searing, burning sensation of the knife, as he had so often remembered it since being found by Ethan Rawley. Remembered and vowed that Bryce would pay for what he had done. He would pay and then he would die!

Glancing at the rack filled with expensive clothes Ethan had placed there for his use, Saul allowed himself the smile he only ever used when alone. Bryce would die, but he, Saul Marsh, would live in comfort. For the rest of his days!

But he must play his hand carefully, not rush, leave an ace in the hole ... until he was ready!

Touching his fingers to the soft cashmere and smooth velour, feeling the richness of mohair, he smiled again. In a way Bryce had done him a good turn. It was through him that Saul had been brought to Brade Hall and tasted a very different side of life. If things went on as they had up to now he could well find himself staying here, and thence to a permanent home with the pretty Edwina. A home he intended to have, a home he was prepared to kill for!

But you move slowly and tread softly to catch a rabbit ... or a woman. Returning to the bedroom, he pulled on the fresh night clothes Baxter had brought for him. There would be plenty of time for wearing fine clothes later.

'I thought I might catch you doing that.'

'Doing what?' Saul glanced towards the face peering around the bedroom door, indigo blue eyes laughing.

118

'Getting out of bed without help.'

Saul let out a short breath of pretend exasperation. 'I have explained already, I can manage by myself I do not want to be a nuisance to yourself or your staff. You have already been so very kind to me.'

Leaving the door open behind him, Ethan crossed the carpeted room. 'You are not a nuisance. Quite the reverse. It is pleasant to have visitors in the house after so long. Father took my mother's death very hard, and with my loss of speech ... well, he just stopped inviting people. Only Edwina came.' He smiled, remembering. 'Edwina stuck it out.'

'She is a beautiful girl.' Saul affected an apologetic expression. 'I hope you do not mind my saying so?'

'Mind? Of course I don't mind, why on earth should I?'

'Some men would. Not everyone cares to have their fiancée admired by another man, especially when that man is just an acquaintance.'

'Edwina is not my fiancée, though she is beautiful.' Ethan grinned. 'And not just in looks, she has a lively personality and is good company. Which reminds me – she has promised to come and visit you every day while I am away.'

Saul felt a burning excitement run through his veins. Rawley was going to be away. He would be left to entertain the pretty Edwina! Things were working out very nicely.

'Will you be away for long?'

'Eh?' Ethan answered from the dressing room, and when he emerged it was with a heavy wool

119

dressing gown over his arm.

'Will you be away for long?' Saul repeated the question.

'I am not off on a visit, old chap!' Ethan laughed, holding the dressing gown so Saul could slip his arms into it. 'Father has decided that it's time for me to begin to take part in the business. It wasn't possible before. Well, if you cannot speak, you cannot tell men what to do. But I did learn the book keeping side of things.'

A stifled groan continued Saul's careful charade as he rose slowly to his feet. Half stooped, as if to spare himself the pain of straightening, he fastened the belt of the gown then sank back on the bed, breath escaping in short staccato bursts.

'Please thank Edwina.' He paused, his breathing deliberately ragged. 'But I will not be able to avail myself of the pleasure of her company. Like yourself, Ethan, I have to start work.'

Crouched before him, Ethan slipped Saul's feet into soft leather slippers matching the deep red of the dressing gown. 'Work?' he said, rising. 'Don't talk rot, man, you can hardly stand.'

'That ... that is simply because ... because I have been lying about too long.'

'Rubbish!' Ethan fetched a hairbrush from the dressing room, shoving it into the other man's hand. 'It is because you are not completely well yet. Castr–' He paused awkwardly, the word half formed on his tongue. Swallowing hard as he saw Saul's fingers tighten about the brush, he went on, 'An injury such as you have had takes time to heal. You cannot expect to go back to work so soon.'

This was the moment. What he said next could make or break Saul. His head sunk on his chest, fingers clenched about the brush, he drew in a long breath. Then, teeth clenched together, he rasped, 'I will not take your father's charity any longer! For God's sake, Rawley, I may no longer have my manhood, but I still have my pride!'

Looking at the figure hunched on the bed, Ethan tried to stem the tide of pity that rose in him. This was a proud man. The thought of accepting another's charity must be abhorrent to him, yet at the same time he was in no fit condition for work.

'Would that pride prevent you from staying here while accepting employment from my father?'

His head still lowered, Saul's eyes gleamed. He had played his hand ... and won!

'Who is the person in the wheelchair?' Miriam had left the garden immediately she heard people approaching. Having no knowledge of any home she might have had she did not use her free afternoon for visiting, so Mrs Baxter had given her permission to use the gardens, provided she did not do so when the Rawleys were present.

Rising from her comfortable chair, the house-keeper reached two long white sleeve cuffs from a drawer in the dresser, pulling them on over her arms, easing them around her elbows and wrists.

'That be the fellow young Ginny be always going on about.' She held her arms out to Miriam who fastened the buttons of the cuffs, catching the nod of the head that said the top few would not come together. 'I know.' The several chins wobbled despairingly. 'They won't button up. Still, they keep the flour from the sleeves of my blouse.'

Giving a stream of instructions, she glanced up as Miriam fetched flour and salt to the table. 'You wasn't seen?'

Bringing lard and stewed lamb from the cool room, she set about dicing meat, stripping off cold creamy fat and laying it aside for rendering into dripping.

'No, I wasn't seen. I heard them talking a way off and came indoors at once.'

'At once, was it?' Sally Baxter's eyes stayed on the bowl into which she had tipped the flour. 'Then how come you knows about a person in a wheelchair?'

Miriam's cheeks flushed a vivid shade of pink. 'I ... I did take a peep through the hedge, but it was a very quick peep and I wasn't seen, I am certain of that.'

Fingers moving dexterously, mixing lard into flour, Sally answered sternly, 'Let's hope you be right. The less you be seen by the master or Mr Ethan, the better. Don't you go taking any chances!'

'I'm sorry.' Miriam turned to the range where potatoes and onions bubbled in a pot set above the fire. 'I just wondered who it was Mr Ethan was wheeling into the garden?'

'You know what curiosity did!' Sally poured half a cup of milk mixed with water into the flour mix, using her hands to mould it all together.

122

'Still, I suppose the more you know, the less you'll go ferreting about looking through hedges.

'That young man in the wheelchair be the one that Mr Ethan found lying out on Derby's Hill. Seems he was badly cut up.' Sally turned the mixture on to a floured board, taking up the rolling pin placed ready. 'Not that I seen it for myself, Baxter were the one put him into bed and helped the doctor do what had to be done. Same as he has done on each of the doctor's visits. But Baxter told me it were no ordinary stabbing, if *any* sort of stabbing could be called ordinary. It be my opinion whoever it were attacked that man had more than just a grudge.'

Draining potatoes and onions through a colander, Miriam transferred them to the table. 'Ginny said he had been drinking, him and another man, then they argued...'

'Ginny Jinks has a mouth as big as a parish oven and a brain the size of a bibble!' Sally banged a metal pastry cutter into the sheet of floury pastry. 'What does her know about it, was her there? No, of course her weren't! But it seems her don't have the sense to realise folk would know that – and you should have more sense than to go believing her.'

'We were only talking.'

'Arrh, so you might have been, and Ginny Jinks talking of summat her knows nothing about.' Gathering pastry circles, Sally passed them to Miriam who quickly began placing them in pie tins she had already greased with a knob of lard. 'There was no smell of drink on that man, I

123

particularly asked Baxter that, so it were no drunken brawl. And neither were his clothes ripped as they might have been had he been set upon and knocked about by a gang. He has never said what it was happened, leastways not to Baxter, but if you asks me it were a fight between two, him and one other. Though whether it were a fair fight...'

Meat and vegetables firmed into the pastry-lined tins, Miriam topped them with lids. 'Do you think it might not have been fair?'

'Wouldn't be right of me to say one way or the other.' Sally looked up from rolling a fresh batch of pastry. 'But to use a knife ... and in the way that one was used ... that don't be fair on any man.'

Carrying pies to the baking oven, Miriam placed them inside. Ginny had hinted darkly at all manner of horrible injuries, but this was not an opportune moment to mention the other girl's speculations.

'He'd far better have been killed outright.' Sally shook her head slowly. 'Would have been kinder than leaving him that way. But kindness had no place in the heart of the one that done that to him. More like it were filled with jealousy, probably over some woman or other. Tom cats could take a lesson from men when two have their sights set on the same woman, and it be likely that what caused that young man to lose what he did.'

'Do you mean he was robbed?'

Sally bent over her pastry board, her cheeks bright pink. 'He was robbed all right, poor bugger! Robbed of that a woman shouldn't rightly talk of, but this much I will say: the man sitting out in that wheelchair ain't never going to be a father!'

Chapter Nine

Pulling the calico night gown over her head, Miriam smoothed its all-enveloping folds. How long? She stared down to where her hands rested on her stomach. How many months had she carried this child? How many more before it made its entrance into the world? She had no way of knowing without remembering when...

Raising her head, she stared at her face in the mirror: at the wide, green eyes darkened with anxiety; the mouth that trembled with fear. Who was the man who'd fathered the child within her? Why did she wear no wedding ring?

Each hour of the day the same questions plagued her, and each night they remained, gnawing, tormenting, answers concealed in the deep mists that shrouded her memory.

'*Three months, maybe a little longer,*' Mrs Baxter had said. Then she would have to leave this house. And go where? '*Leave it with me,*' the housekeeper had said. But were those words uttered just to ease her mind, try to soothe the worry that must show? But why should a woman she had known only a few weeks trouble to reassure her? Why had she not had her sent from Brade Hall?

Kindness? She blinked, sending tears rolling down her pale cheeks. Why was it that kindness from a woman felt so foreign to her?

'She promised,' whispered Miriam, spreading her fingers protectively over the slight bump in her stomach. 'She promised you would not be born under a hedge, and now I give you my promise. No matter what it takes, no matter what I have to do, you will not be reared in a workhouse!'

Wiping away the tears with the back of her hand, she took the hair brush from the washstand, drawing it through her hair. That man in the wheelchair ... he'd had hair of an unusual colour.

The image of that figure almost swamped in rugs tucked well up around his shoulders returned to mind. He seemed to be tall even sitting in that chair, and though he was well wrapped the width of his shoulders was clear. But it was not his body that had caught her attention. It was his hair.

Miriam felt a tremor of unease. She had only caught a momentary glance as he was wheeled into the garden, and his face had been turned from her. But the hair! That tremor again. That particular colour, so like butterscotch...

Ginny had tried to describe him in their moments together. He was so handsome, she enthused, so thoughtful and charming; and that hair, that lovely golden hair... He was like the Grecian god Apollo in a story her teacher had once told.

Replacing the brush, Miriam climbed into bed. Reaching towards the oil lamp set on a small table, she stared into its golden heart and suddenly her own turned to ice.

All of that he may be, she could not say without having spoken to the man.

...that lovely golden hair...

Golden it definitely was. But why did it fill her with so much fear?

Turning out the lamp, she lay back on the pillows. The light was gone, leaving the room wreathed about in shadows, but they were no darker than those imprisoning her mind.

What lay behind them? Supposing she were not married ... had she lain willingly with a man or was her child the fruit of rape? The bruises on her arms could well point to that. Throwing one arm across her eyes, she tried to blot out the horror that thought aroused. Being fatherless was enough of a burden for any child, but to be one whose father could never be named, one who was not even known...

Oh, Lord, she prayed silently. Help me to rear this child. Help me to give it the happiness every child deserves. I promise I will love it with all my heart, I will try to make up for the terrible wrong I have done it. It will be born a bastard, and I know that what I ask now is wrong. I should not pray for help in a lie, but grant this not for my sake but for an innocent child's. Help me shield it from the stigma of its birth, hide the truth of its conception. Do with my life as you will, but please never let my child discover it is a bastard.

Black shadows already paling to grey as dawn

127

entered the window of her bedroom, Miriam's silent prayers lingered in her mind and tears lay damp on her cheeks. But the name that trembled on her lips as at last she fell asleep was spoken aloud.

'Ralph,' she murmured. 'Oh, Ralph!'

'C'mon, wench, put some elbow grease into it. We have dinner to prepare once this kitchen be scrubbed!'

Bent over the table, Miriam tried to scrub faster but her head whirled and the strength seemed to ebb from her body. Somewhere in the distance Mrs Baxter's voice sounded irritated but she could not answer. Mist rolled in on her, taking her breath, her strength, closing her off from life.

'Emma ... Emma wench. It's me, Sally.'

The words seemed to drift slowly towards her, calling her from beyond a vast darkness.

'Emma, you be all right. Wake up, c'mon, wake up.'

She should follow the sound. Go to where they beckoned, but she was too weary, it was restful here in the darkness, she would be safe here.

'Emma! Emma wench.'

The slap to her face was gentle. It should not be. It was hard, always hard. It would be hard next time, bringing the stinging pain it always did, then the slaps would turn to punches ... she had to wake up.

'There you go. It be all over now.' Glancing towards her husband, Sally nodded for him to leave the kitchen. She had called him to help lift the girl into a chair but now she could manage alone. 'You be all right now,' she soothed as Miriam moaned softly. 'Just you sit still while I get you a drink. A nice hot cup of tea and you will be right as ninepence.'

'What happened?' Her head whirling afresh, Miriam allowed herself to be pressed back into the chair.

'A fainty turn!' Sally scalded tea leaves always ready and waiting in the china pot on the hob.

'I fainted?'

'Arrh, you did that. Right out, like a snuffed candle. But it's nothing for you to worry over, it's only natural seeing your condition.'

'But I have never fainted before. At least I...'

'You haven't been pregnant afore,' Sally returned as Miriam broke off. 'And I would swear to that whether you remembers or not.' Stirring a generous spoonful of sugar into a cup she handed it to Miriam, then taking a cup herself she sat in a chair facing hers. 'I reckon you have turned.'

Miriam's brows drew together as she struggled to understand.

'Lots of women faint when they turn.' Sally smiled seeing the confusion in the girl's eyes. 'Halfway to full term the child turns in the womb. Gets into a comfortable position, you might say. It fair knocks a woman back when it happens but it don't do any harm. You'll be feeling good as ever in no time.' She hesitated, eyes sharp as they examined the girl. She was no fatter than a sparrow, a puff of wind would send her flying. If only she could remember. Till that day all the care in the world would not bring colour to those cheeks or life to those eyes.

'You will feel the child move regular in the time left,' she continued to explain. 'The kicks can become quite strong so you should expect that.' She sipped at her tea, her glance dropping first to Miriam's breasts and then her stomach. 'There still be precious little to you as yet, the child be nowt but a scrap, but it'll be big enough when it comes, and if my reckoning be right that should be round about late-November or early-December.'

A few more months and her child would be born. Miriam stared into the tea she had not tasted. Would her memory have returned by then? Would she know who the child's father was? Or would she remember some stranger attacking her, raping her...

'Here, don't you go fainting on me no more!' Sally was on her feet as Miriam's cup began to rattle in its saucer. 'One faint to each pregnancy is all Sally Baxter allows.'

Miriam met her smile. 'I am not going to faint. I ... I was just thinking, wondering who...'

'I know, wench, I know!' Sally touched a hand to the thin shoulder. 'It be more than hard what you be having to bear, but the Lord listens when we speak to Him. He knows what you be going through and when the time be right, He will put an end to it. All you have to do is ask.'

'How can I?' Miriam tasted tears against her lips. 'How can I ask that, seeing what I have done?'

'Maybe you sinned, maybe you didn't. But it be

all the same in His eyes. *"Ask and it shall be given unto you."* They were His words, and they meant forgiveness for any that asked for it truly.'

'The child,' Miriam sobbed. 'It will pay as well as me. Pay for a sin it did not commit.'

'You be a fool if you believe that!' sniffed Sally. 'Each of us be called upon to answer for our own doings and no other's. That child will come innocent into this world.'

For several moments Sally stood with her hand on Miriam's shoulder, her own tears thick in her throat. Who could do this to a girl? What sort of a man ... what sort of parents?

'Drink up your tea, wench,' she said, swallowing her tears. 'It won't do you much good gone cold. Then get you out and sit in the garden for a while. The master and Mr Ethan both be out and that one upstairs can bide in his room till they get back, so there'll be none to see you.'

'But the scrubbing?'

Sally flapped her hand. 'That be no trouble, it be almost done, and Ginny will be back from her mother's in time to give me a hand with the dinner.'

The afternoon sun warm on her face, Miriam walked between the beds of roses, their brilliant colours glowing like gems in a setting of green jade. She breathed deeply, appreciating the perfume that hung heavy in the still air.

Half hidden by a curtain a figure watched her from an upper window, yellow hair contrasting sharply with the blue velvet. Saul Marsh watched the girl's slim shape beneath those brown skirts, her back turned to him, and felt a familiar twitch in his loins. It was still faint – faint as it had been when plain-faced Ginny had bent over him earlier, pretending to fuss with the sheets on his bed. But faint as the feeling was, it was definitely there. He had thought, that first time, it was a trick of his imagination, the product of his own desire for what he could no longer have, that which he'd thought never to experience again. But that twitch was there, low in the base of his stomach, a feeling a man only got with the urge for sex.

Watching the girl pause, bending to smell a rose, he smiled slowly. Ralph Bryce had thought to take this from him forever. *'One testicle gone, and the other...'* The doctor had raised his shoulders in a non-committal gesture during his final examination. He was lucky not to have lost more, had the knife come down at a different angle. As it was...

The rest had been left unsaid. Left to feed on him like a serpent, its poison growing ever stronger as days passed into weeks; a poison which in its turn fed hatred to the point of obsession. But now the serpent could die. The twitch that followed each movement of the girl below proved that. The poison he would keep and nourish until it could be poured out, poured over the prostrate body of Ralph Bryce!

In the meantime... A smile eased across Saul's face, smooth as oil on water. Meantime the servant was willing. More than that, she was eager. True, her face was not pretty, but the hair... He had never seen her with that awful cap off. He looked at her now, walking away from him, seeing the sunlight touch sparks of gold among the rich, near auburn curls. Surprisingly, the girl might yet prove enticing.

Pretty or not, little Ginny would serve to strengthen that part of him struggling to return to life. And Edwina? She would get a bonus!

A movement beyond the hedge catching his eye, Saul drew a little further back behind the curtain. Ethan was back from the steel works his father owned at Rounds Green. He would no doubt be up in a few minutes to see the invalid.

Turning away from the window, Saul returned to bed. He did not want it known just how far his recovery had advanced. Not yet. He did not feel sufficiently confident of pretty Edwina's affections. A few more visits to the sick bed... But the other thing, that twitch in his loins, he felt that well enough. Well enough to practise ... and soon!

Bent over a rose, its deep red petals resting in her fingers, Miriam breathed in the musky fragrance, the stillness of the garden soothing, if only for a few moments, the fear that weighed heavily on her heart.

'How I wish I could paint.'

Taken completely by surprise, Miriam snatched her hand from the flower, at the same time turning towards the speaker.

'I ... I am sorry, Mr Rawley,' she stammered. 'I shouldn't be here. Forgive me, please. I'll go at once.'

'Hold on!' Ethan Rawley laughed. 'Who said you should not be here?'

'Mrs Baxter. She said I might have a few minutes in the garden but only when you or your

133

father were not at home. I did not know you had returned, I'm sorry...'

'You already said that.' Ethan laughed again. 'Besides, I am the one who should be sorry.'

'You? I don't understand.'

Looking deep into eyes green as the first leaves of summer, he felt an emotion new to him. 'I am the one who should be sorry – sorry I cannot capture such a scene on canvas but must make do with holding it in my mind.' Putting out a hand yet not touching her as she made to turn towards the house, he smiled. 'Don't go.'

'But I must. Mrs Baxter will be cross if she finds I have disregarded her instructions.'

'Mrs Baxter never stays cross for long. I was always disregarding her when I was young, and she would threaten all manner of dire consequences but never made them good.'

'That was different.'

'How?'

Miriam cast an anxious glance towards the house. The kitchen was to the other side, looking on to the vegetable gardens, but as the housekeeper said, little went on in Brade Hall that she did not get to know of.

'You are the son of the house, I am but a servant. You have every right to be here, I have none.'

Stepping in front of her, preventing her from passing him without treading on the carefully tended beds, Ethan grinned. 'Then I give you that right. From now on you may come and go in the garden as much as you please, and I will tell Mrs Baxter so.'

'No!' Miriam looked up into laughing eyes that sparkled like dark sapphires. 'Please, I would rather you did not.'

That troubling emotion – one of just wanting to look at the girl staring up at him; just wanting to walk beside her – rising high in his chest, Ethan let the grin fade from his mouth. 'If that is what you want,' he said gently, 'but in return you must promise not to run away should I come on the scene.'

Looking into the face of the man who had picked her up following that accident on the road, who had brought her here to his own home then visited her several times, always in the company of the housekeeper, to ask after her welfare, Miriam felt no urge to escape. She had felt no fear of this man then and felt none now.

With a smile that brought a fleeting light to her eyes, Miriam nodded. 'I promise. Though I cannot promise to stay long.'

Blue eyes twinkling as the smile returned to his handsome face, Ethan broke a rose from the bush, holding it towards her with mock solemnity. 'Accept this in token of our bargain?'

Meeting those eyes, Miriam could not help but return the smile in their depths, but still she turned away.

'Have you remembered your name?' Ethan asked.

'No.'

Catching her hands, he swung her round to face him. 'So what do they call you in the kitchen? I cannot conceive of Mrs Baxter allowing you to be addressed as Wotsit!'

Surprised by her own laughter, Miriam let her hands lie in his. Had she laughed often before the accident, had smiles come easily to her? Thoughts of what she did not know spoiling the brief moment of release from the shadows of the past, she withdrew her hands. 'No,' she said softly. 'Mrs Baxter would not have me answer to that. She calls me Emma.'

'Emma.' Ethan watched tears sparkle suddenly on downcast lashes, watched the tremor about the lovely mouth. He had thought her pretty when visiting her sick bed, but here in the full light of day he could see he had been wrong. This girl was beautiful. Hair of dark Titian complemented skin as creamy smooth as alabaster, curling softly around a face whose features were exquisite, offset by eyes the colour of fresh meadow grass.

'Emma,' he repeated softly. 'That's a beautiful name. But not as beautiful as the girl to whom it was given.' Watching her as she returned to the house, he saw again the look he had briefly glimpsed in her eyes. Forgotten memories ... forgotten lies? Maybe. But *he* had not lied. She was beautiful, and no matter what her true name it could not possibly be more so.

Ethan began to make a habit of coming to the garden, one that soon became known to others. Sally Baxter whisked a mixture of eggs and hot milk with fierce energy. She still had not seen him but reports had reached her just the same. Reports of laughter, a touch of the hand, the two of them sitting side by side in the summerhouse.

136

Laying aside the fluffy mixture, she sprinkled a handful of dried fruit over buttered bread she had placed in an earthenware dish.

She ought never to have given the girl permission to spend her free time in the garden. What would the master say if he found out? And find out he would unless Sally put a stop to it – now.

Taking up the egg mixture, she poured it over the bread, filling the kitchen with the delicious smell of vanilla.

She could tell the girl that what she was doing was in nobody's best interest, that it would be wisest if she didn't go into the garden again. Emma was a sensible girl, and biddable. She would see that no slight was meant, and would agree.

Placing the bread and butter pudding in the slow oven of the carefully blackleaded range, Sally closed the cast-iron door, her plump face flushed from the effort of bending.

The girl would agree, but what of Ethan Rawley? He was no longer a mute child. He was a man, with all the feelings of a man judging by the way he sought the girl's company. But it was company he ought not to keep; polite and well mannered she might be, but class was class and that girl wasn't in the master's. Ethan had regained his speech, he could argue, but it would all come to naught against his father's opposition. Ethan was stubborn but then so was Clayton.

Returning to the table, Sally reached for a clean mixing bowl, spooning sugar into a white mound over a lump of rich yellow butter. If only she had not given permission! But that was like wishing for the moon. Now she could only pray the pain that lay ahead for Emma would not be too hard to bear.

'How be Ginny feeling?' She looked up as Emma came into the kitchen, tray in hand.

'Still snuffly but her forehead feels cooler. I think she's over the worst.'

'Silly girl!' Sally attacked butter and sugar with a wooden spoon. 'You would have thought she would have seen that storm coming and set off from her mother's earlier, instead of waiting till the last minute. Soaked to the skin and an hour's walk before her! I sometimes think her don't have the sense her were born with!'

Her own common sense telling her not to argue, Miriam took the tray to the scullery, washing cup and saucer, and the plate that had held a tea cake. Ginny had scoffed it with the relish of a starving man. Smiling to herself as she returned to the kitchen, she thought of Sally's words yesterday: *Feed a cold but starve a fever.*' It was fortunate for them all that Ginny had not developed a fever!

'Nights be starting to draw in.' Sally reached for the eggs set ready for her, breaking two of them into the bowl. 'There already be a nip in the air. I fear winter will be off to an early start this year; might be for the best if you don't go sitting in the garden any more. We don't want you going down with cold, same as Ginny.'

Lining buttered tins with rice paper Miriam recognised the real meaning behind the words.

Mrs Baxter did not want her taking any more walks with Ethan Rawley. But he was so easy to be with and so very kind! He had come almost daily to spend a few minutes with her; she would miss his pleasant company. But Mrs Baxter's warning, though unspoken, was clear enough. Nothing could come of her friendship with the master's son. He was the heir to Brade Hall while she was a paid servant. And carrying another's child.

Handing across baking tins to be filled with sponge mixture, she met the other woman's meaningful glance. 'I felt a chill in the air yesterday evening,' she agreed diplomatically. 'I think it best to take your advice. The garden is getting a trifle cold for sitting out in, I will not be going there again.'

Yes, this girl was sensible all right. Sally filled the tins with the creamy mixture. There would be no need to say more on the subject.

Going about the business of clearing away the baking utensils, Miriam thought again of those conversations with Ethan. He had told her of his mother, her gentle ways and loving nature. How they'd spent much of their time together, the things she'd taught him of the countryside and how she'd dissuaded him from catching butterflies, saying how much more beautiful they looked flitting among the flowers. He had gone on to describe the riding accident that had killed her, voice breaking as he told of her arms seeming to reach for him, as though to hold him one last time, his name on her lips as she died.

Carrying spoons and bowls to the scullery, she

began to wash them with hot water from the kettle.

Ethan's mouth had been compressed into a tight line for many seconds as the pain she realised had never left him seared through him, and she had sat silent, unwilling to leave while he still struggled for control.

'Not once,' he went on, unshed tears making his voice hoarse, 'did my father condemn our riding on the heath, though even then I knew his fear of it, of the treacherous unmarked pit shafts. No one was to blame, he said, no one could have foreseen ... but I should have foreseen, I should have known!'

He had dropped his head into his hands, breathing ragged, and she had touched his sleeve. 'Do not blame yourself,' she'd said softly. 'Neither your father nor your mother would wish you to do that.'

Now, reaching a white huckaback cloth from an airing line stretched across the scullery, she began to dry the dishes, stacking them on a wooden tray.

Ethan had looked up as she touched him, catching her hands in his, eyes dark and serious. 'I never thought I would say this to any woman, but you are so like my mother. You have the same gentle ways, the same understanding, the same delicate beauty – so fragile and so very, very beautiful. One I want to hold and keep with me forever.'

She had tried to pull away then, not wanting him to say more, but he had held her there in the shelter of the summerhouse. 'I never thought to know this love again,' he had murmured, 'but I love you. I love you so very, very much.'

Draping the damp cloth over the airing line, Miriam emptied the bowl of water, wiping both it and the draining board with a dishcloth. Then, taking the tray, she went back into the kitchen.

He had stared deep into her eyes, reading the workings of her mind. 'I know,' he had said, touching his lips to each of her hands, 'you are a servant. But, believe me, that will make no difference. I love you, Emma, and I want you for my wife.'

He had let her go then, not following or calling after her as she ran towards the kitchen.

He loved her!

The words Ethan Rawley had spoken in the garden had plagued her for days, and plagued her still.

From her bed, Miriam watched moon shadows play across the ceiling. She had not gone to the garden since that night and when Ethan made an excuse to come to the kitchen, Mrs Baxter had told him quite sharply that it was no longer the place for him.

He had been puzzled by that. Miriam had glimpsed it in his face. Sally Baxter had always welcomed him into her kitchen, yet suddenly she was chasing him away.

Miriam remembered the hurt in his eyes as she too had turned from him. He had left the kitchen then, left without another word, and had not been back since.

Squeezing her eyes shut, she held back the sobs

that rose in her chest. He had been so kind to her and now she was denying him.

But she was not denying him! She sat up suddenly and opened her eyes, staring hard at the patterns traced above her head. She was so like his mother. Were not those his own words? It was not love for *her* he felt, but the love he still held for his mother which was responsible for his words to her.

And if it were not...?

Miriam felt tiredness sweep over her. The tiredness brought on by hours of mental conflict. But at the end of it the answer was always the same. She could not allow herself to accept Ethan Rawley's love, nor him to give it. He knew nothing of her background and she could tell him nothing, except for the fact that she was with child.

And by whom? Always the same thought, followed rapidly by the next. Was she a willing partner, was she married to the man ... did she even know him?

'*...you are a servant. But, believe me, that will make no difference ...*'

In the silence of her mind the words rang clear.

Ethan was a fine man. Nothing could be more sure than that. And perhaps, despite their difference in class, he would marry a servant. But a servant with the child of another man already in her arms? That was the sort of bouquet no bride of Ethan Rawley's should carry.

'*...I love you ... I want you for my wife.*'

'I could love you too, Ethan.' Her whisper soft as the moonlight invading her bedroom, Miriam smiled gently back at the handsome face pictured in her mind.

'It would be so easy. But I could never hurt you, and no matter how many times you said the child made no difference, I know that it would. How could it be otherwise? Each time you looked at it you would feel the pain of knowing, just as I myself would know that you were not the father. I will not cause you that pain, Ethan. I can never become your wife.'

Turning her face into the pillow, she felt tears well beneath her lashes. Would she ever become any man's wife? The answer was elusive. She could marry no one until she remembered. Remembered who it was had fathered her child. And if that man had rejected her, or if he were already married? Supposing she *never* remembered!

Miriam pressed her face harder into the pillow.

Then not only would her child be born a bastard, it would remain one ... all its life.

Chapter Ten

Leah Bryce gathered the plates from the table. It had been all of three months since the girl had left the house, three months since Ralph had spoken a civil word. But words, civil or otherwise, had not bothered her since...

Placing knives and forks on the plates, she carried them to the scullery and placed them in the shallow brownstone sink.

'*I'm sorry, Leah, truly I am.*' Words spoken so long ago returned to mind, bringing with them the same hurt and hatred they had then. '*But I love her and I have to go with her.*'

He loved *HER!* Leah leaned against the sink, both hands gripping its chipped edge. He loved that girl with the shining auburn curls and pretty doll-like face. But what of her, Leah? Only two months before he had said the same words to her.

Words! She poured water from the kettle, watching steam rise from the plates, only to disappear quickly in the cool scullery, like mist in the wind. Just as he had gone, leaving her nothing but the memory of his words. Since that time words had not bothered her, nor had the lack of them, for the words *he* had spoken were always with her. She heard them spoken again and again, feeding the lust for vengeance that was meat and drink to her.

Returning to the kitchen, she placed the dishes on the dresser as Ralph reached for his jacket, hanging on the door peg.

'Should you be going out?' his mother asked. 'There be a haze dropping over the heath, it could turn to fog later.'

'Then I'll ask Banjo for a bed in his beer house.'

'It don't be no beer you be going out for!' Leah snapped. 'It be to look for her, your sister!'

His fingers falling still, Ralph gave her a contemptuous look. 'Something you have not done, not once these three months!'

'Why should I?' Leah returned a stare of equal contempt. 'I didn't tell her to leave, nor to get

144

herself pregnant!'

'Nor did you tell her to stay. Oh, I know you say you did not see her go, but I don't believe that. You wanted her out, and would have made no attempt to stop her.'

'No, I would not have stopped her. I will have no bastard born under my roof, and no trollop eating at my table!'

The sound of the tin clock ticking on the mantelshelf above the fireplace seemed to hold them in limbo, each staring at the other. Then, eyes still fastened on his mother, Ralph finished buttoning his jacket.

'You be chasing a dream.' Leah moved to the fireplace, settling herself into one of the chairs drawn up beside it. 'You'll no more find her this time than you have in all the searching you've done.'

Tucking the ends of his muffler beneath the buttoned jacket, Ralph turned to leave. 'At least I'll have tried.'

Oh, he had tried! Leah's eyes remained fixed on the door that closed behind her son. But just what had he convinced himself he searched for? A sister? Switching her gaze to the fire, she stared into its crimson depths. Yes, that was what Ralph Bryce told himself he looked for – when all the time he was searching for that denied him by man and God. Miriam was his sister, she would always be his sister, she could never be what he yearned for her to be. His wife.

'It will be a Godsend when that girl be on her feet again.'

145

Sally Baxter looked up from rubbing salt into the rind of the leg of pork she was getting ready for the oven. 'It fair makes a difference having a pair of hands taken out of a body's kitchen and no mistake.'

'Then let me do Ginny's work.' Miriam peeled the last of the potatoes, rinsing it in the bowl of clean water set on the table. 'It can't be so difficult, surely?'

It wasn't difficult. Sally placed the potatoes around the meat, spreading each with a liberal helping of dripping. But it was upstairs work and she had not wanted the master to see too much of this girl. She had not wanted the master's son meeting her over much either, but it had happened and in her inner heart she felt it had been momentous.

Sprinkling a little salt on the potatoes, she nodded for Miriam to place the roasting pan in the oven.

Ethan Rawley might be a man grown but he was vulnerable. He had been without the love of a woman for many years, except of course her own; but she was not what you might call beautiful, neither was she some six or seven years younger than him. It would be easy for him to imagine himself in love with this girl, especially as he felt responsible for her already.

Sally watched as Miriam set the meat to cook. Even swathed in an oversized apron, her hair caught beneath a cap there was an essence about her, a beauty that went deeper than looks. In other circumstances she might secretly have condoned the young master's courting of her, but there was always the child.

Spooning flour into a bowl, Sally added salt then egg and milk. To be fair, she had to admit the girl stayed no more than five minutes whenever he joined her in the garden. But it did not always take five minutes for a man to think himself in love, and though these weeks spent living close to the girl she called Emma led her to be certain the girl would not take advantage of anything that young man might have said to her, who could say that would stop him?

Whisking the batter for Yorkshire puddings, she glanced over to where the maid sat peeling sprouts.

Suppose the young master persisted in hankering after her, what then of Miss Edwina? The two had been thrown together from childhood, Edwina happily doing the talking for them both. His father must have hoped, as Sally herself had, that one day the two would marry. But now ... she watched as Emma rose, setting aside a colander filled with sprouts all ready for the pot. Yes, the girl was lovely, but she was not the girl for Ethan Rawley.

'Will I take Ginny a drink and something to eat?'

Sally glanced at the clock. It wanted four hours till dinner was served. The master and Mr Ethan would not be home until an hour before that, and that yellow-haired Mr Marsh had been taken out for a ride in the chaise and was not back yet. She felt the same rush of distaste she experienced each time that man was mentioned. It would be no loss if he never returned to Brade Hall.

'Arrh.' She nodded, pushing away thoughts of the man who brought a tingle of mistrust to her spine. 'It be near enough four o'clock and teatime. You brew a pot of tea and I'll cut some bread and butter, and we'll have a slice of yesterday's baking.'

'Ginny has a particular liking for your cherry cake.'

'And so does Baxter.' Sally smiled, fetching bread from the crock in the pantry. 'Reckon he won't say no to a slice, but you can take his to him. The master asked him to do an inventory of the wine cellar. I'll take Ginny's tray.'

She was being over cautious, Sally told herself as she climbed the stairs that gave first on to the corridor that housed the main bedrooms, then on up to the servants' bedrooms at the top of the house. The Rawleys were out at the brickworks or the coal mine, and the man who claimed not yet to be fully recovered from his injury was not in the house, so why had she not let the girl come upstairs with the tray ... why the feeling that to do so was to court trouble?

Reaching the landing she paused to get her breath, ears pricked for sounds that did not come. But what was she listening for? There was no one in this part of the house. Yet still her spine prickled as she went on up the servants' stairs.

'Is Ginny feeling better?'

Miriam was already back in the kitchen when Sally returned, red-faced from her exertions.

'She be nigh on well.' Sally plonked herself thankfully into a chair, taking the tea Miriam held out to her. 'I think she can get up tomorrow,

148

and a good job too. It be no easy job trawling trays that far up. And I'll have to be going up again in the morning for to change bed linen.'

'It could just as easily be done now?' Miriam suggested. 'Everyone is out so it's not likely to inconvenience any of them.'

'That be right enough.' Sally sipped her tea. 'But I ain't much in favour of climbing all them stairs again just yet.'

'Then let me change the beds? I know I'm not an upstairs maid, but just this once...'

'I be tempted.'

'I'll have it done before you finish your second cup.' The girl gave one of her rare smiles as she went to collect sheets from the linen cupboard.

The house was so quiet. Almost afraid to disturb the silence, she moved along the corridor Sally had told her held the main bedrooms. She had not been to this part of the house before and now looked in wonderment at gleaming woodwork, carpet thick as a folded blanket, and on the walls pictures half the size of...

Half the size of what? It had been there on the brink of her mind, hovering just beneath the surface. But it fell back, lost again in the greyness that engulfed her past.

The second door along led to the master's room. She followed the housekeeper's instructions. It helped not having to remember right or left for each room faced on to the beautifully worked balustrade that ran from the stairs the entire length of the gallery.

Her movements deft and sure, she changed bed linen, putting used sheets and pillow cases into

149

the string-necked bag brought with her for that purpose.

Afterwards, glancing at each closed door in turn, Miriam counted to the sixth. This was the room of the man Ethan had talked of one evening in the garden. The man she had seen being wheeled outdoors. Her hand on the handle, she paused. She had only glimpsed the back of his head but it had given rise to a strange feeling in her, almost a tingling of her nerves and now she felt it again – a cold touch like ice against her spine.

Unlooked for a picture of that yellow hair rose to her mind and her stomach lurched. Clutching the fresh bed linen, she forced herself to take a long, slow breath. This man had done nothing to her, they had not even met. What she was feeling was probably just due to the child stirring inside her. Sally had said to expect a few uncomfortable moments. Calmer yet not fully convinced, Miriam opened the bedroom door. Five minutes was all it would take. Five minutes and she could be back in the kitchen.

One glance about the room with its blue carpet and velvet drapes showing her it was empty, she crossed quickly to the bed, pulling off the blue silk eiderdown and placing it on the low chest that stood against the foot of the bed, following it with the soft white blankets.

Reaching for the pillows, she caught her hip against the bedside table, setting the crystal water carafe wobbling against the drinking glass. Catching her breath sharply she steadied the delicate crystal, her heart thumping. Why did she feel so nervous about being in this room?

Stripping off the sheets, she rammed them hurriedly into the linen bag. It would be a relief to have the bed re-made and herself away from this room.

It was as she ran a final smoothing touch over the eiderdown that the hand fastened over her mouth.

Almost paralysed with shock, Miriam could not move as an arm encircled her waist, holding her immobile.

Ethan? Had he returned and come to his friend's room only to find her there?

Miriam struggled to free herself but behind her a man's throaty laughter shattered the quiet of the room.

Surely Ethan would not grab her in such a way? He had not tried to take her in his arms the evening he'd told her he loved her, only gently kissed each hand. This was not Ethan, something inside her protested.

Then who? One hand pulling at that which sealed her mouth, the other dragging at the arm about her waist, she tried to wrench them away but they were strong as steel.

'You don't have to pretend.' The voice was low and husky, lips pressed to the nape of her neck. 'I've seen the look in your eyes each time you brought me a meal. Noticed your hands linger each time you smoothed the sheets about me as I lay in that bed.'

Feeling a tongue trace a line along her neck, Miriam tried to cry out, but the hand tightened, stifling the sound before it could leave her throat.

'Not yet.' The arm about her waist inched upward, still holding her in an unbreakable grip, the hand closing over her breast. 'It isn't the moment to cry out yet. That will come later, when you get what you have been wanting for weeks.'

The voice murmuring against her ear sent waves of fear coursing along her veins. Miriam tore at the hand fastened over her breast, but it served only to excite the man further as he pulled her hard against his body, hot breath fanning her cheek.

'You know the game, don't you, my little Ginny? You've played it before, haven't you?'

The mouth against her ear traced a line of kisses against her cheek up to her temple. He thought she was Ginny! Whoever this man was he had grabbed her believing he was holding Ginny. Miriam clawed again at the arm that pinned her, hearing the throaty laughter as she tried to twist herself loose.

'Yes, you've played before.' The laughter ceased abruptly. 'But have you played this way?'

The question ripped out on a rush of breath and at the same moment the hand was withdrawn from her mouth, the arm that circled her waist released; but before she could move he hooked one foot about her ankle and drove his fist between her shoulder blades, sending her toppling face down on to the floor.

Vaguely aware of glass rattling on the bedside table, Miriam felt the weight of his body sprawled across hers, felt him tear her blouse away then shove her skirts up to her waist.

152

'Not yet.' Hot breath rasped her skin as she cried out. 'I told you, not yet.'

One hand pressed her face into the thick carpet. The other grasped the waistband of her drawers, pulling them slowly downwards.

'Have you done it this way before, Ginny?'

Her senses screaming, Miriam felt the drawing down of her bloomers, heard the man's breath quicken, then felt his hand slowly stroke her bare buttocks.

'Have you, Ginny?' he whispered hoarsely. 'Have you felt a man drive into you this way...'

Miriam tried to heave herself up, to dislodge the man lying half across her, give herself a moment where she might be able to roll away from him. Then, a gasp of absolute terror stifling her, she felt his fingers trail over her bare skin, forcing themselves into the hollow between her legs.

The baby? The thought broke clearly and logically through the barriers of fear. If he succeeded in raping her, what would happen to the baby? Fear, no longer for herself, drove a clear path through her mind. If she could reach the table beside the bed, maybe she could dislodge the carafe, tumble it to the floor then grab it and hit him on the head.

Trying desperately to ignore the hand probing her flesh, the hot breath on her shoulders, she eased her arm forward. He must not know what was in her mind, he must not guess.

Twisting her head a few inches beneath the pressure of his hand, she gauged the distance to the table. She could reach it ... she had to reach it.

Three more inches ... two... Her arm snaked over the carpet, stretching until her shoulder shrieked from the strain; then her fingers touched the stubby leg of the table and she pulled.

For an eternity of seconds it seemed her plan must fail. He would succeed in raping her and her child would die. The thought, stark and raw, added strength to her bid and she shook the table hard, bringing the whole thing crashing on to the floor.

'Be you all right, Mrs Baxter?'

Behind them the bedroom door opened and Ginny's face peered enquiringly around it.

'What the...!' Her mouth falling open, she stared at the figures on the ground, the girl with her clothes torn away.

His body twisting so he could look towards the doorway, the hand dropped from Miriam's mouth.

'My baby...' she sobbed. 'Please! You will harm my baby!'

Understanding flashing across Ginny's face, she was in the room in an instant, her foot shooting out to land solidly against the spine of the man sprawled across her friend.

'You bastard!' Disgust flaring in her eyes, she kicked him again. 'You filthy bastard ... get off her! Get off her!'

Running to the fireplace, she grabbed one of the heavy brass fire irons, bringing it up high above her head.

Quick as she moved the man moved quicker, his back already against the closed door as she turned.

Relief sapping her strength, Miriam pulled her underclothes about her, hands trembling as she pushed down her skirts to cover her legs.

'You filthy swine!' Ginny spat. 'Wait till the master gets to hear what you've done, he'll take a horsewhip to you!' The poker still held menacingly above her head, eyes never leaving his face, she moved slowly to where Miriam sat huddled, her face hidden in her skirts. 'It be all right, Emma,' she said, her voice gentle but her eyes spitting venom. 'Mr Bloody Yellow Hair Marsh won't touch you no more!'

Yellow hair! It seemed to echo the torment of her mind. The man in the wheelchair ... yellow hair ... yellow hair ... he had yellow hair. Spinning faster and faster the thoughts became a whirlpool in her brain, pulling her into darkness, sucking her down ... he had yellow hair ... bloody yellow-haired Mr Marsh ... he had yellow hair. Her head jerking up, she stared at the man with his back against the door.

'Saul!' she gasped. 'Saul!'

Lowering the poker, yet still gripping it ready to use should he make a move, Ginny watched recognition flood into Saul Marsh's eyes.

'Miriam!' He glanced from one girl to the other. 'But I thought...'

'I know what you thought!' Ginny shielded the other girl protectively as she rose unsteadily to her feet. 'You thought you was in for a good time. Her being only a servant wench, nobody would care if you raped her. Well, both Mr Rawleys will care. If one don't beat the life out of you, the other will...'

'Neither of them will do any such thing.' A small scar at one corner of his mouth adding to the slight downward droop of his lower lip, Saul tugged at the bottom of his fawn cashmere waistcoat then brushed casually at his light cavalry twill trousers. 'In fact, they'll not do anything, for the simple reason they will not hear of it.'

'Oh, yes they will. I'll...'

'You will say nothing!' His eyes moving slowly from Miriam to Ginny, Saul Marsh's tone was sibilant with threat. 'You see, they'll not believe you. For how could a man who's been castrated rape a girl?'

'Castrated? You mean...?' Ginny's brow creased.

'Yes, I mean just that. They believe the injury I suffered before Ethan found me took away any possibility of my imposing myself upon a woman, so you would both be accused of lying and dismissed from your posts. But that would not be the end of it for either of you.' Eyes glittering, lips curled into a travesty of a smile, he stared at Ginny. 'Wherever you went, I'd find you and kill you!'

That smile as much of a threat as his words, Saul let his glance rest momentarily on Ginny's frightened face then on Miriam's, seeing the conflicting emotions in her eyes.

'Then I shall come to Brade Farm.' He spoke slowly, savouring the fear that leaped to her chalk white face. 'I shall come for *him*, Miriam, for your brother. He will die for what he did to me.'

Ralph, Brade Farm, her mother... Suddenly the

156

barriers were swept aside and memory returned, great flooding waves of it rolling in on her, chasing away the cobwebs of forgetfulness, clearing the shadows. 'Ralph?' she whispered.

'Yes, Ralph.' Saul's voice held all the hatred of ages. 'He thought he'd killed me, leaving me there on Derby's Hill. But he will be the one to die.'

'You ... you did not come.' Struggling amid the torrent of memories, Miriam barely heard his threat. 'I waited for you in the hollow, but you did not come. Ralph took me home. My mother said you would not want...' She looked across at him, her eyes dazed, not yet comprehending everything she now remembered. 'She said you would not come. But Ralph promised to find you, and when he could not he put my letter in our secret place ... but you did not find it.'

'Oh, I found your letter!' Saul laughed mockingly, smoothing a hand over his ruffled yellow hair.

'But you ... you did not come?'

'Did you expect me to? Did you honestly expect me to?'

Miriam's brow furrowed as if she were having difficulty in understanding what he had just said.

'I wasn't having your bastard foisted off on me. I had no intention of coming back. I didn't want you and I certainly didn't want your child!'

Staring at him, Miriam's head jerked as if he had struck a blow to her mouth. 'Not just *my* child, Saul,' she gasped, 'it is *your* child too.'

He laughed again, this time soft and sneeringly. 'That is what you'd like me to believe, isn't it?

157

You and that brother of yours, to say nothing of your sour-faced mother. Well, I'm sorry to disappoint you but you'll have to find another nail to hang that one on. You won't hang it on Saul Marsh.'

'But the baby...'

'Is not my problem.' The cruel smile widened. 'You went out to play and came home with a bastard. Don't expect me to give it my name.'

Eyes wide and steady on his, Miriam drew herself upright, ignoring the blouse that hung halfway down her arms, the physical pain of his attack swamped by that of his words. Hands and lips trembling, she drew a long breath. 'I will not expect anything of you, Saul.' Her words fell into the silence that had followed his denial. 'Neither will my child. I would sooner it remained a bastard than have it call you father.'

'Then we shall both be content.' Standing aside, Saul Marsh opened the door. 'Now leave my room or I will ring for Baxter and tell him how the pair of you tried to involve me in some devious little scheme you had cooked up in order to extort money from the Rawleys.'

The disclosure of Miriam's pregnancy having taken her by surprise, Ginny had stood for the last few minutes in silence. Now she was over it and her hackles rose with his blatant lie. 'The master would never believe that! He knows we would never try to rob him.'

'Are you sure of that, Ginny?' Saul drew the door open a mite further, his voice a little louder. 'Shall we ask Mr Baxter to come up?'

'No.' It was Miriam who spoke. Appearing

strangely calm despite what had happened, she took the other girl by the hand, drawing her towards the door. 'There will be no need to call Mr Baxter.'

'Remember,' he said as they reached the door, 'the Rawleys will hear nothing of what has gone on in this room. You will say nothing!'

Freeing her hand from Miriam's, Ginny shoved her sharply into the corridor, at the same time raising the poker she still carried. '*We* will say nothing!' she hissed through clenched teeth. 'But what about this, you swine?' Swinging the poker down, she struck him a blow to the side of his face. 'Try saying nothing about that, you sly bastard!'

Holding a towel to his cheek, Saul Marsh gazed at his reflection in the mirror above his washstand. That girl Ginny would neither forget nor forgive. His soft new life was at risk while she lived. Not to mention the life he now planned. A life that would contain everything he'd never enjoyed before ... he would make sure of that. Sadler's money would be put to the kind of use the old man had never dreamed of, there would be no luxury Saul would deny himself. But before he could achieve any of that he must marry Edwina, and one hint, one murmur from that slut of a maid, would put paid to any hope of that.

Easing away the towel, he looked at the purpling bruise along his cheek. Ginny was a danger to his ambition, a hazard he could well do without. He must think of a way to remove that hazard... And Miriam? She would say nothing for fear of bringing harm on that brother of hers.

Wincing as he replaced the towel, he saw the eyes staring back at him turn dark with hatred. Ralph Bryce had not wanted him dead. If he had then one thrust of that knife deep into Saul's heart would have seen to that. No, Ralph Bryce wanted him to live. Live the life of half a man. But he had failed. Cruelly as it had been wielded the knife had not done what was intended, as had been proved in this very room.

Throwing the towel from him Saul felt the acid rise in his throat. Ralph Bryce had failed.

Raising a foot he brought it hard down on the towel.

But Saul Marsh would not!

Chapter Eleven

She would have received the letter he had written by now.

Glancing at the clock in his bedroom, Saul pulled on a sapphire blue cashmere jacket. He made a handsome sight, the colour of the coat enhancing his yellow-gold hair. He would catch the eye of many folk in Dudley.

But he wanted to catch nobody's eye. He must not stand out from the market-day crowd any more than could be helped. Stripping off the jacket and pale grey trousers, he chose instead a severe black suit. That would not be so eye-catching. He would be seen simply as one more employer selecting workers from the line. Taking up a matching top hat, he set it on his head. It felt strange after years of wearing nothing but a greasy flat cap, but it helped to conceal his hair, providing the anonymity that was so important. Soon the colours he chose to wear, and the headgear he chose not to wear, would no longer be of any consequence. But right now...

Glancing again at the clock, he picked up a pair of pigskin gloves. She would come. She would be there waiting for him beside the fountain on Castle Hill.

The Rawleys had swallowed his tale about living in Dudley. He had told them both his parents were dead and that he'd lived with his grandmother. They had offered to bring her here weeks ago but Saul told them she was bedridden, that he would write and assure her of his safety and visit her the moment he was well. That was where he was supposed to be going the several times he had been out alone. Today he would bring the sad news of her death. That and the tale that the house they'd lived in had been given to a quarry worker and his wife would put an end to the need to invent any more stories, either for the Rawleys' benefit or Edwina's.

Climbing into the trap the stable hand held ready for him, Saul flicked the reins, offering no word of thanks. From today such would be his due, and he would thank no servant.

He had chosen the day well. Wednesday was market day in Dudley. Many people brought produce to sell and many more came looking for

161

work. One more would not be noticed among the crowd.

Leaving the trap at the Castle Hotel, he walked the several yards to the large, ornate stone fountain erected close to the grounds of ruined Dudley Castle.

'Saul! Oh, Saul lad!' Amy Marsh gasped, as she recognised the well-dressed figure.

Grabbing the hand that reached for his, he shoved it back beneath her woollen shawl.

'I told you not to speak. I said to act as if you didn't know me!' His voice harsh, he glanced about, but no one showed any interest as they bustled about the market stalls. 'Over there!' he ordered, indicating the spot where a line of men and women of mixed ages stood grouped together, hoping to be selected for a day's hire.

Pretending an interest in a horse for sale together with its foal, Saul waited several minutes before wandering across to the line. After questioning several others he reached a middle-aged woman, the hands holding the shawl over her head attesting to the fact that she knew what hard work was.

'I need a washerwoman.' He came to a halt before the figure, drab in dark skirts that did not totally conceal her shabby boots. 'Have you experience in that line?'

'Arrh, sir.' Amy Marsh did not lift her eyes to her son's face. 'I been a washerwoman nigh on thirty year.'

'So why are you here seeking employment?' Saul allowed his glance to wander over several other likely-looking women. It would serve his purpose better to pretend to be weighing one against the other.

'I worked at Oldbury, sir, at the Hall there, but with the passing of the mistress there ain't no place for me any more. The Hall be closed and none to live in it.'

'I see. But you have a reference?'

'Oh arrh, sir.' Amy kept her glance on the ground while feeling for her son's own letter which she had stuffed into her pocket. 'When the mistress felt her time were near, her had references wrote out for each of her servants. I have it here with me, sir.'

'Later.' He dismissed the reference with a careless flick of his hand. 'Right now I'm in a hurry. I will take you on a week's approval. If your work proves unsatisfactory you will be dismissed. The pay is four shillings a week and your keep. Are you agreeable?'

Pushing the letter back into her pocket, Amy dropped a quick curtsey. 'I be agreeable, sir, and thank you.'

Without another word he began to retrace his steps to the hotel, his mother a subservient two yards behind.

'What do you think you be about?' Amy Marsh snapped as they rounded the corner, but Saul brushed the query aside, keeping silent until they were in his trap and on the road.

'Well?' She had held her peace long enough. Now anger burst free. 'What bloody game be you playing at, letting me think you were dead?'

Keeping the horse to a comfortable trot, Saul quickly outlined all that had happened to him,

163

leaving out any mention of Miriam Bryce or the fact that it was her brother who'd attacked him.

'But didn't you see who it was did such an awful thing?' All her earlier anger forgotten, tears of pity rolled down Amy's work-lined cheeks.

'I saw nothing until I woke up in Brade Hall.' Saul skirted expertly around the truth. To tell her who it was who had left him bleeding on the heath would only be to send her round to Brade Farm with knife in her own hand; and that would wreck his plans. Ralph Bryce would not go unpunished but that punishment could wait.

'But why didn't you send for me? Why didn't you send word sooner?' Wrapping one hand in the corner of her shawl Amy wiped it across her cheeks.

'Listen, Mother.' Saul hesitated, raising his whip in answer to a shouted greeting from a carter travelling in the opposite direction. 'I've got the sort of chance I never thought to have – the chance to live the life of the mine owners.'

'You ... live like monied people?' Amy wiped the shawl once more over her face. 'That can't be right. You ain't never had no more than two halfpennies for a penny all of your life.'

No more he had. Saul's fingers tightened about the reins. But now he had the chance to change that and nothing was going to take it away from him, not even his own mother.

'I tell you, it can happen.' He continued to explain. 'I already have the offer of a job working for Clayton Rawley...'

'Be it a good 'un?' Amy glanced hopefully at his face. 'An overseer p'raps?'

'Talk was of my managing Grace Mary mine.'

Amy caught her breath. 'Manager of the Grace Mary? But be it only talk?'

'No. The offer's real enough. But I shall not take it.'

'Not take it?' Twisting sideways she glared at him, disbelief closely followed by anger. 'Be you out of your mind? There be men standing the line day after day with no hope in hell of getting work, and you say you won't take on the job of manager? Whatever happened to that brain of your'n?'

Flicking the reins, Saul suppressed a smile, forbidding it to rise to his mouth, allowing it to take form only in his mind.

'It is working, Mother,' he answered softly. 'For the first time in my life it's working properly.'

'I don't know how you make that out!' Amy pulled her shawl about her with a sharp disapproving tug. 'Being offered the job of managing a mine when all you've ever done is scrape your backside digging coal in one? Then you turn round and say you ain't going to take it. Don't tell me that be using your brain! You ain't likely to be offered such a job again.'

No, he was not likely to be made such an offer a second time, Saul conceded. But then, soon he would need no man's employment. 'Why work at another man's mine when you can own one?'

'Own one?' Amy's brow creased, anxiety clouding her eyes. That injury had done more to him than physical hurt. 'Saul, lad, you be talking wild.'

His mouth tight, he stared ahead. 'No, Mother,

165

I am not talking wild. Once I am married to Edwina Sadler, I shall as good as own the Hange collieries and the brick and tile works, and they will be mine completely once her father is gone. I shall be a mine owner in my own right and a match for the Rawleys or any other family in the Black Country.'

Holding the shawl about her, Amy felt the blood drain from her veins. He was talking marriage, but how could he? How could he think of marrying when...

'You can't seriously be thinking to wed any girl, not seeing the way you be.'

'The way I be?' he grated, mouth twisting. 'I presume you mean my injury?'

'Of course I mean your injury.'

'But why should that make any difference?'

'Why!' Amy threw up her hands. 'You knows full well why. But if you want me to say it then I will. How can you take a woman in marriage in the full knowledge that all you can bring to her bed is an empty pot!'

The smile he had suppressed now pulled at his mouth, drawing the downward curving lips almost into a grimace. 'The pot, as you put it, Mother, is not empty.'

'But you said...'

'I was severely injured in the groin. At first I thought never to function as a man again, and the doctor thought the same. He said the parts that were left to me were useless. Time has proved him wrong, but no one other than you knows that and that is the way it must remain.'

A tide of feeling rushed through her, bringing a

166

warm glow of relief.

'But surely you have told the Rawleys you be well? That ... that your body be near enough as it should?'

'No.' Saul shook his head. 'I have said nothing to them.'

Glancing sideways, Amy caught the smile that pulled again at her son's mouth. That smile had only ever meant one thing: that he was up to no good. But she knew better than to question him. Since his father's death, Saul Marsh had been a law unto himself But why leave people to think he was deprived of his manhood? He may deny it but he was playing some game, and judging by the look on his face it was a dirty one.

'Repeat nothing of what I have said to you,' he insisted. 'I have my reasons.'

I be sure you have, thought Amy as he drew the trap to a halt at the point where the road diverged. Climbing down, she lifted her shawl, draping it about her head.

'I have told the Rawleys I have no family other than a grand-mother.' He watched her tie the ends of the shawl beneath her breasts. 'She will cease to exist today along with the home we shared.'

Raising her head, Amy looked at the well-dressed man sitting in the smart trap. He had learned so quickly, learned to like the life that wealth could bring. He sat there in his borrowed finery as if he had known such clothes from birth. Yes, Saul had learned to like the life fate had dealt him, but with every rose there was a thorn, everything in life had to be paid for. What price would her son be called upon to pay?

'And me?' she asked. 'Do I have no existence for you after today?'

Saul heard the hurt in her words but weighed against what he had to lose the impact of it was insignificant. If his mother came to Brade Hall, saw Miriam Bryce there, possibly at a time when the girl's pregnancy was undeniable, she would put two and two together. Amy Marsh was not dimwitted. She would guess who it was had taken a knife to him and why, and with her sense of right and wrong she would not be slow to say to whom his marriage should be. Not that she could force him to marry the Bryce girl, but would she tell what she suspected to the Rawleys, and through them Edwina? That was his very reason for not contacting her sooner. He could not take the risk.

'It will only be until after I am married,' he returned. 'Once that is achieved I will send for you. Believe me, Mother, it is better this way.'

Better for whom? Amy watched the trap take the turning that led to Brade Hall. Not better for his mother, she could be sure of that. Saul Marsh had only ever held any true regard for one person, and that person was himself.

She watched the trap out of sight. She did not know Edwina Sadler but already her heart ached for the poor girl.

'But, Saul, you cannot possibly leave, you are not yet fit enough.' Edwina Sadler's long white fingers twined together anxiously in her lap.

With a regretful smile, Saul gave that well-rehearsed twitch of the mouth designed to

168

disguise the truth from a listener.

'I will not take any more from Clayton Rawley. He has already done more for me than I can ever repay, and so has Ethan. I can no longer accept their charity.

'Yes, Edwina, charity it is.' Dropping his eyes, he played out the charade to the full. 'Oh, I know it is well meant but it is charity none the less, and I cannot be a man and live off another.'

'But I thought ... I hoped...'

A blush staining her cheeks, she broke off. Saul allowed a silence to fall between them.

'Will you return to Dudley?' she asked at last.

Lifting his eyes, he saw the remnants of the stain in her cheeks, and the undisguised anguish in her brown eyes. So he had not read her wrong these past weeks. Edwina Sadler had fallen in love with the injured stranger. Now she feared herself about to lose him. If the moment were all, now was his time.

'I do not know where I shall go.' He kept his voice soft, seemingly on the edge of breaking. 'Wherever I go, it makes no difference without...'

Seated opposite him in the tastefully furnished sitting room of her father's house, Edwina looked at the handsome face, one she pictured every night as she drifted into sleep. If only she could say what was in her heart, tell him she loved him. But to speak so openly might cause him to think ill of her.

'Without what?' she asked instead.

Pushing himself out of his chair, he crossed to the window, running a hand through his hair, seemingly in agitation.

169

'Nothing,' he said, getting the right degree of despair into his voice. 'It is of no matter.'

Plucking at the skirts of her turquoise voile dress, Edwina fought the tears of disappointment gathering in her throat. 'Then it can be of no matter it is not kept a secret. So will you not tell me what it is makes no difference?'

'Telling you can't help.' Saul kept his back turned.

'How do you know? I thought we were friends? Surely one friend can be permitted to help another?'

He heard the plea in her voice, the tears underlying her words. It was going the way he wanted.

'Please, Saul, let me help.'

Still with his back to her, he cleared his throat, throwing back his head a little. Every inch of him spoke of a weight he found hard to bear.

'You can't,' he said huskily. 'No one can.'

'If it is the thought of taking employment with the Rawleys that is bothering you, then my father...'

'It is not working for the Rawleys bothers me!' It was almost a cry as he threw himself around to face her, his face holding the same pretence of pain. 'I would willingly sweep the streets if...'

Lifting eyes brilliant with the dew of tears, her voice tender with the love she thought hidden, Edwina asked softly. 'If what, Saul?'

He let his eyes play over her, as if drinking in a picture that must last him a lifetime. Then, his voice stifled with emotion, he let the words tumble from his lips. 'If ... if only I could be with you!'

'Oh, Saul!' She was on her feet and running to him across the room. 'Oh, Saul, you *can* be with me. You can work for my father...'

'No!' He caught her hands, holding her at arm's length. 'I could not work for your father any more than I can work for Clayton Rawley. I said it was that man's charity I could not accept and I spoke truly. But it is more than that, much more. I could not take employment anywhere I knew you were close by. To see you, maybe speak to you, yet know I could never touch you, never hold you, would be a torment I could not stand.'

Allowing a hint of sadness to curve his mouth, he stared deep into her eyes and when he spoke again his voice was throaty with the suggestion of latent tears. 'I could not do it, Edwina.' He let go of her hands. 'I have not the courage.'

'And I do not have the courage to let you go.' Eyes shining like stars through rain, she reached again for his hands. 'Stay with me, Saul,' she murmured.

'Edwina ... oh, my dear!' Chin dropping to his chest, Saul gave a strangled sob, his triumph carefully hidden. 'Don't ask me to do that, please ... don't ask me.'

'But I do ask it.' She pulled his hands around her waist, holding them there, any thought of his thinking ill of such forward behaviour drowned in the love that swept through her. 'I want you to stay with me.'

'And watch as you marry someone else?' He kept his head lowered. 'That would kill me.'

Loosing his hands, she lifted his head. 'No, not to watch me marry someone else,' she whispered, 'but to marry *you*, become *your* wife. I love you, Saul.'

'Edwina ... oh, God, Edwina!' The words tumbled out on a carefully measured rush of breath as he tightened his arms about her, holding her close to him. 'I never dreamed ... I never let myself hope ... how could I ever expect you to love me?'

'But I do.' She lifted her face to his. 'I do love you, Saul.'

His eyes holding hers, he lowered his head, the movement infinitely slow and sensual. 'Oh, my love,' he murmured as his lips brushed hers. 'My own sweet love.' He felt a tremor shake her from head to toe and as his mouth took fierce possession of hers he smiled inwardly.

'She ain't there, Mrs Baxter.' Ginny Jinks almost tumbled into the kitchen. 'I've been up to her room like you said, but she ain't there.'

'But her were there when you took up a bite of breakfast?'

'Arrh.' Ginny nodded, the all effacing cap waggling on the back of her head. 'I told her you said to have a couple of extra hours in bed, seeing as she wasn't feeling too well. I said you thought she had likely picked up my cold.'

'Colds spread all too easy. I can't have either of you going about the house coughing and sneezing, that influenza ain't something to be trifled with.' She could have added, Especially when a girl is pregnant. But that part Sally kept to herself. The less Ginny Jinks knew, the less gossip would be peddled down in the village.

172

'Maybe she's laying the fire in the...'

'And maybe she ain't!' Sally returned sharply. 'That girl don't have any duties in the house other than here in the kitchen. She only helped out yesterday 'cos I was run off my feet with having you laid up. Like as not she'll be in the privy, so till her comes back you can get on with slicing them onions to go into the bread sauce. The master enjoys that with a slice or two of fresh chicken.'

A glare silencing Ginny's protests that she was an upstairs maid and therefore shouldn't have to do kitchen chores, Sally took the roasting pan from the slow oven, basting the partly cooked chicken before replacing it.

Straightening from the gleaming black range, she glanced at the clock. It was unlike Emma to take advantage. She should have been here in the kitchen nigh on an hour ago. Ginny had said she'd had a bit of a fainting turn yesterday. She had heard the noise, apparently, as Emma bumped against the bedside table in Mr Marsh's room.

Wiping her hands on a square of huckaback taken from the airing line above the range, Sally looked thoughtful.

It wasn't right for a woman to go fainting all over the place even if she was pregnant. Sally felt the same quickening in her veins she had felt yesterday when Ginny had come down to say the girl felt unwell. The same intuitive stirring that told her now that she had not been given the whole story.

'Tell me again exactly what happened in that

173

bedroom yesterday, Ginny? I have my doubts that I've heard it all.'

'I'd best put this in the larder and then wash my hands, the smell of them onions be awful powerful. I don't want to go carryin' it upstairs.' Grabbing the dish of onions, Ginny skipped quickly into the scullery. Sally Baxter could smell a lie a mile off. But she had not told a lie. Ginny pumped cold water over her hands. Then again, she hadn't told all of the truth!

Chapter Twelve

Huddled in the summerhouse Miriam drew her shawl about her. She had been careful to dress only in the clothes she had worn the day she had left Brade Farm; all except for the blouse Saul had torn from her back.

She shivered as memory of that attack came flooding back. Why was Saul Marsh still here in this house if his injuries were healed? And who was it could have harmed him so as almost to have killed him?

The first of her questions she could see no answer to, but the second... The hands clutching the shawl trembled. Could it really have been Ralph who had done that to him? Was she right to judge her brother capable of committing such a horrible deed? Ralph had always been liable to punish anyone he thought had given offence to her, giving many a lad a bloody nose. But this!

Almost to castrate a man! Would he go so far?

Swallowing the sickness that thought brought in its wake, she remembered the words her brother had said: *'I will find him.'*

Beyond the summerhouse a pair of blackbirds sang their goodbye to summer but Miriam was deaf to all but the turmoil inside her.

What if Ralph had found him and Saul had refused to own the child as his? What if her brother's anger had proved too much to bear? Ralph would not take kindly to a man seducing his sister then refusing to accept the consequences; if Saul Marsh had said the same to him as he had said to her in that bedroom, told Ralph he did not want her and most certainly did not want the child...

But to go so far! Would anger carry her brother to such an extreme?

'...Then I shall come for HIM, *Miriam, for your brother. He will die for what he did to me.'*

She choked back a sob as the words rang ominously in her mind. Saul had proved himself a liar in many ways, so why did she feel so sure that in this he had told the truth?

He wanted to kill Ralph.

Saul Marsh intended to kill her brother.

Oblivious of the cold she stood up, her inner vision revealing a scene that was far from these gardens: Brade Farm, and the woman who lived there. A woman with sandy hair fading to ash grey, eyes almost colourless, like lifeless pools in those sharpdrawn features. A woman with her hand raised to strike...

The mental picture causing her to tremble,

Miriam hesitated. She could not go back to that house! But what if her brother were in prison ... or even worse had been hanged for what he had done?

The thought terrifying her, she swayed, striking her shoulder hard against the door jamb. Pain, sharp and biting as smelling salts had the same restorative effect, calming her nerves and bringing back common sense.

Saul Marsh had been in this house since the night he'd been injured. He had not lodged any complaint with the police or if he had she would have heard of it, for had not Sally Baxter told her that little went on in Brade Hall she did not know of? And what the housekeeper did not chatter about, Ginny most certainly did, whenever they found themselves alone. So if no complaint had been lodged then her brother could not have been arrested.

Miriam drew in a long breath, the tang of autumn spicy in her lungs. But who could say how long Saul Marsh would wait to take his revenge? Not by any lawful means but on his own account.

Ralph had to be told. She had to return home. Drawing the shawl more firmly about her, Miriam walked from the summerhouse.

'I had thought to leave without telling anyone.' Miriam sipped gratefully at the hot sweet tea Ginny had made for her. 'Then I realised how wrong that would be. I must at least say thank you to Mrs Baxter, and of course to you, for all the kindness you have shown me.'

'But you don't have to leave, just 'cos you have your memory back. Mrs Baxter...'

'You did not tell her?' Miriam looked anxiously at the girl busy setting china on a tray.

'Only that you had your memory back.'

'Nothing else? Nothing about...'

'About what that filthy swine tried to do to you?' Ginny shook her head, setting the large cap bobbing. ''Course I didn't, not after you made me promise not to. Though I still think you should shop the pig, tell the master what he were up to, that's what I think you should do.'

'But what if Mr Rawley doesn't believe me?'

'I'd be there too.' Ginny added cutlery to the tray, first scanning each knife and fork for the slightest blemish. 'I could confirm what I saw.'

'And if the master thinks we've cooked up a story? If he believes not us but Saul Marsh? You'll be out of a job, and without a reference might not easily find another.'

'Sod the job!' Ginny retorted, banging dessert spoons on to the tray. 'I lived afore ever I took this post and I guess I can make my living again if it be took from me. Anyway, I'd be willing to chance it. That Marsh should be made to pay for what he did, not allowed to get away Scot free. What if he tries it again on some other poor wench?'

'He won't. I think he's learned his lesson.' Miriam dropped her glance to her cup. Ginny was right, of course, Saul Marsh should be denounced. But if she did that then he would almost certainly have her brother arrested for attempted murder, and wrong though it was to

177

conceal so despicable an act, she could not bring herself to expose Ralph to danger.

Lifting the tray from the dresser, Ginny carried it to the table. 'I only hope you be doing the right thing,' she said placing cutlery at regular intervals along the spotless white cloth. 'That you don't come to regret it.'

'Come to regret what?' Returning from inspecting the table Ginny had laid in the upstairs dining room, Sally Baxter came into the kitchen and caught the last of the housemaid's words.

With a coolness that revealed Ginny had often been similarly caught out, she followed up the cutlery with the plates, keeping her reply airy. 'I were just saying, I hope Miriam don't come to regret not staying in bed. That she don't take cold.'

'Miriam!' Sally's hands went to her ample hips. 'And who is Miriam?'

'It's me, Mrs Baxter,' she answered before Ginny's apologetic grimace could give way to words. There had been enough half truths and innuendos, she could not let the girl go on covering for her. 'I've remembered my name.'

'Eh, wench! That be good news.' Sally bustled further into the kitchen, beaming beneath a white cap starched to the rigidity of iron. 'Did it happen this morning?'

Miriam glanced quickly at Ginny before answering. 'No. It happened yesterday after ... after...'

'After you felt faint?'

Mrs Baxter supplied her own answer and Miriam did not contradict her. The woman

178

would not be so easy to keep silent on the subject of attempted rape as Ginny. She was more likely to tell Clayton Rawley as soon as he returned to the Hall.

'P'raps it was that knock you took against the table? They do say that a bump can often cure the ill another one gave rise to. But whether it did or it didn't, I'm glad you have your memory back. Now you can...' Leaving the sentence in mid-air the housekeeper glanced at Ginny who had finished laying the table for the servants' lunch.

'I can name the father of my child?' Laying aside her cup, Miriam looked at the older woman. 'It's all right, Mrs Baxter. Ginny knows about my being pregnant.'

'Ah, well, it was bound to come out sooner or later. Mind!' Sally threw a warning glance at the maid. 'You watch your mouth, Ginny Jinks. You'll not go trumpeting this down in the village. It be nothing to do with folk down there, nor with you! So keep your mouth closed.'

Helping herself to a cup of tea, Sally carried it to her favourite chair beside the range and looked over at Miriam, sitting twisting her hands together in her lap.

'You don't have to go deciding on anything right away,' she said, grey eyes filled with compassion. 'You have a home here with us till your time be further along, after which my sister in Tividale...'

'No, Mrs Baxter. Thank you but I have to go home.' Standing, Miriam took up the shawl that had been draped over the back of her chair. 'I

179

have a mother and a brother.'

'I understands, wench.' Sally nodded. 'They must be fair beside themselves with worrying what's become of you, any mother would be.'

Any mother except mine. Miriam felt the bitterness of that thought sting like acid. The only worry Leah Bryce might have would be of her daughter returning home.

As if hearing the thought, Sally Baxter laid aside her cup. 'Should it be you find that all is not well ... that perhaps you don't be so welcome any more, then you come back here; there will always be a friendly greeting, and like I said, my sister over in Tividale be ready to help.'

Tears catching in her throat, Miriam threw the shawl about her shoulders. Why was it that Sally Baxter, a virtual stranger still, could show her such kindness when her own flesh and blood, her own mother, had never shown anything but harshness?

'I will remember, Mrs Baxter. Thank you for all you have done for me, and please thank your sister. I don't know what I would have done had you not taken me in.'

'It be Mr Ethan and his father you have to thank for that.' Sally smiled. 'This be their house.'

Crossing the shawl over her chest and around her still narrow waist, Miriam tied the ends into a knot. She lifted her glance once more to the kind grey eyes regarding her steadily across the kitchen. 'I will thank them, of course, but first I must go home. Please, Mrs Baxter, will you do me yet another kindness? Will you give the

180

Rawleys my thanks and tell them I will write to them and thank them myself in a little while?'

'Of course I'll tell them.' Sally pushed herself up from the chair. 'They'll understand your eagerness to return to your own home.'

'Mr Ethan ... I wouldn't want him to think I had turned my back and left without a word.'

'You leave Mr Ethan to me,' Sally said, giving her a hug. 'I'll tell him what you said.'

But I will tell him no more. She hid the thought behind a smile as she watched the younger women embrace. The girl had given cause for nothing but admiration and praise during her stay in Brade Hall, despite her condition. But there was class and class, and Sally had never known the mixing of them to bring anything but regret. Nice girl Miriam might be, but she was not of an equal standing with Ethan Rawley. He would be told the girl had left, after sending him her thanks, and nothing more.

Would he see her today? Hear word of her from someone who had seen or perhaps spoken to her?

Reaching the lock up a way from Fishers Bridge, Ralph paused. He had searched in each direction for miles around, but with no result. Miriam seemed to have vanished from the face of the earth. Glancing at a narrow boat as the huge lock gates slowly opened, he felt a surge of hope. Maybe this time...

'I ain't heard of no wench such as you describe,' the boatman answered his query, hand on the collar of the heavy cart horse tied by a long leading rein to the barge.

181

Ralph had not mentioned the fact that she was carrying a child. By this time it must show and that might well alter the description he had given of Miriam.

'She has hair some might call copper-coloured,' he repeated, then as the man shrugged, added, 'she was expecting a child.'

The bargee glanced sharply at him, fresh interest on a face etched deeply with lines. 'Be she your missis?'

'No.' Ralph shook his head. 'She's not my wife, she's my sister.'

Lifting his flat cap, the man scratched his greying hair. 'Got herself in the puddin' club then slung her hook when her family found out?'

Ralph felt his insides twist at this crude summary, that somehow made his sister appear little more than a prostitute. But she had got herself pregnant and she had run away.

'It happens all the time, lad,' the man went on, replacing his cap. 'I've no doubt her'll be home soon enough when her finds out there be none to keep her. It ain't so easy for 'em to take a man's eyes with a babby holding on to their skirts.'

Resentment cooling to brittle anger, Ralph retied his muffler with fingers he wanted to curl into fists. To strike the bargee would bring a certain satisfaction, but how long would that last when it was taken from the wrong man? This was not the one he truly wanted to harm, this was not the man who had used his sister then cast her aside. Fists and anger under control, Ralph thanked the man and was turning away when a girl of about ten years came to stand at the bargee's side.

'We'll be back along here day after tomorrow.' The man took the horse's leading rein. 'If we see anything of her, where can I leave word?'

Pointing left, Ralph indicated the squat low-roofed building that was the Blue Ball Inn. 'There,' he said. 'Leave word with Banjo, the landlord. If there is any word he will tell me.'

'Oh, arrh?' The bargee smiled, showing gap teeth. 'An' how do you get him to stop playing that banjo long enough to tell you anything?'

'It isn't easy,' Ralph replied as a jangle of music drifted towards them on the evening quiet.

'Well, if we see her...'

'See who, Father?' The girl's bright eyes were on Ralph.

'None of your business, my wench, get you back to your mother.'

'She might have seen Miriam.' Ralph clutched at the faint hope.

'Seen who, Father?' Beneath the rim of her grey cotton bonnet, the girl kept her eyes on Ralph.

'I would take it kindly if you would let me ask your daughter?'

Swayed by a politeness not usually given to those many folk thought of as 'wharf rats', the bargee glanced at a woman who came out to stand beside the tiny living cabin.

'He be speaking about his sister. Wants to ask our wench if she might have seen sight of her.'

The woman nodding, he turned back to Ralph.

'What does your sister look like, mister?' The girl was quick to act on her mother's permission.

Reaching into his mind Ralph saw clearly the

picture Miriam made walking across the heath, her shawl falling loose about her elbows, the sun lighting her hair to dark flame.

'I'm not much for describing clothes.' He smiled at the young girl whose eyes never left his. 'She always wore dark skirts though sometimes her blouse would be white or maybe a sort of blue ... but she is beautiful and her hair is dark auburn.'

'Would that be red?'

'Sort of,' her father answered. 'A bit like your mother's fancy table, the one her won't have you put a pot on.'

'You mean mahogany!' The girl pronounced the word proudly. 'That table is mahogany. Is that the colour you mean, mister, a sort of reddish-brown?'

Ralph smiled. 'I think that is as near as I can describe it, but in the sunlight it does appear more red than brown.'

'I know what you mean, mister, and I have seen a woman with hair that colour.'

'Where? Can you tell me where?'

'I can tell you, mister, but I can't say as you'll know the place.'

'I've lived here for a long time, I know quite a few places.' He tried to keep the urgency out of his voice.

'So, tell the gentleman where it was you think you seen this woman.

'I don't *think* I seen her, Father, I *know* I seen her.'

Clucking his tongue softly as the horse shifted its hooves, scattering tiny pebbles across the towpath, the bargee glanced at the girl, who reached barely to his shoulder. 'So what makes you so sure the woman you seen was this man's sister?'

'I didn't say it was his sister, Father,' she answered, a tiny smile touching her mouth. 'I got no way of knowing who it was I seen, but I do know the colour of her hair was as he tells it. I took particular notice 'cos I thought it was the most beautifullest hair I ever did see.'

'You be sure now,' her mother cautioned. 'You be sure you ain't just wanting to be helpful. You won't be helping none unless it be the truth you're telling.'

She stepped to the edge of the barge, her own grey bonnet strings fluttering in a sudden breeze.

'Our wench likes to help,' she said, a hint of apology in her voice. 'But she be young yet, and a mite eager.'

'I ain't putting no varnish on it.' The girl turned to face her mother. 'It be the bare truth. I did see a woman and her hair was that colour. I remember thinking, the Princess has hair that colour.'

'Now how would you know that?'

Turning back to her father, the girl answered quickly, "Cos I seen a picture of her, a picture all painted with colours, it were hanging on a wall in that police station in Dudley. I was looking at it when Mother and me paid the fine for you getting drunk and punching a copper ... it were a policeman told me the picture was of Princess Alexandra, and her hair was au-auburn.'

'Well.' His smile humorous, the man placed a hand on his daughter's shoulder. 'Seems you knows what you be talking about. Now tell us where it was you spotted the woman?'

'It were while we were alongside the wharf taking on bricks from the Phoenix Brick and Tile works.' The girl's eyes swept back to Ralph. 'That be near where the Dudley Road splits off to Tividale. Mother had sent me to get flour and bacon and when I were coming back, I seen the woman I told you about. Her were going the way of Tividale. She had dark skirts and a white blouse – I seen it when the wind caught her shawl and blew it back from her shoulders. But it was her hair I noticed particular, it shone so. I think it were even beautifuller than Princess Alexandra's! Is your sister as beautiful as the Princess?'

'I think so.'

'And do you think it be her I seen on the Tividale road?'

For the first time in weeks, Ralph's smile rose easily to his lips. 'I can only hope so. At least, it is the first information I have been given. But this I can say – you are just as beautiful as either my sister or the Princess.'

A blush creeping slowly beneath the bonnet, the girl jumped lightly aboard the barge, hand raised in silent farewell as the horse pulled them on.

His steps quickening, Ralph followed the Dudley Road. Passing the high wrought-iron gates of Brade Hall, he glanced sideways, taking in the well-kept trees that lined a drive curving away out of sight. He envied no man such position or wealth, content with what God had given him. Ralph would have only one thing changed in his life. Pulling up his collar against the promise of a cold night, he thrust the thought away. Miriam had been born his sister. A mountain of wishes and an ocean of yearning could do nothing to alter that.

Reaching the spot the girl had named, he took the branch of the road that would lead to Tividale. It had taken just a couple of hours for the barge to cover the short distance from here to Brade Hall Lock. How far could Miriam walk in that time ... where had she been since leaving home ... and why was she going to Tividale?

Questions playing like a fountain in his mind, he walked on. Maybe it was not Miriam the barge girl had seen. Maybe...

But all the maybes he might think of would not stop him. His eyes racing ahead, he scanned the road bordered now by rough heath to one side and the canal to the other.

Some day, somewhere, he would find his sister.

Unbidden the image of his mother rose in his mind. How would she react when he did? Laughter, grim and hollow, echoed in the depths of his soul. She would react in only one way, that being once more to deny the girl the shelter of a home, to try to drive her away yet again. But should he find Miriam, should God see fit to give her back to him, then their mother would accept her daughter or see the last of both of her children.

Would that be any real burden to Leah Bryce? It felt almost as if someone else had asked the question, someone outside of himself, but the answer that welled up from Ralph's heart was all his own. She had no real love for either of her children. Never to have to look at them again would cause her no grief Leah Bryce's eyes looked back – back to a girlhood that was blighted. She had never seen the present and was blind to the future. The love and fulfilment each could have brought her was lost to resentment and pain, submerged in a jealousy that drowned all the good in her. How different she was from Amy Marsh. Not once had Leah searched for her daughter, nor asked her whereabouts of a living soul, and certainly not of any saint or God. She had written her off, blotted her out of her life, whereas the mother of that swine Saul Marsh had gone on asking; every carter, every pack man, even the gypsies who parked their wagons on the heath. She asked them all the same question: 'Have you seen my son?'

For Marsh had disappeared too. Not for the first time, Ralph found himself wondering what had happened following that fight over on Derby's Hill. He had brought the knife slicing down. Felt flesh come away in his hand.

Deep in the pockets of his jacket, his hands clenched at the horror of the memory.

Marsh's eyes had seemed to widen unnaturally as he realised what that knife was about to do. He had watched the hand that brought it down, then he had screamed. The sound had bounced off the grass and rocks, swirling along the gullies between like the howl of some hell-released banshee. Then the blade had found its mark.

Inside his pocket his right hand seemed to experience afresh the slight hesitation, the faint resistance the knife had met on contact with the flesh. Snatching both hands free Ralph flexed all his fingers, shaking away the memory. He had meant to kill Saul Marsh, wanted the man who had shamed Miriam dead.

But there had been no body found. He had searched the heath to both sides of Derby's Hill and there had been no sign of Marsh, dead or alive. So what had happened? It was as if he, like Miriam, had been swept away.

Like Miriam. Strange, but up until this moment the thought had not occurred to Ralph. Vanished ... like Miriam. Could it be they had met up somewhere on the road and left together?

A tightness in his throat, he tugged the muffler free from his neck and stuffed it into his jacket pocket. But it was no scarf that kept the air from his lungs, it was the old tightness that came each time he thought of Miriam being with another man.

But the time *must* come. He lifted his face to the sky, wanting to cry out his secret heartache. One day she would marry. One day she would be gone from him.

Only not yet!

Slumping to his knees, the smell of the damp heath in his nostrils, he released the cry of anguish building inside him.

'Dear God, not yet! Don't take her from me yet!'

Chapter Thirteen

She had meant to return home. To go back to the house above Brades Village.

Miriam held the shawl close about her, huddling into its worn folds, trying to fight off the chill of the fast-encroaching dusk.

Ralph had to be told, to be warned of the threat Saul Marsh had made. She had told herself that repeatedly, used it to bolster her resolve as she left the Hall, repeated it in her mind over and over again as she had walked that long half mile to the road. Only when she reached it the resolve had melted away, gone like a thief in the night, and she had taken the Tividale turn.

But where could she expect to find a sheltering roof in that town? Was it even a town or just a huddle of houses like her home village? She had eight shillings in her pocket, money Mrs Baxter had insisted she borrow. 'Pay it back when you can,' the housekeeper had said, pressing eight silver coins into her hand. But how long would that be? Who would give employment to a woman eight months pregnant? And without work, how would she repay Sally Baxter?

Maybe she could manage without spending any of the money. If she could find work on a daily basis, taking just one meal as payment. But then where would she sleep, and how would she get a letter to Ralph and the Rawleys unless she

190

bought pencil and paper and then a couple of penny postage stamps?

Perhaps if she saw a carter, he might take a letter for nothing? Supposing she bought paper from him, he would surely lend her a pencil ... perhaps, perhaps! Miriam caught back a sob. There were too many such words in her life. If only it could all go away.

But it wouldn't. She forced herself to go on, placing one foot mechanically in front of the other. It was her own actions had brought her to this, her own naivety. She should never have believed Saul when he'd said they would be married. But she had. She had swallowed all of his lies, greedily wanting more. Like a child with sweets, she thought, each one promised to taste better than the last. And then suddenly there were none left and the packet was empty.

Just as she was left. She had nothing but the memories of the lies he had told, that and a child she must care for alone.

Would she not be better off at home, even with her mother's dislike of her so painfully obvious? At least the child would have shelter. There would be a roof over its head, and Ralph would...

Her courage slipping, Miriam's steps slowed. Then words, each like a blow to her brain, slammed into her mind.

'There'll be no bastard born under my roof!'

Her mother had been adamant, and Ralph obstinate. For her to return to that house would mean mother and son living forever at odds with each other, and the child at the centre of it. She could not put her brother through that and she would not put an innocent child through it either.

Leah had made her childhood little more than living misery, and with her father's death seven years ago had made her girlhood more so. No child should be made to suffer as she had, to feel so unloved, so terribly unwanted; despite all her brother had done to make it up to her, the absolute denial of her mother's love had long ago broken Miriam's heart.

'It will not happen to you.' Beneath the shawl, she touched a hand to her stomach. 'I will never let that happen to you.'

'You'd best hurry if you mean to be home afore moonrise!'

Lifting her head at the call, Miriam saw the wagon pass, its candle jars already winking to each side. Lost in her own thoughts, she had not heard the crunch of its wheels on the hardpacked ground.

'It ain't good to be on the road after dark.' From the driving seat, a man wearing a muffler over a flat cap then tied in a knot beneath his chin spat tobacco-stained saliva noisily on to the road. 'It be all too easy to get run down with one of them carriages bringing iron masters and mine owners home from Dudley.' He spat again, 'Racing along as though they had a wasp in their breeches. Think nobody should be on the road 'cept them! You watch yourself, young woman, or it'll be as I say, you'll find yourself run down!'

Muttering to himself, the man drove on. Miriam watched the cart move off into the shadows then turned on her way.

It had happened before. The cart Ethan Rawley had ridden in had caught her in the back, taken her unawares ... just as that attack in the bedroom had taken her unawares.

She had not known Saul was there. Icy shivers touching her spine, she tried to rid herself of those dark memories, to force them from her mind, but try as she would they remained, reviving the terror of those moments, rekindling the fear that had not truly left her since his attempt to rape her.

In her mind's eye she saw the bedroom again. Blue velvet falling the length of the windows to rest in folds on a blue carpet, the chair drawn up beside a fireplace holding brightly burning coals, the bed with its matching side tables ... he had not been there.

Yet he had attacked her!

Like watching a drama on a stage she saw herself bend towards the bed, reach out to give the covers a final pat, saw the tall figure move silently across the room, one arm hook itself about her waist, a hand go across her mouth, that voice thick against her ear ... those hands on her skirts ... touching her...

'Miriam?'

He was saying her name, he was here now, behind her! He had followed her and this time...

A scream half choked with terror caught in her throat. This time there would be no help.

'Miriam!'

It came again, soft and deep, as strong hands grasped her arms, beginning to turn her about.

'No ... o ... o!' Somewhere deep inside herself,

Miriam found the strength to struggle. 'Not again, Saul, please ... not again!'

But the hands continued to turn her and as the arms went about her she felt herself slide into a tunnel, wide and dark, a tunnel with no end.

'She would not have left without good reason, Father.'

Watching his son's restless movements, Clayton Rawley felt uneasy. Ever since Ethan had brought that girl to the house there had been a difference in him, a change of character almost. True, recovering speech lost from boyhood could account for much of the happiness that of late had radiated from him; much, but not all. Clayton had thought at first that being able to talk and laugh with Edwina as they had done when children ... then he had thought that possibly having another man, one nearer his own age, to converse with ... but it seemed it had been neither of those things.

'She would not leave without telling me.'

Without telling *him!* Selecting a cigar Clayton lit it, blowing a stream of pale smoke towards the ceiling. With no woman in the house it had become a habit of his to take a cigar in the sitting room. Why should the girl say anything to Ethan? Yet the words had been specific. Without telling *him!*

Was there something between his son and that girl? Had Ethan behaved foolishly with her, perhaps compromised himself? And how would that affect his relationship with Edwina?

Clayton watched another stream of smoke drift

upward. Sadler would take a dim view of any such behaviour. He doted on his daughter, gave her everything she ever asked for. But giving her a man who had messed around with a servant girl! What father, however doting, would want such a man as husband for his daughter?

'What could have caused her to leave so suddenly?'

The words cutting into his thoughts, Clayton lowered the cigar, tapping ash into a heavy crystal ash tray.

'I thought Mrs Baxter made that perfectly clear. The girl's memory returned and she wished to go back to her own home. Surely that is not only understandable, it is perfectly natural?'

'Of course it is.' Ethan came to a standstill facing his father. 'I can understand her wanting to return home, but not without so much as a word!'

'She asked Mrs Baxter to convey her thanks to us,' Clayton observed. 'That is correct enough. Maidservants are not often called upon to speak directly to the master or mistress of a house...'

'Emma was not a maidservant!' Ethan returned sharply. 'Not as such anyway.'

Lifting the cigar to his mouth, Clayton drew smoke deep into his lungs. A grey cloud engulfing the word, he asked, 'Emma?'

'That was her name ... well, probably not her real one. It was Mrs Baxter who gave it to her, she said.'

'She said?' Clayton's glance rested on his son.

'We talked sometimes.' Feeling the enquiry behind his father's glance, Ethan crossed to the

195

fireplace, standing with one foot on the hearth, staring into the fire. 'I would see her in the garden or in the summerhouse. I said Mrs Baxter would never agree to having her addressed as Wotsit, and she said I was right. Mrs Baxter had said they would call her Emma until her memory returned and she remembered what her real name was.'

'So you would talk to this girl sometimes?' Clayton made a mental note to speak to his housekeeper on the subject of servants using the garden. 'Why should that lead you to expect a personal explanation of her leaving the house?'

Straightening his shoulders, Ethan faced the older man. Telling the truth had never been difficult between them yet at this moment he somehow felt it would not be welcome. Blue eyes meeting grey, he said simply, 'Because she knew I loved her.'

Showing nothing of his dismay, Clayton laid the cigar in the ash tray. Ethan had said the girl knew he loved her ... *knew* he loved her! How? Just what had taken place in those meetings in the summerhouse?

Keeping careful check of the concern beginning to take hold of him, Clayton forced himself to relax. To have a shouting match would achieve nothing right now. His son thought himself in love and at this moment nothing would be gained by his father dismissing it as a flash in the pan; though hopefully it would prove to be just that. Holding that gaze already tinged with defiance, he asked levelly, 'You told the girl so, I take it?'

Ethan's head lifted fractionally, bringing his

chin forward, the movement a subconscious challenge. 'Yes. I told her.'

'May I ask what she said?'

There was no anger in the query, no censure, the calmness draining away the defiance Ethan had not realised he felt. His shoulders sagging a little, he sank into a chair opposite his father's.

'Nothing,' he said, staring at the floor. 'She didn't say anything. She just walked away. She didn't come to the garden after that so I went to the kitchen a couple of times, but on each occasion Mrs Baxter made it clear I was not welcome there.'

Keeping his appreciation of his housekeeper's actions from showing on his face, Clayton rested his hands on the arms of the chair. What he was about to say must be asked, whether or not it found acceptance with Ethan. If that girl had been wronged whilst in this house then he must know about it. 'Ethan.' He looked squarely at his son. 'Have you in any way taken advantage of Emma?'

If he expected his son to jump to his feet and raise his voice in anger or self-justification, he was proved wrong. Instead Ethan's head was raised slowly and the honesty glowing from his eyes was almost painful to see.

'I am sorry if I have given you cause to think so, Father. I would never have treated her that way, nor would I hurt you by doing such a thing. All we ever did was talk, and that only for a few minutes each evening.'

Feeling almost like a child who had been gently reprimanded, Clayton was tempted to ask no more, yet he had to. He had to satisfy himself that there was no real foundation to what his son professed to feel for the girl.

Clayton watched the shadows of unhappiness cross his son's face, dancing in rhythm with the thoughts that must be passing through his mind; the same unhappiness that had clouded his features for too many years following his mother's death. Unhappiness Clayton had never wanted to see there again.

'Ethan,' he asked gently, 'can you be sure that what you feel for Miriam ... that, apparently, is the name she said she remembered ... can you be sure it is not that you feel so responsible for her seeing that it was the cart you were riding in which knocked her down? It is sometimes possible for us to misconstrue our emotions.

'I know what you are saying, Father.' Ethan gave a wry smile. 'I too thought that maybe it was guilt which gave rise to what I was beginning to feel for Miriam, but it was not. I do love her, Father, and I intend to find her. And when I do, I shall ask again if she will be my wife.'

Ask again! Clayton felt a fresh jolt of alarm. Ethan had already asked that girl to marry him ... it had gone that far! So why had she, a girl obviously without a penny to her name, with God knew what family or background, walked away from such a proposal? Why had she given no reply to his declaration of love? Unless of course she thought that he, Clayton, would have no liking for such a relationship. That by seeming to refuse Ethan she would win his father's approval and later possibly his consent! Penniless she might be, but brainless the girl was not.

'If that is what you must do.' Clayton nodded in seeming acceptance. 'But have you given a thought to the effect that will have on Edwina? It has always been understood that one day you two would marry.'

'Understood by you, Father, and by the Sadlers, but never by Edwina or myself. We are very fond of each other and we will, I hope, always be friends, but neither of us sees the other as a marriage partner. Besides, she has her sights set on Saul Marsh.'

'Saul Marsh!' Clayton's laugh was half in astonishment, half disbelief 'You can't be serious?'

'I am, Father.' Ethan smiled, this time with more conviction. 'She told me she was going to speak to her father, ask his permission to marry Marsh.'

'Should Marsh not do that for himself?'

'He should do.' Ethan's eyes recovered a little of their twinkle. 'But trust Edwina to know they might do better if *she* did the asking.'

'I see their point.' A smile hovered about Clayton's lips too. 'She always could twist Sadler around her little finger. One hint of a tear and he'd give her whatever she asked; though in this I am willing to wager it might take a sob or two.'

'If there are any wagers then mine goes on Edwina.'

'Likely you would win.' Clayton nodded his head. 'Though whether she will... Marriage to a man she knows next to nothing about, and with that injury...' He paused, the smile leaving his face. 'A man does not get himself castrated for simply refusing to hand over his money!'

From a corner of the elegantly furnished room a Louis XV clock ticked long seconds away while the men stared at one another.

'Does Edwina know the nature of Marsh's injury?' Clayton broke the silence. 'Does she realise the full implications of it?'

'She has said nothing of it to me.' Ethan's reply was a mixture of apology and embarrassment. 'I ... I was so tied up in my own feelings I never gave any thought to it.'

'I see.' Reaching for the tapestry pull that hung beside the fireplace, Clayton gave it several tugs. 'You could not have broached such a subject with Edwina and I have my doubts that Marsh will have intimated the fact that any marriage to him can be no marriage at all, no real marriage, that is. I shall ask him, and if he has said nothing then I shall. To Sadler himself.'

'But, Father ... if they really love each other, then maybe it ... not being able to have children will not make any difference.'

'Make no difference!' Clayton no longer made any attempt to keep the anger from his voice. 'I am sorry, Ethan, but you do not know what you are talking about. Being able to father children is only a happy coincidence of marriage, only one part of it. It is about being able not only to feel love for a woman but also to show her that love in its physical form. Merely being together is not always enough. Women as well as men have needs, as Edwina may come to realise when she is lying beside a man incapable of fulfilling them.

What she does can in the end be only her decision but that decision must be made in the full knowledge that Saul Marsh is a eunuch!'

Breaking off, Clayton glanced at the butler as he entered the room.

'Baxter, please tell Mr Marsh I wish to see him at once.'

Surprised at the curtness of one who was usually so polite, the butler gave the faintest inclination of his head. 'Mr Marsh is not at home, sir.'

Clayton's mouth firmed, irritability beginning to take its toll. 'Not at home! Did he say where he was going ... when he would be back?'

'No, sir. He did not mention either of those things.'

'Well, what time did he go out?'

Tucking away his curiosity for future investigation the butler answered urbanely. 'I believe it was just after the kitchen maid left, sir.'

'Which maid?' Ethan had a sudden inexplicable feeling of presentiment.

Not immune to the sharpness of the question, Baxter filed it in his mental cabinet. The behaviour of both Rawleys was decidedly out of keeping, it would be interesting to know why. It was not only his wife liked to keep abreast of all happenings at Brade Hall.

'Mrs Baxter referred to her as Emma, sir. Though I believe the name she recalled as being her own was Miriam. Mr Marsh took it upon himself to go to the kitchen to ask for fresh towels to be placed in his bathroom.'

'Didn't he ring for them?'

Returning his glance to Clayton the butler retained the illusion that hid the interest. 'I thought he must have done, sir, and that the bell in his room had not been working, so I checked it myself with the help of Mrs Baxter.'

'And?' The demand was abrupt.

'It was in perfect working order, sir.'

Clayton glanced at his son, a frown drawing his brows together. Then he looked back at the butler.

'Mrs Baxter apologised for not having answered his bell, even though she said later she was certain it had not been rung. She told Mr Marsh that with the kitchen maid leaving she had been left short-staffed but that Ginny would take some towels upstairs at once. Mr Marsh then asked if it was the maid with auburn hair who had left, and confirmed it a second time. When he was assured it *was* that girl who'd left he said he must go out at once. I saw him leave myself, sir. He took a horse from the stables, though he was not dressed for riding.'

'Very well, Baxter, thank you.' Clayton raised a hand to dismiss him. 'Perhaps you will tell him when he returns that I wish to see him?' With the door closed he looked at his son. 'Where do you think he went in such a hurry?'

'I don't know and I don't really care.' Ethan rose to his feet. 'Miriam is all that concerns me. I have to find out where she went. I have told you already: when I do find her I shall ask her again to be my wife. I hope you will not allow that to come between us, Father? I love you but I also love Miriam.'

The ultimatum was out. Accept the girl or risk losing his son. Clayton stared thoughtfully into the fire as Ethan left the room.

Was it that the girl's leaving had Marsh following her? They had both been brought here that same night. Could there be a connection, albeit he had been found on Derby's Hill and she on the Dudley Road? He watched flames dance into the darkness of the chimney. Derby's Hill and the road to Dudley ... and between them, Brades Village! It was not inconceivable that the girl had come from there, nor that Marsh lived there too, despite his claims to the contrary.

Both of them on the same night ... Clayton's mind ran on, asking questions, providing possible answers. A man on the heath, claiming his horrific injury was due to robbers though it was clear from his clothes he had nothing worth the stealing. Then the girl. Where was she headed, alone at that time of night, with nothing but the clothes she stood up in? And they, too, poor enough to mark her as having nothing.

A girl who showed all the signs of running away from home, and a man with his manhood sliced away... Could one have any bearing on the other ... could one have been caused by fear, the other retribution?

If so there could be only one feasible explanation. The girl was with child. By her own consent or otherwise? Clayton turned the question around in his brain, chasing it with another. Had her lover refused to own to his seduction of her, refused to be named the father of the child she might be carrying?

Had that refusal cost him his manhood?

Unthinkable? Not to a father.

Watching the flames whirl and dart in their brilliant dance, Clayton knew his questioning of Saul Marsh would not be confined to the subject of his marriage to Edwina.

Miriam had not gone the way of Brades Village, thought Saul Marsh, trotting his horse into the stable yard. Leaving it to the care of one of the stable boys, he strode towards the Hall. That stupid Baxter woman had been vague as to how long it had been since Miriam had left. But even with her head start of an hour or more, he should have overtaken her, she walking while he was mounted. He had ridden fast, stopping just short of the village and waiting. If somehow he had missed her on the road, he was bound to see her pass from his vantage point behind a tall outcrop of limestone. But she had not passed, though he had stayed there until dusk began to gather. No! He tapped the short riding crop against his thigh. She had not returned to the village, which meant his secret was safe for now. There would be time to deal with Miriam Bryce later. And with her whelp.

'Excuse me, Mr Marsh?'

Baxter seemed to appear from nowhere as Saul crossed the large square entrance hall. Irritated by the form of address, Saul waited without turning. The man made a deliberate point of not calling him 'sir', but one day soon he would. Oh, yes, they would all call him sir!

Equally irritated, Baxter stood several yards

away instead of deferentially approaching him. The man was a nothing, a nobody. That in itself would not have affected his behaviour towards any man, but Saul Marsh was an upstart. He had an eye to the main chance, but the manners to go with it? Not judging by the way he spoke to the household staff. Young Ginny had seemed taken with him at first, but then young Ginny Jinks hadn't sense enough to see through his pretence.

Unable to resist the barb he had already noticed stung this guest who treated the Hall as his own, Baxter placed slightly more emphasis than necessary on the first of his next words.

'*The master* asked me to tell you he wished to speak to you.'

Shoulders stiffening, Saul's head lifted, the light from the central gasolier dusting his yellow hair with a thousand points of gold. The barb had found its mark.

'I am dusty from riding.' He still did not turn. 'Tell Mr Rawley I will join him once I have washed and made a change of clothes.'

Baxter hid a smile. The man had cheek! You had to give him that, cheek or ignorance. But both elicited only contempt from the shrewd old butler. Marsh would overplay his hand sooner or later. He would overstep the mark and then his stay here would be at an end. Once more emphasising the words, he spoke quietly.

'*The master* said at once. He told me to inform you the moment you returned.'

Sensing a kind of pleasure in the way the butler said those words, Saul felt his nerves tauten. Was there something wrong? Had he done something to annoy Rawley?

Satisfied that the unspoken point had been made, Baxter returned his voice to a level pitch. 'He's in the study. I will inform him of your return.'

'There's no need!' Saul swung quickly round, his handsome face twisted into a frown. He was aware of the butler's dislike of him and now it was mirrored in his own features. 'I'll tell him myself.'

'As you wish.'

The absence of that 'sir' grated on Saul as the butler walked away towards the servants' quarters. One day he would sing a different tune. One day he would be forced to say 'sir' when addressing Saul Marsh.

'Mr Marsh, please sit down.'

Clayton Rawley made no attempt to smile at the man who entered his study. He had given him hospitality and provided him with medical care, yet somehow down the weeks he had been unable to feel any real warmth towards the man with whom his son seemed so taken. Jealousy? He laid down the pen he had been using. Perhaps. His son had been silent for so long, maybe Clayton did resent sharing him with someone else now.

'Baxter tells me you wish to speak to me, sir?' The words were politely spoken, Saul Marsh was no fool. Set Rawley against him and marriage to Edwina could become fraught with uncertainty. Old Sadler and Clayton Rawley, he knew, had long been friends – and friends, as his mother was fond of saying, 'piss in the same pot'.

'My son tells me you and Edwina Sadler have

plans to marry?'

It was abrupt and to the point. The hours spent waiting had not blunted Clayton Rawley's concern or his determination.

'Edwina and I are in love.'

An impatient movement of the hand sent Clayton's pen rolling across his well-polished desk. 'That does not concern me.

Then what does? Saul met eyes that were cool and penetrating, eyes that seemed to read his mind. He kept his own gaze steady and unflinching.

'What does is how much Edwina does, or does not, know about the injuries you sustained from that ... robbery.'

The hesitation was momentary, so brief it might not have been made at all, but Saul heard it and interpreted it well enough. Clayton Rawley did not believe his story about being the victim of a robbery. The question was, how much else did he disbelieve?

'I can understand your concern, sir.' Wanting to tell Rawley to go to hell, that it was none of his business, Saul decided that path would prove fraught with danger. Better by far to maintain a deferential air, gall though it was in his mouth. 'And I appreciate it. I know how much Miss Sadler means to you and to Ethan, and I assure you I would be nothing but a loving husband to her.'

'That is my point exactly. Just how much of a loving husband can you be? How can you be the husband a young woman needs?'

Saul smiled inwardly. He knew what it was this

man wanted to say to him, but he would make him say it nonetheless, every single syllable!

'Should her father do me the honour of giving Edwina to me, then I hope to give her all the love that is due to her.'

Across the desk Clayton Rawley's breath was expelled in an exasperated rush. 'Let's not play with words!' he snapped. 'You are old enough, and to my mind wise enough, to know full well what need I refer to. How can *you* make love to a woman? How can *you* father children when you are ... when you are not a man in the truest sense of the word?'

He did not know! Saul smiled inwardly. The accusation had been made. When the time came to apologise, Rawley would choke on those words. But Saul could afford no denial at this stage. One word from those below stairs and his plans might yet blow up in his face. Rawley believed he was a eunuch. For a while longer he must go on believing it.

'I love Edwina, and will make her happy regardless...'

Clayton's hand came down sharply on the desk, rattling the crystal ink wells in their silver stand. 'Rubbish! I don't know what you have told yourself or led Edwina to believe, but a marriage needs children. Women need children. If you think otherwise then you are a fool!'

Rawley could not be falling more deeply into his hands were he being pushed. Saul's satisfaction mounted.

'Forgive me, sir, but Edwina and I do not think so.'

'Maybe not now, but what of ten years ahead? What of the time you both find yourselves wishing for a son, a child to carry on your name? What then, eh? It is already too late for you, and God knows you have my sympathy, but don't make it too late for Edwina also. Tell her – tell her you can never give her children.'

'Edwina is aware of that fact.'

He had said it quietly, but had he screamed the words they could not have had a deeper effect. Saul watched first disbelief then consternation settle on Clayton Rawley's face.

'I know it is a subject a man does not usually discuss with a young woman, sir, but a marriage built on lies could be no marriage at all,' Saul went on smoothly. 'She had to be told and having no ... no parents,' he swallowed in just the right place, '...to explain my injuries, the responsibility became mine. I told her everything. I also wanted to tell her father but Edwina was adamant on that point. It was no one's business but ours, she said.'

And you, no doubt, let her have her way on that. Clayton remained sceptical. He may have guessed wrongly when thinking Marsh had said nothing of his injuries, but he was not wrong in his estimation that the fellow was after money, Edwina Sadler's money.

'It is no business of mine.' He picked up the implied reprimand. 'But Edwina has been like a daughter to me. I would not wish to see her hurt in any way.'

Like a daughter! Saul laughed silently to himself. And you hoped it would go on that way,

209

hoped she would be a daughter-in-law! But hopes were flimsy craft, easily dashed.

'I would not see her hurt either. That is the reason I went to her home today. I went to see her father. Wanted to be sure he had been told everything.' Lies dripping like honey from his tongue, Saul gave a faint, almost bleak smile. 'I love Edwina too much to allow her to mislead her parents.'

'You told Sadler?'

Saul nodded.

'Has he...?'

Watching incredulity crease the other man's brow into a frown, Saul almost laughed aloud. Instead he nodded again. 'Given his consent? Yes, sir, he has.'

Christ! Clayton felt the shock of it strike him between the shoulder blades. He would never have expected that of Sadler. True he was soft where his only child was concerned, but to giver her to ... a eunuch! To know she could never furnish him with grandchildren. No, he would never have believed Sadler would go that far. But he had and now the subject must be allowed to lie. He could not add to what his old friend's true feelings must be by ever discussing it with him.

'I hope you and Ethan will not take our engagement unkindly?'

Saul's downturned mouth lent his face an expression that could be interpreted as anxious, even though his mind was shouting in triumph. Instinct told him the direction of the older man's thoughts; his lies would go unchallenged.

No real warmth in his voice and with no true

alleviation of the bitterness he felt at such a union, Clayton gave a brief shake of the head.

'Of course not. I am sure my son, like myself, will wish Edwina happiness.'

There had been no congratulation for him. Saul felt the snub and filed it in his memory. Rawley, like his butler, would be made to pay for these slights. And much sooner than they thought.

'When is Sadler making the announcement?'

'It is Edwina's birthday in a little under a month.' Confidence in every inch of him, Saul met his host's steady glance. 'Edwina's mother thought it would be fitting to announce our engagement then. A combination of two happy events, she called it.'

It will be no happy event for Connie Sadler. Clayton hid the thought behind a nod of acknowledgement. Her daughter marrying a man without even his own balls to his name!

'You and Edwina must allow me to give a small dinner party before the date. A private little get together to give her our good wishes.'

You would prefer to be giving her your sympathy, Saul thought, while aloud he offered his thanks.

'Shall we say the night before the official announcement?'

'Thank you.' No trace of his true thoughts showing, Saul nodded. 'I am sure Edwina will be delighted.'

'One moment more.' Clayton raised a hand as Saul made to rise from the chair he had taken on coming into the study.

Inside the leather boots, on permanent loan

211

from Ethan, Saul felt his toes curl. Rawley had conceded defeat with one hand, was the other about to strike?

'Mr Marsh, since you have been good enough to answer my questions so far, perhaps you would do so once more? Baxter tells me you went riding some time ago – tell me, while you were out, did you by any chance see anything of the maid who left this house a little before yourself?'

Saul bristled with alarm. Just how much did Rawley know? What had that bitch of a girl said? His eyes giving no indication of the apprehension he felt, he answered Clayton.

'No, sir.' Despite the inner panic, his voice was calm and even. 'I did not see Ginny at all. Is there some concern?'

'Not for Ginny. But then, it is not Ginny to whom I was referring.'

'I was not aware of any other maid,' Saul lied smoothly. 'Apart from Ginny, and of course the Baxters, I have seen only stable hands.'

'That is because I no longer keep a large indoor staff. After the death of my wife we live very quietly.' Clayton shrugged slightly. 'There was no longer the call ... the Baxters manage well between them. But this girl I speak of was brought here to the Hall on the same evening as you. The cart my son had you put into knocked her down. It happened just outside the village. Ever since then Ethan has felt a certain responsibility for the girl, for this ... Miriam.'

The use of that name set his nerves jangling again, but Saul kept his tone light. 'She could just be late returning from her home.'

'She will not be returning to the Hall. The girl walked out at a moment's notice. My son is concerned something may have happened to upset her. He just wanted to reassure himself on that point.'

So they did not know! Saul felt himself relax. Neither Miriam nor the other one could have told what had happened in that bedroom. Had they done so Rawley would have thrown him out before now.

'I will go and help look for her, sir.' He stood up. 'If I may have the use of a horse, I will leave straight away. Maybe I will find her.'

'No, Marsh.' Clayton too stood up. Coming around the desk, he led the way from the study. 'Let the matter go. I understand she has recovered her memory so it stands to reason she must know where she is going.'

And she also knew I would go there! Saul followed him from the room. That explains why I did not find her. She obviously took the other road, the one that led to Tividale.

But you will not escape that way, Miriam.

You will not escape Saul Marsh!

Chapter Fourteen

Kneeling on the ground, Ralph cradled the still form in his arms. Miriam had been terrified, so terrified she had fainted. Again he heard the echo of her scream in his mind. There was no need to

213

ask who it was had put the fear of God into her. She had called his name: Saul! It was Saul Marsh had terrified Miriam, but how? What had he done to her?

Ralph's body, already chilled by the night air, shuddered as his veins ran with ice. Had Marsh threatened her, struck her, or tried to... He looked down at the face so pale in the light of the rising moon. If Marsh had tried that again, then this time he *would* kill him.

'Miriam.' He breathed the name, his voice no louder than the heath breeze. 'Miriam, wake up.'

Held against his chest she moaned softly, then as her senses returned the moan turned into a frightened cry and she struggled to free herself

'Miriam.'

'No...' Her eyes blind with sharp tears, she struck out with both hands. 'No ... please, Saul. No...'

'It's all right, it's all right!' Ralph folded her close to him, the sobs that wracked her body wracking his soul. 'It's me, Miriam. Me – Ralph.'

He repeated the words over and over, rocking her in his arms as he had so often as a boy, comforting his sister after Leah had administered one of her beatings. How often in that loveless boyhood had he thought of running away and taking Miriam with him? But each time he had changed his mind, telling himself the hardship of homelessness would be too much for a girl; but as boyhood had changed to manhood he had recognised the truth. It was not Miriam it would be too much for, it was himself. Not the fear of being without a home, that was not the new

214

chain that forged itself about him, preventing him from taking her away. It was rather the suspicion, then the confession, of the secret he held inside him. He loved his sister. The danger was, he loved her too much.

'It's all right,' he murmured again, feeling her struggles subside. 'You're safe now. I've got you. Shh!'

'Ralph?'

He felt her hands clutch his jacket but she did not look up.

'Yes, Miriam.' He bent his head, bringing his lips against her hair. 'It's me. You're safe now.' Then, so softly only his own heart could hear, he added, 'You are safe, my love.'

He had to release her, to open his arms and let her go. Hesitating one more half moment he drank in the warmth of her, the feel of her nestling against him. Then, the very act tearing him apart he held her away from him. 'Yes,' he said, his voice unsteady. 'It is Ralph, you are quite safe now.'

'How?' She held on to his arm, still so weak he had almost to lift her to her feet. 'How did you know ... were you looking for me?'

'If you mean, how did I know you were here on this road, then I didn't.' His hand was half outstretched ready to catch her should she find herself too weak to stand. 'As for my looking for you, I have done that every free minute since you disappeared. Why? Why did you run away? Was it because of Mother?'

'I had to.' She looked up at him imploringly. 'I could not stay in that house, not after she knew.'

Her tears twisted the soul within him. Ralph brushed them gently from her cheeks. 'It doesn't matter who knows. You're coming home with me and there'll be no more beatings. Mother is aware of what will happen if she strikes you again.'

'No, Ralph. There would be nothing but arguments between you and Mother. I can't be the cause of so much hurt to you.'

His fingers gentle, Ralph lifted her shawl, draping it about her head. 'You will cause me more hurt if you do not return. There can be no peace for me not knowing where you are or even if you are safe.'

Removing his jacket, he guided her arms into the sleeves then buttoned it across her thin body. He had not asked where she had spent the last months, that would come later. Nor had he asked with whom she had spent them, but somewhere among it all Saul Marsh figured. One arm supporting his sister, he turned in the direction of Brades Village. Her cries had been a testament to that and to the fact that Marsh had frightened her badly.

No, he had not asked about Saul Marsh nor did he need to. But that did not mean he would forget.

Leah stared at the figure raising and lowering the wooden dolly, struggling to pound it against the linen in the round wash tub. He had found her! After all these weeks he had found her and brought her back to this house. Back here to spawn her bastard!

Been living up at the Hall, so she said. Leah snorted to herself. Ralph was a fool if he believed such a story, but then that one was fool enough to believe anything Miriam told him. To him his sister was above lying, above doing any wrong. But she had done wrong, and admit it or not it was a wrong that tore the heart out of him. She could never be his, that he must own to. But to play the whore!

And the man she had played with: Saul Marsh. He had never been near this house, but then had Leah herself not predicted that? But he had gone missing shortly after Miriam had admitted her pregnancy, disappeared like mist in sunshine. His mother had asked everyone passing through the village, that much she'd learned when picking up meat from the butcher, or groceries from Bella Longmore's shop. Not that Leah stayed in that one longer than necessary, there were too many inquisitive folk gathered there, women who would be much better given to tending their homes as well as their own business. But they would not tend that of Leah Bryce. She gave them short shrift when they tried to poke their noses where she did not want them, and she did not want them asking after her daughter. Brades Village had already had its amusement, taken long ago when... But that was in the past. There would be no more to add to it, no gossip behind her back, no finger pointed her way again.

The child would come in its time. It would be born into the world as it had to be – but in the same breath it would leave it.

'Don't touch Miriam again!' That had been her

217

son's warning, and it was one Leah would live by. But a bastard child! He had said nothing of that, and that she would not endure.

No one in the village knew of the unborn child, and none would know. What had been sown would be reaped, but the harvest would not be kept! So many children were born already dead, and many who were not were nudged quietly into a grave that had waited nine months to take them. A hand over a tiny mouth not yet drawing a first breath ... a blanket smothering a face ... there were ways a-plenty, and she would use one of them.

Turning her back on the silent figure wrestling with the heavy dolly, Leah returned to the scullery, gathering dusters and a tin of Mansion wax polish from a chest of drawers.

Carrying them upstairs, she set about polishing the linen chest and wash-stand that had been her mother's, buffing them until her face was reflected in the mahogany. They were the only two pieces of worth in the whole house, that and the lamp that she had saved so hard to buy. It had been part of her bottom drawer, part of all she had collected ready for her marriage to him... But he had gone off with another, a girl prettier than her, a girl with red-brown curls, and she had been left to bear the brunt of the sniggering of the women of Brades Village. *'Serves her right,'* had been their dictum. *'Has too much of a bob on herself does Leah Thompson. That'll take her down a peg or two!'*

She had heard it all and more besides, but it had not brought her down to their level. She had kept herself aloof, as she did now. She turned towards the double bed, staring at the brass rails kept bright as a new pin. The bed she had shared with William Bryce. She had never loved him. She had washed his clothes and kept his house but there had never been any love in it. Not for her. Any he might have had before marrying her was dead even before his first child came.

Her hands falling to her sides, Leah stared into yesterday. Her soul had withered that day *he* had left the village, turning her life into dust. But the need for vengeance did not fade so easily. It had stayed with her through the years of heartbreak until it became the very blood that flowed in her veins.

A sound from the yard took her to the window. The dolly was rolling on the ground and Miriam, bent double, was gripping the rim of the tub with both hands.

It was time. Her steps unhurried, Leah returned to the scullery, replacing the polish in the drawer then setting aside the dusters to be washed later in the week. The child was coming. She smiled inwardly. It could not be a better time. Ralph was going straight from the colliery to Brade Hall, something about returning eight shillings to the housekeeper there. Let him go. He would soon learn it was a lie, that his sister had never been to the place let alone been lent money by its housekeeper. But his going was a blessing. With luck the child would be born, and be ready for burial, by the time he got home.

Going into the yard she watched Miriam haul herself upward, her face bleached of colour, one

hand clutching her stomach, the other still gripping the wash tub.

'The baby!' She gasped. 'I ... I think it's
coming!'

Wordless, her own face devoid of pity, Leah
picked up the dolly, setting it on its end by the
wall of the brew house. Lifting shirts and blouses
from the hot soapy water, she dropped them into
a large enamelled bowl, carrying them into the
scullery where she rinsed each one in the shallow
sink.

Once more in the yard she heard the gasp and
strangled groan of pain as Miriam slumped again
over the tub. Holding each dripping garment,
Leah fed them through the wide wooden rollers
of the mangle, her upper body rising and bending
as she slowly turned the huge iron handle.

As each item passed through the rollers, Leah
shook it then folded it before sending it through
again, repeating the process until every drop of
excess water had been squeezed from it.

Behind her Miriam tried to stifle a cry but a
fresh spasm of pain ripped it from her.

'Mother ... the baby!'

'You didn't need me when you were putting it
in there, and you needn't call on me to get it out!'
Filling her apron pocket with pegs, Leah picked
up the wicker basket of folded washing and took
it to the line strung the length of the yard.

Breath coming in tiny terrified gasps, Miriam
held on to the tub. Her mother had spoken
hardly two words to her since Ralph had brought
her home, but surely she would help now?

The first waves of pain passing, Miriam drew

herself upright, eyes fastened on her mother. She had walked away! Left Miriam standing there in pain while she carried on with the laundry! How could she be so uncaring ... did she have no feelings at all?

The last garment pegged to the line, Leah walked back across the yard, eyes hard as stone as they met those of her daughter. Childbirth was hard and it was not uncommon for mother as well as child to go under. What if that were to be the result here? Hoisting the empty wicker basket higher on her hip, she felt no pang of fear at the thought. Her heart knew only one emotion.

Depositing the basket in the brew house, she took the tub, heaving it over on to its side, watching the soapy water splash across the flags and into the narrow channel that carried it to the soakaway.

The last of the water tipped from the tub, she rolled it on its side to stand against the wall of the brew house. Then and only then she looked at the girl whose eyes mirrored fear and pain.

'Get yourself up to your room,' she snapped. 'Unless you want Marsh's filth dropped here in the yard!'

Tears hot on her cheeks, Miriam turned towards the scullery. She would get no help from her mother. Once inside she caught on to the sink, waves of nausea in close attendance on the pain that wracked her.

Ralph had said he would bring someone from the village when the time came, but she had thought there was another month yet. Another month before her child would come.

They had talked it all over sitting in the kitchen-cum-living room, she and Ralph, their mother a silent witness until he had taken pen and paper, yellow with age, from the cupboard beside the fireplace. Leah had stared at the pen and paper, the colour draining from her face, her mouth thinning to a line even narrower than before. And then, still without a word, she had walked out. Miriam had written a letter thanking the Rawleys for their kindness and Ralph had promised to deliver it to the Hall along with the eight shillings Mrs Baxter had lent her.

They did not need to borrow money, he had declared, returning pen and paper to the ceiling-high cupboard that surmounted several shelves. He had enough to buy what a baby needed.

Her breathing easier as the pain receded, Miriam straightened up. She had thought to have a month yet before the child came. Time enough, Ralph had said, for him to go to Dudley. He would not be recognised in that town. He would find a pawn shop and buy gowns and vests, binders for the baby's stomach, all the things it would need. Maybe a warm shawl to wrap around it in the drawer it would use as a cot.

Beyond the scullery window, Leah carried a shovel filled with hot embers raked from beneath the copper, throwing them on to a heap that sat like a small grassless hill beside a corner of the wall that closed off yard from heath.

Tears she had swallowed returned to fill Miriam's throat. She would get no help from her mother!

The village... If she could reach the village then

someone would help. Starting for the living room, she gasped as pain, sharp and searing as before, shot through her again. She would never make the village, yet there was no help here. She must fend for herself. But she knew nothing of childbirth, her mother had never told her anything of such matters, she had no knowledge of how to help herself or the child!

The realisation, almost as sharp as the pain, took her breath away.

Maybe Ralph would come home, return from Brades Hall before the baby came? And if he did not? Fear, cold and stark, filled every vein, yet with the fear came reason. She had no one to depend on until her brother came home, and the child had only her. Whatever was done must be of her own doing.

Slowly, ignoring the ache in her lower back, she walked into the kitchen. The child would need to be washed. Checking the kettle and seeing it was full, she carried it across the room, pulling open the stairs door. One foot at a time, her boots loud on the bare wooden steps, she was halfway up when a fresh surge of pain tore the kettle loose from her hand, showering her skirts with boiling water before it rolled and clattered down the stairs.

'Oh, God!' she cried softly, bending against the agony slicing through her. 'Oh, God, it was me. *I* did wrong. Please don't let my baby pay for my sins.' Sinking to her knees, her breath held fast, she waited for the pain to pass. How long did this torture last, how long did it go on for? There was no way of knowing unless her mother ... but Leah would give no advice, no comfort, she had made that clear.

It may only be a matter of minutes. Miriam could not give birth on the stairs! Drawing a long breath, she placed both hands on the step above, pulling herself on all fours to the top. Reaching the tiny landing, she tried to stand but sank down as a wave of sickness engulfed her. Yards away her bedroom door stood slightly open.

Mists of tears and pain clouding her vision, she reached one hand towards the wall, levering herself to her feet, clenching her teeth against the weight that seemed to be forcing its way between her legs.

Using the wall as a prop, leaning the whole of her body against it, she dragged herself inch by inch into her room before dropping heavily to the bed. Perspiration running faster than tears down her face, she fought the onslaught of pain. She must not give in, she must not give way to the fear that waited ready to devour her.

Teeth clenched, finger nails biting into her palms, she tried to think. She had no clothing in which to dress the child, yet it had to be kept warm. She had to find something to wrap it in. Through the miasma of sickness that fought ever harder to cloud her brain, she remembered the cotton petticoat in the chest of drawers, the lace-edged one only ever worn beneath the special dress she had not been allowed to wear on Sundays but only at Christmas or Easter.

Praying the pain would not take her again, she pushed herself up from the bed and crossed to the chest. Pulling the drawer out completely, she placed it on top of the chest. The dress was already small for her even had she wanted to wear it again. But she would not. She did not deserve to wear pretty clothes after what she had done. But the child ... the dress would make a warm lining for the drawer that would be its bed.

Laying aside the underwear she took out the petticoat, holding it crushed against her stomach as another red hot pain threw her against the chest of drawers. She must hold on. She had to make herself ready. But how, what did she do?

Almost senseless with fright, she staggered back to the bed. If only she could rest. Somewhere deep within the chaos of her mind a dark cavern opened up. A still, shadowed place where she could hide, where the pain would not reach her, where fear would have no reality. In its warm darkness she would be safe, there would be no mother to beat her, no Saul Marsh to rape her, no baby...

'But there is a baby!' The cry pushed back the longing, the need to escape. 'There is a baby and it deserves to live!'

Her cry seeming to give fresh strength to her limbs, she laid the petticoat across the foot of the bed, then unfastening her skirt let it fall to her feet, followed by her bloomers. Heaving herself on to the bed, she lay back on the pillow.

How long had she lain there? When would it all be over? Tossed by waves of pain she glanced towards the window. Outside the darkness was deeper, throwing her room into greyness. Would Ralph be home soon; home in time to help her, to help her child?

Caught in a nightmare of pain that convulsed her thin body, she tried to hold back the scream that nevertheless erupted from her mouth in a low protracted groan.

'You'll be needing this.'

Veering back from the chasm that threatened to swallow her, Miriam opened eyes that had screwed themselves tight shut against the incessant throbbing agony.

'Mother,' she sobbed, 'help me!'

'There's water to wash yourself when your business be done.'

Leah glanced at the girl, the petticoat stuck to her stomach with sweat, emphasising the mound beneath, emphasising the bastard that would shortly be born. Her face devoid of sympathy, cold eyes holding no vestige of pity, she turned to the washstand, emptying the contents of the kettle into its platter bowl. The heavy china would cool the water soon enough, she need bring no more.

At her back Miriam cried out again, a long drawn out cry of sheer agony, but Leah did not look round.

'Please, Mother!' Anguish in her cry, Miriam reached a hand towards the figure by the washstand. 'Help me ... don't leave me, please ... please don't leave me ... please!'

The plea was cut off by a pain that snatched it from Miriam's mouth.

But it was a plea that found no answer as Leah closed the door behind her.

Rawley had believed him, swallowed his story whole. Saul looked at himself in the mirror in his dressing room. Now he must get Edwina to the altar as soon as possible. His host had believed him but that did not mean Saul could not be discovered. It would only take that frumpy maid to say one word, even suggest he had attacked the Bryce girl in this bedroom. What if she had already said as much to that housekeeper? Mrs Baxter wouldn't hesitate to tell her husband who would take great delight in telling his master. But as yet no one had spoken. That little interview with Rawley said as much, but while the threat hung over him, while the possibility that they might remained...

The mouth reflected in the mirror thinned until only the droop at one corner remained. Something must be done about Ginny Jinks, something final, as it must with sweet Edwina.

Running his eye over a line of cravats, Saul chose one of palest blue silk, teaming it with a coat of rich burgundy. The colours highlighted hair that glowed golden as honey. This way of life, with all its comforts, suited him very well. It was one he intended should continue, one nobody would snatch from him. And supposing that meant another losing their life...? Saul's eyes hardened to steel. If that was what it cost, then that was what he'd pay.

Seating the jacket comfortably about his shoulders, he flicked a hand over perfectly tailored trousers just a shade more blue than grey.

But that did not include Edwina. Or not, at

least, until *after* their marriage.

Studying his reflection in the mirror, he curled his mouth into a slow calculating smile. There were other, pleasanter ways of buying silence. Ways that, for the likes of the Rawleys and the Sadlers, were every bit as final.

Selecting a handkerchief of matching blue from a drawer that seemed to hold handkerchiefs of every possible colour, he patted it into his breast pocket, allowing the smallest corner to peep above it. That would please Edwina who had told him the finishing touch appeared to be very fashionable in London.

'Oh, I'll be fashionable,' breathed Saul, his hand resting momentarily against the pocket as he eyed his reflection. 'Your money, my dear, will keep me very fashionable.'

But first that money had to be his. As his mother had always told him: *'Don't go counting your eggs till they be sitting on your plate!'*

Well, all that Edwina Sadler had, all she stood to inherit, might not sit on his plate until after that marriage service, but it would be well and truly in his pocket long before.

The hollow beneath the rocks of Derby's Hill had served him more than once and would serve him well again. Edwina followed his every suggestion, swallowed every word like a starving man. What did it matter if those words stemmed more from his imagination than the truth? She would thrill to the thought of slipping away across the heath. He would even 'find' them a private hideaway. Forbidden fruits were always sweetest!

The smile that came back at him held the essence of slyness.

Edwina Sadler would taste all of them, but Saul Marsh would receive their benefit. Hers would be one pregnancy he would not deny. And should sweet Edwina fail to conceive...?

The fact the Sadlers' daughter was no longer a virgin, and the threat of having such voiced abroad, would have an equally favourable effect. One way or the other, tonight would see Saul Marsh secure for life.

Chapter Fifteen

Sweat and tears mixed with red hot waves of pain, Miriam watched the bedroom door close. Leah Bryce had gone, turned her back, leaving her child alone in fear and pain.

But was that not what she had always done? Left her alone in the darkness, the sting of another beating smarting, whispered words of hate echoing in her young ears. That was how it had been whenever her father was not in the house. Then Ralph had come to her, to hold her in his arms and soothe away the nightmare of fear.

'Come now...' Her words were almost silent, held in check by teeth clenched in agony. 'Come now. Please, Ralph, come now...'

Downstairs Leah heard the scream. It would be soon. She glanced down at a piece of old sheet folded into a square, a bobbin of thread placed on top. Miriam had called her brother's name, called him to comfort her as she had called when a child; and he had always come running. But this time he would not come, there would be no brother to hold that slut's hand or protect her bastard. Ralph had gone to Brades Hall. It would all be over before he got back. The child would be dead!

In the grate the fire settled, small coals falling into its glowing centre, sending a shower of tiny sparks into the darkness of the chimney. Leah stared at them, dying one by one, their beauty spent, brief glowing life snuffed out. Her life had been like that. A short time touched by the beauty of love, glowing in the knowledge she too was loved. Then, like sparks from the fire, that beauty had died, extinguished as the love she'd thought hers had been given to another. And inside too she had died, her life in ashes as if that brief beauty had never been.

But it had! It had, and the embers of it still lay in her heart, lay where they would always lie until she took them to her grave. *He* had done this to her. *He* had taken the brilliance of her life and snuffed it out. Then he had left, gone with his pretty new love, with curls the colour of a dying sun.

But she would make them pay, make them both pay!

Overhead a long drawn out cry broke the comforting dreams and Leah reached for the square of linen and spool of thread. She must be there ... ready.

Washed in and out of consciousness by waves of searing pain, Miriam's head lolled to one side, the fingers of both hands clenched, white-knuckled, against the rumpled bed cover.

'Ralph, thank God you have come...'

Looking down at her daughter, Leah's face twisted with spite. 'It don't be Ralph,' she said viciously. 'He won't be coming back, not till it be too late. Too late for that which is fighting to be born.'

Turning from the bed, she set cloth and thread in the basin on the wash-stand then walked to the window, sitting down on the chair set beneath it.

In the semi-darkness of the bedroom, Miriam's breathing was short and fast, broken every few moments by long groans as pain clawed at her stomach. But the sounds found no echo of pity in the hard-faced woman. Hands folded in her lap, Leah watched the frail figure writhe and twist. It was no more than she deserved; no more than either of them deserved.

At her back, beyond the window, the sky had changed into its black gown of night, enveloping the room in deeper grey. She would need light for what she was to do.

Going back to the bed, Leah took a match from the table beside it and lit the meagre oil lamp. Beneath its sallow gleam Miriam's eyes stared up at her, pain robbing them of recognition. Then even as Leah turned away a long, hollow moan carried the girl into unconsciousness, the child sliding from her.

Going quickly to the wash-stand, Leah grabbed the reel of thread and snapped off a long piece.

231

Back at the bed she glanced once at the unconscious figure of her daughter, then, thread
outstretched between her hands, bent towards
the child.

The woman had been more than civil, asking
Ralph into the kitchen, wanting to make him tea.
She had nodded, taking no offence when he
returned the eight shillings, approval on her
plump face as he had thanked her then explained
that Miriam was his sister and as family he would
pay for what she and her baby needed.

He had shown her the letter Miriam had
written for the Rawleys and asked to see them to
give his sister's apology personally. But the
Rawleys were both out, the housekeeper had told
him. He could rest assured, though, she would
tell them both that he had called and what he had
said.

They had talked for a few minutes more,
mostly of Miriam, but he had volunteered no
information, guessing his sister would have told
all she wanted them to know; and all the while
Ralph had felt a strong desire to be gone, the
same inner voice calling him as it had when he
was a young boy; the voice that called each time
his sister needed him.

It was that which set him running back over the
heath towards the farm, instinct guiding his feet
where eyesight could not, and all the while the
feeling inside him mounted until he could almost
hear the voice that meant so much to him, the
voice of Miriam calling out for help.

Leah would not harm her surely, not when she

knew what he would do in return? But there was no telling with his mother. No telling what her spite would lead her to.

Breath harsh in his chest, heart thudding against his ribs, trusting long years of walking the heath to keep him out of the way of mine shafts that had crowned in, their sunken shafts a certain grave, Ralph ran on.

Off to his right the village was revealed by circles of yellow light where people had lit lamps against the darkness; cheerful welcoming light that called to him. There was no cheer at Brade Farm, no feeling of welcome, only his mother's constant malign presence, a tightly maintained corrosive bitterness of which she never lost sight; a bitterness that had helped his father to the grave and would willingly help Miriam to the same end.

Miriam! He stared into the night, eyes probing the darkness for the house set apart from the rest of the village, but no patch of friendly light danced in the deep-shadowed heath.

From where he stood it appeared the house was in darkness, empty. But Miriam was there ... there was nowhere else she could be, unless ... but Leah would not take her to the village, stubborn pride would prevent that.

So why was the house without light?

The fear that had encroached while he was at Brade Hall surged in him like a living thing, reaching for his throat, an icy unnameable fear that sent him running for the house.

The touch of her hands against the tiny body

seeming to bring it to life, the child gave a weak cry. Leah hesitated, glancing again at the face of her daughter. Miriam was still unconscious, she would not have heard the child cry, never know it had come into the world alive. No one would know! It would take only seconds, then it would be finished. A hole just beyond the wall of the yard, the place where the heath began ... she would put it there.

In the half light Leah smiled, an expression that might have been mistaken for happiness had it not been for the cold glitter of malice in her eyes.

Sweet revenge overwhelming her like the blare of trumpets, she did not hear the sound of boots on the stairs or the bedroom door being thrown open.

One glance showed Ralph the clothes abandoned on the floor; then his sister, so small and still, blouse and petticoat soaked with sweat sticking to her chest and legs, strands of hair plastered across her unmoving face.

'Miriam!' The cry had not fully left his lips before he was at the bedside.

Surprise slackening her fingers, Leah loosed the child, letting it fall back on to the bed and bringing another cry from the tiny mouth.

'The child ... thank God it is alive!' Dropping to his knees, Ralph touched one hand to his sister's brow as he glanced up at his mother. 'Miriam, is she...?'

Frustration almost choking her, Leah found it hard to speak the words. 'That one is alive, same as this!'

What ill wind had brought him home so soon?

Why should heaven cruelly ordain that her suffering should go on? One more minute, that was all it would have taken, just one more minute. Yet it still might not be too late! He was so concerned for his sister, he would not see... Cotton concealed in her hand, Leah bent once more towards the child.

'What's that for?' Detecting a covert movement, Ralph's glance swept to his mother's hands.

'The cord. It has to be cut, don't it?' She answered, voice sharp with fresh frustration. 'Child can't be left with it dangling from its stomach.' Her fingers surer now, she deftly twisted the thread around the umbilical cord, pulling it tightly until it severed.

'You can't go kneeling there, you be in my way. They both of them need washing and tending. Get you downstairs,' she said as the child wailed again, 'and leave me to do what has to be done.'

Turning to the wash-stand, she picked up the piece of worn sheet. The chance might yet be hers!

Wrapping the baby in the cloth, she laid it on the foot of the bed. 'Let the child bide there till I've seen to its mother.'

Its mother! The words pulling at his heart, Ralph looked at the face of his sister, dark circles surrounding the closed eyes, the marks of pain still about the mouth. She was the mother of the child that lay there, swaddled in cloth. If only the father...

But it was not him and never could be! They had been born brother and sister, banned from marrying by the law of God and man; but neither God nor man would prevent him from loving Miriam and her child. He would care for them both so long as he had breath in his body. Rising to his feet Ralph picked up the tiny bundle, cradling it gently in his arms.

'I will take the child,' he said softly, 'it can be washed downstairs.'

'You can't look to it!' his mother snapped, seeing her opportunity slipping away.

'No, but I can care for it, keep it warm until you have finished with Miriam.'

Holding the child in the crook of one arm, he touched the tip of his finger against the tiny puckered face. If only...

The door safely closed, Leah glared her hatred at the girl on the bed. She had brought water, intending to leave her to wash herself, but Ralph would come back, would not remain downstairs or go to his own bed before seeing his sister again. Leaving her to care for herself would alert him, perhaps set him wondering about the welfare of the child. A mother who would not help her daughter might also have no care for her own grandchild.

Not that she had. Leah reached for the basin of water, long since turned cold. She held no love for Miriam or the fruit of her defilement, but she must make some show of feeling, some pretence; it would last only until the child could safely be done away with.

Ralph watched his mother bathe the child then dry it with the piece of huckaback spread across her lap. Her movements lacked gentleness, matching the harshness of her tight-lipped mouth. They raised in him the old unease; the feeling of fear he had always had for his sister's safety, and now her child's.

No bastard will be born under my roof... The words returned to his mind. In that his mother had been proved wrong. But she had also said: *No bastard will eat at my table...* The silent shadows took on a paler gleam, a beacon of warning that glowed inside him.

'You can shift that, it be finished with.' Leah nodded towards the basin of soapy water. 'Tip it down the drain in the yard.'

Glancing at the basin then back at his mother, Ralph did not move.

'Did you hear?' she demanded, sprinkling the tiny body with a dusting of Robin starch. 'I said for you to empty out that water.'

'I heard what you said.'

'Then do it!'

'Why the hurry, Mother?' Suspicion flooding through him, Ralph remained seated. 'Could it be you want me out of the house?'

Wrapping a triangle of cloth about the tiny buttocks, securing it with a safety pin fastened above the navel, Leah reached for the rest of the worn cloth that had once been a sheet, flicking it deftly in half while still balancing the child on her knees.

'Why would I be wanting you gone from the house?' She wrapped the child in the cloth that must serve as its shawl and clothing, passing it firmly about its head and body, holding down

237

arms and legs, leaving only the tiny face free of the binding.

'Not from the house, Mother.' Ralph gave vent to the fear that sat like ice in his stomach. 'Just from this room. That would give you time enough.'

The child wrapped tight as a parcel and held in her lap, Leah felt a tremor of unease. Could he know what she planned, could he have guessed?

'Time enough for what?' she snapped.

Leaning forward, he took the child from her, his hands almost swamping the tiny body. 'Time to put an end to this child's life. That's what you intended isn't it? Perhaps you'd hoped to do it upstairs, only I arrived before you could.'

'Don't talk so idiotical!' Leah's eyes flashed.

'Am I talking like an idiot, Mother, or am I saying what you hoped I had not guessed? But it is no guess when I say you want this child gone and forgotten. I know you too well to think otherwise. You would like to see them both dead, wouldn't you, Mother? Miriam and her child.'

'Yes!' Leah was on her feet, all pretence gone as she faced her son. 'Yes, I'd like to see them both dead. And, yes, I would have destroyed the filth you hold in your hands had you not come when you did.'

'As I thought.' His voice was very quiet. 'I warned you once what would happen should you strike Miriam ever again. Now I repeat my warning. Lay a finger on either of them, try to harm them in any way, and you will pay. Dearly.'

Leah glanced at the child.

Anger giving way to gratification, her mouth

eased into the travesty of a smile. She rose to her feet. Lightly shaking the cloth on which she had dried the child, she hung it over the airing rack strung above the fire. Then, still smiling, she turned to face her son.

'I'll not have to lay a finger on that which you hold in your hands, that which your heart longs to be your own. There be no need for me to touch it for the hand of death be already reaching out for it.'

'What do you mean?' Ralph exclaimed in an anguished voice.

'Look at it.' Leah smiled viciously. 'It has the yellowness of death on its face. It hasn't cried apart from the first minutes after birth, it breathes but only just, and doesn't turn its head in search of the breast. No, I'll not need to point its way to the grave. It stands on the edge already.'

'No!' Ralph tightened his hold protectively about the tiny scrap of humanity. 'What you say is lies, the child will live.'

'Take it then.' Leah laughed, the harsh sound grating in the quiet of the room. 'Take it up to *her*, its mother. Watch over it together, it will make no odds. Though you never take your eyes from it, nor let it out of your arms, still you will not keep it. Death hovers beside that child, and though it may not claim it tonight or tomorrow, it will take what it has come for!'

Carrying the child up to Miriam's room, Ralph looked down anxiously at the face already pale as marble, the tiny eyelids veined with purple, and deep within himself he shivered. But his mother's words would not prove true, he would not let them. The child *would* live.

Clayton Rawley had proposed a quiet family dinner party to mark the eve of the engagement, reflected Saul, waiting for the horse to be harnessed to the carriage. But what would the owner of Brade Hall say if he discovered that engagement was as yet only a figment of Saul Marsh's ambitious imaginings?

His welcome here was beginning to wear a little thin; true nothing had been said of his leaving, and the generosity of the Rawleys was as marked as ever, hence the use of this carriage, but for how long would it continue? Should it end before he could turn those lies into truth, what then? He could hardly expect to be taken into the Sadler home and hadn't the money to rent the house or buy the clothes he would need to keep up appearances.

Edwina had seen him in nothing but the clothes lent to him by Ethan, nor would she see him in anything less expensive. It did not matter that he had lost the home he'd shared with his grandmother she'd said. Saul smiled, congratulating himself on the convincing way he had lied. It did not matter, she had told him, her soul in her eyes, it did not matter that he was not wealthy. But by the time it did, it would be too late. She would be his wife, and, more importantly, her money would be his.

'You watch your step, my wench.'

Saul's ears pricked at the sound of Sally Baxter's voice floating from the open door of the kitchen.

'I will, Mrs Baxter.'

The answering voice was younger, pitched higher and lighter, the words delivered in an almost sing-song fashion.

'Remember what I said. Half-past nine and not a minute later.'

'I'll remember, Mrs Baxter.'

'Well, just see as you do or you'll find the door locked. When I says half-past nine, I means half-past nine, not a quarter to ten, so don't you go thinking I do.'

'I won't, Mrs Baxter. Tarra.'

Saul stepped casually to a place where he could see the rear of the house. Sally Baxter stood on the whitewashed doorstep, watching Ginny Jinks walk down the servants' path which he knew eventually met the main drive halfway down its length. Fate was playing into his hands.

Stepping smartly back, he kept out of sight as the housekeeper turned indoors. Glancing at the sky, he smiled. The sun already hovered over the horizon.

Out of sight of the house, he drew the carriage to a halt. He must not catch up with the housemaid too quickly. A carriage accident on the drive would lead to too many awkward questions being asked. Barring visitors, only the Rawleys' carriage used the main approach to the Hall. If no visitors called tonight and the Rawleys had not used the carriage, then he would automatically be suspect; even if nothing could be proved it was better to avoid suspicion at all. Yes, somewhere along the Dudley Road was ideal. That saw plenty of carriage traffic. An accident to a girl day dreaming as she walked ... it had happened before. The reins idle in his hands, Saul laughed. It was about to happen again!

Two birds with one stone. Five minutes later he flicked the reins, setting the horse to a walk. Tonight would see the end of the threat of Ginny Jinks and also solve the problem of his engagement. He laughed again, low in his throat. Ginny and sweet Edwina, he would take them both, only one would enjoy the experience more than the other; as for Saul, he would enjoy both equally.

That would still leave Miriam, and of course her brother. He would never really be secure with them around. True, they could do little once his marriage was achieved, little except gossip, but gossip was dangerous and he did not intend to allow it.

Which one should he see off first? Keeping the horse to a walk, he mulled over the problem.

Miriam? She was the one who could harm him most. She was the one who had almost been raped. Her word could put a halt to his dreams. Yes, Miriam was the one who should die first, and that way ... the smile returned to his mouth, a slow malevolent spreading of the lips ... that way her loving brother would suffer the additional pain of loss. And the more pain he could cause Ralph Bryce, the more satisfied he would be. The man had deliberately held back from ending the life he could so easily have taken that night; instead he had thought to destroy it a different way. He had thought to cause Saul Marsh to die a thousand times over, die each time he looked at a pretty girl, each time he knew he could never love a woman again!

'But it didn't work, Bryce,' he murmured into the gathering dusk. 'Saul Marsh isn't a eunuch and he's not dead! You'll wish you had put an end to him when you had the chance, for you will know who it was killed your precious sister, and you will also know she need not have died. That it was your fault.

'Your fault, Bryce!' Delighted by his own reasoning, Saul's low cynical laughter travelled on the breeze. 'You will know she would not have died had you used that knife differently. Yes, your sister will be the first, and then ... then I shall come for *you!*'

The carriage had followed the curve of the drive and was now on the final quarter mile that gave on to the tall wrought-iron gates. Saul's gaze travelled ahead, scanning the road for sight of the girl. With a lift of his spirits he caught sight of a figure, skirts swinging from a waist topped by a neatly fitting jacket, hat set on hair loosed from the coil that had held it when last he'd seen the girl wave to Sally Baxter. Ginny was obviously set for a few hours' entertainment. A pity she would not live to enjoy it.

Keeping the same slow pace, he saw her face briefly as she turned to look round at the sound of a vehicle. The carriage was no danger to her, she would think. Poor Ginny! It would be the last she would ever think.

No more than a hundred yards now. He watched the jaunty swing of her stride that revealed a hint of white petticoat below darker

243

skirts. He must not overtake her before she passed through the gates.

He glanced at the sky. Its surrender to dusk was almost complete but as yet no moon claimed sovereignty. Lighting the carriage lamps would afford him the time he needed.

Calling the horse to a halt, Saul dismounted. Taking a box of Swan Vesta matches from his pocket, he flipped up the top of one of the glass side lamps then struck a match.

What if the girl turned now? Would she recognise him? She would if the flame lit his hair. Ethan Rawley did not have yellow hair.

Swiftly cupping a hand about the flame, he trapped the light, holding the match so no light reached higher than his chest. Maybe the carriage lamps were not such a good idea after all. But if he failed to light them now the girl might turn back, thinking he needed assistance.

Feeling the heat of the flame near his finger tips, Saul dropped the match. The girl had not stopped nor was she looking behind her. But the longer he could delay the lighting of these lamps, the farther away she would be, and the more difficult for her to see who it was driving the carriage. Not that it would really matter in the end. The dead did not talk.

Giving one more glance at the figure swinging down the drive, he struck a second match, holding it to the wick of the lamp before throwing it aside.

The second lamp lit, he climbed back into the driving seat, clucking his tongue in soft command for the horse to walk on.

How would he do it? He savoured the thought. Bring the carriage up at a trot, make her run? No, she might take to the heath and he could not follow if she did that. The chances of himself finishing up a hundred feet down the shaft of some abandoned gin pit were too great. He must forego the pleasure of the chase, of running her down slowly. It would have to be done quickly, at a sudden gallop!

Thirty yards ahead the figure passed through the open gateway, skirts tossed by the quick skip of the girl's step.

A few minutes more and she would be clear. He could not afford to idle along. She could become lost among the shadows, then he would not know which direction she had taken. A flick of the reins set the horse into a jog. He must judge just right; not too close, not too far. The girl must be given no cause for fear.

He would need to slow the horse, take it through the gates at a walk in case of other vehicles being on the road which was the one link between the towns, being used by carters as well as carriages. But carters tried not to travel at night, and with luck the mine and quarry owners would not be returning from business just yet.

The pillars that supported the gates loomed to either side of the carriage. Saul felt his heart quicken. Which branch of the road had she taken? Squinting in the gloom, he searched for sight of the girl. There, to the left, towards Brades Village, and she was running.

Why? Saul watched for a brief second, his thoughts keeping time with those flying feet. Had she turned while he was lighting the lamps? Had she seen and recognised him, and if so guessed what he intended to do?

She could run, but not escape. He would pass the wheels of the carriage over her fallen body. Guiding the horse on to the empty road, he fastened his eyes on the running figure.

'Run, girl,' he whispered. 'Run. You will soon be doing it for your life, but you won't run fast enough.'

The thought was pure stimulation, sending a flush of heat to scour his veins. This was more pleasurable than a night in Banjo's beer house, more intoxicating than his best ale.

Flicking the reins, Saul held the horse to a trot. Closer. He watched the figure ahead, skirts dancing as she ran. He would draw closer and then, a touch of the whip and the horse would break into a gallop.

Blood surging with the heat of fever, he judged the distance.

Now ... it must be now!

Gathering the reins in one hand, he reached for the driving whip. Eyes fixed on the running figure, he closed his fingers around the stock, drawing the whip easily from the mount. Breath caught in his throat, mouth half open at the sensation sweeping through him, he raised the whip slowly above his head holding it in mid-air as the girl was swept into the arms of a man waiting in the shadows.

Chapter Sixteen

Holding the child close to his chest, Ralph carried it carefully upstairs. His mother had spoken true, albeit from malice. The child did have a sickly yellowness to its skin, and so far it had not cried for milk.

But surely that did not mean it would die? Yet there was a quietness about it, an almost unnatural stillness. Even given the sheet wrapped firm about its limbs, he would have thought it would try to move.

Dressed now in a plain calico night gown, her face washed clean of perspiration, hair brushed back from her brow, Miriam smiled weakly as he entered the bedroom.

'Is ... is the baby all right?'

Ralph nodded, not wanting his fear to show in his voice. Time would bring the answer. Miriam's worries would begin soon enough.

He held the tiny bundle out to her, not missing her wince of pain as she levered herself higher.

'You have a daughter, Miriam.' He smiled, the love in his heart reflected in his eyes. 'Now I have a sister and a niece to care for.'

'And to worry over.' She took the child, touching her lips to the tiny head covered in red down. Then, lifting her gaze to his, she added, 'I am so sorry, Ralph. I never meant for it to be like this. I thought ... I hoped...' She had hoped that Saul

247

Marsh would come to her, tell her they would be married, but that had not happened. Instead he had denied the child and tried to rape her.

Seeing the glint of tears, Ralph turned away.

'It doesn't matter what you thought,' he said gruffly. 'All that does is that you are home, your baby is born and you are both safe.'

'We will not be a burden to you, Ralph,' Miriam replied, voice heavy with tears. 'I will find a place to live and a job. I will work to keep myself and her.' She lifted the bed covers, drawing them around the child, feeling the tiny body against hers.

'You could never be a burden to me, nor the child neither. And my only worry would be your not being where I could care for you!'

'But Mother...'

'I know.' He cut the protest short. 'We both know, so I will not try to hide the fact. She does not want the child under her roof. But Mother is going to have to accept it. At least until you are strong enough to move, then we'll both leave. I will find work in Dudley or we could go further, say Walsall or even Wolverhampton. There'll be places there we can live.' Ralph smiled but inside he worried. He had no idea whether he could find work in any of those areas; they were towns he had only heard of, nothing more than names to him.

'Did you see either of the Rawleys?'

He shook his head. 'The housekeeper said they were not at home. She took the letter you had written and said she would see they got it. She also said thank you for the return of the money she'd loaned you, but you had no need to worry about returning it so quickly.'

'She was not offended?' Miriam looked up sharply.

'No. In fact she seemed a friendly type. Pleased you were back with your family.'

'He would not own to the child.' The statement came as suddenly as the soft tears that spilled down her pale cheeks. Miriam bent her head, bringing the tiny face against her own. 'He does not want the baby, and does not want me. I was a fool to believe him. To believe anything he told me.'

He would not own to the child. Did that mean she herself had spoken to Marsh of the baby she carried? She had cried his name when Ralph found her alone on the road to Tividale, cried it out as though she were terrified of him. Had Saul Marsh come across her on that road, or had he known she was at Brade Hall and gone to her there?

'He was there, at Brade Hall.' Wiping the tip of her finger gently across the brow of the sleeping infant, Miriam brushed away the tears that had fallen on it. 'It seems he was taken there the same evening I was. He had been involved in some sort of accident and was found by Ethan Rawley. I did not know it was him, not until...'

'Until?' Ralph felt the blood freeze in his veins.

Telling her brother of Saul Marsh's attempt to rape her would only cause more anger, more violence; and it would not wipe away the hurt or the memory. They both of them had enough painful memories. It would serve no purpose, handing her brother one more.

'Until my memory returned.'

'So why did you leave?'

Brushing her lips across the downy head, Miriam did not meet the challenge in her brother's eyes, but the harshness of his voice contained the unmistakable undercurrent of anger.

'I ... I wanted to come home.'

'So badly you rushed out like a cork from a bottle of ginger beer!' He banged one fist against the chest of drawers. 'You wanted to hurry back home ... is that why you were going in the opposite direction?'

'I ... I was...' Miriam hesitated. She did not want to lie, but neither did she wish Ralph to know what had taken place in that bedroom.

'It *was* Marsh, wasn't it? He was the one sent you scurrying away like a scalded cat!' Ralph went on, his glance taking in the expression that flashed across her face, the fear that was the answer to his question. 'Did he ... did he touch you? Did he try to harm you? If so, by God I'll kill him!'

'No, Ralph, please!' Miriam lifted her head to look at him, the yellow light of the oil lamp highlighting the shadows in her drawn face. 'He ... he did not hurt me. Merely said he did not want me or the baby. Now I just want to forget him and make a life for my daughter. I want no more of Saul Marsh.'

She could try to forget Marsh, Ralph thought as she bent again over the child lying silent in her arms. Try to forget what it was he had done to her. But while his sister might try to forget, he never would. It may be a while in coming but the day of reckoning would dawn, and when it did Saul Marsh would pay his debts in full.

A house and the position of general manager of Sadler's coal mines! There were eight of them in all, shifting several hundred tons a week. Saul Marsh smiled, satisfaction glowing inside him. Not bad for a start. But he would not be really satisfied until the whole of Sadler's business was his, and not just as manager.

'I've no objection to my wench taking a collier for a husband,' Sadler had said over the dinner table, though his wife's face had been cold as yesterday's custard. 'Just so long as you takes care of her and works hard. I came up on the cheeks of my backside meself, first digging coals and doing wi'out meals so as to save money. Then, when I had enough to buy pick and shovel and timbers for shoring, I sunk my first pit shaft. I ain't looked back since. You prove as good a worker and I'll have no cause for complaint.'

It had been no challenge at all after that. Edwina seemed to have her father in the palm of her hand, and Saul had Edwina in his. Yes, life was going to be good for Saul Marsh.

The house was Edwina's own. Left to her by her grandmother, it stood on a small hill at Tipperty Green, overlooking the farms and cottages that went with it. It was large enough. Guiding the horse and carriage towards Brade Hall, Saul nodded to himself as he thought of the fifteen-room red brick house. It was still not large enough to house his mother as well. She would remain a part of all he had left behind; she would never be a visitor to Glebe House. There must be nothing to remind him of the poverty of his life in the village, or threaten the stability of the one he would have from now on. But Miriam Bryce and his child! Why should they be a threat to him when they could so easily be got rid of? And Ralph Bryce... He too would suffer the same fate. Nothing and no-one must stand in the way of Saul Marsh.

But the girl, Ginny Jinks, there he was not so sure. She might open her mouth at any time. He should have run her down in the driveway. It would have been a simple matter to have lifted her into the carriage and then have dumped her body on the road somewhere else. But it was easy to be wise after the event. Saul felt his satisfaction slip away. There had been no chance since that evening, but he would find a way. So long as she remained at Brade Hall, or until his marriage to Edwina was finally accomplished, he would not feel thoroughly at ease.

But he need no longer worry that the latter would somehow fall to materialise. Tonight had set the seal on their marriage as surely as any signature on a set of marriage lines. Maybe in a few months' time he would be the father of a second child.

Edwina had already carried a mental picture of herself, gowned in white, being welcomed home to Glebe House, this time with the new master beside her. She had eagerly showed him over the elegantly furnished old house. She had even been ready to anticipate that marriage.

She would show him over the house herself, she had said, dismissing the equally old caretaker back to his cottage in the grounds; and she had showed Saul all around it, the pleasure and excitement of doing so apparent in her voice as she gave him a brief explanation of the history of each piece of furniture. Her grandmother had obviously had a liking for the finer things of life. Not that he would know one style from another but the whole house had an aura of luxury he'd found intoxicating.

'That is by Turner.' Edwina had pointed in the direction of a painting. Then, passing another, 'And that one is by Constable.' So it had gone on, her revealing of the house for his inspection, an anxious note lifting her voice as if she asked for his approval. And he had approved, making a mental note to have everything valued. You could never say when a swift discreet sale might become necessary. It would be in his interest to know the value of each possession before hand.

'This was the room I always had whenever we stayed with my grandparents.'

She had led the way along one of the dual landings hung with family portraits.

'I don't want to talk about that.'

Saul smiled into the darkness, remembering the look of dismay that had flashed to her face.

'Oh, Saul!' She had turned to him instantly, clinging to his arm. 'I did not mean to upset you! Oh my dear, I am so sorry.'

Upset him? A dry laugh rang out into the night as he thought of it. If only she had known –

known she was playing straight into his hands!

'Please, my dear.' She had almost begged. 'Say you are not truly upset?'

'But I am.' He had touched a hand to a doll's cradle draped in flower-sprigged muslin. 'I can't lie to you, Edwina. I am unhappy.'

'But why, Saul?'

'Because,' he had murmured softly, 'I did not know you then.'

'Oh, you sweet darling!' She had pressed her face close against his chest, arms going about him. 'You should not be unhappy about that.'

'But I am.' He had stepped away from her. 'I regret every moment of my life when I did not know you, and I can't bear to think of a life that does not have you at its heart.'

Her smile tender, voice soft with feeling, she had answered gently. 'You do not have to think of me any other way. Just two weeks now, and we will be together for always, we will be the centre of each other's life forever.'

Catching the hands that would again have gone about him, he had held them against his chest, his voice harsh with assumed emotion. 'No, Edwina. I was not strong enough to say this before ... I could not face the thought of not seeing you again, not hearing your voice say my name.' He had broken off then, a sob catching in his throat.

Saul laughed again, remembering. That was a touch she could not resist. It had brought a quick cry from Edwina as she'd struggled to free her hands, but he had held tightly to them, using his superior strength to hold her just far enough away. 'But now,' he had continued, hurt ringing in his voice, 'Now I see that I must. We cannot be married.'

Her strangled gasp had echoed through the quiet house. 'I don't understand. Why ... why can we not be married?'

He had fastened his gaze on her upturned face, eyes travelling over it as if to imprint it on his mind. 'Because I have nothing to bring to it. I have no money, no property. Your father was good enough to offer me a position and to accept me as your husband, but even given all of that I could not keep you as you are used to being kept, and it would break my heart to think I denied you anything. In fact, I will not allow that to happen. I will not let you give yourself to a man who can give nothing in return.'

Her cry had been one of sheer misery. 'But ... but you said you loved me?'

'And I do.' His deep gaze had held her as easily as it had held many a village girl before, and he could see the end result promising the same reward. 'I love you too much to let you sacrifice all you have for me, when all I can offer is my heart.'

Edwina had released herself from hands that seemed suddenly to have lost all strength, all will. Bringing her body close to his, she had clung to him, her words whispered. 'All I want is your heart, my darling, that is all I will ever want. You can never give me anything I could value more. Say you will marry me, take me as your wife? Nothing else matters. If you do not wish to work for Father then you shall not. I have enough money from my grandmother to keep us, we shall want for nothing. I will want for nothing – just so long as we are married. Don't deny me, Saul. Please do not deny me!'

Her words had been cried in torment but they had sent a warm feeling of relief through him. He had taken a gamble, given her the perfect opportunity to withdraw from the match, but she had not. He had uttered her name then, the catch in his voice making it seem his heart was breaking, then his arms had gone about her and he was raining fierce kisses on her eyes and mouth.

'My sweet love ... my sweet love.' His murmurs had been soft and heady, snatched between moments when their lips were apart. And she had returned his kisses and given way to the pressure of his body as he lowered her slowly to the floor, curving herself into him as his hand explored her softness. Then slowly, every move calculated to overwhelm her, he pushed her legs apart. 'Edwina! Oh, my love ... my dear sweet love.' The words brought his mouth to hers again, closing off her cry as he entered her.

Guiding the carriage between the high gates and along the drive that led to the Hall, Saul Marsh laughed deep in his throat. Edwina Sadler had enjoyed playing the role of mistress of Glebe House, one he would have her play again several times before leaving church as his lawful wedded wife.

Calling softly to the horse, he smiled into the darkness. Ethan Rawley had no knowledge of where his portrayal of the Good Samaritan would lead that night he had found him on

Derby's Hill; nor had Ralph Bryce when he had left him there.

Eyes reflecting the worry eating at her Miriam glanced at her mother, busy at the table that dominated the small room.

'She will not feed, she just turns her head away.'

'Hmmph!' Leah plunged both hands into a basin of flour.

'She did not feed in the night either.'

'So what do you want me to do about it?' Leah's glance, hard and hostile, met that of her daughter.

'Tell me what to do? If you will not help me, at least help my baby.' Miriam choked back tears. 'Don't let her die, Mother. Show me how to feed her and I will leave this house tomorrow, say nothing to Ralph ... you have my promise.'

'You will leave this house regardless of your brother!' Leah rubbed cubes of fat into the flour. 'He might think himself the mainstay here but this house is mine and I'll have no whore nor bastard living in it. I worked to keep myself before I was wed, and since I've been a widow. I need no son to earn my bread and will suffer none holding a sword above my head. So you can take your by blow and go wheresoever you please, just so long as I don't have to set eyes on you ever again.'

Weak from the birth and lack of sleep, Miriam felt a wave of weariness wash over her. Ralph had sat all night on the chair in her bedroom, just as he had sat through the nights of her illness following that awful night on the heath. Oh, he had said it was their mother who'd sat with her, but on each of Miriam's wakings it had been he who had come to her. Just as he had been there to hand her the child from its bed in the drawer or to bring her a hot drink, his words soothing the fear rising in her heart. The fear of her child refusing to feed. But Ralph could not be here all the time, he must work until mid-evening; and she knew if she were to keep her strength she must be up and about for Leah would not tend to her needs.

'I cannot take the child away until she accepts food!' Miriam's answer rang out with newfound strength. She had never spoken to her mother in such a tone before, but she had never had a child to fight for before, a tiny life that depended upon her. 'I will not leave until I am sure I can keep my baby safe.'

'You can never keep her safe!' Leah spat venomously. 'You can never keep her at all!' Both hands resting on the rim of the basin, Leah stared at the girl she had never loved. 'Look at her. Look at the colour of her skin. You ask why she will not take the breast? It is because she's dying ... that child is dying.'

'No!' Lifting the baby high on her chest, Miriam held her own head protectively over the tiny one. 'Why do you say such a cruel thing? Take out your hatred and your spite on me, but why say that of a child less than two days old? A child who can do you no harm!'

Behind Leah the tin clock ticked, its sound filling the room like the beat of a drum. Miriam lifted terrified eyes to where it stood on the mantelpiece. Was it ticking away the seconds of her baby's life?

'The hatred that will take that child's life is no hatred of mine,' Leah went on, ignoring the girl's chalk white face. 'It is the hatred of wickedness. The Lord will not suffer the fruit of your wickedness to live. It is He who has set the finger of death on that child and no works of mine or of yours will save it! You will leave this house but the child will not go with you. You will leave it behind in the ground.'

'That's not true!' Daughter held close against her, Miriam turned away, shielding the frail body from her mother's gaze, her own sobs keeping time with the clock. 'She will not die ... she will not.'

'Wait and see.' Leah returned her hands to the mixture in the basin. 'The Lord will not be denied. He will take that which His hand has marked, and I will not be one to go against His word.'

He could not want that? Miriam ran up the narrow stairs. God would not let her carry a child for nine months only to snatch it away a few days after its birth. He would not take a tiny life to pay for a sin it had played no part in committing. She gathered together a few things and bundled them beneath the child.

Carrying the shawl-wrapped bundle close against her breast, she touched a finger to a cheek tinged yellow. 'I won't let you die, my darling,' she murmured. 'I won't let you die.'

'Where do you think you be going?' Leah looked up as Miriam came down the stairs and went to the door.

Her own shawl wrapped about the child and her things. Miriam reached for her mother's then withdrew her hand. Taking it would only fuel further argument. But the defiance she had felt earlier surged up in her again and she turned to confront the older woman.

'You will not help my baby so I must find someone who will.'

'And who do you think will lift a hand to help a bastard?'

'I don't know.' Miriam's voice was strangely calm, and the eyes that looked back at her mother held nothing but pity. 'But not every woman in Brades Village can be as heartless as you.'

'You'll bring no village woman to my house. I'll have no tongues wagging about my business.'

'It is not your business they will wag over, Mother, it is mine.'

'They will talk of nothing that has gone on in this house.' Leah's eyes sparked with fury. 'You keep clear of Brades Village, you hear me, girl? You keep well clear of that place.'

'I hear you very well, Mother.' Miriam lifted the latch that held the door closed. 'But my daughter needs my help, and unlike you I will give it to her. All your anger will not stop me.'

'It will do no good.' Leah laughed, a harsh brittle sound. 'There be no woman in the village can do anything to save that child. No, nor any doctor in Dudley. The only help you should look for would be a priest, one to say the last words over her. But no priest will come to pray over a bastard, no priest will baptise it into the Church and none will give it burial in holy ground. It will be cast out, unwanted in the Kingdom of the Lord. And it will be *your* fault.'

Pulling the door open, Miriam felt the blast of winter cold bite into her bare arms and pressed the baby even closer to her own body. Her mother's heart must be every bit as cold. 'I have taken your word all of my life,' she said, her back to the woman she addressed, 'but this time I shall take someone else's. As I said, Mother, there must be a woman in the village not as heartless as you.'

'And I say you will fetch no woman to this house!' Even as she screamed the words Leah had grabbed the poker from the hearth and was across the room with it, raising it above her head as she ran.

Chapter Seventeen

'I could not leave her, Ralph. I tried to lift her but she was too heavy. I made her as comfortable as I could but I could not get her up to bed.' Miriam looked at her brother, worry darkening her eyes.

'What happened?' Ralph Bryce looked down at his mother, lying on the floor, head on a pillow, body swathed in blankets.

'I did not see her fall. I was just about to leave for the village ... going to try to get help for the baby. I heard mother call and ... and then she fell.'

261

'You were going to the village, and Mother was no doubt waving you off when she fell? What was she chasing you with? A knife or a hammer?' His tone was scathing.

'Ralph, she...'

'Don't bother!' With a quick shake of his head, he bent to lift his mother in his arms. 'We both know she would die before letting you go down to the village with the child, so don't tell me any lies. I can guess what happened.'

'I should have gone for a doctor but I was too afraid to leave her.' Miriam followed him up the narrow stairs, turning back the covers on her mother's bed for Ralph to set her down. She'd been afraid to leave her mother lying unconscious on the floor, and even more afraid for her baby who had rolled from her own arms when she had fallen under her mother's blow.

'There's no doctor nearer than Langley and if he's out then the nearest place is Dudley. You could not have walked that far with the child.'

She should have tried. Loosening the pearl buttons that ran down the front of her mother's blouse, Miriam was overcome with the guilt that had ridden her for several hours.

She herself had lain senseless for some minutes and when she awoke her first thoughts had been for the child. Fear thick in her throat, she had struggled to her feet, head swirling with dizzying waves of pain.

She remembered peering through blurred eyes, fear holding her rigid as she looked at the bundle lying so still on the stone-flagged floor. Was this the death Leah had predicted? Was her baby dead, killed by the fall from her arms?

She had stood there staring, throat dry, heart beating louder than the tin clock. Then her daughter had cried, a pitifully weak mewling cry, but it had forced Miriam to move and she had scooped the bundle into her arms, tears of relief washing the tiny face.

It was only as she turned that she had seen her mother. Crumpled into a heap, head to one side, eyes closed in a face that might never have known colour. And her hand flung slightly outward, still curved about the iron poker.

Miriam had laid the baby in the drawer from her chest, brought down to the living room, then knelt beside her mother. There was no movement, no life seemed to remain in that spare body, but the faintest stirring of breath escaped through the thin lips.

That was when she ought to have gone for help, she acknowledged guiltily. But she had not. She had not gone to the village. Why ... why? She had been prepared to go and find help for her daughter so why not for her mother?

I was afraid to leave her. What if she woke and needed me...

'I will get the shelves from the oven if you can manage to undress her.'

Ralph's voice bringing her from her thoughts, Miriam nodded. Slipping a voluminous calico night gown over her mother's head, she forced the limp arms into the sleeves, tying the cotton ribbons threaded through the wristbands.

Her mother had struck her with a poker! Suddenly the nightmare of it closed about her in a

263

thick choking miasma of fear that had her gasping for breath. Leah had risked killing her to prevent her from going to the village.

Lost in black thoughts she did not hear her brother come back into the room. Watching her standing beside the bed, her gaze somewhere beyond his knowing, her whole body shaking like a leaf in the wind, he realised what he had guessed from the beginning. There was more to their mother's fall than Miriam had said. But now was not the time to demand explanations.

Placing the oven shelves he had wrapped in pieces of huckaback beneath the sheets, he slid an arm gently about his sister's trembling shoulders.

'Come away now. I will sit with her. You go and get some rest.'

'No.' Miriam drew a long steadying breath. Striking a match from the box set on the bedside table, she held it to the lamp. 'We must get a doctor.'

'I want no doctor!'

The sallow gleam of the oil lamp lit the pallid face but left the eyes as small pools of glistening black as Leah's eyelids slowly lifted.

'Bring me no doctor.'

The words were slurred, the mouth tight and pulled down on one side, but there was no mistaking the determination in the dark eyes that stared up at them.

'But you need help,' Miriam was the first to answer.

'I want no doctor, I tell you,' Leah slurred. 'I won't pay good money to hear what he'll tell me.

264

That I have been overdoing things. Take bed rest, he'll say. Then who'll do what has to be done? I be tired, that's all. Tomorrow will see me back on my feet.'

Miriam turned to her brother. 'But the doctor should check her.'

Glancing at the figure in the bed, Ralph drew her away as his mother's eyes closed.

Downstairs he fed the fire with fresh coals then sat facing his sister across the table.

'What she said was true,' he said softly. 'Folk do get so tired they just keel over. I've seen it a couple of times before down in the village. All the doctor ever said was for them to be kept warm and not to let them get all fretted up. You'll see, she'll be up and about again come morning, and no doubt her temper as sweet as ever.'

'I should have gone for the doctor.'

'Stop that, Miriam!' Ralph's voice rose sharply. 'You did what was best. You wrapped her up and stayed with her. Had you left her, anything could have happened. She could have vomited or choked – who knows? Blaming yourself is not only wrong, it's useless. It will do neither you nor her any good. If anyone is to be blamed it should be me. I should have taken you away from this house long ago. I should not have brought you back here to have your child.'

As if in answer a thin wail came from the drawer laid alongside the hearth and Miriam picked up the baby.

'Has she taken milk today?'

'A little,' Miriam answered, rocking gently. 'But she does not feed as she should. A few drops and

265

she turns her head away.'

'Let's try her with this.' Reaching into his pocket, he drew out a small paper bag. 'I got it from Longmore's shop on the way home.'

Taking a cup from the dresser, he carried it into the scullery, half filling it with milk from the cool jar. Then back in the living room he diluted it with water from the kettle. Placing the cup at Miriam's elbow, he withdrew a glass pipette from the paper bag.

Testing the heat of the milk against her lips, Miriam filled the slim phial then inserted it into the baby's mouth.

'She seems to like that.' Relief in her smile, she refilled the tiny glass tube. 'Please God she will not die after all.'

'Die?' Ralph frowned, anger turning his grey-blue eyes to dark slate. 'Is that what Mother said – that your baby would die?'

She did not answer, but then she didn't need to. Their mother would say such a thing and delight in doing so. Though her words might yet come to pass, and God knew he felt they would, there was no call to trumpet them and break Miriam's heart in the process. But then again, wouldn't their mother delight in doing that as well?

'I'm afraid, Ralph.' Her voice cracking on a sob as the child refused to swallow more than the first few drops, Miriam laid aside the pipette. 'She's so very tiny, so helpless. What if she should die without a name? Without being christened?'

Dropping to his knees at her feet, he took the child's tiny hand, holding it gently between finger and thumb.

'She will have a name, and she will be christened. I will go to St Matthew's and make the arrangements just as soon as she gets a bit stronger.'

'Mother said no priest would baptise a bastard.' Miriam looked into the eyes lifted to hers. 'She said none would come to say the prayer for the dying nor give her burial in holy ground. She said my baby would find no place in the Kingdom of the Lord.'

'God Almighty!' Ralph sprang to his feet, his face livid. 'Does that woman never stop!'

'But it's true, isn't it? Should my baby die it would not be buried in the churchyard.'

Too full of emotion to answer he turned away, staring into the scarlet flames of the fire.

'Why?' she asked softly. 'Why would they do that to a child? Why cast it from God when it has done no harm?'

'*They* can't cast it from God!' The words were rasped out, his fist coming down hard on the mantelshelf. 'No one can cast a soul from God but God Himself, and that He would do to none. He will not bar your child from His Kingdom, name or no name. It will not matter to Him whether the words of a priest have been said over her or not. A few mumblings and a dribble of water make no difference to His love.'

He turned to face her, the tears on her cheeks assuaging his anger.

'What good is there in believing in a God who could turn away a helpless babe?' he asked gently. 'A God who would revenge Himself on any child is not worthy of the love of man. If you

267

believe in the Lord, then you must believe He will not turn from a child too young to know even the meaning of sin!'

Watching her lift the baby, holding it against her cheek, tears glistening like jewels in the lamplight, Ralph knew deep inside that his sister believed in God, but in her fear the words of her mother ranked more strongly in her mind.

Snatching jacket and muffler from the hook on the back of the door, he strode out into the night.

A little way from the village Ralph hesitated. He had kept to the heath since leaving the house but to get to his destination meant crossing the junction of Salop Street and passing between the houses that lined both sides of Albion Street. The chances of his meeting somebody from one or other street was high, and he did not wish to. He could take the tram, ride to where the main road passed the end of Albion Street. There was empty ground that end, the houses ending where they abutted the church. People from Brades Village used the tram but rarely. Money was too hard earned to go spending it on tram rides when they could walk.

Touching his fingers to his pocket Ralph felt the small bottle he had taken from the brew house in the yard, thankful his mother had a tendency to keep things she thought might have a use.

Casting a glance toward Banjo's beer house, already pouring out the tinny sounds of a banjo that floated across the silent heath, he saw no sign of movement; still he would wait here. The tram could be seen long before it reached him giving him time to sprint to the road.

'Evenin'.' The conductor touched his cap as Ralph swung on to the tram. 'It be a cold 'un, I reckon we be in for some snow.'

'I think you're right.' Taking a halfpenny from his pocket, Ralph exchanged it for the ticket the man punched in the machine strapped about his waist. He did not feel like talking but not to answer would draw attention.

'Best place on a night like this be at home with your feet in the hearth.' The man smiled, his teeth white beneath a nose red from cold. 'Another couple of hours and I'll be off there meself. Home where you be going?'

'It is.' Ralph peered through the darkness, looking for his stop.

'Arrh, well, you'll be there soon enough.' Raising a hand to the leather cord that ran the length of the tram, the conductor pulled once on it, nodding to Ralph as the bell tinkled. 'This be Albion Street.'

Murmuring goodnight, Ralph jumped clear of the small square platform, stepping back as the gears crashed and the tram lumbered forward. A couple of hundred yards, that was all it was. Chances were he could be there and back without anyone seeing him.

All around the church of St Matthew tombstones rose like grey ghosts, the bare branches of trees reaching out like skeletal fingers. Pausing in the lee of the building he listened, but no sound other than the rustle of branches sounded in the night air. From the windows the faint glimmer of

269

candles scarce pricked the darkness. The church was empty, as he had hoped.

Treading cautiously, feet making no sound on the soft ground, he moved to the front of the church, pushing open the smaller door set into one of the huge oak double doors only opened on Sundays.

Stepping inside, he waited for his eyes to become accustomed to the deeper shadows of the building. At the farthest end of the nave tall sconces, invisible in the gloom, held candles whose points of light appeared to hang suspended in mid-air, gleaming like yellow stars in a midnight sky.

But what he sought was not beside the High Altar. Taking the bottle from his pocket, he eased the cork slowly from its neck. It would be here, near the door.

Each step taken with care, following the map of memory, he took several paces to the right. Allowing a few moments for the soft glimmer of the candles to fade from his vision, he made out the shape of the wooden stand. Memory had served him well though he had not set foot in this church since his father's passing.

Holding the bottle firmly, he reached it towards the stand, plunging it into the basin of holy water that stood in a recess at the centre. Miriam's child would not do without the benefit of the church. Given or stolen it would be hers.

Laying the sleeping child in the drawer that served as a crib, Miriam stood for a moment looking down at the tiny jaundiced face, the fringes of dark lashes resting like shadows on the cheeks. The child was growing weaker, she needed help; if only Ralph had not gone off like that she would have asked him to stay with their mother while she took the child to the village. Surely someone there would know what to do?

Behind her the lid of the kettle began to jig. Turning it, she swung the bracket back from the heat of the fire. She would see if her mother was awake before making a drink. Exchanging the kettle for the pan of barley broth made earlier in the day, she swung it into position atop the glowing coals. Ralph had not eaten on coming home from the mine, he would need something hot.

Reaching a piece of cloth from the airing line above the range, she took two blue bricks from the slow oven. They were always kept there when the oven was not in use, absorbing heat to be used as warmers for the beds.

Gently withdrawing the shelves Ralph had placed at Leah's feet, she replaced them with the hot bricks.

'There be no need for dancing attendance on me.'

The slurring of the words gave them a strange, eerie sound and despite herself Miriam shivered.

'You would do better to tend that spawn of Saul Marsh's. It don't have long for this earth.'

Clutching the oven racks in her arms, Miriam looked at her mother's twisted malevolent face.

'Why do you say that, Mother?' The words burst from her lips. 'What harm can my child do you?'

Leah's teeth came together so the next words were hissed behind them. 'It be a bastard!'

'And for that she should die? Is that what you hoped for when you struck me with that poker, to kill the two of us?'

'No ... o ... o' It was a long slow drawn whisper and for a moment pleasure glinted in Leah's empty eyes. 'It was not your death I hoped for – that blow were a warning. Now I give you that same warning again. You go to the village, you let them know of the shame you have brought to this house, and I will see you in the ground, you and your bastard.'

Her breath held in her throat, Miriam turned towards the bedroom door. On the pillow Leah's head followed her. 'I want you to know why I kept that poker from your head.'

Miriam felt the words follow her, sliding behind her, venomous and ruthless as some malignant serpent.

'I want you dead, that I will not deny. But I want that death to be long in coming. I want it to come slow, prayed for night after night as mine has been prayed for. I want you to feel as I feel, to know as I know what it is to live with death in your heart.'

Standing on the dark landing, Miriam struggled to release the breath from her locked throat, yet still she held it, for to loose it would be to scream and go on screaming for all the pain of her childhood, for all the days and nights she had never known her mother's love, for a bitterness that held her at its centre.

Hearing the latch lift, she walked slowly down

the stairs. Ralph was beside the table in the middle of which stood a small green bottle.

The shelves in their wrappings still held to her chest, Miriam glanced at the bottle, her brows coming together.

'It is for her.' Drawing off jacket and muffler, he returned them to the hook on the door. 'For the child.'

Quickly pushing the shelves back into the oven, Miriam picked up the bottle. 'Medicine! You got her medicine?'

'No!' Ralph felt his heart twist as he caught the hope in her eyes. 'It's not medicine, but maybe it will work as well as anything a doctor could give. It is holy water. I got it from St Matthew's.'

'The priest gave it to you? But I thought ... Mother said...'

'The priest did not give it to me, there was no priest there to ask.'

'You stole it!' Her fingers closing tight about the ribbed body of the bottle, Miriam's eyes widened.

'Some might say that.' Crossing to the hearth, Ralph looked down at the tiny form in the drawer. 'There was no priest to ask it of so I asked it of the Lord. The church is His house so I reckoned the water was His to give. Water used at a christening would be no different from that which is in that bottle, except it would be in a font; the blessing given over it would be the same, making both as holy. You understand, Miriam.' He swung round to face the girl watching him. 'If the church will not baptise your child, then we must.'

'But ... but we can't!' Shock reducing her voice to a whisper, she placed the bottle back on the table, drawing her hand away with a quick guilty movement.

'Why can't we?' he demanded loudly. 'Wearing a long gown and a collar turned back to front can't have *so* much influence with the Lord. If what you say comes from the heart, then He will listen. Is that not what we were taught in school and on all those Sundays we spent sitting on hard benches, listening to sermons that went on for-ever?'

Her glance going from the bottle to his face, she whispered. 'It ... it might be a sin.'

'Any more of a sin than leaving a child un-baptised, allowing it no place in heaven or on earth?' His tone softened. 'The real sin is in not being brave enough to do it, Miriam. But think of the child, think of your daughter.' Bending over the makeshift crib, he lifted the baby, handing her to his sister. 'You must decide.'

Half hidden by the shawl, the tiny eyelids traced with veins were closed; the flesh stretched taut over a face pale and anaemic in the sallow gleam of the oil lamp.

What if her mother's words were true? Miriam lifted a tiny hand, pressing it to her lips. What if her baby should die without the benefit of baptism, be nameless forever?

'Help me, Ralph,' she whispered on a sob. 'Help me name my daughter.'

Fixing his eyes on a face somehow made more beautiful by the sorrow upon it, Ralph felt every muscle tighten in his stomach, and in his heart he

274

spoke to his God. *If there is sin in what we do then that sin is mine. Visit it on me alone.*

As Miriam bent her face to the child, crooning softly against the downy head, he took a small china dish from the dresser, emptying the contents of the bottle into it.

'Unwrap the shawl.' He smiled, trying to give confidence to the girl whose hands shook as she did as he asked.

On the mantelshelf the tin clock ticked somnolently, its sound the only hymn that rose as Ralph touched his hand to the dish. 'I am no priest,' he said quietly, 'but I bring this child to Thy mercy.'

Taking the baby, he held it cradled in one arm, searching his memory for words he had heard only once in his life and then only as a six-year-old boy.

'Who brings this child to be baptised?'

Catching his nod, Miriam answered, 'I do. Miriam Adena Bryce.'

It had seemed to him as a child that the christening of Miriam had gone on for hours. He knew he could not reproduce the full proper ceremony. But they were only words; a few well meant would serve as well as a thousand said for effect. But knowing their importance to his sister, he would do his best.

'What name is given to this child?'

Name! Only now did she think of that. She had not chosen a name. Had her life been that of a daughter beloved of her mother then the name chosen would have been that of the child's grandmother; but she had never been loved, and Leah

275

would not welcome her name being given to a bastard child. Confusion darkening her eyes, Miriam shook her head.

'I don't know. I never thought to choose one.'

'May I choose?'

The question taking her a little by surprise, she looked up. The love reflecting from the blue-grey depths of his eyes gave her the answer. Her brother had cared for her, protecting her wherever he could, and he would care for and protect her child; he should choose her name. With a smile, she nodded.

Beneath his sister's gaze, Ralph glanced at the child crooked in his arm. All around them silence settled, subduing the ticking of the clock, blotting out the hiss of the kettle.

Blood pounding in her temples, breath tight in her throat, Miriam watched Ralph stretch his free hand towards the dish.

Who was right, her mother or her brother? She watched the hand rise from the dish, seeming to see its movement in slow motion. Would the church have rejected her child, condemned it to live without the love of heaven, or was it as Ralph said, that God would love a child regardless of its birth? And what they were doing now? She watched the hand hover above the tiny head. Was that right or wrong? No doubt the church would see it as a sin.

One more sin! The pounding in her head grew louder, filling it until she rocked on her feet from the pain. One more sin for her baby to carry ... she couldn't ... she must not let it happen!

She could stop him. Say the word and Ralph

would stop. She felt her mouth open but the words stayed locked inside.

As if outside herself she watched him reach into the dish, saw the finger rise again into the air.

Behind him a coal slid through the bars of the grate, sending a shower of scarlet sparks bursting into the hearth. Miriam felt a shiver run through her body; the flames and the sparks, it was so like the word pictures painted by her Sunday school teachers. Was it a warning, an omen of what lay in wait for them if they continued? Again she felt herself try to speak but it was Ralph's voice, low and husky, that penetrated the thudding in her head.

'Angela Miriam.' The finger was lowered, tracing the sign of the cross on the tiny forehead. 'I baptise thee in the name of the Father, the Son, and the Holy Spirit.'

'There, it's done!' Almost shoving the baby into Miriam's arms, he swept up the dish, carrying it into the scullery.

Why? Why! Leaning over the shallow sink, Ralph allowed anger and despair to wash over him. What cruel fate had ordained his life should be like this? That he be torn and twisted by a desire that could never be satisfied; plagued with emotion which could never know release; damned with a love that could never be fulfilled.

Seated by the hearth nursing the child in her arms, Miriam smiled as he returned to the living room, her earlier fears forgotten. 'Angela's a name I have not heard before. What made you choose it?'

Returning the dish to the dresser, he kept his

back to her as a fresh tide of emotion threatened to dislodge the defences he had so carefully erected inside himself

'I thought it suited her. It is a beautiful name and she is a beautiful child.'

Forcing himself to turn around, Ralph watched the light play over the auburn head bent over the sleeping child. Angela. What better name for a child one step away from death?

Chapter Eighteen

Her baby was going to live. The weight that had pressed on her heart for several days had lifted and Miriam almost smiled as she carried her mother's supper tray downstairs. The child had twice taken milk today, just a little but it was a start.

Carrying crockery into the scullery, she washed and dried it then took it into the kitchen to replace it on the dresser.

It was like a miracle. She glanced towards the drawer set alongside the hearth. She had been so afraid when they had said the words of baptism, but since the moment Ralph had touched her baby's head with holy water it seemed the process of healing had begun. Already the tiny face had lost some of its awful yellow colour. It seemed Leah's terrible predictions would not come true.

'I'll take Mother's tray up if it's ready?' Ralph

opened his eyes, stretching himself to wakefulness.

Watching her brother extend his long legs across the hearth then push himself from his chair beside the fire, she saw the lines of weariness shadow his eyes. He had insisted he should be the one who sat through the nights at their mother's bedside, as he had sat beside Miriam's, saying she needed rest if she were to have the strength to care for the child and for Leah while he was at work. But the toll it was taking was evident in his face.

'Mother has already had supper,' Miriam said gently, a world of love in her voice. 'I'll make the cocoa then I think you should go to your bed.'

'I'll sit with her till she's well.'

'She does not need you to do that.' Miriam spooned cocoa into heavy china cups. 'She'll call if she needs one of us. You need your rest, Ralph, and you can't take it propped in a chair. Believe me, Mother is much better. In fact, it took me all my time to persuade her to stay in bed.'

Taking the cup from Miriam, he sank back into the chair, gaze resting on the glowing coals. 'Since when did Mother allow herself to be persuaded into anything? She only stayed in bed because she doesn't have the strength yet to climb out of it.'

'Then let me sit with her.'

'No.' He shook his head. 'You have the baby to see to.'

'I can take Angela with me to Mother's room.' Miriam savoured the name on her tongue. Ralph had chosen well.

279

'That would have her out of her bed quicker than a dose of salts!' He smiled grimly. 'Either that or she would die trying. Best not take the child in there.'

Of course, she had not thought of that. Relief at seeing the improvement in her daughter, knowing she was going to get well, had swept other thoughts from Miriam's mind. But her brother was right. To take the child into her mother's room would give rise to nothing but harsh words and bad feeling.

Swallowing the last of his drink, Ralph set the cup on the table. 'If you see to the lamps then I'll carry the child up to your room.'

Miriam nodded then opened the stairs door as he picked up the drawer that held the sleeping child. Ralph was so gentle with her, kissing the tiny head the moment he came into the house, rocking her tenderly in his arms when she cried. He should marry, have a child of his own. But would he do that if it meant leaving his sister in this house?

Closing the door softly, she scooped up the empty cups. Ralph was entitled to a life of his own, a life without a dependent sister and her child ... a life without Leah. Rinsing the cups, she felt the weight creep back into her heart. She must not ask any more of her brother. As soon as their mother was fully recovered, she would take her child and leave.

Miriam woke with a start. The room was bathed in a grey light, it was almost dawn. Was it the baby who had woken her? She listened for several seconds but no sound broke the stillness. Yet something had startled her. Leah? Was it her mother who had called?

Slipping from the bed, she shivered in the cold air. Catching up her shawl, she wrapped it about her shoulders as she bent over the drawer. The child was sleeping, it was no cry from her that had caused Miriam to wake so suddenly.

Deciding against turning up the lamp in case the light disturbed the sleeping infant, she opened the bedroom door, treading softly to her mother's room. Outside she listened. There was no sound, yet as she turned to go back to her own room something seemed to draw her back.

Turning the handle, she pushed the door slowly inward. Ralph slept lightly, the slightest sound would disturb him. The curtains, unlike those of her own room, were drawn close across the windows, shutting out the cold grey light, but beside the bed the lamp burned on a low wick that sent shadows flickering darkly over the walls. Miriam had always been afraid of this room, never readily coming into it as a young child. And now ... the fear that had held her then still remained.

Her eyes becoming accustomed to the dimness, she picked out the shape of the chair beside the fireplace, the embers of the fire only just showing red, the figure of her brother slumped in it. Her mother could not have called or Ralph would have heard, but they were both still sleeping. It had been purely her imagination.

Her hand still on the door handle she glanced towards her mother's bed – the breath snatched

from her lungs at what she saw. From the whiteness of the pillow a shadowed face was turned
towards her, the light of the lamp picking up the
black gleam of two glittering eyes, lips drawn
back in a venomous smile.

'You think all to be going well with that spawn
of Saul Marsh...'

The whisper was no more than a breath in the
silence but the sheer malevolence of it struck
with the force of lightning. Miriam's fingers
gripped the handle as she recoiled, her own eyes
held by the glistening triumph in her mother's.

'...but you be wrong. The mark of the devil has
been wiped away. The fruit of evil is destroyed.'

Breath still held in her throat, she felt the
magnetism of those watching eyes, felt them
holding her while they sought into her soul.
Then, slowly, the lids lowered and she was free.

You think all be going well ... but you be wrong...

The words hammered against her brain. But
this time there was no truth in what her mother
had uttered. Her child was on the mend.
Whatever had ailed it from its birth was over
now; Angela had taken milk from the pipette at
supper last night and was still sleeping.

Still sleeping? The fear that had never been far
from her since her daughter's birth returned,
chilling Miriam to the bone. The child had not
woken for some ten hours. Surely that was not as
it should be? Were newborns not supposed to
feed every three or four hours?

Fear turning to blind terror she ran back to her
own room, dropping to her knees beside the
drawer that served her baby for a crib. In the

shadow of the blanket wrapped about the tiny head she saw the lashes of closed eyes and lips that were slightly parted.

Her mother *was* wrong. Her baby was well and asleep. Relief chasing terror, her breath released with a choking gasp, Miriam leaned over the drawer, touching a finger to the child's brow.

Beyond the window the grey pre-dawn changed to a pale pink glow, throwing a flushed light into the room – and over the face of the child, and its mother whose mouth had widened in a silent scream.

'Let her go, Miriam. Let me take her.' Ready to leave for the mine, Ralph had brought a cup of tea to his mother, then seeing his sister's bedroom door wide open had called softly to waken her. He had called several times then gone to the door to find Miriam rocking back and forth on her knees, the child clutched to her breast.

'You have to let her go, Miriam.'

Gently, his own heart twisting with pity, he prised her arms from around the small bundle.

'It was my fault...' Eyes swimming with tears were lifted to his. 'I killed her! I killed my own child!'

Feeling the coldness of the tiny body already stiff within its wrappings, Ralph laid it back in the drawer.

'It was my fault...'

'It was no one's fault!' Pushing himself to his feet, he turned quickly, his voice sharp. If Miriam were allowed to give way to hysteria there was no telling what she might do.

'It was.' Choking on her own sobs, Miriam's

hands struck out as Ralph grabbed her shoulders. 'It was me ... my sin caused her death ... Mother said...'

'Mother said!' He spat the words. 'I've never known her say anything not meant to hurt.'

'But it's true! She said the Lord would not suffer my child to live, that He would...'

'Miriam, listen to me.' Pulling his sister gently into his arms, Ralph held her against his chest. 'The Lord has not taken your child because of what you did. He does not take the life of the innocent to pay the price of sin.'

'But I...'

'You made a mistake,' Ralph told her softly. 'You thought Saul Marsh was in love with you. Neither heaven nor I can blame you for that.'

'But Mother...'

Ralph's arms tightened around the trembling frame of his sister. 'Mother would blame you if the sun failed to rise.'

Words fighting their way out between sobs, Miriam pulled away from him.

'But she *knew*,' she whispered. 'She *knew* my baby was dead ... Ralph, our mother *knew!*'

'The fruit of evil is destroyed.'

Once more Miriam saw those words being mouthed at her, the black eyes glistening from the shadowed bed, and again she trembled. Her mother had wanted the child dead, that was why she had prevented Miriam from going to the village for help; and she had allowed it to happen. She may not have killed her baby by having it out of wedlock, but she might have caused its death by not getting a doctor. Heaven might well

284

forgive one sin but it could not overlook the other!

'Come downstairs.' Ralph took her arm.

'No.' Miriam tried to pull free. 'I can't leave her, I can't leave my baby.'

'She will take no more harm.' He turned her gently, holding her firmly as she tried to return to the child. 'Come and have some tea, it will warm you.'

Passing her mother's open door, Miriam glanced in. The same glistening dark eyes locked on hers and the thin mouth parted in a mocking smile that was purely evil, the same smile she had seen in the grey dawn.

A smile that said, *I told you so.*

'If you don't want to cause her more suffering you will do as say.'

Leah Bryce looked at her son. The few hours since the death of Miriam's child had marked his face with the lines of years.

'If I could rise from this bed, I would do it myself. As it is you must be the one. I tell you, an unchristened soul will not be taken into the church yard. And that child of your sister's were not only unchristened, it were a bastard!'

'A child cannot be punished for the circumstances of its birth.' Ralph looked at his mother, guilt rising in him at his own revulsion. Why did she hate Miriam so, her own daughter?

'Try telling that to the priest along of St Matthew's!' Leah smiled. 'I've no doubt as to the answer he will give, but even should he agree there are those in Brades Village won't stand to see such as that child laid in consecrated ground. Far better heed what I tell you. It must be buried out on the heath.'

'But we can't ... it would break Miriam's heart.'

Like her broke your own when her lay with Saul Marsh on that same heath. Leah kept the thought tight in her heart. Like it would go on breaking every day of his life. Like hers had broken so many years ago.

'And hearing the priest say no to the burying of her child, to have it turned away from the church, will that not break her heart?'

Was his mother speaking the truth? Ralph looked at her, her skeletal body hardly raising the covers of her bed. Or was it merely another of her vindictive plays, another way of piling grief upon grief?

'You said the church would not agree to take a child who was not christened,' he said quietly. 'But Miriam's child *was* christened.'

Beneath him, staring up from the pillows, his mother's eyes narrowed to dark slits. 'That spawn of sin were christened? You lie! No priest would...'

'Maybe no priest, Mother,' Ralph interrupted. 'But I would and did. I christened Miriam's daughter.'

'*YOU!* You baptised that child?'

'Yes.' Ralph felt the heat of his mother's anger. 'I did it the night before last.'

'And you think that makes it acceptable in the eyes of the Lord!' Leah's laughter was harsh as she sank back into the pillows.

'I don't care what is or is not acceptable in the

eyes of the Lord, it was my sister's eyes that counted with me. I did it for her.'

'But it would do no good, you must both have realised that? Given no priest to speak the words, it would still take water that had been blessed, holy water, to anoint the child's head. Without it all words are null and void, and you had only water from the scullery pump.'

The triumph that gleamed from the usually dull eyes, the satisfaction threading her voice, brought a coldness to Ralph's spine and a hardness to his heart. Whatever had happened in the earlier years of his mother's life, her blatant exultation over the possible damnation of an innocent babe was an appalling spectacle. He felt nothing for her but revulsion.

'I am *not* sorry to disappoint you, Mother.' His cold smile matched Leah's. 'But the water I used to anoint the child's head was holy water.'

'Don't think by lying you can fool me!' Leah smirked. 'Your saying words over a basin of water counts no more with the Lord than any mutterings you might have made over that child.'

'Perhaps.' Ralph allowed himself a bitter smile. 'But then, you see, Mother, I am *not* lying. The water I used was as holy as any used in a baptismal font. It had been blessed by a true minister of the church, and even though I am not consecrated to use it, my doing so could not take that blessing from it. It remained holy no matter who used it or where.'

'But how?' Disbelief took the place of mockery. 'The priest would give no holy water for such ... such an offence to the Lord.'

'No priest was asked. I took the water from the church.'

Leah's eyes widened a fraction, showing the return of triumph. 'You stole it!' It was almost joyful. 'You stole holy water from the church? Then the baptism you performed with it serves no purpose. It will find no favour with the Lord!'

'Yes, I stole that water!' His voice throbbing with the strength of his emotions, Ralph stared down at his mother. 'And if that finds offence with the Lord, then so be it. But if you believe He would refuse His love and mercy to a babe baptised in it, then you and I worship a different God.'

He strode to the door then turned back, his eyes going to those that followed him. 'A different God, Mother,' he said softly. 'But when death claims me I will be ready to face mine with my sins, sure of His mercy. But you ... how will you answer for yours? What mercy can you expect from a God who shows no love for a child innocent of sin? Think of that, Mother. Think of it very carefully!'

Clearing the table of the meal his sister had not touched, Ralph glanced to where she had sat, still as a statue, since early morning. She had not wept since he'd brought her downstairs but neither had she spoken. Yet he knew that deep inside her soul she was screaming.

So how could he tell her what their mother had said: that her child must be put into an un-marked grave, buried in secret out on the heath?

Carrying dishes into the scullery he washed

them, his fingers unused to such a task and clumsy in the operation.

He could not do that to Miriam. Returning the dishes to the dresser, he glanced again to where she sat, the light from the fire gilding her hair. But what if the child were refused burial by the church, turned away like some parasite, would that not hurt Miriam even more? One way or another, the child *must* be buried.

Going to his sister, he dropped to his knees before her, taking into his hands that despite the fire were cold as ice. 'Miriam.' He spoke softly, as if waking her from sleep. 'Miriam, the child. She ... we have to...'

He broke off, the words like stones in his throat, too hard for him to speak.

'I know, Ralph.' Freeing one hand, Miriam laid it on the head that had dropped into her lap. 'She must be buried.'

He had expected tears and wild cries but her voice was empty of feeling, a strange calm pervading it, and when he lifted his face the only tears were his own.

'I know that too,' Miriam said softly. 'I know what Mother said. The church will give no burial. So I must do that for my daughter. But I don't know if taking her on to the heath ... I don't know if I can do that alone.'

Staring into a face as pale as that of the child lying dead in its makeshift crib, Ralph felt his heart twist.

'You will not be alone.' He felt the words catch in his throat, tears he could not hold back warm on his lashes. 'You will never be alone, Miriam.

289

Not so long as I live.'

He made for the brew house, tears blinding his eyes and making his steps uncertain. Casting about, he found an empty box stored in a corner and for the second time in as many days was grateful for his mother's habit of hoarding things.

In the yard he brushed the fine film of cobwebs from the box. It was made from wood and sturdy. It would serve their purpose well enough.

Once more in the scullery, he halted. He would rather take the box straight upstairs, place the child in it and carry it away; sparing Miriam the heartbreak of seeing it. But to get to the bedroom he must pass through the kitchen. Concealing it as best he could, he re-entered the room which was darkening now as shadows encroached. Yet enough light remained to show him the silent agonised intake of breath and the trembling mouth as his sister rose to her feet at the sight of her child's coffin.

'No.' He shook his head. 'Stay there, Miriam, I will do what has to be done.'

The trembling about her lips did not stop though her voice was calm as before. 'You are so kind to me, Ralph, and to Angela. But who better to tend her daughter for the grave than her mother?'

Knowing it useless to argue, Ralph took his sister's cold hand, holding it tightly as they walked up the narrow stairs together.

Teeth clenched against the tears that threatened to burst her heart, Miriam washed the tiny body with water from the jug on her wash-stand then

290

wrapped it in a fresh piece of huckaback, winding it about the cold little arms and across the tiny chest; but as Ralph held out his hands to take the child she clutched it to her breast, holding her face to the icy cheek.

'I love you,' she whispered. 'I will always love you. Oh, my sweet darling, I'm sorry. So very sorry...'

'Miriam.' Ralph's hand touching her shoulder, she kissed the face of her daughter for the last time.

Across the landing Leah's voice came, harsh and strident in its demand to know what was going on. But it was ignored as Ralph laid the body in the crude wooden box.

'No!' Miriam seemed to wake suddenly from some dream that had held her half waking since finding her child dead. 'Not like that. I don't want her to ... to leave like that.'

'What be you two doing?' Leah's voice, alive with frustration, came in at the open door.

'Go to her, Ralph.' Miriam walked over to where the box stood on the chair beneath the window. 'Go to our mother. Tell her what she wants to hear – that the child of the daughter she detests is dead and will lie in an unknown grave.'

Recognising that it was as much a plea to be given a few last moments alone with her child as it was for him to satisfy their mother, Ralph turned from the room.

Going to the chest of drawers, Miriam took from it the warm woollen dress that had been her brother's gift, then the Sunday best petticoat she had not taken with her the day she'd left this house. Lastly she withdrew the narrow silk maroon-coloured ribbons that had been her childhood treasure.

'Now they will be yours, my darling.' Tenderly she smiled down into the face that seemed carved from yellow wax, the lips still slightly parted. Lifting the baby, she held it to her, feeling the coldness of it through the huckaback, reaching through the cotton of her own blouse to fasten about her heart.

'I have to let you go, my precious one,' she murmured against the down-covered head. 'But you will always be with me in my heart. No one can ever take you from there.' Then, her face still against the child's, she lifted her gaze to the window.

'Please,' she murmured, 'please don't turn my child away. Don't punish her for the sin that was mine. Let her namesakes bring her to You, please, Lord. Take my own angel into Your keeping.'

Carrying the stiff little body and laying it on the bed, she folded the dress, fitting it in a soft layer in the box, hiding the rough discoloured wood. Then, every movement a blow to her heart, she draped the petticoat about the still form, arranging the deep lace of the hem around the waxen face. Laying the child in the crude coffin, she folded the silken ribbons into bows to decorate the little breast, then leaned down to kiss the tiny mouth.

'You look very pretty, my darling,' she murmured, tears at last bursting through the barrier she had raised. 'The angels will not be able to resist loving you, just as I do.

'Please,' Miriam prayed again, 'take my daughter into Your keeping.'

Straightening up, she lifted her eyes to the window. Beyond the panes the edges of the dark clouds turned to brilliant silver.

Chapter Nineteen

'Wrap yourself warmly, it's bitterly cold out on the heath.'

Ralph glanced at his sister. She was so pale, so fragile-looking, her face full of anguish and despair. The urge to hold her burned strongly in him; the love he felt for her threatening to break the chains he had bound about it.

He watched as she reached for her shawl, throwing it about her shoulders. He had reasoned with her, wanting her to remain here in the house. What was to be done, he'd told her, could be done by him alone; there was no need for her to go with him on to the heath.

She had looked at him then, lovely eyes swimming with tears, mouth trembling, and he had realised there was every need. Miriam needed to be with her child at the end, to be with it at its burial.

'Mother must be told.' The pain in his sister's face matched by that in his heart, Ralph turned, reaching for the box of matches that stood behind the tin clock on the mantelpiece. It was an excuse to look away from her. There were matches in the brew house but he could not look at her much longer without telling her – telling her he loved her, not as a brother but as a man loves a woman he wants for his wife; telling her that no matter what had gone before, Marsh ... the child ... he, Ralph, loved her and would always love her.

Her eyes fixed on the small box lying open on the seat of a chair, Miriam stared at the face of her daughter. She would never hold her again, never feel the warmth of that tiny body against her breast or feel those perfect fingers curl about her own. She would never hear her laughter, never dry her tears. They would walk together once across the heath but her child would not see the hoarfrost that gowned the gorse in silver; she would not feel the touch of the breeze in her hair or the nip of cold on her tiny nose. For her daughter was dead.

Miriam stepped closer, stretching out her hand to touch a finger to that cold cheek. 'We must say goodbye, my darling,' she whispered. 'We have to part. But you will never leave my heart. I will love you always. Goodbye, my little Angela, my own sweet angel. Goodbye.'

Ralph had not watched his sister but her low whisper caught his ears, the sobs shaking her voice touching his heart. If only the child had been stronger, if only it could have lived for Miriam's sake! He would have cared for it, helped in the raising of it as though it were his own.

His own! His fingers tightening about the match box, Ralph stared down at the hearth. There would be no child of his getting, no woman would bear his children, for the one he loved was beyond his reach; he had loved her all of her life but she was forbidden him.

Need and denial clashed in his throat so the words rasped harshly he spoke without looking up.

'Mother has to be told we will be leaving the house for a while. She might call and wonder why we give no answer. Will you go up to her?'

'Yes. I will tell her where ... where we are going.'

Hearing her tread on the stairs, Ralph took up the box that lay on the chair beneath the window. The lid had to be fastened down but not in front of Miriam. She must not see the nails driven in, endure the agony of seeing her baby being closed away, the memory of that beautiful little face being covered forever would live with Miriam all of her life, but his sister had suffered enough, this at least he could keep from her.

Carrying the box into the brew house, he laid it on the rough bench he had once helped his father to build. Then, memory guiding him in the darkness, he located the candle that was kept standing on a saucer. The matches from the living room still in his pocket, he did not bother to grope along the unseen shelf to find the box kept there. The candle lit, Ralph reached for the tool chest that had been his father's.

Selecting a hammer, he took a handful of short iron nails from a tin box, laying them beside the makeshift coffin. Reaching for the lid that had stayed in the brew house, he hesitated, looking for the last time at the tiny face cradled in a froth of lace.

She was so small, so perfect, this child of his sister's. Together they would have given her so much love, so much happiness; given this child all that their mother had never given them. She would have been the child Ralph could never have. Now even that had been snatched away.

The heart inside him feeling it would break, he touched his lips to a face that was cold as marble. 'Goodbye, my little one,' he murmured. 'Goodbye, my little love. May heaven protect you.'

Placing the lid on the box, he glanced at the painted words picked out by the light of the candle. Sunlight Soap. The irony of it stung. The child it held had never seen the sunlight, never felt the warmth of it on her face. He brought the hammer down in a vicious, angry blow. *The sins of the fathers...* The words of so many Sunday school lessons returned to him now. The child in this box had paid that price, paid for the sins of the father she would never see.

One by one, Ralph drove the nails home, closing the child into her eternal home. She would never see Saul Marsh. But he, Ralph Bryce, would see him. Driving the last nail into the soft wood, Ralph stared beyond the flickering shadows into the blackness.

Yes, one day *he* would see Saul Marsh.

In the living room, Miriam waited, her shawl drawn tightly over her head and crossed beneath her breasts. Looking up as Ralph entered through the scullery, the tears that marked her ashen face glinted like crystals.

Seeing her stiffen as she caught sight of the box, Ralph reached for her hand. It would be a pathetically small following that took the child to its grave, but it would be done with more love than accompanied any king.

Without speaking a word, he led his sister out into the night and across the silent moon-washed heath. Coming to a spot from which the house could just be seen, he laid the box on the ground.

Using the heel of his boot, he chopped at the hard ground. Having loosened a large enough patch he knelt, and with the moon his only light, his sister's sobs the only sound, clawed at the earth with his bare hands. The cold and damp of the hard ground bit into his fingers, making the task slow and painful.

Beside him, Miriam caught up the pathetic coffin, sheltering it beneath her shawl, holding it to her, the rough wood hard against her chest. The hole that Ralph was digging, the dark mouth opening in the cold ground, was for her baby; this was the cradle she would lie in. Clutching the box with tight protective arms, she rocked back and forth, face resting against it as she sobbed.

Judging the hole deep enough Ralph leaned back on his heels, his hands tingling from the grip of the frost.

'I'll take her now, Miriam.' Unable still to refer to the coffin, Ralph held out both hands.

'No!' Miriam clutched her burden more tightly, eyes drowning in tears glistening like silver lamps in the moonlight. 'No, I can't. I can't leave my baby. I can't ... I can't!'

The agony of her cry tearing at him, Ralph got to his feet. 'It has to be done, Miriam,' he said softly. 'You know that, don't you? The child must be laid to rest.'

Just as gently, every movement cutting into his own heart, he parted the folds of the shawl, prising the box from her arms.

Dropping again to his knees, he lowered it into the ground.

'No!' Her cry one of sheer agony, Miriam flung herself face down, reaching towards the tiny coffin. 'No ... oh, dear God, not here ... please, not here.'

For a brief moment Ralph stared at the sobbing figure of his sister hanging over the dark opening in the ground. Then, his mouth hardening, he lifted her to her feet.

'No, not here, Miriam. Your child will not lie here. She will lie in St Matthew's church yard.'

'But how? The priest...'

Retrieving the little coffin, Ralph stood up.

'There is a way,' he answered, voice heavy with emotion. 'None but us and one other will know, but you have my promise – your daughter will be buried with benefit of book and priest.'

Scraping the loose earth back into the hollow with the side of his boot, he stamped it down, then began the walk back across the night held heath.

Insisting his sister stay in the house, Ralph followed the same route to the church as he had a few nights before. The box he carried, half hidden beneath his jacket, raised no enquiry from the conductor of the tram. The folk of Brades Village often asked for their groceries to be packed in a box, soap or otherwise. The wood could be used afterwards, warming many a cold grate.

Leaving the tram, he walked the short distance to St Matthew's, breathing a sigh of relief when he met no one along the way. Beyond the lych gate the church rose black and compelling against the sky, but that was not where Ralph's steps led. Glancing first to right then to left, hesitating only to listen for footsteps, he continued on past the ornate arch of the gate, going instead to where a small house stood, squat and low-roofed, close beside it.

His glance taking in the faint gleam of a lamp that shone somewhere inside, Ralph turned up the collar of his jacket, pulling his muffler across his face so only his eyes were visible. He walked quickly around the side of the house, coming to the narrow confined space that was boasted of as a yard. Knocking on the scullery door, he stepped back against the lee of the brew house, using its shadows further to disguise himself.

'Who be there?' Yards away the door of the house scraped open.

Noah Billings, short frame and stooped shoulders giving him the look of a vulture, was revealed in the light of the lamp held above his head.

'Be there a buryin' in the offing?' Ralph kept his voice low, giving it a rough rasping sound, using the local dialect more than was usual for him.

As sexton for the church and also its grave digger, Noah was not unused to such visits late at night, nor unfamiliar with their cause or the poverty that prompted them. Not everybody could afford the services of a priest.

'Ar, there be one in the mornin'. Who be askin'?'

Ignoring the question, Ralph reached into his pocket and as he stretched out his hand the moonlight shone on the silver coin in its palm. He as well as Noah knew of the practice of slipping a still-born child into the grave along with the coffin it was meant for; he also knew the price the old man asked, sixpence, but the payment he offered was twice that. For a shilling Noah Billings would ask no more questions.

'There be a box that goes along of this.' Ralph's tone was guttural, eyes fixed on the man though keeping in the shadows. 'Will you be takin' of both?'

There was no hesitation. The old man's free hand shot out, gnarled fingers closing over the coin.

'Set the box down along of where you stand.' Noah pressed the shilling deep into the pocket of his waistcoat. 'Then get you away. You need 'ave no fear as to Noah Billings not holding to a bargain.'

Deciding against the tram, Ralph walked home, the wind keen and cutting against his face. No, he need have no fear of the sexton forgetting his promise, though it had not been put into words. Tomorrow Miriam's child would find its rest in holy ground. God grant it bring them both peace.

Cresting the small rise that gave on to the house, Ralph stared at its dark silhouette, feeling the old familiar bitterness rise in his throat.

God grant it bring them both peace.

He would ask no less for Miriam or for the child so soon to lie in someone else's grave. But what peace could there be for him?

Standing there, the wind cutting through his thin jacket, he laughed – a low, almost derisive sound. A laugh that held all his pain, all his hurt, that recognised the hopelessness of his situation. There could be no peace for Ralph Bryce, a man in love with his own sister.

So the child was dead. Leah stared at a ceiling swathed in deep shadow but made no move to put a match to the lamp beside her bed. The feeling that had come to her in the night had not been wrong. And now they were out there on the heath, brother to bury his sister's bastard. Thin lips drew back in the semblance of a smile but it was one that held no mirth and knew no pity.

It was as it should be, as she had wanted, as the Lord willed. But despite the last thought, Leah felt a shiver against her spine.

'What mercy can you expect?' The words her son had thrown at her returned but they brought no fear with them. She had stopped asking for mercy long ago and expected none now. But what did that matter! Her life had been little short of a living hell since *he* had chosen another woman over her, what difference would eternity in purgatory hold? None! Leah stared into the shadows. It would be worth the reckoning.

So the child had been baptised with holy water? She laughed softly, hearing it echo back from the silence of the empty house. But though Ralph might believe that to make a difference, Miriam

301

would not. The strength of her religious up-bringing, the faith the church and Leah herself had instilled in her, would bind her mind with ties too strong for her to break. And though much of Leah's own instruction had been mis-leading it had served her purpose, her one true purpose ... revenge.

Lifting herself from the pillows, she threw back the covers but as she tried to move her legs the left one remained still as a felled tree. Leah stared at it. That was not all the damage her fall had bequeathed. The left side of her face was numb to the touch, as was the whole of that side of her body.

A stroke! She needed no doctor to tell her that. She had seen her husband die of the same. After several weeks of illness he had gone quickly with-out regaining consciousness, but she ... how long must she live chained to a chair or bed?

In the darkness she seemed to hear the mock-ing words her son had spat. *'A different God!'*

Grasping the covers with one hand, Leah drew them over her legs. Lying back, she closed her eyes but that did not shut out the memory of that tall figure beside her bed, grey-blue eyes glinting like tempered steel as he looked down at her. Nor did the pounding in her temples drown out the memory of the words he had spoken to her then.

'You deserve what has happened to you, but you do not deserve to die. You should lie there for the rest of your life, and perhaps you will. Is this the mercy of your God, Mother? Maybe, like your son, you should have worshipped a lesser one!'

'I beg your pardon, sir, but there is a matter I believe I should bring to your attention.'

Clayton Rawley was averse to being disturbed whilst in his study and irritation showed in his abrupt reply. 'You deal with it, Baxter. That *is* what I pay you for, isn't it?'

The butler waited one second. 'I believe, sir, that this is a matter you would prefer to deal with yourself.'

Throwing down his pen, Clayton looked up, exasperation clear on his face. 'For God's sake, man, can't you see I'm busy! Oh, well, what is it?'

'It concerns your guest, sir, Mr Marsh.'

Marsh! Exasperation gave way to interest. Clayton was still not satisfied that young man was all he pretended.

'Close the door, Baxter.' He beckoned the butler further into the room.

'It is something Mrs Baxter and the girl Jinks said to me, sir, something rather disturbing.'

'Well?' Clayton was in no mood for dramatic intervals.

Clearing his throat, Baxter gauged his employer's mood. Should what he was about to say be a lie after all then he as well as Ginny Jinks would be seeking a new post.

'It appears that Mr Marsh tried to rape the girl who left here a few weeks ago, the one Mr Ethan found wandering on the road. That is what triggered the return of her memory, sir.'

'Like bloody hell it would!' Clayton exploded. 'Supposing it were true, which is impossible.'

'Mrs Baxter assured me of it, sir.'

'I am not disputing the fact, your wife might

303

well believe what Jinks told her, but I *know* Marsh could not have committed any such offence. Come to that so should you, Baxter. You helped nurse the man. Speaking plainly, you know very well he was emasculated. The fellow who cut his purse also cut off the man's balls! So there is no way he could have done what he is accused of.'

Baxter maintained his customary deference but beneath it his voice was firm. His wife was not easily taken in by the prattling of the staff, and though the girl Jinks might have varnished the truth a little, his Sally would not have let him come to Rawley unless she were convinced there was something to the girl's story.

'Forgive me for contradicting you, sir. I can only assume that was the diagnosis you were given by the doctor, and that was certainly the impression he gave me. At first.'

Clayton surveyed the man who had served him faithfully for many years. Baxter would not lightly make an accusation against any man.

'The doctor told me Marsh had lost his manhood. What does that make him if not a eunuch?'

Baxter nodded slightly. 'What indeed, sir? Were it true.'

A frown appearing on Clayton's brow, he leaned forward on the desk. 'Are you telling me he did not lose it?'

A little of his earlier apprehension fading, Baxter felt himself on firmer ground as he saw the glint in Clayton's eyes. Whatever the master had been told of Marsh's condition, it appeared to have fallen somewhat short of the truth.

'Yes, sir.' His answer was firm. 'That is what I believe. Mr Marsh suffered the loss of one testicle, that much is true, and the weapon used on him cut the other – but not so deeply as to sever it. The angle of the blow fortunately deflected the weapon sideways. Instead of finishing the job it was intended to do, it came down on to the inner thigh. In a subsequent examination the doctor told me that, barring infection, there was a good chance of a partial recovery. There was no infection, sir.' Baxter paused but when Clayton remained silent went on, 'I am sorry you were not kept more fully informed. I assumed the doctor gave you his report...'

'Yes ... yes.' Clayton waved one hand.

'I did not feel it my place to discuss Mr Marsh's condition with you, sir.' Baxter sounded apologetic. 'I beg your pardon if that was wrong of me.'

'Wrong ... of course it was not wrong!' Clayton banged a fist hard down on the desk. 'It is not you who did wrong, it is Marsh. He led me to believe he was totally castrated. But why?'

'If I might suggest, sir – could it have been as a cover, to protect himself against just such an accusation as Jinks has made?'

It was more than probable, Clayton thought. Was that also the reason for his telling Edwina the same lie ... or had he told her nothing at all?

Glancing up, he said, 'Bring the girl Jinks in here, and ask Mrs Baxter if she would be so good as to come too.'

An hour later, having listened to the maid tell

her story, Clayton reached for his pen. Sadler should know just what sort of man he was getting for a son-in-law.

Saul Marsh sat the horse with ease. He had acclimatised quickly to the good life, but there was one thing about the old one that intrigued him, and the more he thought of it the more interested he was. The child Miriam Bryce carried ... his child. It was due about this time. He calculated quickly in his head. Yes, it should be born now. He was a father. He smiled slowly, urging the horse forward with a touch of his heel. What was his first born, a son or a daughter? Not that it mattered overmuch, he would be having no contact with it. But its mother... The smile widened, the slight droop at one corner of his mouth giving it a twisted look. Miriam Bryce would provide him with a little casual entertainment.

Keeping to the heath, he followed a wide circle that would bring him to the back of the old farm house. He wanted no chance meeting with anyone from the village. And if the widow Bryce were home... Saul's smile disappeared. He knew how he would deal with that harridan. A sharp blow with his riding crop and she would give him no trouble!

The whole place seemed deserted. Hitching the reins to a post that had once been part of a fence, Saul cast a quick glance about the empty yard. It might almost seem the family had up and left; almost, except for the sheets pegged to the washing line.

Soft leather boots making no sound on the cobbles, he crossed to the brew house, the smile returning to his mouth.

The interior was deep with shadow, the watery afternoon light squeezing in at the door having little effect on the dimness. Saul studied the confined space. A tin bath hung from one handle, an enamelled bowl complete with a pair of wooden laundry tongs sat in a shallow brown sink, and beside the copper a zinc bucket gleamed in the semi-darkness. In the farthest corner a large washtub stood with its base to the ceiling, crowned with a heavy dolly.

Despite its greyness Saul could see the cleanliness of the little room, quarry tiles still glowing red from a recent scrubbing; he smiled, but grimly as he remembered his mother's slip-shod house, each room dotted with flutters, litter left lying about, nothing having its specific place, and nothing returned to it supposing it had. But all of that was over for Saul Marsh. He had found his place in life and would not be changing it. Master of Glebe House! No, he would not be changing that.

The wetness of the quarries bore witness to the fact that someone had only recently been at work in the brew house, yet now it was empty. Saul stepped back from the door. The one he sought must be in the house.

Footsteps kept deliberately soft, he crossed to the scullery, making no sound as he entered and none as he stood at the door of the kitchen.

The table, part covered with an old blanket folded to give extra thickness, was spread with a pillow case set for ironing. Glancing towards the fireplace, he saw Miriam lift a heavy flat-iron from the bracket where it had stood heating against the coals, their light reflected in the deep auburn of her hair. Yes, he was going to enjoy a little casual entertainment.

Keeping silent he watched as she touched a finger to her tongue then to the iron, testing its warmth. Then, still not moving, he spoke softly.

'So you came home after all, Miriam?'

Her eyes flew to him, the iron dropping heavily on to the upturned saucer used as a stand. The crack of splintering china sounded like a gunshot in the quiet house.

'Why are you here?'

'Why?' His tread soft, wary as a hunting cat's, he moved forward into the room. 'Why, to see you, of course.'

Miriam felt herself tremble. Saul Marsh was not here to enquire after her health.

'Then you have seen what you came to see. Now please leave.'

'Tut, tut, Miriam. Did your mother not teach you? That is no way to greet a guest.'

Her hand still fast about the handle of the iron, Miriam stared into his eyes, the light from the fire revealing the mockery that illuminated their depths. A mockery that only added to the revulsion already stirring within her.

'A guest is a guest only so long as he is welcome,' she said, clinging to the words, using them for support. 'After that he becomes an intruder. You are an intruder in my mother's house, I ask you to leave.'

308

'Oh, yes, your delightful mother. Where is she?'

'Upstairs. She can't move from her bed.'

Miriam realised her mistake as soon as the words came from her lips, but it was too late.

'And your brother is at the mine.' Saul moved towards the table, his body sinuous, threatening. 'That leaves you and me, Miriam, just us two together ... as I had hoped.'

Her fingers tightening their grasp on the rapidly cooling iron, Miriam lifted it, holding it before her like a weapon. 'Go away,' she breathed. 'Go away now.'

'Or you will do what?' The derisive smile still playing about his mouth, he drew out a chair, settling his long frame on to it. 'Hit me with that iron? I don't think so, Miriam, violence is not your style.'

'Please, Saul!' It was almost a sob, her shoulders slumping as she replaced the iron on the bracket. 'Please, go away!'

'Oh, I will, Miriam, I will. When I have what I came for.'

'What ... what did you come for?' Fear taking away the last of her strength, she leaned against the table.

'Nothing you have not given me before, and if I remember correctly, enjoyed the giving...'

The sorrow and loss of the previous days weighing upon her, Miriam felt her knees buckle.

'...the same as you would have enjoyed again had not that housemaid interrupted us. But there will be none to interrupt us here...'

He was speaking of his attempt to rape her, making it seem as if she had been a willing party and would be again!

'But first let me ask about our child. Just what is it I am father to? Do I have a son or a daughter?'

He had owned to the child at last! The thought beat dully in Miriam's terrified mind. Named himself father to her baby. How she had once longed to hear those same words, but now they meant nothing. They were empty as her heart was empty, dead as her child was dead.

'Well ... what have I sired?'

Glancing at the hand lying casually on the table, Miriam seemed to see it from somewhere outside herself, detached from reality as she noted the clean finger nails, the skin devoid of coal dust. And his speech... Saul no longer used the dialect that distinguished the people of Brades Village. He was intent upon learning the ways of the gentry, but in other ways he had not changed. He was here to seduce or rape, and she knew it would matter little to him which it turned out to be.

'I ... I had a daughter.'

'A daughter.' He lifted his fingers in a dismissive gesture. 'Too bad. So where is it?'

Tears welled, filling her throat at the memory of the tiny body she had held against her own, the little mouth that had not been given time to smile at her, the mauve veined lids closed over eyes that promised to be beautiful, the small jaundiced face cradled in white lace.

'Angela is ... is dead. She died a week ago.'

'A sorrow or a blessing?' He saw she was holding the table for support.

'How can you talk like that, as if the child's life counted for nothing?' Eyes green as grass met those whose indifference mocked her, tearing down the fences she had built about herself since laying her child in its paltry coffin. Now her whole body shook with the sobs that rose from her soul. 'Unlike you, I wanted my child. I loved her... I loved her.'

Rising slowly, Saul edged the chair away with his heel, eyes never leaving the sobbing girl. 'So you loved our daughter and now she is gone? But I am nothing if not generous, Miriam...'

Grabbing her by the shoulders, he spun her into his arms. His mouth coming close to hers, he ripped her blouse away.

'What has been taken from you, I shall replace. We must see that you have a second child.'

Chapter Twenty

'She seems to have disappeared from the face of the earth!' Ethan Rawley's finely sculpted features were marred by a frown as he paced his father's study. 'I have searched every town for miles around but it seems no one has seen or heard of her.'

Clayton listened. He did not want to tell his son what Baxter had reported. The girl was not what he wanted for Ethan, she was from a class entirely different from their own. Marriage to her could bring no advantage. Yet could it bring his

311

only son happiness? Was it wrong to withhold what he knew of the girl? It was little enough after all; it would not tell Ethan where she was or who were her family.

'The girl obviously did not want to be found,' he tried again. 'Had she wanted you to follow her, she would have said where she lived. But she did not. Surely that tells you enough? The girl was not in love with you, she did not wish to become your wife.'

'I can't believe that, Father. I will not believe it!' Ethan turned to the man seated at the desk, grey eyes watching him with concern. 'Something frightened Miriam, I feel sure of it. She would not have left so quickly otherwise. I have to find her. I love her, Father, and I want to marry her.'

Seeing the torment in the handsome young face, Clayton felt his resolve melt away. Going to the fireplace, he tugged at the bell cord. Let Baxter repeat what he'd said earlier regarding what had taken place in this house, then let Ethan make what he would of it.

'You are certain Marsh did not ... did not...' Ethan spoke only upon the butler's finishing the story he'd been asked to repeat.

'If what the girl Jinks says is correct, then no, Mr Ethan, Marsh did not succeed in harming the young woman.' Baxter, tactful as ever, replied to the question Ethan could not ask.

'Did Miriam – Miss Bryce – say where she was going ... where she lived?'

'I believe not, Mr Ethan.' Baxter heard the

urgency in his voice but not by the flicker of an eyelash did he show it. 'Perhaps you would like to speak to Jinks yourself?'

'Yes, I would. Have her come to the study. If that is all right with you, Father?'

'Perfectly.' Clayton nodded. 'But it could prove a little frightening to the girl to be summoned in here. Perhaps you should ask your questions in the drawing room – the atmosphere is not so heavily masculine in there. She may feel a little more relaxed.'

Doubtful as to the housemaid's feeling anything like relaxed when faced with her employer's questions, Baxter returned to the servants' quarters, waiting while Ginny replaced her already clean apron with another. Then, followed by the trembling maid and his wife who doggedly maintained that as the girl's superior she should be present during her interrogation, and would tell Clayton Rawley so, he led the way to the drawing room.

'Thank you for coming too, Mrs Baxter. Perhaps we would all be more comfortable seated?' Clayton smiled at the trio before him, glad of the foresight of the older woman. The girl would feel more at ease in her presence.

'Ginny.' He used the girl's Christian name, his tone gentle. 'My son would like to hear from your own lips what happened the day Miss Bryce left our employ?'

Seated on the edge of her chair, hands folded one over the other, Sally Baxter urged the trembling maid to speak. 'Tell Mr Ethan exactly what you told me ... speak up, girl. The master don't have all day to wait on you!'

'Don't be afraid, Ginny.' Clayton leaned back in his chair, apparently unconcerned though inside he felt furious that his hospitality had been thus abused and his servants must be questioned. 'Just tell us exactly what you told Mrs Baxter.'

Her voice quivering with nervousness, Ginny retold her story, finishing with, 'And that be the truth, sir. All of the truth.'

'Thank you, Ginny.' He nodded. 'Would you mind if Mr Ethan asked you a few questions now?'

'No, sir.' Ginny nodded. 'I don't mind answerin', supposin' I 'ave the answers.'

'Ginny.' Ethan sat forward in his chair. 'I know you have done your best, there can be no doubt that what you have said is exactly what you saw and heard, but did Miss Bryce tell you where she was going when she left the Hall? Where she lived?'

Ginny squirmed in her own seat, gaze falling beneath Sally's steady look. 'I ... I ain't sure, Mr Ethan.'

Her reply sharp and instant, Sally's spine straightened. 'You was sure enough in the tellin' to me!' she snapped. 'And the girl certainly said nothin' of where she was bound when last *I* spoke to her.'

'I am sure she did not,' Clayton intervened, soothing ruffled feathers. 'But Ginny did say she walked Miss Bryce from the house. I thought maybe something was said then that later became forgotten?'

'Try to remember, Ginny.' Ethan spoke before

314

the housekeeper could resume. 'I would be so grateful.'

Keeping her eyes averted from Sally's face, Ginny twisted her fingers in her lap. ''T'weren't much, Mr Ethan, and I don't know if it be of any use. But Miriam ... her said ... her told me her lived along of a farm house above Brades Village. But her said to promise not to tell nobody!'

'I'm sure she will not mind your telling me.' Ethan rose to his feet, adding a quick after-thought. 'Just as I know Mrs Baxter will approve of your having kept your promise until now.'

Following as the servants left the room, Ethan strode into the stables. At last he knew where Miriam had gone.

Above the kitchen, Leah heard her daughter's cry. Unsure her ears were not playing tricks on her, she listened hard and when Miriam's scream echoed again through the house, threw off the covers, trying to lift herself from the bed. The pounding in her head increasing, she willed her legs to move as a man's laugh, deep and throaty, followed quickly in its wake.

'Why should your arms be empty and you cry over something it will give us both pleasure to replace?' Saul's mouth pressed down hard, cutting off Miriam's cry, another vicious tug ripping away the remnants of her blouse.

As the cloth came away in his hand Miriam turned, but Saul was quicker, his hand fastening on to the strap of her chemise.

'Noo...' Her hands struck out blindly but he knocked them away, bringing the flat of his hand

315

down hard on her cheek. Half senseless from the stinging blow she stumbled back, then his hands were on her again, weight bearing her down until she lay on the brightly patterned pegged rug before the hearth.

Terror rising in her, Miriam felt the snap of the flimsy straps as he snatched at her thin cotton chemise, tearing it away from her breasts. She felt the warm dampness of his tongue as it played over her bared nipples.

'Please ... oh, God, please, no...' Squeezing her hands beneath his chest she tried to push him from her, but she had not the strength. He would rape her! The thought seared her mind. Saul Marsh would rape her and she could do nothing to stop him.

Cries mingling with sobs, she felt him lift himself up from her. He was leaving ... pray God he was leaving! Opening her eyes she saw the face she had once thought so handsome staring down at her, features flushed and distorted with lust.

He was not leaving! Seeing him throw aside his belt, hands releasing his trousers, she cried out afresh, brain reeling as one hand came smashing down against her temple.

'Cry out!' His weight pressed down on her body as he lowered himself on to her, hand fumbling beneath her skirts. 'Cry out all you want, it only adds to the pleasure.'

Against her face his breath came in quick harsh gasps, one hand inching slowly over her leg and thigh, fingers closing on the waistband of her cotton bloomers. Almost subconsciously Miriam stretched a hand towards the fireplace, searching for the poker.

From overhead Leah's voice called her name, a sharp imperious cry that brought momentary hope to Miriam, but it was followed by a thump on the ceiling and then by silence.

Saul had lifted his head at the call. Now he laughed, a vicious sound. 'Seems your mother must have taken a tumble. Let's hope it's only her neck that's broken!'

'Let me go to her.' Miriam clutched at one last straw. 'Please, Saul, she is ill. She needs me.'

The laugh rattling again in his throat, he wrenched at the bloomers, stretching the band to its fullest. Cursing when it did not break he loosened it, only to twine his fingers in the cotton. Worn thin by years of wear it tore with the first violent tug.

'I need you!' The words issued from lips slackened by the lust riding high in him. 'What I need I take, whether it please or no. Now I'm going to take you and this time there is no Ginny to spoil the fun, and no brother will take me by surprise. Next time he tries to kill me, I will be ready, and you can be sure it will be he who dies.'

Her hand still searching for the poker, Miriam shuddered as his hand touched her beneath the torn bloomers. If only she could keep him talking just a few moments more... Words jerked from a throat constricted with fear.

'Ralph need never know. If ... if you go now...'

'I'll go when I'm good and ready! And if you have any care for that brother of yours, you won't mention my being here. So either way he need never know.'

'You will never be any good, Marsh, but by God you had better be ready!'

A snarl breaking from him, Saul rolled sideways. In the open doorway Ethan Rawley stood tapping a riding whip against his leather boot.

'It will make little difference Miss Bryce telling her brother, or not telling him, of what you tried to do to her at Brade Hall and again here today. *I* know and I intend to make you pay for it.'

Ethan's eyes were black with anger. They caught the flickering light of the fire, seeming to burn like the coals that fed it. His finely drawn features pinched with fury, he raised the whip as Miriam scrambled to her feet, her torn clothing hanging in tatters from her shoulders.

Hindered by his trousers hanging loose about his legs, Saul struggled to find his footing. Across the room Ethan watched. Rage contained inside him like a capped volcano, he held the whip at head height. He would not strike his first blow at a man on the ground.

'What am I supposed to have done at Brade Hall?'

Feeling his comfortable new life slipping away, Saul tried to bluff his way out.

'There is no supposed about it, Marsh.' Ethan kept his eyes locked on those that watched him. 'Ginny told us all that happened. You are no longer welcome in my father's house, and when Sadler hears of this I have no doubt your engagement to Edwina will be ended.'

'Leaving her free for you?' Saul's face twisted into a sneer that pulled his mouth downward. 'Well, let me tell you this. Your marriage bed will not be the first she has shared with a man. Sweet Edwina is no virgin. But then, neither is Miriam...'

The whip snaked out, whistling as it sliced through the air, bringing a high-pitched scream from Saul as it bit into his face.

Retching deep from her stomach, Miriam stumbled into the scullery. Leaning over the sink, she clenched her mouth into a tight line, fighting an urge to gulp at the cool air, knowing that in doing so she would give vent to the screams rising within her.

From the kitchen another whine of leather on air brought a second shout of pain. Miriam shook with fear. Saul Marsh was a strong man; he had spent many years at the coal face wielding a pick axe. Ethan could be no match for him. She ran the few steps to the next room, clutching the rags of her chemise over her breasts as she felt the sickness rise again from her stomach.

Saul was half crouched, his arms crooked at the elbows, hands spread like claws. One cheek lay open from the whip, blood running down his chin, staining the fine white lawn of his shirt with crimson.

Miriam screamed as the whip rose once more, causing it to falter as Ethan glanced towards her. That was all Saul needed. Like a caged tiger newly freed, he sprang. Both hands fastening about the stock, he wrenched the whip loose, dropping it as Ethan smashed a fist hard into the cut on his face.

Livid at the knowledge that his marriage to Edwina would not now take place, that he had

319

lost all that he had schemed for, Saul made a dive for the whip. Reading the move, Ethan kicked out, shooting it across the stone-flagged floor.

A snarl on his lips, Saul gazed wildly about the room; moving slowly, aware of Ethan raising both fists in a boxer's stance, he edged towards the dresser.

As if caught in a nightmare, limbs heavy with fear, Miriam watched him back against the dresser, watched the hand that went behind him, the fingers close over the knife she had left there. Only when he brought his arm up did the bonds holding her throat loosen. But it was too late. Even as she screamed a warning the knife arced through the air, burying its blade in Ethan's chest. Then, as Saul moved towards the fallen man, fear for Ethan lent her strength and Miriam was across the room, the heavy poker brandished in her hands.

Anger and resentment lending her strength, she glared at the man who had fathered her child then twice tried to rape her. Teeth clenched, she raised the thick iron bar. 'Go, Saul, go now. Try to touch either of us and I will bash your brains out with this poker!'

A few feet away, Saul Marsh came to a halt. His eyes swept the girl, one hand holding the tattered chemise over her breasts, the other brandishing a poker. He sneered. 'You don't know what you're talking about.'

'Maybe not.' Miriam stood her ground, ignoring the moans of the man slumped at her feet. 'But I am willing to find out ... are you?'

For long moments he stood watching her, eyes

shadowed by the fast-fading afternoon. Feeling each moment stretch into eternity, her arm trembling from the effort of holding the heavy poker above her head, Miriam panted for breath.

'It's not over,' Saul said at last, lips hardly moving. 'It's not over for Rawley ... or for you!'

Turning he ran from the house, just as Miriam's knees buckled and she sank to the floor.

Nausea overcoming her in waves, Miriam clamped both hands to her mouth. Her eyes pressed shut, she crumpled up, head pressed against her chest. When would it stop ... when would it ever stop? First Saul's rejection of her, then his assault followed by the death of her baby, and now this. She could face no more ... no more!

'Miriam.' The voice was low but it could not be ignored. As if hauling herself back from a far off place, she dragged herself into reality as her name was repeated, the voice that spoke weak.

Opening her eyes, she saw Ethan reach out towards her. Then he fell back, head lying awkwardly against a corner of the fireplace.

For a moment she could not think what had happened, then as memory returned she was on her knees beside him.

The knife still protruded from his chest, handle glistening in the firelight. Miriam stared, mesmerised with fear. Had it buried itself in his heart? Had Ethan died saving her? No, he was not dead, he could not be. He had spoken her name just seconds ago.

But a man could die in seconds!

The knife should be removed. She stared at it, blood oozing beneath its blade, staining shirt and jacket in a dark tide.

'The knife,' Ethan breathed, his eyes closed. 'Take it out.'

Miriam felt her heart turn over.

'Take it out,' he whispered again.

Summoning every ounce of strength, she reached for the knife then drew back as nausea rose, hot and acid in her throat. 'I can't,' she sobbed. 'I can't! Oh, Ethan, I can't … I can't…'

His face drawn and pale from loss of blood, he tried to lift himself but the effort left him gasping with pain.

'Miriam,' he panted. 'It … it has to come out. A towel … get a towel to staunch the blood.'

Given something definite to do cleared her mind. Getting to her feet, she reached a clean piece of white cloth from the airing line above the fireplace. Folding it into a pad, she glanced at the kettle hissing quietly above the coals. The wound should be washed, but in the time that took would he lose so much blood he would not recover?

Questions whirling in her mind, she glanced at the man lying at her feet. He already looked as though death held him in its arms.

'Miriam…'

'I'm here, Ethan.' She knelt again, bending over him.

'Take it … out.'

Teeth sinking into her lip, Miriam watched his eyelids try to open, a mere flutter against his pallid cheeks.

322

'You need a doctor, Ethan. If I try to remove that knife it ... it could kill you.'

A faint smile touched the colourless lips. 'I will die if you don't. There's no time for a doctor. You have to do it, Miriam, and do it now, please ... it's my only chance!'

His only chance? What if Ethan were mistaken ... what if he were *not!* He had been so kind to her, she could not live with the thought that she had contributed to his death.

The thought bringing sickness flooding into her again, shuddering violently Miriam reached for the knife.

The carriage lights faded slowly, the horse moving at a gentle trot. They were taking Ethan home. Watching the twin lights, blinking like yellow eyes in the gathering evening, Miriam felt tears course down her cheeks.

'Let him live,' she whispered. 'Please God, let him live.'

She had drawn the knife from his chest, her stomach heaving as she felt the flesh cling stubbornly to the blade, then the fountain of blood spurt over her as it finally came free. Then she had held pad upon pad of cloth to the wound, holding it so it could not slip, talking to him all the while, though now she could remember nothing of what she had said.

But she remembered what Ethan had said. The carriage lights dropping out of sight in the dip of the track, she turned back into the house, his words echoing in her mind.

'I love you, Miriam. I tried so hard to find you, to

tell you. Say you will marry me? Say you will be my wife?'

Taking his head into her lap she had begged him not to talk, begged him to save his strength, but he had gone on, his hand holding hers until he'd drifted into unconsciousness. And she had not answered. Not told him the love she felt for him was that for a dear friend, not that on which to found a marriage. Any love she had once thought she held for Saul Marsh was dead forever. She stared at the fire that had almost died. Like her heart. Never again would she love a man. Never again would she hold a child of her own to her breast.

'I love you, Miriam.'

They were his final words as he slid away from her into some far region from which she could not draw him back. She had panicked then, seeing the last vestige of colour slip from Ethan's face, his breathing so shallow it might already have stopped.

That was when she had run from the house, her feet flying across the heath, fear that she might meet Saul again thudding in her chest she made for Brade Hall.

She had met the carriage just above the village, the Hall having been alerted when Ethan's horse, spooked by an animal or sound, had returned riderless to its stable. Clayton Rawley had glanced at Miriam from the window, then almost dragged her inside.

She felt a sweep of warm colour in her face as she recalled how he had removed his coat, and without a word draped it about her. In her anxiety for Ethan she had been oblivious to the state of her clothing. Only when Clayton Rawley had stared at her naked shoulders, at the straps of her torn chemise hanging forgotten over her breasts, then covered her with his own coat, had she remembered.

Then, still silent, he had listened to the account of Saul's attack upon her, and how Ethan had come upon them and sprung to her defence.

In the grate the dying coals settled lower into the mound of grey ash, but the picture Miriam stared at was the one in her mind, the picture of Clayton Rawley's face as he asked, 'Did my son tell you the reason for his visit?'

She had wanted to say nothing, to let what Ethan had mumbled remain hidden in her heart, but somehow she found she could not lie to the man watching her from the opposite seat of the carriage.

'Ethan said... She had brought her head up then, meeting those grey eyes. 'He asked me to be his wife.'

The carriage had raced along for several moments. All the time their eyes held.

'And may I ask your reply?'

'I did not give it.' Her breathing was still laboured after running so far but her voice was steady.

'I see.' Clayton Rawley had raised one eyebrow, but apart from that gave no visible reaction.

'Mr Rawley.' Having started, Miriam rushed on, 'I did not give your son my answer. He slipped into unconsciousness before I could. But when he is recovered enough to hear it I shall give it to him. I will be forever grateful to him, as I will be to yourself for the kindness you both showed me. But gratitude is no basis for marriage. I would like to think of Eth– of your son as a friend. I hold a deep respect for him, and, yes, a deep affection. But that affection could never become the deep abiding love that he deserves, the love he should be given by a wife. I could not love him as a husband. My answer to Ethan will be no, I cannot marry him.'

Clayton had said nothing more to her.

The light of the fire growing dimmer, the shadows advanced boldly into the room. Deep in her thoughts, Miriam sat on, oblivious.

Clayton Rawley had said nothing more to her, not even after they'd reached the house, not looking in her direction until Ethan had been laid carefully in the carriage. Then it had been only a simple 'thank you', but the eyes which met hers had held a thousand questions. Yet he asked none of them. Taking the coat she had exchanged for her shawl, he turned towards the door and hesitated.

'Are you alone here, Miss Bryce? I can have one of my men stay here until we can get a woman to come.'

'No.' Miriam had refused the offer. 'My mother is here with me. She ... she must have gone to ask for Ralph ... for my brother ... to be allowed to come home early.'

The twinge of guilt she had felt on speaking the lie returned now as she remembered it.

'Your brother!' His voice held a note of query but he gave no voice to it. Instead he asked about

Ralph's employment, nodding as she told him the name of the colliery. Then he had walked from the house to where his carriage waited. Walking past it to the bed carriage where he turned to her again, his eyes sweeping her face, his voice soft with emotion, he had touched a hand to hers.

'I thank you for what you have done for my son, Miss Bryce. I shall not forget this day nor the part you played in it. Had it not been for your care, Ethan might well have died. I almost lost him once before when ... when my wife was killed. As it was, shock and grief robbed him of his tongue and me of hearing his voice. I would not live with that sorrow and loneliness again. If my son lives you will have saved me from that; no words of mine can ever tell you of my gratitude.'

Withdrawing his hand, he climbed into the carriage, settling next to Ethan whose chalk white face was barely visible above warm blankets. Then, his eyes brilliant with tears, Clayton had looked again at her, the merest shadow of a smile touching his mouth.

'Maybe it would have been more of a blessing than I had thought, to have a daughter-in-law from Brades Village.'

The fire settled lower in the grate, cinders falling down between the bars. A faint pink glow faded quickly as the last of the heat died, leaving ashes cold and grey as the feeling inside her. She should make the fire up, fetch coal from the yard and build it high, make it burn hot and bright, light the lamps so they drove back the shadows.

But Miriam ignored the message of her mind,

gazing into the dying fire.

'Maybe it would have been more of a blessing than I had thought...'

What blessing would Clayton Rawley count a daughter-in-law who had carried another man's child, one who had given birth to a bastard?

Laying aside her shawl, Miriam pulled the tattered remnant of her ruined blouse over her head. Then, sliding out of her torn bloomers, she gathered both garments in her hand and, without glancing at them, threw them in the fire.

Reaching for the kettle that hung on the bracket she lifted it free, and without a backward glance carried it up the narrow stairs.

Once in her own bedroom she poured the bubbling water into the bowl on the tiny wash-stand, then stripping off the rest of her clothes, scrubbed every inch of her body until the skin burned on her bones.

His hand had trailed along her leg.

She scrubbed harder, using the sting of it to erase the memory from her mind, wash it free of the stigma of his touch, of what he had done to her. But the stain of it had gone deeper than soap and water could remove. It had bled down into her soul, and there it would remain.

He had grabbed the waistband of her bloomers.

Stubbornly the thoughts returned, each more vivid and alive than the one before, forcing her to relive the horror of that attack.

Drying herself, Miriam lifted the bowl, setting it on the floor.

He had snatched the bloomers, tearing them half off her then stopped as her mother had shouted her name...

Her mother! One foot in the china bowl, Miriam stood stock still. She had forgotten her mother! In the fear and turmoil of what had happened she had forgotten that Leah had called. Or had she? Was it only in Miriam's imagination she had heard it?

Washing both legs quickly, she grabbed fresh clothing from the chest of drawers, fingers still fumbling with buttons as she ran towards Leah's bedroom.

Her mother lay with her head turned sideways on the pillow, eyes closed, breath hardly stirring her chest. Coldness clutching her stomach, Miriam's glance took in the heavy brass candle holder which had fallen on the floor.

'What were all that?'

Leah's head turned slowly, the glint of her eyes visible in the shadows.

A sharp sob escaping her, Miriam moved to the bed. Her mother's face was the grey of ashes except for the red flush colouring her forehead.

'What were all that shouting?'

The words were slurred by her twisted mouth, but the same note of command rang in them.

'It was nothing. Nothing for you to worry over.'

Avoiding those bright eyes, Miriam smoothed the sheets about her mother's still form, then bent to retrieve the candle holder Ralph preferred to use during his nightly vigil in this room. Replacing it on the bedside table, eyes still averted from those she felt burning into her, she asked, 'Can I get you anything, Mother?'

Ignoring the question, the devil's own anger

glaring from her eyes, each word struggling past her lips, Leah stared accusingly at her daughter.

'It were nothing?' she demanded. 'Nothing for me to worry over! It were too noisy to be nothing, and since when did you do anything that caused me no worry? I'll tell you when – *never*, that's when! Every moment you have lived you've been a worry to me. It be no surprise you can't look me in the face, no surprise at all, for I heard you down there. Your voice and a man's, laughing together.'

Leah sucked at the air, chest heaving as it rattled in her lungs.

'It were him, weren't it? Him - Marsh! Don't bother to tell me any lies for I heard the two of you rolling and banging about on the floor. You heard me call and there be no denying it, but you didn't come – the reason being you were too wrapped up in your filthy games, too busy pleasuring yourself and him, too far gone in your own lust to bother to see to your own mother.'

'No!' Miriam's cry was loud, her denial as strong as her mother's accusation. 'It was not like that, not what you think...'

'Not what I think!' Leah's eyes glittered with the pleasure of indictment. 'I know what my own ears told me. I know who it was were with you in my own house. I know the filth you were up to, the fornicating...'

'No!'

Miriam drew away. Outside her mother's bedroom she leaned against the wall, hands covering her face. It was not like that ... it was not!

But it would be little use trying to get her

330

mother to believe that. Nothing she could say would alter what Leah chose to think.

Pressing her hands to her mouth, Miriam stifled the dry sobs rising in her throat.

Leah would listen to none of it, nothing but what her own warped mind told her. Trying to explain, to get her to acknowledge that nothing that had taken place had been of her daughter's doing, that none of it was her fault, would be like blowing in the wind: it would all come back in her face.

Tears stinging the backs of her eyes, Miriam walked slowly down the stairs.

In her bed, Leah's eyes burned fever bright as she listened to the tread.

'You be naught but a trollop!'

She rolled her head on the pillow, eyes resting on the shadowed wall.

'You be naught but a trollop. Just as that other one were a trollop!'

Chapter Twenty-one

Handing in his lamp and number tag, Ralph called a quick good night to those miners who had ridden the cage with him to the surface. He was in no mood for talk or company.

Clear of the pit head, he glanced up at the moon sailing full and silver-white against waves of scudding clouds. A hunter's moon. He breathed deeply, filling his lungs with air that tasted sweet and fresh; air that was not laden with choking black dust and the foul smell of the coal trench.

Dotted about the heath, gorse bushes stood sentinel against the darkness, their shape given depth and line by the borrowed finery of the moon. He had always loved the heath by moonlight, its beauty and total serenity, shadows hiding its man-made scars. But it was the peace there he valued most. Even as a child he had used the heath as a retreat, a quiet refuge from his mother's acid tongue. But as the years passed he seemed to come to the heath less and less often, hurrying home as soon as his shift was finished, hurrying to shield his sister from that same vicious tongue.

Miriam! He breathed again, deeper, using the crispness of the winter night to chase away the emotions in his warning body. She was his sister and he loved her, with a love that was not that of a brother.

But he could not turn his back on her now, leave the house as he had long ago realised he should. He could not leave Miriam alone with their mother. Nor would things be any better if he left taking her with him as he had promised he would. He would still love her, long for her; but he would still be her brother.

Tucking his empty snap box under his arm, he thrust both hands into the pockets of his jacket. He would take the long way home, the path around the marl hole; perhaps by the time he reached the house the pain in his heart would have eased.

From the place where he had run after stabbing Ethan Rawley, Saul Marsh watched the figure approaching, silhouetted tall and black in the moonlight. In the shadow cast by the lee of a jutting rock that edged the marl hole, he peered into the distance. It couldn't be Ethan Rawley. He had done for that one with a knife in the chest! The only journey he would make now was to the cemetery. Nor, he guessed, would it be the father searching for him. He would have his minions and the bobbies doing that. But they would not find Saul, he knew the heath too well. He would be well clear of Brades Village before they had searched even a part. But he was going to need money. He should have asked for that before trying to take the Bryce girl. That mother of hers must have had a penny or two stashed away. But it wasn't too late. The brother would be off to work in the early hours ... Saul could make another call then. A night in a barn somewhere must do until then.

A dozen or so yards away the tall figure stepped into a patch of moonlight and Saul felt his pulses race. Whatever god was in heaven was on his side! He might be forced to leave the village but he would take the satisfaction of revenge with him. He had sworn to kill Ralph Bryce ... now he would do it.

Pressing himself back against the rock, making use of the shadows, his hand felt about, mouth drawing up into a smile as his fingers closed over a large stone.

The sister and the brother. Saul waited for Ralph. He would take both!

333

'I said I would kill you!'

Stepping forward as Ralph passed, Saul brought the stone down with all the force in his arm.

After years spent underground, every sense attuned for the first faint sounds that heralded a cave in, Ralph caught the scrape of a foot on loose shale. Instinct leading him to shield his head, he had already half turned away when the blow fell, deflecting it on to his shoulder.

Stumbling from the force with which it had come, he half fell against the rock, the snap tin clattering to the ground.

'You thought I was done for!' Saul leaped forward, hands fastening around Ralph's throat. 'You left me here on the heath after you cut my balls off. But you didn't take it all. You left enough for me to fill your sister's belly a second time, enough to leave her with another bastard!'

Marsh! It was Marsh who had struck him. Marsh had been to his home ... to Miriam. Rage such as Ralph had never felt before throbbed through every vein, drumming in his head, tingling in his fingers as he freed his hands from his pockets.

'...*leave her with another bastard.*'

Every syllable clamoured in his brain. Marsh had not been satisfied with trying to rape Miriam at Brade Hall, he had gone to the farm. He had...

Suddenly the heat of anger turned to ice, a vicious need to kill taking its place. The fingers pressing at his throat, cutting off breath, seemed no longer to bother him. Placing his palms together, Ralph forced them up between his chest and Marsh's until his forearms were level with their faces. Then, with a sharp outward thrust, he broke the grip on his throat.

'I made a mistake all those weeks ago.' His own feet steady beneath him, Ralph saw his attacker stumble then regain his footing. 'I should have finished the job.'

'But you didn't!' Saul moved crablike in a semicircle about the man who had tried to castrate him. 'Happily for your sister. She enjoyed what I gave her today.'

'Like I am going to enjoy what I give you!' Ralph rode the taunt, recognising it was intended to throw him into a rage that would blind him to his opponent's moves. 'This time there will be no mistake. I won't leave you to be found alive.'

Bending swiftly, Saul scooped up a handful of the loose shale that bordered the marl hole. Throwing it, he laughed, 'You or me, Bryce, it makes little difference which of us dies. But somehow I don't think it will be me.'

Dust filling his eyes, the sharp grit stinging his face where it sliced the skin, Ralph blinked and in that moment Saul was on him: fists pummelling his head, a knee in the groin driving the breath from him as he fell to the ground.

Drawing both knees to his chest, he rolled away. He needed a moment to recover.

Saul's outline was hazy against the silver-black of the flooded hole. His vision clearing, Ralph drew in a long ragged breath, watching the other man search the moon-washed ground.

'I'm going to finish you, Bryce, here and now!' Saul straightened up, in his hand a sharp-edged flake of limestone. 'But not before I take from you what you took from me. But I won't leave you with one testicle – there'll be no need. You won't live to use it. Not like me. I've had your sister, there in your own home, and I shall have her again before I finally say goodbye to this Godforsaken hole!'

Ralph lay still, the cold earth beneath him no match for the freezing need inside him. Eyes almost shut, he listened for the tread that would tell him the moment was right.

'I wonder what that sour bitch of a mother of yours would say to having her son's balls sent to her in the post?'

'You'll never know, Marsh!' Rolling on to his back, Ralph kicked out with one foot, sending the stone spinning from Saul's hand. Then, with the agility of a cat, he was up, his fist crashing into Saul's face. A second blow then a third followed in rapid succession.

'Lie there, you bastard!' His chest heaving, Ralph stared at the man crumpled in a heap on the ground. 'But you won't be unconscious when I cut the other one off! You are going to scream as my sister must have screamed. You are going to feel the fear she has felt, suffer the pain you made her suffer!'

Pulling the muffler from about his neck, he went to the edge of the quarry to soak it in the slimy water. Returning to Saul, he slapped it on the man's face.

'Wake up!' he hissed. 'Wake up, you filthy swine! I want you to see as well as feel.'

Casting a glance about the ground lit by a

brilliant moon, he searched for the splinter of rock Marsh had held. It must have fallen further away, but where one had been there would be another. Moving a few feet from the fallen man he poked the coarse grass, the toe of his boot feeling for a similar shard.

Only as he bent to pick one up did the sound come to him. Still crouched, he whirled to face it.

Saul had risen to his feet. Swaying from the blows that had dropped him, he glared at Ralph.

'You shouldn't have turned your back,' he hissed.

Ralph stayed low. Even as the last word slid from Saul's lips he raised one arm, throwing the lump of stone that had been concealed by his fallen body.

Instinctively Ralph shielded his head, bringing up both arms to cover it as the stone whistled past, splashing into the water at his back.

Not knowing which way Saul would follow up his renewed attack, Ralph stayed crouched for several seconds, glancing up only when no assault came. Saul had gone.

Gingerly, alert for any sudden movement, Ralph eased himself to his feet. Eyes accustomed to working long hours in the bowels of the earth cut through the silvered darkness, but he could see no sign of the other man. But ears that were able to detect the slightest creak of pit stays, the merest whisper of sound from tunnels of exposed seams that ran away into blackness, picked up the scratch of boot against rock. His head remaining perfectly still, giving no clue that he had heard anything, he allowed only his eyes to lift.

Several yards above him, Saul Marsh's outline showed stark and black against the night sky. Bent double, using hands and feet, he was climbing up the overhang of rock.

Silent as a cat, his own movements swift and sure, Ralph followed. He must reach the flat crest at the same time as Marsh, otherwise a kick to the head as he topped the rise would send him hurtling if not to death then to crippling injury.

Ignoring the jagged surface that bit deep into his palms, slicing into the tips of his fingers, he hauled himself over the lip of rock. Only to look up into Saul Marsh's mocking face.

Clayton Rawley sat at his son's bedside, fingers tightly bunched, mouth set hard. It was a miracle Ethan was alive, the doctor had said. Only someone's efforts to prevent the bleeding had saved his life, but even now it could prove touch and go. He must be nursed day and night until the danger was past. But that was the least of the problems that faced Clayton for two nurses were already hired to care for his son around the clock. Clayton leaned forward as a slight moan came from the sleeping figure but the nurse coming swiftly across the room warned him against speaking.

Warned against speaking to his own son!

Clayton rose and left the bedroom.

Warned against trying to bring Ethan out of that world of silence, a world he had lived in for so many years already.

Suddenly Clayton was back in the past, watching the face of a small boy, blue eyes brilliant with unshed tears as his mouth worked to bring out words that would not come.

The strident ringing of the door bell bringing him out of his reverie, he walked down the stairs to the hall just as Baxter admitted two uniformed policemen. Clayton smiled grimly. If fortune favoured him he would find Saul Marsh long before the law. *That* was the most pressing task that awaited him.

But the girl ... would she want it known what Marsh had almost done to her? Would his giving that information to the police serve any purpose other than to bring the questioning eyes of the village gossips upon her? Doubtless they would lay the blame for the attempted rape at her door. She would be named as culprit ... they would say she had led him on and have a field day regardless of the girl's innocence.

Leading the way to the study, Clayton knew he would say nothing of that part of the day's events. Marsh would pay, and with his life, but it would not be the law would take it!

'You shouldn't have followed me up here'

Above Ralph's head, Saul's foot lifted. 'Was it the stone I bounced off your head or hearing of what your sister and I did together in your mother's house that drove the sense from you?' His laughter rang out, dark and ugly as the thoughts behind it. 'Was it the pictures in your mind that sent you scuttling up here? Pictures of the sister you've always been so protective of, lying on that rug, legs spread wide, her arms about my neck? I hope so, Bryce. I want that to be the picture you take with you ... to eternity!'

Laughing again, Saul brought his foot viciously downward.

The same quickness of mind that had saved him from pitfalls served Ralph now. With a half roll, he brought his body level with the leg on which Saul stood balanced. Lying on his left side, he reached to grab Saul's ankle and jerk it with all his strength.

One foot already in the air, and thinking the other man at his mercy, Saul was pulled off balance, crashing heavily on to his back.

Needing only that moment, Ralph hauled himself the last couple of feet on to the rocky plateau. Then his hands were on the lapels of Saul's jacket, dragging him to his feet.

'It won't be a picture of Miriam lying with you, or any other man, will stay with me.' Ralph felt the pain of his own lie. 'It will be one of you alone ... lying dead at my feet!'

With the agility of an acrobat, Saul dropped his upper body forward then twisted beneath Ralph's arms, the fine serge of his jacket ripping.

'You're still the boy you were at school, Bryce.' In the silvered shadows, Saul's eyes glittered like some watchful animal's, waiting a chance to seize its victim. 'Defending your sister. Only this time you were too late. She will marry with a child already hanging on her skirts – *my* child!' He laughed loudly, the sound shattering the silence. 'That is if she can find a man willing to marry a whore!'

Strips of cloth fluttering from his hands, Ralph lunged for the mocking figure, swearing softly as

Saul sidestepped.

'*Still* the same dull boy!' Saul jeered. 'A lot of brawn but not much else... It worked on those kids at school, but this one has grown up, Bryce. This one uses his brain to get what he wants, whether it be a woman's virginity or a man's life. And I shall have taken both before the next few minutes are past.'

Scaling the tall rock had been no effort for Ralph, but now he sucked hard at the cold air. Marsh was no beginner at the game he was playing. Goad your opponent with words, drive him out of his mind with innuendo, find his weakness then probe and stab until every trace of reason and control were gone.

But Marsh was not the only one who'd left childhood rashness behind. Ralph too had grown up, though the hot blood of the boy he'd been still raced in his veins. But he must not let it rule his head; not give way to the anger that ran with it. Marsh would be counting on that. Ralph sucked again at the night air, taking its coldness deep into his lungs. This time Marsh's calculations would be way off the mark!

His senses clear now, mind centred on one thing, Ralph ignored the mocking laughter. A short distance from him, moonlight outlining his body in sharp silhouette, Saul's every move was clearly visible.

'Maybe I will give her a place to live, a place I can go for a little nightly entertainment.' Saul edged further back as Ralph came on. 'I shall have more than enough money to keep your sister as my mistress. You see, Bryce, unlike her I

341

used my time well during my stay at Brade Hall. I became engaged to Edwina Sadler. Oh, that's all over now!' He stepped further back, teeth shining as the moonlight caught his smile. 'There'll be no marriage. But Sadler will pay, and plenty, for my silence concerning his daughter ... you see, I took her virginity as I took Miriam's.'

Judging the distance between them with every step, Ralph edged further forward.

'That was always your style, wasn't it, Marsh?' He spoke softly. 'Always so eager to get beneath a woman's skirts. Well, never again.'

'Not quite right.' Saul sniggered. 'Not in your sister's case. It was not her skirts I thrust into, nor was it my head I used, it was...'

'I know what it was you used, you bastard! But you will never use it again!'

Drawing back his arm, Ralph drove his bunched fist forward, but Saul was ready. Stepping swiftly back he laughed as the blow sailed harmlessly past his face, one foot sliding behind him to support his weight. Finding no foothold, he tottered back over the lip of the rock. For several seconds he seemed to lie against the night sky, arms spread wide, then he was gone, one long terrified scream piercing the night and dying away.

'Like you said, Marsh,' Ralph muttered as the awful sound settled into the stillness. 'It doesn't much matter which one it is.'

Stepping to the edge of the overhang, Ralph looked down at the black waters of the flooded marl pit. Rippling silver circles marked the resting place of the fallen man. Staring into their inky depths, Ralph smiled grimly.

'It doesn't much matter which one it is!'

A few days and Saul Marsh might well be found, floating dead in those sour waters. Or maybe not. It didn't much matter, there was none but his mother to mourn his passing. Ralph turned away, beginning the long climb down to the heath below.

Chapter Twenty-two

Her mother had believed Miriam to be Saul Marsh's willing partner, that she had brought him into the house and lain with him of her own consent!

Miriam raked ash from the dying fire.

It had been useless trying to explain; each time she had gone up to her mother's room, Leah had screamed abuse at her, calling the wrath of heaven down upon her head, vowing that this time Ralph would see the evil in her, that he would send her from the house. Her mother's body may have lost some of its strength but her tongue was vicious as ever. It scalded as it always had, the scars it left just as deep and painful.

Bringing coals from the scullery, she fed them on to the glowing embers, then, her movements that of an automaton, refilled the bucket from the yard and placed it beneath the scullery sink.

This time Ralph would believe their mother. Rinsing her hands beneath the pump above the sink, Miriam dried them on a square of huckaback. He could not be expected to believe that Saul had attacked her for a second time, and here in her own home; after all, he would reason, she had been a willing partner once before so why not again?

Back in the living room, Miriam leaned heavily against the table, eyes closed against the shame flooding through her. Ralph would believe their mother ... believe his sister was a whore.

She could not face that. Her mother's spite and lies she could endure, *would* endure, but the look she would see in her brother's eyes ... that she could not bear. It seemed she had brought so much worry and discord to this house, feeling since earliest childhood she was at the heart of her mother's bitterness and her father's unhappiness. But Ralph too had known suffering, she could not cause him any more.

Blind with tears, she stretched out a hand for her shawl hanging behind the door, a shudder going through her as it was enfolded by cold hard fingers.

'Let me go!' Terror engulfed her as she was caught in arms as strong as steel bands.

'Why?'

The question rang in her ears, adding to the fear that had swallowed her, burning in her as she tried to twist away.

'Why should I let you go, Miriam?'

It was said softly. But the horror was too strong, too violent, to be overriden.

'Why, Miriam?' It was asked again, as softly as before. 'Because you are afraid of what I might

344

think, that I might believe what I hear, that I might take the word of scum like Marsh before that of my own sister?'

'Ralph! Oh, thank God! Thank God, it's you!'

Realisation of who it was robbing her of strength, Miriam slumped against him. Then, as what he had said penetrated the fear, she pushed away, looking into his face. 'Then ... then you know?'

His arms still about her, Ralph led her back to the fireside, lowering her gently into a chair.

'He came... Saul came here to the house.' Choking between sobs, the words she had not wanted him to hear came tumbling out. 'He said he wanted to see the child.'

In her lap her fingers twined restlessly, but it was her expression that held Ralph's gaze. The pain and fear and shame she felt were more than he could bear to see. The cold rage he had felt became icy hatred. Should those waters have spared Saul Marsh then Ralph would kill him some other way. Nothing would induce him to let such vermin live.

'He insisted on seeing the child,' Miriam went on brokenly. 'Then, when I told him she had died, he said he said he would give me another.'

Ralph's heart lurched inside him. What Marsh had thrown at him there on the heath, had not been a boast, it was the truth. He had raped Miriam!

Looking down into her eyes, drowned by an ocean of tears, his own pain submerged beneath her own, he drew her into his arms, feeling her body quake as he held her against him. But he could not tell if the anguish that swept through him was from listening to her words or from being so close to a woman forbidden to him.

'I tried to push him away,' she sobbed against his chest. 'I tried...'

As her voice rose on a note of hysteria, Ralph stroked one hand against her hair, murmuring gently against her ear as he had done so often during her childhood. Then as she calmed he lowered her again to the chair and knelt at her feet, his hands clasping hers. But he did not urge her to silence. He must hear all. Break his heart as it would, he must hear all that Miriam could bring herself to tell.

'I told him that if he left without ... without doing what he threatened ... you need never know.'

But he *did* know! Ralph stared over the top of her bent head, seeing none of the lights dancing from its auburn curls, only the silver moonlight glazing the pitch-black waters of the marl hole; the spreading ripples reflecting its gleam.

Marsh had gloated, revelled in the pleasure of his telling, gloried in the knowledge of the pain it caused; throwing it at Ralph again and again, giving him blow upon mental blow, stabbing at him as Miriam stabbed at him now. But Ralph knew he could not ask her to stop, could not protect himself from the pain of those words. He must know from Miriam herself the truth of what Marsh had said.

'But it made no difference.' Dejection replacing hysteria, she went on. 'He threw me to the floor and would have done what he intended had not

Ethan Rawley come just at that moment.'

Ethan Rawley! Ralph stared at the white washed wall. Saul Marsh had not mentioned Rawley.

Forcing himself to speak quietly, to keep the hope from his voice, he asked, 'Ethan Rawley ... he came to this house?'

Freeing one hand, Miriam brushed away the tears streaking her face.

Behind Ralph the coals settled lower into the bed of the fire sending a shower of sparks dancing over the pegged rug, yet he paid them no heed but remained holding on to his sister's hand, waiting for her answer.

'Yes,' she nodded. 'He came just as Saul...'

'Did Marsh ... did he hurt you?'

'Not in the way you mean.' Miriam held her head low. 'He would have, even though I begged him not to. It was only Ethan's arrival that prevented him.'

Thank God! Ralph's heart swelled. Marsh had not done what he claimed, Miriam had not been raped. Relief warm inside him, Ralph remembered the vile taunts the other man had slung at him, knowing all the time he lied.

'Ethan dragged him away.' Each word cost Miriam dearly. 'There was a fight and ... and Ethan was injured.'

He would be little match for Saul Marsh. Ralph listened in silence. A man needed more than strength to fight that one. He needed to know how to use the same dirty tactics Marsh had learned as a boy.

'Was he badly beaten?'

Miriam lifted her head, eyes full of fear. 'Saul did more than beat Ethan,' she whispered, 'he stabbed him.'

'...*that is all over now ... there will be no marriage.*'

So that was what Marsh had meant. The reason for his stabbing Rawley would of course come out and in so doing destroy any hope there had been of marrying Edwina Sadler.

'I tried to help Ethan, but there was so much blood, and when he lost consciousness I was afraid he would die. That was when I ran to fetch his father. Ethan looked so pale, so very near to death. Oh, Ralph, it's all my fault!' Sobs wracking her shoulders, Miriam buried her face in her hands. 'It's all my fault.'

'None of it is your fault!' Anger bringing him to his feet, Ralph kicked at the fireplace, sending poker and brass-mounted companion set clanging into the hearth. Overhead the noise was echoed by that of the heavy candle holder hitting the floor. Ignoring both the noise of the falling objects and the sound of his mother's faint call, Ralph turned to his sister.

'Marsh was nothing but a swine. He would use anyone and anything to get what he wanted, no matter who was hurt in the process!'

'It doesn't matter the hurt caused to me.' Miriam sobbed through her fingers. 'I deserve it after what I have put Mother and you through, the disgrace I brought on you.'

'You were easily deceived.' Ralph looked down at her drooping head, his whole being filled with the need to hold her. 'But no more so than many a young girl. I won't lie by saying what you did was not wrong, but a mistake is a mistake and must be judged as such. No matter what others might say or think, that is how I will look at what happened to you. You are my sister and to me you neither bring nor bear disgrace.'

He had wanted to say, 'You are my sister and I love you.' But realising that to speak the last of those words would awaken an emotion too strong for him to hold back, he had resisted. 'You say you went to fetch Rawley's father?'

Miriam nodded. 'He was already very near the village. Ethan's horse broke loose and ran back to its stable. That warned the groom something was wrong and he alerted Mr Rawley. He knew where I lived, knew of this house from his maid, Ginny Jinks. He was already coming to take Ethan back to the Hall. But, Ralph, he looked so desperately ill ... the wound in his chest...'

'Rawley will be all right.' It was probably a hope without foundation, but Ralph said it anyway. 'He'll have the best possible care.'

Yes, Ethan would have the best care. Miriam stared into the fire. But was that enough to save his life?

'I tell you, her be nothing but a whore!' Leah Bryce glared at her son sitting in a chair drawn up to the fire in her bedroom. 'I heard them both down there in the kitchen, tumbling and rolling, setting things clattering with their dirty games. I know what it was they was after doing.'

'It wasn't what you think,' Ralph answered acidly, eyes fixed on the dancing flames.

'That's all you know, 'cos it be all you wants to

349

know!' Leah spat. 'No doubt her's filled your ears with her own version of the tale, but it be lies, all lies.'

'How do you know she lied, Mother?' Ralph asked quietly. 'Seeing as you were not there to hear. And how can you claim to know what happened between them when you were not present to see?'

''Cos I know the likes of Saul Marsh,' Leah snapped. 'I know there be only one thing would draw him to this house. And I know your sister. Her was more than willing the time afore, and her were willing this time!'

The time before! Ralph's heart squeezed in on itself. He could not argue with his mother on that point. Miriam had gone to the heath of her own accord, lain with Marsh out of her own desire.

'No!' His denial rang out, but it was more a denial of his own thoughts than of his mother's accusation. 'Miriam was not to blame, she had no idea Marsh was in this house until he attacked her.'

In the semi-darkness of the room lit only by the flames, Leah's eyes glittered.

'Attacked!' She pronounced words with difficulty, each becoming a little more slurred than the one before. 'Attacked? That be what she told you, was it?' She laughed, a terrible gurgling sound that rattled in the back of her throat. 'When a woman is attacked then her screams. Why didn't your sister scream?'

Ralph's fingers tightened about the arms of his chair.

'I called for her when I heard them cavortin'. I

called but there came no answer except for their laughter. Even when I knocked that candle holder to the floor they never stopped their evil game.'

'Miriam would have answered, would have come to you had she been able.'

'Defend her if you will.' Her mouth a twisted caricature, Leah tried to smile. 'You always did. But I were here, lying in this bed, and I heard it all, every filthy sound. And I tell you it were not your sister's mouth that Marsh were covering. And I say again, her gave no scream.'

The lie pressed home Leah watched the firelight flicker over her son's face as he sat with shoulders hunched. But there was no touch of remorse in her heart, no feeling of pity for what she saw: hurt and pain, sorrow and anger. She had sown the seeds of doubt. They would sprout and grow, and she would tend them, nurture them, until the harvest of her hatred was ready. Then would come her own fulfilment. She would reap what *he* had sown. Miriam would pay the price of vengeance.

Ralph closed his eyes against his mother's words, but images still rose to taunt him. Could what she had said be true? Could it be that the shame his sister felt for her own actions, and fear of his retribution, had caused her to lie to him?

Dropping his head into his hands, he fought the doubt edging into his mind. Miriam had never needed to fear him. From babyhood she had seemed to know implicitly that *he* could never harm her or even speak harshly to her. And she had never lied to him until...

Angry with himself for allowing the thought to slip into his mind, Ralph dropped his hands, sitting sharply upright.

Miriam would have screamed. She would not willingly have accepted Marsh.

'*...her was more than willing...*'

It was not true! He rose to his feet, trying to drive away the thought. Miriam had never lied, while his mother ... she would not think twice about telling the blackest of lies if it would hurt either Miriam or him. But though he repeated this reasoning over and over, doubt still hovered in the secret reaches of his heart.

'I can guess what her told you.' Laughter rattled once more in Leah's throat. 'But then, what else would her say? If Marsh has left her breeding another bastard then her needs to cover the part her played in the getting of it; her must pretend there were no pleasure for her in what they did, that it were against her will. Her knows Marsh will not wed her no matter how many bastards he gets on her. So her tells you it was done without her consent, against her will. But I heard them and I knows that sister of yours made no complaint.'

'Ethan Rawley came before ... before anything happened!' Ralph forced himself to speak, to say the words that would drive those pictures from his mind, the torment from his soul.

In the semi-darkness of the room Leah's eyes glittered like chips of jet, the scorn in her voice matching their blackness.

'That be what her said, was it? And you believed her! But then you always did. And why

'... ask yourself why?'

Watching him, she sensed his hesitation.

'You make no answer.' She made no effort to hide the mockery in her voice. 'And I know the reason for that as well! You can't bring yourself to say it so I will say it for you. You believe everything her tells you, every lie her feeds you no matter how obvious. You believe her because you be in love with her. In love with your own sister!'

'Leave it, Mother.' Across the room his eyes glowed a warning. 'Don't ... don't say any more!'

Her every word a barb in his flesh, he dropped back into his chair.

It was true! Anguish almost forced the words from his mouth. He loved his own sister, with a love he would never hold for any other woman, a deep abiding love. But it was a love forbidden. One that neither God nor man could sanction.

Leah read his thoughts, and smiled.

She had waited almost half a lifetime. They had gone, the two of them, leaving her behind to suffer the pity that hid the laughter of Brades Village; to marry William Bryce. But for him she could feel no love, as she felt none then for him who had jilted her. But she felt something else, something so powerful it filled her, drove her on with its strength. She had fostered it, nourished it, and now it would reward her. It would give her all that she deserved, all that had been due to her from the moment of *his* leaving.

Smile widening, Leah relaxed deeper into her pillows.

A harvest of hatred and she would reap it to the full.

A falling cinder rattling into the hearth recalled Ralph from his own silent world. Glancing to the candle standing on the table beside his mother's bed, he could see it was more than half burned away. If only it could stay night forever; if only he did not have to face the world ever again.

Deep in the shadows his mother's breathing was short and fast, each draught of air sucked into her lungs with a heavy rasping sound. Reaching for the poker to stir the dying fire into brightness, he turned as she called his name.

She had never called to him before. Not once in any of the nights he had sat with her. Returning the poker to its stand, he crossed to the bed. In the dim candlelight it seemed her face had sunk in on itself. Dark hollows where once cheeks had been, mouth drawn sideways, a thin streak of saliva oozing from its corner. Only the eyes were the same. Glittering, dark and full of malice, they stared up at him.

'You won't ever have her.'

It was so quiet, each word laboured, but Ralph caught them all.

'Leave it, Mother. You need rest, we both need rest.'

'We don't always be given what we need, nor what we want.' Leah breathed hard, though the effort barely lifted her chest. 'And you won't be given that which you want more than life, though you could have had it, you could have had...' She broke off, a cough grating like pebbles in her throat.

What could he have had? Turning up the wick of the paraffin lamp, he held the candle flame to it. Then, as the light fell across his mother's face, he turned thought into words.

'You could have had her ... Miriam.' Leah's brow burned a dull angry red, the rest of her face a bloodless white. 'But you won't ... you won't.'

'What do you mean?' Ralph stared into eyes that had taken on a brighter gleam, glittering like black sequins in the yellow glow of the lamp.

'I mean the girl sleeping in that room across the landing was not born of my body, nor was her seed that of him that fathered you. The one you know as Miriam Bryce is no daughter of mine and no sister to you!'

The fingers that held the lamp tightening, Ralph stared down at his mother, his brain refusing to accept what she said. It couldn't be true. He remembered Miriam being born. No, he remembered getting up one morning to find her lying in a drawer set against the hearth in the living room! But that did not necessarily mean she was not his sister; in their walk of life women were up and about the day after giving birth, just as Miriam had been following the birth of Angela. What his mother had said was lies. Even now she could not resist causing him pain.

'Why do you say such a thing?' he breathed. 'Why do you hate Miriam so much you even deny her birth?'

Beneath the glow of the lamp, Leah's brow reddened as if touched by a branding iron. Her breath was snatched in quicker, shorter gasps, yet still her eyes glittered bright and evil as a serpent's.

'I say it because it is the truth. That girl was not

355

carried in my womb, it was not I who gave her birth.'

'Then who?' The question was sharp as Ralph placed the lamp beside the candle holder.

'It were hers, given to her by the one who should have been mine...'

Seating himself on the bed, Ralph leaned forward as his mother's voice faded to a whisper. Lies or not, he must hear it all.

'She came to the village flaunting her pretty face, her hair the colour of autumn berries. She could have had any of the Brades Village men, but when she made her choice she took the one betrothed to me. She took Tom Shaw. When her father finished his work up at the Hall, they left the village and Tom Shaw went with them.'

At the corner of Leah's misshapen mouth spittle shone in the sickly yellow light.

'They left together, the pair of them, with never a word to me. I was left to face the gossip of every woman in the village. It were your father, William Bryce, who wed me then. I became his wife though I held no love for him. But each night I prayed the Lord to give me vengeance, to repay what had been done to me.'

Straining to catch the whispered words, Ralph wanted to ask so many questions. But to interrupt her now might set the seal on the silence she had kept for so many years.

'It seemed my prayers were to go unheard. That the Lord would hold vengeance unto Himself. Then came the letter. You were nigh on six years old. She was dead, the letter told me, dead from childbirth two weeks since; and he, Thomas

Shaw, dying of the consumption. Would William Bryce, his true and best friend, take his child from the orphanage where she had been sent? Would he give her a home and rear her as his own daughter?'

Fingers clawing the sheet, Leah stared at her son.

'I was given no choice. William Bryce left the same day, returning from Wolverhampton with the child. *Her* child! He gave it his name but it was me saddled with the caring of it. Then I came to realise the workings of the Lord. Her that had robbed me of my life had been robbed of her own.'

Laughter scraped against Leah's throat.

'"*As ye sow, so shall ye reap!*" She took mine, the Lord took hers. I could not make her pay as I'd yearned to do, she was beyond my vengeance, but the child she had borne was given to me in her stead. The Lord was giving me my revenge.'

'You let me go on thinking Miriam was my sister!' Ralph shook his head, disbelief in his voice. 'Even after Father died, you let me go on believing it, even though you knew my feelings for her. You could have put an end to the torment but you did not. Instead you added daily to the agony of it. You took your hatred out on an innocent girl, made her life a misery to salve your own twisted pride. You vented your spite on your own son, putting him through hell. And all the time you kept your own lust alive! A lust more potent and evil than any you accused Miriam of holding.'

At his sides his fingers clenched into tight fists.

'What you have done is more than cruel, it is evil. If what you have said is the truth – and believe me, Mother, that is the one thing I count you a stranger to – then why hide it so long?'

Against the pallor of her cheeks, the crimson stain across Leah's forehead seemed to glow. 'Oh, it is the truth,' she murmured. 'The truth is in every single word.'

All these years!

Anger and resentment near to bursting in him, Ralph turned away. She had known ... for years his mother had known his real feelings for Miriam! She could have removed the pain of his self-recrimination, the feeling that by loving Miriam so much he committed a sin. But Leah had said nothing. She had watched his suffering, taking perverse pleasure in the pain of her own child.

As the horror of it struck home, Ralph swung back to the bed, bitterness in his face as he stared down at his mother.

'All these years and you said nothing. Well, you will say it now. You are going to tell Miriam what you have just told me!'

Her fingers relaxing on the sheet, eyes glittering, Leah watched her son stride from the room.

Chapter Twenty-three

'Will you be wanting a last minute with your mother?'

Miriam shook her head as one of the village women touched her arm. 'Come you away then, wench. You'll not want to be seeing any more. You'll have enough sorrow to remember this day without heaping more on the top.'

Glancing at her companion the woman gave a slight tilt of her head, indicating the direction of the scullery. Placing Miriam between them, they ushered her gently from the living room.

Enough sorrow to remember this day.

Standing silently between the two women, Miriam felt the irony of the words. She would not remember her mother's funeral with joy, but it would be only one more sombre day among hundreds she could remember; one more day without joy.

'Be it all right to carry on?'

Miriam looked at the man who, cap in hand, came to stand at the scullery door.

'Arrh, you carry on,' the second woman answered as Miriam stood silent. 'We'll keep the wench in here. Far better her don't see what has to be done.'

Blankly, Miriam watched him pick up the hammer and nails that Ralph had brought in from the tool box, seeing yet not registering the look of understanding pass between him and the women.

'Try to bear up, me wench.'

Putting a motherly arm about Miriam's shoulders, the first woman spoke comfortingly as the banging of the hammer resounded through the quiet home. Her whole body trembling, each stroke of the hammer like a blow to her head, Miriam dropped her face into her hands.

Her mother was dead! Leah Bryce was dead! Even now she could not accept the strange feeling of emptiness inside her. The days of torment were over. Never again would she hear the abuse, the eternal accusations, never again feel the sting of that hand striking her across the face. But where was the relief she had always thought would come when she was finally free from her mother? Where the happiness? This was not the way she had dreamed her release would come, not through death. Leah Bryce had never given her a mother's love, never shown her tenderness, but through it all Miriam had never wished for freedom this way.

'We be ready.' The man returned the hammer, putting it discreetly behind the coal bucket.

'Come on, Miriam wench.' The woman stood with her arm about her, giving her a comforting squeeze. 'It be hard, we all knows that well enough, we've been through it ourselves. It ain't never easy, but it has to be done. Come on, wench, put a brave face on it, if only for the sake of your brother. The lad is taking it very hard. He looks little better than a walking corpse hisself. But then, it be understandable...' She glanced at the woman who, with herself, had washed Leah's body, dressing it in a white cotton night gown, brushing her long hair and tying it in plaits. '...men don't have the same strength as women. Oh, they can mine coal or puddle iron, but when it comes to this sort of thing, then they don't have the strength we women have.'

'That be the truth and a half!' The other woman nodded. 'A woman has to be strong enough for herself and for the men in a case like this. They never finds it easy to handle death.'

'None of we do.' The first woman too nodded her head as she gathered Miriam closer. 'None of we do, and the younger you be the worse you feels it. But the pain passes, Miriam wench, take the word of one as knows. It takes time but it passes eventually. It be hard for you now and it will be for weeks, there ain't no denying that, but heart-breaking as it be to lose your mother, the grief will ease. Now, try to hold back the tears for your brother's sake. What must be done had best be done soon. The quicker it's over, the better it will be for the both of you.'

The pain passes...

Miriam grasped the words, holding them in her mind. *The pain passes...*

But where was the pain? Why did she feel nothing but emptiness in her heart? A cold aching emptiness that had come not with her mother's death, but with her brother's decision.

The woman's arm still about her shoulders, Miriam returned to the sitting room. The wooden door resting on the seats of two chairs still lay beneath the window, but the coffin it had supported was gone.

'Come on, wench, you has to go.'

Feeling her hesitation, the woman urged Miriam gently on, walking with her over to where Ralph stood behind the hand cart holding his mother's coffin.

Eyes drawn to the plain deal box, Miriam stared at the single small wreath set at its centre. She had not thought of wreaths, had no last offering to accompany her mother on her last journey, just as none had gone with that soapbox.

Her daughter had been given no wreath. Miriam stood with eyes fixed to the small tribute made from greenery collected on the heath and fashioned by village women. Red berries of butcher's broom glowed beside fat purple berries of myrtle. Twined between sprigs of blue-grey juniper, bedded in the dark glossy green of holly, they gleamed in the dull light of winter. Nothing so pretty had been placed on her daughter's tiny coffin.

Two men taking the handles of the hand cart, two more walking one to each side, all with heads bare, the group of women following, they moved off towards the village, feet and cartwheels crunching on the frost-bitten ground.

Beside her, Ralph walked in silence. Why did he not take her hand? Why had he left it to others to comfort her? He had always been so caring, always there for her. But though he walked at her side now he was not close to her. He was in that distant place, the one he had drawn himself into after finding their mother dead, a place he would not allow her to enter.

Along the streets the little cortège was greeted by the murmured blessings of women who crossed themselves with quick fingers, and old men who raised their caps as the coffin passed by. From many of the houses the same salute came from curtained windows.

Bringing the hand cart to rest beneath the arch of the wooden lych gate, long blackened by coal smoke rather than age, the four men hoisted the coffin on to their shoulders, carrying it into the church.

Miriam had come here every Sunday with Leah, each week until her mother had learned of her pregnancy. She had always thought the church beautiful, the colours of its stained glass streaming like the ribbons of May Day banners over the dark oak pews; the glint of polished brass candlesticks gleaming on an altar draped with red velvet. The church had been a place where, for a short time, the bleakness of her life had been forgotten, submerged beneath blessed serenity.

Ralph no longer attended. From leaving school he had turned his back on religion, teasing her whenever she spoke of it. She glanced at him now as he sat beside her, but his face was closed, eyes staring directly ahead.

The service was brief but long enough for the chill of the church to strike at the bones. With the whispered Amens she felt grateful for the release.

At the open grave, Miriam found herself glancing about the tiny cemetery. Which tombstone marked the place where her baby lay? Whose body covered it in that cold ground?

'*Ashes to ashes...*'

The vicar droned on as the verger, clad in the same dark robes, held a small wooden box toward Ralph.

'*...dust to dust...*'

Reaching into the box, Ralph took a handful of the soil that lay in it. Stepping to the edge of the yawning hole that held their mother's coffin, he sprinkled it over the wooden surface; but when the box was held to her, Miriam turned away with a strangled sob.

Closing his prayer book, the vicar glanced at them over heavy spectacles. He gave a brief nod and a murmured goodbye, indicating the funeral service was at an end. Turning away, he was followed quickly by the small group of women who had escorted the coffin to the grave, shawls drawn over faces pinched with cold. Leah Bryce had never been a popular member of the community, but duty was duty; she had been one of their own and as such would be seen to her final resting place. But that done they were quickly gone.

Her own shawl held close, one corner clutched across her nose and mouth, gave Miriam scant protection from the biting wind sweeping across the heath and into the church yard. Flurries of hoar frost trailed like petticoats peeping beneath invisible gowns. Usually Miriam would have appreciated this delicate finery but today it passed by unseen.

Her mother lay in that box at the bottom of the grave, soon to be hidden by the earth. No more would she vent her spite on either of them, yet even now Miriam felt the resentment that had always been present in Leah. The virulent bitterness that had been so much a part of her dealings with her daughter was present still.

Miriam shivered as she turned to look once more at the open grave. It seemed to draw her to it, as if in some unseen, unknown way the presence of her mother was with her yet.

Nervously, she touched Ralph's sleeve. Like the women and the priest, they should leave. But he seemed not to feel the touch. Like herself a moment ago, he was staring fixedly at the open grave.

'Ralph.' She touched his sleeve again. 'It is time to go, we have to leave her ... I'm sorry, dear, but we have to leave her.'

He did not turn his head to look at her, nor did he give any answer. Miriam felt her heart twist painfully. Had their mother's death affected him more deeply than she could have expected? Or was he blaming her for Leah's death?

The thought overwhelming her, Miriam pressed the shawl against her mouth, stifling the sob that rose to her lips.

Ralph did not want her here, did not want to share the grief that held him. He had turned his back on his sister.

Taking one last glance at his drawn features, she made to turn away. As if the movement had suddenly brought him back to life, Ralph stepped closer to the edge of the neatly dug hole. Staring into it, he laughed. Miriam shivered at the harshness of it.

'A different God!' He laughed again. 'Remember, Mother – a different God!'

Crossing the heath in silence, Miriam matched her steps to his. Maybe he would speak before they reached the house, end this awful quiet that had come between them since that night.

Then Ralph had burst into her room. Shaking her awake, he had literally dragged her from her bed, hauling her after him as he strode out again. She must hear what their mother had to say, she must hear it now, he'd insisted. It could not wait until morning. Then, as she grabbed her shawl from the foot of her bed, he had taken her hand, pulling her across the corridor to their mother's room.

'*Tell her!*' he had yelled pushing her before him to the bedside. '*Tell Miriam! Tell her what you have just told me!*'

Her breath misty on the frosty air, she shuddered. But it was a shudder that stemmed as much from her memories as it did from cold.

Leah was still on her pillows. Hair her own tetchiness had prevented Miriam from plaiting and coiling about her ears, as she had always worn it, was spread across the pillows, their whiteness yellowed by the spill of lamplight. Her thin lips were slightly parted in a twisted smile, made the more grotesque by the droop her illness had bequeathed. But it was the eyes that were the most arresting feature.

Miriam felt her body tremble afresh as those eyes stared at her again from the darkness of her own mind.

Those eyes had watched them come into the room, watched Ralph push Miriam to the

366

bedside. Malign and venomous, their gleam bitter as it had ever been, Leah Bryce's eyes had stared at her daughter.

'Tell her!'

Ralph had grabbed the hand that rested motionless on the sheet, shaking it when their mother did not speak. But it had lain in his, cold and unmoving, while the eyes, beady and bright in the reflected glow of the lamp, mocked them both.

Clutching the shawl as the wind caught it, trying to tear it from her body, Miriam heard again the sob that had broken from her brother as he realised their mother was dead. Beneath the cover of her shawl her mouth trembled.

It had been the cry of the damned. The cry of a soul doomed to perpetual torment.

'I ask your pardon, Miss Bryce, I did not know you were in mourning or I would not have called.'

Clayton Rawley glanced at the band of black petersham ribbon circling the sleeve of Miriam's white blouse.

'I am grateful you came.' She moved aside from the door, indicating for him to enter.

Inside the small room, Clayton glanced at the plain furnishings: a dealwood dresser adorned with plain white crockery, the table spread with a matching cloth draped over dark red chenille, the cast-iron firegrate polished to black silver. There was nothing in the room worth more than twopence but the whole of it was sparkling clean.

'My condolences on your loss.' He took a chair

but refused her offer of tea.

Miriam took a seat opposite. Then, wanting only to enquire after Ethan's condition, felt first she must explain her not calling to ask after him at the Hall.

'My mother was taken ill a few days after my return. There was no one else to help nurse her apart from my brother, and he had to work during the day.'

'Of course.' Clayton touched the top hat perched on his knee, his movement a trifle self-conscious. The girl was obviously still very much affected by her bereavement. He should have kept to his first idea of sending a note to this house instead of being swayed by Ethan.

'I felt I could not leave her alone. Her illness left her partly paralysed and confined to her bed. I felt I must be here, should she need me...' Breaking off, she tried to suppress a shudder at the memory of that afternoon her mother had called and she had been unable to answer, over-powered by Saul Marsh.

'She died a month ago.' Miriam's fingers twisted together in her lap. 'I would, of course, have called to enquire of Ethan...'

Clayton smiled as she glanced up. 'I have no doubt of that, Miss Bryce, but the formalities of mourning must be observed. I must not trespass upon your grief any longer.'

'Please!' Miriam spoke quickly as he made to stand. 'Please, Mr Rawley, tell me – is your son...'

The smile returned to his mouth and Miriam saw thankfulness invade those kind eyes. 'My son will recover, thanks to your help, my dear.'

'I'm so sorry. So very sorry...'

All the traumas of the last weeks seemed to press down on her at once, each adding its separate crippling weight to the other. Covering her face with her hands, Miriam tried to hide the tears but they thickened her voice.

'Ethan was trying to help me ... he pulled Saul away ... he would not have been hurt if he had just gone away. Oh, God! It was my fault. *My* fault!'

Clayton leaned forward to touch her arm. 'It was never my son's way to turn his back on anyone needing help. Ethan would never have just gone away; nor would I have wanted him to. What my son did that day was what any red-blooded man would do. I have no complaint on that score.'

'But he could have died!' Miriam sobbed.

'He could have.' Clayton withdrew his arm. 'A knife in the chest, so close to the heart, could easily kill a man. But, thank God, that did not happen. He is making a good recovery but it is slow going – too slow for my son who has a liberal share of the impetuosity of youth. Which is what brings me here. He threatened to leave his bed and come here himself unless I called and asked you to be so good as to visit him. But, of course, under the circumstances that will not now be possible. A lady in mourning cannot make calls.'

Drawing a handkerchief from the pocket of her apron, Miriam brushed it over her cheeks as Clayton Rawley rose to leave.

'Mr Rawley,' her tears under control, she stood

up, head held high, 'we in Brades Village do not let social propriety come before gratitude or friendship. In your world it may not be deemed the proper thing to pay calls until the three months of mourning are passed, but in mine we do not have the same rules. Men and women here must work to live. The only chance they have to grieve is when they are lying in their bed. That being so, I should have made enquiries as to your son's health a month ago. It is down to my own selfishness that I did not.'

'I cannot believe that of you.' At the door Clayton turned back. 'I have not had the pleasure of knowing you very long, Miss Bryce, but judging by the few occasions we have met I find it difficult indeed to think of you as selfish. May I tell Ethan you will call at the Hall some time in the future?'

'If it is acceptable to you, Mr Rawley, I would very much like to visit your son today.'

Clayton Rawley watched the girl sat stiffly on the edge of the seat opposite. Her shawl was pulled tight across her chest, hair glinting auburn fire whenever the pale sunlight caught it, the beauty of it striking.

She had buried her mother a month ago. He let his eyes dwell on the face turned to the passing heath. That was enough to bring sorrow to the heart of any young girl. But there was more than sorrow lurking in those grass-green eyes, there was heartbreak. Whatever had happened to this girl seemed set to destroy her.

Ethan had told him of what had occurred in the

house, of that swine Marsh's assault upon her. But terrible though that was, it had been a failed attempt. Surely that alone could not account for the sadness pervading her? But then, she had seen Ethan stabbed in the chest, had pulled the knife free and held him in her arms thinking he might die there. How many women would have the courage to do that? Each of those things would be sufficient in itself, a heavy enough affliction to bear, yet he felt there was more to it than that. She had suffered a deeper, more profound shock. Somewhere, somehow, Miriam Bryce had lost more than a mother.

'Allow me to thank you once more for coming.' Helping her from the carriage that had brought them both to Brade Hall, Clayton held her cold fingers in his as he smiled down at her. 'I know my son will be most happy to see you.'

Freeing her hand, he half turned to the butler who came to meet the carriage.

'Baxter will see you upstairs. Forgive me for not joining you but I have an appointment. Though I feel Ethan will not be unhappy at my having to leave you solely in his company.'

Following the butler along the thickly carpeted corridor that led to the bedrooms, Miriam felt again the cold fear that visited her every night. Passing the room that had been Saul's, she felt a touch of ice against her spine, trembling at the memory of his breath against her face, his hand tearing at her clothes.

'Are you all right?' His hand raised to tap at Ethan's door, Baxter paused.

'Yes ... thank you.' Miriam swallowed the bile

371

searing her throat, but beneath her skirts her knees trembled.

'We was all sorry for what happened,' Baxter whispered. 'Mrs Baxter especially blames herself. Says if she hadn't sent you up here...'

'Tell her there is no need to blame herself or anyone.' Miriam tried to smile. 'It's over now, and forgotten. If I may, I will come to the kitchen before leaving the Hall. I would like to see Mrs Baxter and Ginny.'

'They'll be happy to see you.'

Tapping on the door of the bedroom, Baxter opened it and stepped aside as Miriam entered. What had happened to the girl at Brade Hall was over as she'd said, but it was not forgotten. Her eyes betrayed the lie, just as they told him that Saul Marsh's attempt to rape her was not the only horror she had undergone. Miriam Bryce had suffered more since leaving the Hall, proof of that was written plain on her face. The girl had gone through hell, and the gates were not yet closed behind her.

'Miriam, I am so glad!'

Propped on huge white pillows, Ethan stretched out both hands to her as she came to stand beside his bed.

'I wanted so much to see you, to know you are well. That swine Marsh did not return? I remember his running from the house.'

'No, he did not return.' Her knees not yet steady, Miriam withdrew her hands from his clasp, lowering herself into the winged chair drawn close to the bed.

'Thank God!' Ethan relaxed against the

pillows. 'The police have not managed to trace the swine as yet, there is no trace of him, but he will turn up sooner or later. Bad pennies always do. When he does you can be sure he will be sent down, and for life if my father has any influence.'

'I don't think Saul will return to Brades Village. Surely he has more sense than to risk that after what he did to you?'

'You can never tell with a man like him. He's just as likely to take that risk. That is why I had to know you were safe, that your mother is recovered.'

'She is dead.'

Ethan leaned sharply forward, falling back with a faint grunt as pain lanced through his chest. Lifting a hand, he took the one she raised to meet it.

'Miriam, I am so sorry.'

Only the look she gave him speaking her thanks, Miriam returned her hand to her lap.

'But doesn't this mean you are alone in the house?'

Hearing the concern in his voice, she shook her head, not meeting his eyes. Her answer, and it must be given so Ethan could have peace of mind, would not be all the truth.

'No, I am not alone in the house. I have my brother, and also one of the girls from the village has come to live in with me, so I am safe enough.'

'Why not come and live here at the Hall? You could be cared for properly here ... and we could be married. I told you that day as you sat with me in your arms: I love you, Miriam, and I want you to be my wife. Say you will marry me? Say it, Miriam?'

She stared at her fingers, twisting the corners of her shawl. She could marry Ethan, be the future mistress of this lovely house, safe and secure. He loved her, hadn't he said so twice before? He loved her and that should be enough. Only it was not enough, not for either of them. He needed her to love him. And she? What was it she wanted? What was it life was denying her?

No answer in her mind except the one she knew she must give the man watching her from his sick bed, Miriam twisted the shawl tighter around her fingers.

'I can't say it, Ethan,' she murmured, eyes lowered. 'I do love you, it is true. I love you for your gentleness and kindness. I love you for the friendship you showed me from our first meeting. But to make that a basis for marriage would be wrong. I would end up hurting you and that I could not live with. I love you as a dear and cherished friend, but not as a husband should be loved. Forgive me, please.'

'Honesty needs no forgiveness, Miriam.' He smiled but his eyes betrayed the sadness her answer gave. 'You have spoken the truth that is in your heart. I will not say I welcome it but I respect it. I hope that though you will not be my wife, you will always be my friend.'

'Always.' She lifted her eyes. 'Always, Ethan.'

'I can walk home, it is not too far.'

Miriam returned the hug Sally Baxter gave her then turned to embrace a grinning Ginny.

'Mebbe not.' Sally Baxter smoothed her long apron decisively. 'But Baxter will be the next to walk from this house, and that with his bags in his hands and me at his side, should the master discover his orders 'aven't been carried out to the letter, afore I loses my temper.'

'I would not want you doing that.' Miriam hugged the older woman again.

'You're not the only one!' Ginny Jinks laughed.

Extricating herself from Miriam's arms, Sally Baxter took refuge from tears by turning quickly to glare at the house maid.

'You get yourself back inside, Ginny!' she ordered. 'There be plenty for you to apply your 'ands to, and give your tongue a rest!'

Watching the coach door close on Miriam, Ginny waved cheerfully. She had long learned the real danger signals in the housekeeper's irascible behaviour, and so far her words had displayed none.

The coach moving at a steady pace, Miriam watched the heath slip past. Adorned in the splendour of a silver frost its beauty was awesome, but lost before the thoughts that filled her mind.

'You have spoken the truth that is in your heart.'

Ethan's words danced in her memory. But she had not spoken the whole truth. She was not alone in the house, a girl from the village had come to live in, that much was true. But she had not told it all. She had not told Ethan that her brother was no longer there. She had not told him Ralph had left!

Chapter Twenty-four

Coming to the branch of the Dudley road, the coach turned towards the village. But lost as she was in her own thoughts, Miriam saw none of the white-rocked beauty of the heath. She was remembering the last time she'd seen Ralph.

They had returned to the house, the two of them walking from the graveside, no word passing between them.

The kitchen was darker than usual, curtains drawn, closing off the dim afternoon light. The grate was cold and empty as it had been since their mother's passing. Taking the matches, Miriam lit both lamps.

Without removing his jacket Ralph had fetched wood and sticks from the yard, silently lighting a fire. She had reached cups from the dresser, setting them on the table though she could not brew a pot of tea until the fire burned through.

He had been so quiet, so withdrawn since finding their mother dead. Shutting her out of his life as though she did not exist.

He had set the fire, his deft fingers laying sticks in criss cross order, then adding small coals as the flames licked high. Still keeping silent he had refilled the bucket with coals, setting it in place beneath the scullery sink, and all the time Miriam had wondered. After the harshness of their upbringing from the time their father had died, she had not expected Ralph to take their mother's death so hard. But from the very moment of realising Leah no longer lived it seemed some phantom hand had grabbed his soul, that even as she watched it was squeezing the life from his heart.

It was as she offered him tea. Placing the cup before him, she had touched his hand resting on the table.

He was sitting with his arms folded, head resting on them, eyes closed. She had touched his hand gently, thinking he might have fallen asleep, not wanting to wake him; but he had started like a scalded cat, face twisted as if from pain.

'I can't stay here!' The words burst from him. 'I'll get someone from the village. One of Bertha Timms's girls will come and stay with you – most likely she will be glad to get away from her mother's nagging, and Bertha won't say no to the few shillings a week I'll pay her for letting the girl stay here.'

Miriam had stared at him. What had she done that he should want to leave the house? True he had long wanted to do just that, but that had been when their mother was alive. Surely now things were different? There would be no more hard words, no more terrible scenes, they could live happily together.

'Don't you see!' He had kicked the hearth, the way he always did when frustration got the better of him. 'A man and a woman living alone under the same roof ... can't you see what people would make of that?'

Bewildered, she continued to stare as if she had

not heard what he'd said. Then, as it dawned on her, she asked: 'Is it me, something I have done that has hurt or annoyed you, is that why you want to leave?'

The tortured sound of the cry her words brought from him echoed in her mind, the anguish in his face as vivid in her memory as when he had turned to face her.

'It's nothing you have done. Oh, Jesus, Miriam, don't make this harder for me! I'm trying to shield you from the talk that would come from the village, from the lies that would spread faster than summer fire over the heath.'

Still confused she had gone to him, taking his hands in her own. 'But, Ralph, we are brother and sister. We have lived together in the same house all our lives, what difference can there be in continuing to do so now?'

He had gazed down at her.

'The difference is my ... our mother is no longer here!' He had tripped over the words as if they stuck to his tongue. 'While she lived there could be no gossip, no malicious implication, but with the two of us here alone it will be a Godsend to those who are always eager to think the worst of others. And there are a few of that sort in Brades Village. I won't have you subjected to their lies.'

'But how could there possibly be gossip about us? What is there to say? It is perfectly natural for brother and sister to live together in the same house.'

'Miriam.' His fingers had tightened about her own. 'Miriam, we both of us know there would

378

never be anything ... untoward. Nothing that folk could talk about. But they would, believe me they would. True or false it would make no odds, there are always those ready to invent what isn't there, pretend a thing exists when it does not.'

'But, Ralph...'

'Please, Miriam!' His face had twisted as it had a few moments before. 'Think about what I say. A young girl and a man, under the same roof, night after night. It might be all right at first, but soon tongues would begin to wag, remarks would be passed, and that would send the ball rolling.'

But she had not thought about what he was saying. She knew only that he had said he could not stay with her. Her voice breaking, she had stared up at him.

'But it is perfectly natural we should live together, we are brother and sister.'

'No!' He had snatched his hands from hers, pulling away to stand at the window, the curtains closing away the outside world. He had stood there for several minutes, his shoulders drooping. She had wanted to go to him, to hold him as he had held her as a child, to give him the comfort he had always given her. But she had not. Some inner sense seemed to warn her of the barrier he had erected about his emotions; that to touch him at that moment would bring it tumbling, leave him susceptible to the doubt that had racked him since their mother's death.

Then, the words coming with a deliberate calm that told her clearly they were final, he had said, 'There are those who'd let the fact of our being kin make no difference. They would see what

379

they want to see, make what they want to make...'

'But what could that be?' she had cried. 'What can they make of it?'

'They could make you into your brother's whore!'

His words had dropped into the quiet room like a stone. A stone that had smashed her world apart.

Sitting in the coach, Miriam was deaf to the sound of hoofs, the crunch of wheels on the frozen ground, hearing only the silence that had descended on the room.

'I'm sorry,' she had said, understanding for the first time what her brother had tried to say to her. 'I did not think such a thing possible. I would not have thought people could be so cruel, so...'

'So dirty-minded?'

It had sounded so bitter, so hopeless.

'Some folk find it easy as well as entertaining.'

The kettle she had swung across the fire began to steam, jiggling its lid. She had gone across to it, swinging the bracket away from the heat.

'I'm sorry, Ralph.' She had stood staring at the glowing coals. 'I did not think of the position my selfishness would put you into. Of course we cannot share the same house, but I must be the one to leave.'

His sharp intake of breath had been loud in the quiet room and she had turned to look at him. 'No, Miriam. You will stay here.'

'But that is not fair,' she had protested. 'This is your home as much as mine. If either of us has to go, it should be me!'

The sadness with which he had answered had

tugged at her heart. Miriam gripped her hands together beneath her shawl. Just as it tugged at her now.

As he turned from the window he had looked straight at her, the light of the lamps giving his eyes a brilliance that seemed like tears.

'Life is not fair,' he'd said softly. 'None of us really matters. Life takes what it wants from each of us then moves on, leaving the dregs behind.'

She had not understood his meaning, but the pain in him she knew well enough; she had felt that same pain many times.

'Then why make it more unfair on yourself by leaving your home?'

For a moment the trick of the light seemed to drown his eyes in a flood of tears. Then he had laughed, softly and with just a trace of his old humour.

'We could go on like this for hours, you were always better at arguing than me. But this time I mean it. You will stay here in the house. I have got myself a room in the village...'

She remembered the shock that had given her. He had already found another place to live! Had he so wanted to be free of her, free of the responsibility of his unmarried sister.

'...I will continue to support you, to pay for the running of the house. Nothing will change...'

'Except that you will not be here, we will not be together.'

He had started towards her then, but checked himself, coming to lean both hands heavily on the table.

'Help me, Miriam!'

It had been like the cry of a child, a cry that had dragged the heart from her body. She had gone to him, touching his face with her hand, but he had jerked away and when he spoke his voice held a tone she had not heard before.

'For God's sake, will you understand! This is no game I am playing.'

Stunned by the harshness of it, she had made no answer.

'Miriam, I am trying to do what I know is best for us. For you. I want no finger to point at you, no gossip to follow you, unfounded as it might be. The only way I can be sure, the only way I can feel at ease with myself, is to leave this house. But you will not be alone. I have arranged for one of the Timms girls to come and live in.'

'Then if one of the Timms girls is coming here to live, we would not be alone. There would be three people in the house the same as before.'

She had tried one last time, but he had not changed his mind. Ralph had left that same day.

The ache inside her solid and heavy, Miriam remembered the hidden fear in his last words.

'You must never be in the house alone, promise me, Miriam? You will never stay here alone.'

Climbing from the coach, she watched it drive away.

Nothing will change.

The words echoed in her mind. But they had already changed. Her brother had gone. Had it been because of a need for freedom, a need to be released from what he saw as his responsibility for her?

The wind pulling at her skirts, she turned

towards the house. Had she accepted Ethan's offer of marriage then she would no longer be her brother's burden, no longer his responsibility. Ralph could return to the home that was rightfully his. She already felt a kind of love for Ethan. Perhaps in time it would become a different love, the sort of love she had once dreamed of having with the father of her child. But that love would have died. Even if Saul had not killed it, it would have shrivelled away inside her, she knew that now.

But that would not happen with Ethan. He was so kind, so gentle. Surely her love for him could only deepen? He loved her, and in time she would love him in the same way. Marriage to Ethan would give both men what they wanted. To Ethan it would bring the wife he longed for; to her brother the freedom he wanted.

But even as she walked up the path towards the house, Miriam recognised this answer was no answer at all. What if that love for Ethan did not change, if she could not love him as a wife? To break one man's heart so as to mend another's was wrong. The only solution was the one she had tried once before.

She must leave Brades Village. Leave and tell no one where she was going.

'I took everything ... like you said, I took them to me mother. Her was so pleased, said what didn't fit her would come in handy for the little ones. Her could cut them down and alter them round a bit – a ribbon here and there and they would look real pretty.'

Miriam smiled at the girl who shared her home. One of a family of twelve, she had been delighted with the room that had been Leah's. They had cleared it together, the girl commenting on the quality of some of the clothes Leah had long since laid away. 'There's many a year's wear left in them, it'd be criminal to chuck them on the fire!' she had said, fingering a coat and several dresses.

Miriam had said to take anything that was of use, and the girl had beamed. So Leah had given someone a moment of pleasure, albeit that someone was not her daughter or her son.

Helping prepare vegetables for the evening meal, Miriam was only partly aware of the girl's continuous chatter, her thoughts still on her brother. He came to eat with them each night at the close of his shift and she packed him fresh snap for the next day. It was the same as it had always been, except what little joy was once in Ralph's life seemed to have died. His face had grown gaunt. Shadows lay in dark circles about eyes whose only light was one of sadness, and a dusting of grey powdered his temples.

Taking the peeled potatoes to rinse beneath the scullery pump, Miriam glanced at the door that gave on to the yard. The bolts were secured top and bottom but that did not prevent the shiver that ran along her spine or the sudden choking fear from filling her throat. Saul Marsh had entered the house that way, had taken her by surprise, had...

Fear overwhelming her, she leaned blindly over the sink.

'Did you hear what I said... Eh, be you all right?'

'Yes.' Miriam seemed to float back from a long way off, her head spinning. 'Yes ... I'm just tired.'

'Come and sit you by the fire.' Placing an arm about Miriam's waist, the girl helped her to the living room. 'What you be needing is a nice cup of tea. I'll have one brewed before you can blink.'

'So what will I tell him?'

'Tell him?' Miriam looked up blankly as Amy Timms handed her a cup.

'Eh, I thought as how you hadn't heard a word I've been saying!' Taking the tea she had poured for herself, the girl perched on the chair opposite Miriam's. 'I said as how me mother says to tell you the priest along of St Matthew's wants to see you.'

Blood freezing in her veins, Miriam felt the heart inside her stop beating. The priest wanted to see her! Her fingers tightened, the clatter of the cup against its saucer unheard against the pounding in her head.

The priest wanted to see her!

He must have discovered what she and Ralph had done. Her brother's theft of the holy water, the baptism, her child's burial in holy ground.

'Be no need for you to look like that.' Amy saw the colour drain from Miriam's face. 'You haven't been caught pinching the church plate or with your fingers in the poor box, but by the way you've paled anybody would think you had committed a murder and hid the body.'

They had committed no murder. Nausea in her throat, Miriam trembled. But the body of her child had been hidden. Ralph had taken it to the church yard, paid the verger to bury it in someone else's grave, and now it had been found!

'Eh, I can see the cogs turning in your head, same as I can see that cup smashing into the hearth if you're not careful. Look, drink your tea then get yourself down to the parish house. I can see to the meal well enough by myself, Lord knows I've had the practice.'

From the hollow below the house, Ralph watched the woman leave. Her skirts were whipped by the wind that tugged the shawl tight about her head and shoulders. Miriam! His heart wheeled. He had used the excuse of possible gossip for not staying at the house, but that was not the real reason for his departure. The truth of it was he did not know how long he could keep the secret of his feelings for her hidden, conceal the love that was slowly destroying him. But even then he had been unable to make a clean break, to leave the village altogether. He had taken a room telling himself he must stay at the mine, work to keep them both. But that had been a lie, a salve to his pride. He could have found work in other coal mines, taken a room in another town and sent money for the upkeep of the house. But he had stayed, and the reason was Miriam. He could not tell her what had been said the night his mother had died. *His* mother!

A laugh, dry and dead as autumn leaves, stuck in his throat. That was the worst of it. Leah's spite and jealousy, that had lain like a curse over them all of their lives, had not died with her. It was her legacy to him. He laughed again. His bitter inheritance.

She had known! She could have saved him the heartache of thinking himself wicked to hold a love he thought so wrong, so unnatural. But she had said nothing. All those years and his mother had said nothing! Then, with her dying breath, she had taunted him with the knowledge that he and Miriam were no blood kin. And that had been her trump card, her final blow. A master stroke that would see his life in ruins. Her eyes had mocked him as he turned to fetch Miriam, mocked as if she knew the haemorrhage would strike her brain before he could return.

And she had won. He watched the girl's figure draw closer. She must have guessed he would say nothing of what she had told him. For who would believe him? The people of Brades Village? Miriam? No, the truth would stay hidden as Leah had hidden it, finally dying only when he did.

Her head bent against the wind, Miriam did not see him, starting with a frightened cry as he spoke her name.

'It's all right. It's only me, Ralph.' He stretched out his arms to her, dropping them before she could step into them. He had not held her since learning he was not her brother. To do so would be to send his defences crashing.

'Where are you going?' He glanced at her face, its pale beauty marbled by the touch of the risen moon.

'To St Matthew's. They ... the priest ... he knows. He has found my baby's body.'

Eyes green as the sea stared up at him, grinding

his heart like a millstone. 'Who told you this?' He forced his hands to remain at his sides.

'Amy ... her mother said to tell me.'

'Tell you what, Miriam? What exactly did Amy's mother say to tell you?'

'She said...' Fear still upon her, Miriam searched for the words. 'She said her mother told her to say the priest wanted to see me.

'And that's all? She gave no other reason?'

'No.' Miriam shook her head. 'But she had no cause to. There can be nothing else he wishes to speak to me about. It's my baby, I know it is. Her coffin has been found and now I must answer for it.'

Despite his resolve her misery was too much for him. Reaching out, Ralph drew her against him, arms tight about her.

'No, Miriam, you are wrong. It is not the child.' His mouth against her temple he spoke softly, soothing her as he had when she was a child; as he had so often soothed her after their mother's cruelty.

Only Leah had not been *their* mother.

The bitterness that had become a part of him burned fresh as on the night he had learned, too late.

She had been only *his* mother.

'Your baby has not been disturbed. The burial has not been found or I would have heard. The one who took her from me would have sent word. Trust me, Miriam. Your baby is safe where she lies, I made sure of that.'

Lifting her face to him, sobs still shaking her, she asked, 'How – how can you be sure?'

'Because I too had a message from the priest. Like you I feared the child had been taken from her resting place, so I went to the graveyard. I searched every part of it and none had been opened. There was no trace of fresh digging. But had there been, had your daughter been taken from one spot, I would have found another and that too in holy ground. There is no one will take that child from the church, just as no one can keep her from heaven.'

The wind snatching the shawl from her head, Miriam looked up at him. 'Thank you, Ralph,' she whispered. 'You are such a wonderful brother, I do love you.'

A wonderful brother! The irony of it stinging his soul, Ralph drew her against him, holding her for one last wonderful moment, his answer spoken silently in his mind.

'I love you too, Miriam. My God, how I love you!

In the sitting room of the small parish house, Miriam was still too worried to appreciate the comfort of it compared with her own home. Why had she and Ralph been summoned here? Despite her brother's reassurances there could be no reason other than the one she dreaded.

'Let me thank you both for coming. I should have visited you both at your homes but the pressure of parish business...' The priest touched the white collar circling his throat. While it was not exactly a lie, it was a useful excuse.

'I was at the Timms' house today ... one of the girls is coming up for First Communion. While I was there, Bertha – er, Mrs Timms – was taking apart a dress she tells me you sent to her.'

'Yes.' Miriam nodded. 'There were several. They were my mother's. I was going to burn them when Amy said they could be of use. Ralph knew of it.' She glanced quickly at her brother beside her. 'He agreed I should give them to Mrs Timms.'

'Yes, yes.' His assurance returning, the priest shuffled an assortment of papers set before him on a small round pie-crust table.

'I should have dealt with this in the study.' He glanced over the top of his horn-rimmed spectacles. 'But I felt you might be more relaxed here in the sitting room. I hope I did right?'

'Thank you.' Miriam nodded.

'Perhaps you could tell us just why you brought us here?' Ralph had taken all the obfuscation he intended to take. Whatever it was had to be said, it were best said quickly.

Shuffling the papers again the priest cleared his throat, clearly unsettled by what he had to say.

'As I said a moment ago, I was at the Timms' house today. During my visit, Mrs Timms proceeded to take one of the dresses you sent her to pieces, it seemed she thought it would make an excellent Confirmation dress for her daughter.

'Well the outcome of it was, she found these in a pocket sewn inside the lining.'

Ralph eased forward in his seat. 'Those papers were sewn into my mother's dress?'

'That is what I said.' Tone slightly tart, the priest looked at him over his spectacles. 'Mrs Timms gave them to me to read. What I saw,' he tapped the papers, 'led me to ask you both to call here. Perhaps before I say any more, you should both read them?'

Why should her mother sew papers into her dress? Miriam watched the colour drain from Ralph's face. Why hide them where she could not easily read them again? What secret was she trying to conceal, and if it were so awful, why not just burn the papers?

Taking them as Ralph finished reading, Miriam opened the first one.

Dear Friend,

I write this letter in the name of that friendship we shared for so long. Two weeks ago my dearest wife was delivered of a baby girl. The child was born healthy but in giving her life my dear wife forfeited her own. She lived but a few hours after the birth.

We both thanked God for his gift to us even though I knew, as did my wife, that I would not live to have the rearing of her. Then, when it became plain not one but two of us would shortly be leaving this world, my darling wife begged me ask you to take our child. I pray God you will do this, William. Take my daughter Miriam from the orphanage. Rear her as your own. Give her the love we have been prevented from giving her. I commend you to the care and mercy of God, as I commend my child to you.

Your old and dear friend,
Thomas Shaw

Her hands shaking, Miriam looked at Ralph. 'Read the rest,' he said gently. 'Read them all.' Disbelief giving way to bewilderment, she read

391

through each document. A copy of a birth certificate, a letter signed again by Thomas Shaw and by the doctor attending him, which gave permission for 'the child, Miriam Adena Shaw' to be given into the care and guardianship of William Bryce.

Hardly comprehending what she read, Miriam turned from one paper to the next. A document headed, 'The Orphanage of Our Lady', an official stamp occupying a corner opposite a flourishing signature, gave permission for the 'said child to be delivered into the care and custody of William Bryce'.

Lastly she unfolded a narrow rectangular document. Her fingers trembling so violently the words danced on the paper, she read, *Certified Copy of an Entry of Marriage.*

Below she read the names 'Thomas Shaw' and 'Adena Miriam Peveral'. Her eyes travelled across the paper until she came to the words: *Married in the Parish Church, according to the Rites and Ceremonies of the Church.*

Her eyes showing the bewilderment she felt, she looked at the priest watching her. 'Is ... is this real?'

'Most certainly. After reading the papers Mrs Timms handed over to me, I made a thorough investigation. Enquiries at the Orphanage proved that a child, a girl, had been taken into the household of William Bryce of Brades Village, and the paper you now hold is the marriage certificate of the parents of that child. That, too, is perfectly genuine.'

Miriam glanced again at the document in her

hand. At the foot, signed across a red one penny stamp, was the signature, Lionel G. Brown. While written above it was declared, *I do hereby certify that Thomas Shaw, Bachelor, and Adena Miriam Peveral, Spinster, were married this 28th day of June 1867 in the Parish of St. James, Wednesbury, in the County of Stafford.*

The papers dropping to her lap, Miriam whispered. 'I ... I don't understand.'

'You are going to need some time, my dear.' The priest nodded. 'That is only to be expected. What you have read has come as a shock to you. Indeed it has come as a shock to us all.'

'But why show these papers to me? Apart from my father's name, I know none of the people of whom these documents speak.'

'When you say you recognise the name of your father, do I take it that you refer to William Bryce?'

'Of course!'

The priest smiled patiently. 'Look again at the birth certificate. The names it carries are those of your true parents. You are not the child of William and Leah Bryce, you are the daughter of Thomas and Adena Miriam Shaw.'

'No.' Eyes wide with confusion, she swung to Ralph. 'He is wrong. Tell him he is wrong.'

'I can't, Miriam.' Reaching out, he took one of her hands. 'I can't tell him that because he is not wrong, what he says is all true.'

'How ... how can you be sure?'

Glancing at the priest, Ralph caught the nod that gave him leave to carry on. Speaking softly, his eyes never leaving her face, he told her.

'The night my mother died she told me everything. How she had been jilted by Thomas Shaw in favour of a girl who'd recently come to the village. How they left together, then she married my father. But the jealousy never left her, nor did her desire for revenge. Then that letter arrived.' He nodded towards the papers still in her lap. 'She was not consulted, she said, given no choice but to accept the baby girl William Bryce brought home from an orphanage in Wolverhampton. The child of the woman who had ruined her life. The woman who had stolen her love was dead and so was the man who had deserted her. But Leah's spite was not dead, and for all those years she took it out on you ... on both of us. She said you would never learn the truth. Nor would you have done were it not for the papers she'd sewn into a dress and left there.'

'Jealousy is a terrible thing.' The priest shook his head. 'A terrible thing. It can be a mortal sin. Just as it was a sin to leave you both in ignorance for so long, for who can tell when the Lord may summon us to His presence? You might have gone on living in the same house together and that would have been sin indeed, seeing you are no true kin. We must be thankful that Mr Bryce moved from the family home the day of his mother's funeral. Had he done otherwise the situation could have been compromising to your good name, Miriam.'

He rose to his feet, clerical robe swishing against the gaiters it covered. 'As I said, my dear, you will need time to come to terms with what you have learned tonight. But remember, the

Church is there to help.'

Looking at Ralph, he continued, 'Take the papers with you, Mr Bryce. When Miss ... er ... Shaw is more used to their contents then you can decide between you what is best done with them. I mean, whose custody they will remain in. However, I shall on Sunday acquaint the members of the congregation with the fact that you are not the kin you both believed yourselves to be, and that the Church is fully conversant with the details after seeing the relevant documents. There can be no blame attached to either of you for what was solely your mother's decision to remain silent, and only praise for your action, Mr Bryce, in leaving that house when you did.'

Stunned by what she had heard and read, Miriam sat unmoving as the two men shook hands. It was only when Ralph took the papers gently from her that she looked up.

'Come on, Miriam.' His smile gentle, eyes shining with the life that had been reborn in him, he drew her to her feet. 'I'll see you back to the house.'

The breeze cutting across the heath was cold against her face but Miriam did not feel it. What the priest had said, it could not be true ... those papers ... were a lie. She was the daughter of William Bryce. Leah Bryce had been her mother. But the priest would not lie.

Suddenly the enormity of it all came home to her. The full realisation of what it meant. She stood perfectly still.

'Those papers ... he said they were genuine, but how can they be?' She lifted her face to Ralph,

395

eyes wide and silvered by the moon. 'I ... I am your sister.'

Pure joy reflected in his face, Ralph drew her into his arms and this time no guilt touched his heart.

'No, Miriam.' He smiled against her hair. 'You are not my sister. You and I were not born of the same parents.'

'Mother ... Leah ... she told you that?'

'Yes. But not until moments before I came to fetch you.' His arms shielding her from the chill of the wind, Ralph repeated what had passed between himself and his mother the night of her death.

In his arms, Miriam stood quietly, feeling far away. Holding her close was enough for Ralph. Finally he stood as silent as she.

'She had the same name as myself.' At last she spoke, the words soft with emotion. 'The woman to whom those marriage lines belonged. Her name was Adena Miriam.'

In the moonlight his mouth softened in a smile. 'And yours is Miriam Adena. Your mother gave you her own names.'

'I wonder, was she beautiful?'

'Leah said her curls were the colour of autumn berries, the same colour as yours, and that she could have had her pick of any man in Brades Village. She must have been beautiful, as her daughter is beautiful.'

'Her daughter!' Miriam seemed to consider his words, then easing back her head she stared into the face of the man she had always thought her brother, seeing for the first time in many months

396

the light of real happiness shining in his eyes. 'Why didn't you tell me?'

He smiled, one hand bringing her head to rest against his chest again. 'Would you have believed me? Would anyone have believed me without seeing those papers? I think that was my mother's intention. She hid those letters, fully intending that one day they should be found. Probably after one or the other of us had married. She wanted me to know – that can be the only reason she did not destroy them. That is the first and only mistake I have ever known her to make.'

'But I still don't understand, why did she not tell you sooner?'

Drawing a deep breath, Ralph knew the moment had come, the moment when his secret must be told. Releasing his hold on her he stepped away. He could not bear to feel her revulsion at his confession.

'My mother kept your birth a secret from everybody. Perhaps at first she intended I should know when I was of an age to understand. But then, as we both grew older, she realised that not only did I love you, I was *in* love with you. That gave her another weapon to use against her son, to keep him in line. A man in love with his own sister! The idea nauseated me, yet for all I tried, I could not alter my feelings for you. The love I felt grew and grew until I feared it would kill me. God forgive me, Miriam!' He turned away, not wanting her to see the tears springing to his eyes. 'I thought never to say these words, I never wanted you to know, but as heaven is my witness – I love you!'

They were no kin! Reared in the same house by the same woman, but they were no kin! Miriam felt a strange relief sweep through her. Was this the reason she had refused to marry Ethan Rawley?

And the love she'd thought she felt for Saul Marsh? That had proved a brief infatuation, as she had cruelly been brought to recognise. Ethan had not treated her with cruelty, he had shown her only respect and tenderness, yet she could not say she loved him as any more than a friend.

But all of her life she had felt a deep love for Ralph, a different all-encompassing love she did not begin to understand ... until now.

Looking over to where he stood with his back to her, his strong body etched in silver moonlight, she felt her heart swell. Ralph loved her. After all that had happened, he loved her.

And this feeling, this wonderful quiet happiness that had settled over her like a warm cloak, was that the love she had spoken of to Ethan's father, a love that went far deeper than friendship? Smiling softly, Miriam knew that it was.

Stepping close to him, keeping her voice soft, she whispered, 'I love you too, Ralph. I love you as you love me.'

A sob breaking from him, he whirled round to face her. For one long moment he stared into the face he had loved for so long. Then she was in his arms. Holding her against him, he stared out across the silvered heath.

At last his prayers had been answered. At last the love of a sister could become the love of a wife.

This Large Print Book for the partially sighted, who cannot read normal print, is published under the auspices of

THE ULVERSCROFT FOUNDATION